# THE
# EXPECTED
# ONE

# THE EXPECTED ONE

## Book One of the Magdalene Line

# KATHLEEN McGOWAN

**SIMON &
SCHUSTER**

London · New York · Sydney · Toronto

A CBS COMPANY

First published in Great Britain by Simon & Schuster UK Ltd, 2006
A CBS COMPANY

Map by Paul J. Pugliese

3 5 7 9 10 8 6 4 2

Simon & Schuster UK Ltd
Africa House
64-78 Kingsway
London WC2B 6AH

www.simonsays.co.uk

Simon & Schuster Australia
Sydney

A CIP catalogue record for this book is available
from the British Library.

Hardback 10-digit: 0-7432-9532-3
13-digit: 9-780-7432-9532-1
Trade Paperback 10-digit: 0-7432-9534-X
13-digit: 9-780-7432-9534-5

Printed and bound in Great Britain by
The Bath Press, Bath

This book is dedicated to:

*Mary Magdalene,*
*my muse, my ancestor;*

*Peter McGowan,*
*the rock I built my life on;*

*My parents, Donna and Joe,*
*for unconditional love and interesting genetics;*

*and to our Grail princes,*
*Patrick, Conor, and Shane,*
*for filling our lives with love, laughter, and*
*constant inspiration*

To the chosen lady and her children,
whom I love in the truth;
and not I only, but also all who know the truth;
because of the truth which lives in us
and will be with us forever.

2 JOHN 1–2

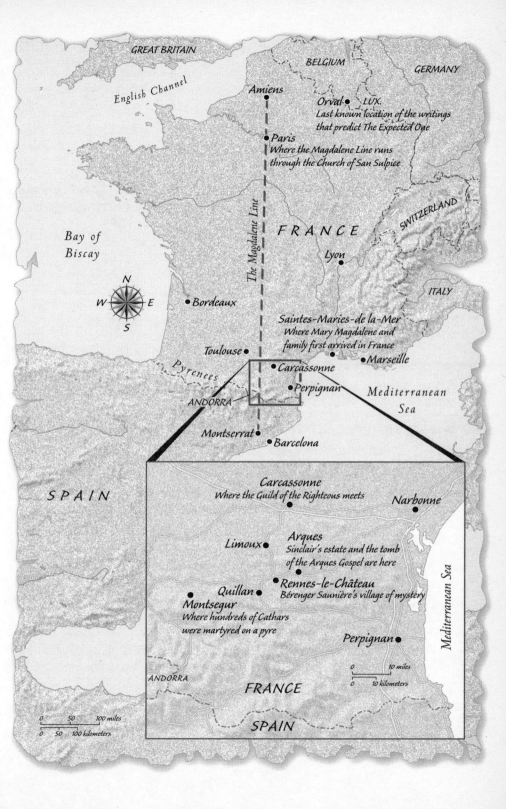

GREAT BRITAIN

BELGIUM

GERMANY

*English Channel*

Amiens

Orval • LUX.
*Last known location of the writings*
*that predict The Expected One*

Paris
*Where the Magdalene Line runs*
*through the Church of San Sulpice*

F R A N C E

SWITZERLAND

*Bay of*
*Biscay*

Lyon

ITALY

N
W E
S

• Bordeaux

Saintes-Maries-de la-Mer
*Where Mary Magdalene and*
*family first arrived in France*

Toulouse •

*Pyrenees*

• Carcassonne

Marseille

• Perpignan

*Mediterranean*
*Sea*

ANDORRA

Montserrat •

• Barcelona

S P A I N

Carcassonne
*Where the Guild of the Righteous meets*

Narbonne

Limoux •

Arques
*Sinclair's estate and the tomb*
*of the Arques Gospel are here*

• Rennes-le-Château
*Bérenger Saunière's village of mystery*

Quillan •

Montsegur
*Where hundreds of Cathars*
*were martyred on a pyre*

Perpignan •

*Mediterranean Sea*

ANDORRA

FRANCE

SPAIN

0        10 miles
0        10 kilometers

0    50    100 miles
0    50    100 kilometers

# THE
# EXPECTED
# ONE

# PROLOGUE

*Southern Gaul*
*the year 72*

There wasn't much time left.

The old woman tugged the tattered shawl tighter around her shoulders. Autumn was coming early to the red mountains this year; she felt it in the marrow of her bones. Gently, slowly, she flexed her fingers, willing the arthritic joints to loosen. Her hands mustn't fail her now, not with so much at stake. She had to finish the writing tonight. Tamar would arrive soon with the jars, and all must be ready.

She allowed herself the luxury of a long, ragged sigh. *I have been tired for a long time. Such a long, long time.*

This latest task, she knew, would be her last on earth. These past days of remembering had drained all of the remaining life from a withered body. Her ancient bones were heavy with the unspeakable sorrow and weariness that comes to those who outlive their loved ones. God's tests for her had been many, and they had been harsh.

Only Tamar, her sole daughter and last living child, remained with her. Tamar was her blessing, the flicker of light in those darkest hours when memories more terrifying than nightmares refused to be tamed. Her daughter was now the only other survivor of the Great Time, although she had been a mere child while they all played their part in living history. Still, it was a comfort to know that someone lived who remembered and understood.

The others were gone. Most were dead, martyred by men and methods too brutal to be endured. Perhaps a few still lived, scattered across the great map of God's earth. She would never know. It had been many years since she received word from the others, but she prayed for them in any case, prayed from sunrise to sunset on those days when the remembering was very strong. She wished with her heart and her soul that they had found peace and had not suffered her agony of many thousand sleepless nights.

Yes, Tamar was her only refuge in these twilight years. The girl had been too young to recall the horrific details of the Time of Darkness, but old enough to remember the beauty and grace of the individuals God had chosen to walk His sacred path. Dedicating her life to the memory of those chosen ones, Tamar's way had been one of pure service and love. The girl's singular dedication to her mother's comfort in these end days had been extraordinary.

*Leaving my beloved daughter is the only difficult thing I have left to do. Even now, as death comes to me, I cannot welcome it.*

And yet . . .

She peered out of the cavern that had been her home for almost four decades. The sky was clear as she raised her lined face, taking in the beauty of the stars. She would never cease to feel wonder at God's creation. Somewhere, beyond those stars, the souls she loved most in the world awaited her. She could feel them now, closer than ever before.

She could feel *Him.*

*"Thy will be done,"* she whispered to the night sky. Turning slowly, deliberately, the old woman returned inside. With a deep inhalation, she examined the rough parchment, squinting in the dim and smoky light of an oil lamp.

Picking up the stylus, she resumed her careful scratching.

*. . . All these years later and it is no easier to write of Judas Iscariot than it was in the dark days. Not because I hold any judgment against him, but rather because I do not.*

*I will tell the story of Judas and hope to do so with justice. He was a man uncompromising in his principles, and those who follow us must know this: he did not betray those—or us—for a bag of silver. The truth is that Judas was the most loyal of the twelve. I have had so many reasons for grief these years past, and yet I think there is but One whom I mourn more than Judas.*

*There are many who would have me write harshly of Judas—to condemn him as a betrayer, as a traitor, as one who was blind to the truth. But I can write none of those things for they would be lies before my pen touched the page. Enough lies will be written about our time, God has shown me that. I will not write more.*

*For what is my purpose, if not to tell the whole truth of what occurred then?*

THE ARQUES GOSPEL OF MARY MAGDALENE,
THE BOOK OF DISCIPLES

# CHAPTER ONE

*Marseille*
*September 1997*

*M*arseille was a fine place to die and had been for centuries. The legendary seaport retained a reputation as a lair for pirates, smugglers, and cutthroats, a status enjoyed since the Romans wrestled it from the Greeks in the days before Christ.

By the end of the twentieth century, the French government's efforts at whitewash finally made it safe to enjoy bouillabaisse without the fear of getting mugged. Still, crime held no shock value for the locals. Mayhem was ingrained in their history and genetics. The leathered fishermen didn't blink when their nets yielded a catch that would prove unsuitable for inclusion in the local fish stew.

Roger-Bernard Gélis was not a native of Marseille. He was born and raised in the foothills of the Pyrenees, in a community that existed proudly as a living anachronism. The twentieth century had not infringed on his culture, an ancient one that revered the powers of love and peace over all earthly matters. Still, he was a man of middle age who was not entirely unworldly; he was, after all, the leader of his people. And while his community dwelled together in a deeply spiritual peace, they had their share of enemies.

Roger-Bernard was fond of saying that the greatest light attracts the deepest darkness.

He was a giant of a man, an imposing figure to strangers. Those who did not know the gentleness that permeated Roger-Bernard's spirit might have mistaken him for someone to be feared. Later, it would be assumed that his attackers were not unknown to him.

He should have seen it coming, should have anticipated that he would not be left to carry such a priceless object in absolute freedom. Hadn't almost a million of his ancestors died for the sake of this same treasure? But the shot came from behind, splintering his skull before he even knew the enemy was near.

Forensic evidence from the bullet would prove useless to the police, as the killers did not end their attack on a note of simplicity. There must have been several of them as the sheer size and weight of the victim required a certain amount of manpower to accomplish what came next.

It was a mercy that Roger-Bernard was dead before the ritual began. He was spared the gloating of his killers as they set about their gruesome task. The leader was particularly filled with zeal for what came next, chanting his ancient mantra of hate as he worked.

"Neca eos omnes. Neca eos omnes."

To sever a human head from its resting place on the body is a messy and difficult business. It requires strength, determination, and a very sharp instrument. Those who murdered Roger-Bernard Gélis had all of these things, and used them with the utmost efficiency.

The body had been at sea for a long time, battered by the tide and chewed by hungry inhabitants of the deep. The investigators were so disheartened by the ragged condition of the corpse that they assigned little significance to the missing digit on one hand. An autopsy, buried later by bureaucracy—and perhaps something more—simply noted that the right index finger had been severed.

*Jerusalem*
*September 1997*

THE ANCIENT AND BUSTLING Old City of Jerusalem was filled with the frenetic activity of a Friday afternoon. History hung heavy in the rarified and holy air as the faithful hurried to houses of worship in preparation for their respective sabbaths. Christians wandered the Via Dolorosa, the Way of Sorrow, a series of winding and cobbled streets that marked the path of the crucifixion. It was here that a battered and bleeding Jesus Christ shouldered a heavy burden, making his way to a divine fate atop the hill of Golgotha.

On this autumn afternoon American author Maureen Paschal appeared no different from the other pilgrims who made their way from distant and varied corners of the earth. The heady September breeze blended the aroma of sizzling shwarma with the scent of exotic oils that wafted from the ancient markets. Maureen drifted through the sensory overload that is Israel, clutching a guidebook purchased from a Christian organization on the Internet. The guide detailed the Way of the Cross, complete with maps and directions to the fourteen stations of Christ's path.

"Lady, you want rosary? Wood from Mount of Olives."

"Lady, you want tour guide? You never get lost. I show you everything."

Like most Western women, she was forced to fend off the unwanted advances of Jerusalem street merchants. Some were relentless in their efforts to hawk their wares or services. Others were merely attracted to the petite woman with long red hair and fair coloring, an exotic combination in this part of the world. Maureen rebuffed her pursuers with a polite but firm "No, thank you." Then she broke eye contact and walked away. Her cousin Peter, an expert in Middle Eastern studies, had prepped her for the culture of the Old City. Maureen was painstaking about even the tiniest details in her work and had studied the evolving culture of Jerusalem carefully. So far it was paying off, and Maureen was able to keep the distractions to a minimum as she focused on her research, scribbling details and observations in her Moleskine notebook.

She had been moved to tears by the intensity and beauty of the 800-year-old Franciscan Chapel of the Flagellation, where Jesus had suffered his scourging. It was a deeply unexpected emotional reaction as Maureen did not come to Jerusalem as a pilgrim. Instead, she came as an investigative observer, as a writer in search of an accurate historical backdrop for her work. While Maureen sought a deeper understanding of the events of Good Friday, she approached this research from her head rather than her heart.

She visited the Convent of the Sisters of Sion, before moving to the neighboring Chapel of Condemnation, the legendary location where Jesus was given his cross after the sentence of crucifixion had been passed by Pontius Pilate. Again, the unexpected lump in her throat was accompanied by an overwhelming sense of grief as she walked through the building. Life-size bas-relief sculptures illustrated the events of a terrible morning 2,000 years earlier. Maureen stood, riveted, by a vivid scene of haunting humanity: a male disciple as he tried to shield Mary, the mother of Jesus, to spare her the sight of her son carrying His cross. Tears stung at the back of her eyes as she stood before the image. It was the first time in her life she had thought of these larger-than-life historical figures as real people, flesh-and-blood humans suffering through an event of nearly unimaginable anguish.

Feeling momentarily dizzy, Maureen steadied herself with a hand against the cool stones of an ancient wall. She paused to refocus before taking more notes on the artwork and sculpture.

She continued on her path, but the labyrinthine streets of the Old City proved deceiving, even with a carefully drawn map. The landmarks were often ancient, weathered, and easily missed by those unfamiliar with their whereabouts. Maureen cursed silently as she realized she was lost again. She stopped in the shelter of a shop doorway, shielding herself from the direct sunlight. The intensity of the heat, even with the slight breeze, belied the lateness of the season. Shielding the guidebook from the glare, she looked around, attempting to get her bearings.

"The Eighth Station of the Cross. It has to be around here somewhere," she muttered to herself. This location was of specific interest to Maureen, for her work centered on this history as it pertained to women. Referring back to the guidebook, she continued to read a passage from the Gospels that pertained to Station Eight.

"A large number of people followed him, including women who mourned and wailed for him. Jesus said, 'Weep not for me, daughters of Jerusalem, weep for yourselves and for your children.' "

Maureen was startled by a sharp knock on the window behind her. She looked up, expecting to see an angry proprietor glaring at her for blocking his doorway. But the face that looked back at her was beaming. An immaculately dressed, middle-aged Palestinian man opened the door to the antiquities shop, beckoning Maureen in. When he spoke it was in beautiful, if accented, English.

"Come in, please. Welcome, I am Mahmoud. You are lost?"

Maureen waved the guidebook lamely. "I'm looking for the Eighth Station. The map shows . . ."

Mahmoud waved the book away with a laugh. "Yes, yes. Station Eight. Jesus Meets the Holy Women of Jerusalem. It is just out here and around the corner," he gestured. "A cross above the stone wall marks it, but you have to look very carefully."

Mahmoud looked at Maureen intently for a moment before continuing. "It is like everything else in Jerusalem. You have to look very carefully to see it for what it is."

Maureen watched his gestures, satisfied that she understood the directions. Smiling, she thanked him and turned to leave, but stopped as something on a nearby shelf caught her eye. Mahmoud's shop was one of the more upscale establishments in Jerusalem, selling authenticated antiquities—oil lamps from the time of Christ, coins with the emblem of Pontius Pilate. An exquisite shimmer of color coming through the window attracted Maureen.

"That's jewelry made from shards of Roman glass," Mahmoud explained as Maureen approached an artful display rack of silver and gold jewelry embedded with jeweled mosaics.

"It's gorgeous," Maureen replied, picking up a silver pendant. Prisms of color darted through the shop as she held the jewelry up to the light, illuminating her writer's imagination. "I wonder what story this glass could tell?"

"Who knows what it once was?" Mahmoud shrugged. "A perfume bottle? A spice jar? A vase for roses or lilies?"

"It's amazing to think that two thousand years ago this was an everyday object in someone's home. Fascinating."

Giving the shop and its contents closer inspection, Maureen was struck by the quality of the items and the beauty of the displays. She reached out to run a finger lightly over a ceramic oil lamp. "Is this really two thousand years old?"

"Of course. Some of my items are older still."

Maureen shook her head. "Don't antiquities like this belong in a museum?"

Mahmoud laughed, a rich and hearty sound. "My dear, all of Jerusalem is a museum. You cannot dig in your garden without unearthing something of great antiquity. Most of the truly valuable go into important collections. But not everything."

Maureen moved to a glass case, filled with ancient jewelry of hammered, oxidized copper. She stopped, her attention grabbed by a ring that supported a disc the size of a small coin. Following her gaze, Mahmoud removed the ring from the case, holding it out to her. A sunbeam from the front window caught the ring, illuminating its round base and showing off a pattern of nine hammered dots surrounding a central circle.

"Very interesting choice," Mahmoud said. His jovial manner had changed. He was now intense and serious, watching Maureen closely as she questioned him about the ring.

"How old is this?"

"It's hard to say. My experts said it was Byzantine, probably sixth or seventh century, but possibly older."

Maureen looked closely at the pattern made by the circles.

"This pattern seems . . . familiar. I feel like I've seen it before. Do you know if it symbolizes anything?"

Mahmoud's intensity relaxed. "I cannot say for certain what an artisan meant to create fifteen hundred years ago. But I have been told that it was the ring of a cosmologist."

"A cosmologist?"

"Someone who understands the relation between the earth and the cosmos. As above, so below. And I must say that the first time I saw it, it reminded me of the planets, dancing around the sun."

Maureen counted the dots aloud. "Seven, eight, nine. But they wouldn't have known there were nine planets back then, or that the sun was the center of the solar system. It couldn't be that, could it?"

"We cannot assume to know what the ancients understood." Mahmoud shrugged. "Try it on."

Maureen, suddenly sensing a sales pitch, handed the ring back to Mahmoud. "Oh, no, thank you. It's really beautiful, but I was just curious. And I promised myself I wouldn't spend money today."

"That's fine," said Mahmoud, pointedly refusing to take the ring from her. "Because it's not for sale anyway."

"It's not?"

"No. Many people have offered to buy that ring. I refuse to sell it. So you may feel free to try it on. Just for fun."

Maybe it was because the playfulness had returned to his tone and she felt less pressured, or maybe it was the attraction of the unexplained, ancient pattern. But something caused Maureen to slip the copper disc onto her right ring finger. It fit perfectly.

Mahmoud nodded, serious again, almost whispering to himself, "As if it had been made for you."

Maureen held the ring up to the light, looking at it on her hand. "I can't take my eyes off of it."

"That's because you're supposed to have it."

Maureen looked up suspiciously, sensing the approaching sales pitch. Mahmoud was more elegant than the street vendors, but he was a merchant all the same. "I thought you said it wasn't for sale."

She began to take the ring off, to which the shopkeeper objected vehemently, holding up his hands in protest.

"No. Please."

"Okay, okay. This is where we haggle, right? How much is it?"

Mahmoud looked seriously offended for a moment before replying. "You misunderstand. That ring was entrusted to me, until I found the right hand for it. The hand it was made for. I see now that it was your hand. I cannot sell it to you because it is already yours."

Maureen looked down at the ring, and then back up at Mahmoud, puzzled. "I don't understand."

Mahmoud smiled sagely, and moved toward the front door of the shop. "No, you don't. But one day you will. For now, just keep the ring. A gift."

"I couldn't possibly . . ."

"You can and you will. You must. If you do not, I will have failed. You would not want that on your conscience, of course."

Maureen shook her head in bewilderment as she followed him to the front door, pausing. "I really don't know what to say, or how to thank you."

"No need, no need. But now you must go. The mysteries of Jerusalem are waiting for you."

Mahmoud held the door for her as Maureen stepped through it, thanking him again.

"Good-bye, Magdalena," he whispered as she walked out. Maureen stopped, turning quickly back to him.

"I'm sorry?"

Mahmoud smiled his sage, enigmatic smile. "I said good-bye, *my lady.*" And he waved at Maureen as she returned the gesture, stepping out again into the harsh Middle Eastern sun.

Maureen returned to the Via Dolorosa, where she found the Eighth Station just as Mahmoud had directed her. But she was disquieted and unable to concentrate, feeling strange after the encounter with the shopkeeper. Continuing on her path, the earlier sense of dizziness returned, stronger this time, to the point of disorientation. It was her first day in Jerusalem, and she was undoubtedly suffering jet lag. The flight from Los Angeles had been long and arduous, and she hadn't slept much the night before. Whether it was a combination of heat, exhaustion, and hunger, or something more unexplainable, what happened next was outside Maureen's realm of experience.

Finding a stone bench, Maureen eased herself down to rest. She swayed with another wave of unexpected vertigo as a blinding flash emanated from the relentless sun, transporting her thoughts.

She was thrown abruptly into the middle of a mob. All around her was chaos—there was much shouting and shoving, great commotion on all sides. Maureen had enough of her modern wits about her to notice that the swarming figures were robed in coarse, homespun garments. Those who had shoes wore a crude version of a sandal; she noticed as one stepped down hard on her foot. Most were men, bearded and grimy. The omnipresent sun of early afternoon beat down upon them, mixing sweat with dirt on the angry and distressed faces around her. She was at the edge of a narrow road, and the crowd just ahead began to jostle emphatically. A natural gap was evolving, and a small group moved slowly along the path. The mob appeared to be following this huddle. As the moving mass came closer, Maureen saw the woman for the first time.

A solitary and still island in the center of the chaos, she was one of the few women in the crowd—but that was not what made her different. It was her bearing, a regal demeanor that marked her as a queen despite the layer of dirt covering her hands and feet. She was slightly disheveled, lustrous auburn hair tucked partially beneath a crimson veil that covered the lower half of her face. Maureen knew instinctively that she had to reach this woman, needed to connect with her, touch her, speak to her. But the writhing crowd held her back, and she was moving in the slow-motion thickness of a dream state.

As she continued to struggle in the direction of the woman, the aching beauty of the face that was just out of her reach struck Maureen. She was fine-boned, with exquisite, delicate features. But it was her eyes that would haunt Maureen long after the vision was over. The woman's eyes, huge and bright with unshed tears, fell somewhere in the color spectrum between amber and sage, an extraordinary light hazel that reflected infinite wisdom and unbearable sadness in one heart-searing blend. The woman's soul-swallowing gaze met Maureen's in a brief and interminable moment, conveying through those improbable eyes a plea of complete and utter desperation.

*You must help me.*

Maureen knew that the plea was directed at her. She was entranced, frozen, as her eyes locked with the woman's. The moment was broken when the woman looked down suddenly at a young girl who tugged urgently at her hand.

The child looked up with huge hazel eyes that echoed her mother's. Behind her stood a boy, older and with darker eyes than the little girl, but clearly the son of this woman. Maureen knew in that inexplicable instant that she was the only person who could help this strange, suffering queen and her children. A swell of intense confusion, and something that felt far too much like grief, moved through her at this realization.

Then the mob surged again, drowning Maureen in a sea of sweat and despair.

Maureen blinked hard, holding her eyes shut tight for a few seconds. She shook her head briskly to clear her vision, not certain at first where she was. A glance down at her jeans, microfiber backpack, and Nike walking shoes provided reassurance from the twentieth century. Around her the bustle of the Old City continued, but the people were dressed in contemporary fashions and the sounds were different now: Radio Jordan blasted an American pop song—was that R.E.M.'s "Losing My Religion"?—from a shop across the way. A teenage Palestinian boy kept time, drumming on the countertop. He smiled at her without missing a beat.

Rising from the bench, Maureen attempted to shake off the vision, if that's what it had been. She wasn't sure what it was, nor could she allow herself to dwell on it. Her time in Jerusalem was limited and she had 2,000 years of sights to see. Summoning her journalist's discipline and a lifetime's experience of suppressing her emotions, she filed the vision under "research for later analysis" and pushed herself to keep moving.

Maureen found herself merging with a swarm of British tourists as they rounded the corner, led by a guide wearing the collar of an Anglican priest. He announced to his group of pilgrims that they were approaching the most sacred site in Christendom, the Basilica of the Holy Sepulcher.

Maureen knew from her research that the remaining Stations of the Cross were contained within that revered building. Spanning several blocks, the basilica covered the site of the crucifixion and had done so since the Empress Helena vowed to protect this sacred ground in the fourth century. Helena, who was also the mother of the Holy Roman Emperor Constantine, was later canonized for her efforts.

Maureen approached the enormous entrance doors slowly and with some hesitation. She realized as she stood on the threshold that she had not been inside a real church in many years, nor did she relish the thought of changing that status now. She reminded herself firmly that the research that had brought her to Israel was scholarly rather than spiritual. As long as she remained focused, with that perspective, she could do it. She could walk through those doors.

Despite her reluctance, there was something unmistakably awe-inspiring and magnetic about this colossal shrine. As she stepped through the mammoth doorway, she heard the British priest's words ring out:

"Within these walls, you will see where Our Lord made the ultimate sacrifice. Where He was stripped of His robes, where He was nailed to the cross. You will enter the holy tomb where His body was laid. My brothers and sisters in Christ, once you enter this place, your lives will never be the same."

The heavy and unmistakable smell of frankincense swirled past Maureen as she entered. Pilgrims from all walks of Christendom surrounded this place and filled the mammoth spaces inside the basilica. She passed a group of Coptic priests huddled in hushed, reverent discussion and watched a Greek Orthodox cleric light a candle in one of the small chapels. A male choir sang in an Eastern dialect, an exotic sound to Western ears, the hymn rising up from some secret space within the church.

Maureen was taking in the overwhelming sights and sounds of this place, and was feeling aimless from the sensory overload. She did not see the wiry little man who eased up beside her until he tapped her on the shoulder, causing her to jump.

"Sorry, Miss. Sorry, Miss Mo-ree." He spoke English, but unlike the enigmatic shopkeeper Mahmoud, his accent was very heavy. His skills with Maureen's language were rudimentary at best, and as a result she didn't understand at first that he was calling her by her first name. He repeated himself.

"Mo-ree. Your name. It is Mo-ree, yes?"

Maureen was puzzled, trying to determine if this strange little man was actually calling her by name and, if so, how he knew it. She had been in Jerusalem for fewer than twenty-four hours, and no one save the front desk clerk at the King David Hotel knew her name. But this man was impatient, asking again.

"Mo-ree. You are Mo-ree. Writer. You write, yes? Mo-ree?"

Nodding slowly, Maureen answered. "Yes. My name is Maureen. But how—how did you know?"

The little man ignored the question, grabbing her hand and pulling her across the church floor. "No time, no time. Come. We wait a long time for you. Come, come."

For such a small man—he was shorter than Maureen, who was herself uncommonly petite—he moved very quickly. Short legs propelled him through the belly of the basilica, past the line where pilgrims waited to be admitted to the Tomb of Christ. He kept moving until they reached a small altar near the rear of the building, and stopped suddenly. The area was dominated by a life-size bronze sculpture of a woman holding outstretched arms to a man in a beseeching pose.

"Chapel of Mary Magdalene. Magdalena. You come for her, yes? Yes?"

Maureen nodded cautiously, looking at the sculpture and down at the plaque that read:

IN THIS PLACE,
MARY MAGDALENE WAS THE FIRST
TO SEE THE RISEN LORD.

She read aloud the quotation from another plaque beneath the bronze:

"Woman, why weepest thou? Who is it you are looking for?"

Maureen had little time to contemplate the question as the odd little man was pulling at her again, hurrying at his unlikely pace to another, darker corner of the basilica.

"Come, come."

They rounded a corner and stopped in front of a painting, a large and aged portrait of a woman. Time, incense, and centuries of oily candle residue had taken their toll on the artwork, causing Maureen to move close to the dark portrait, squinting. The little man narrated in a voice grown deeply serious.

"Painting very old. Greek. You understand? *Greek.* Most important of Our Lady. She needs you to tell her story. This is why you come here, Mo-ree. We have waited a long time for you. *She* has waited. For you. Yes?"

Maureen looked carefully at the painting, a dark, ancient portrait of a woman wearing a red cloak. She turned to the little man, intensely curious now as to where this was taking her. But he was gone—he had vanished as quickly as he had appeared.

"Wait!" Maureen's cry rang out in the echo chamber of the massive church, but it remained unanswered. She returned her attention to the painting.

As she leaned closer to the portrait, she observed that the woman wore a ring on her right hand: a round copper disk, with a pattern depicting nine circles surrounding a central sphere.

Maureen lifted her right hand, the one with her newly acquired ring, to compare it to the painting.

The rings were identical.

*. . . Much will be said and written in time to come of Simon, the Fisher of Men. Of how he was called the rock, Peter, by Easa and myself while the others called him Cephas, which was natural in their own tongue. And if history is just, it will tell of how he loved Easa with unmatched power and loyalty.*

*And much has already been said, or so I am told, about my own relationship with Simon-Peter. There are those who called us adversaries, enemies. They would have it be believed that Peter despised me and we fought for the attention of Easa at every turn. And there are those who would call Peter a hater of women—but this is an accusation that can be applied to no one who followed Easa. Let it be known that no man who followed Easa did ever belittle a woman or underestimate her value in God's plan. Any man who does so and claims Easa as teacher speaks a lie.*

*It is untrue, these accusations against Peter. Those who witnessed Peter's criticism of me do not know of our history or from what source come his outbursts. But I understand and will not judge him, ever. This, above all else, is what Easa has taught me—and I hope he taught it as well to the others. Judge not.*

THE ARQUES GOSPEL OF MARY MAGDALENE,
THE BOOK OF DISCIPLES

# CHAPTER TWO

"Let's take it from the top: Marie Antoinette never said, 'Let them eat cake,' Lucrezia Borgia never poisoned anyone, and Mary, Queen of Scots was *not* a murderous whore. By righting these wrongs, we take the first step toward restoring women to their proper and respected place in history—a place that has been usurped by generations of historians with a political agenda."

Maureen paused as murmured appreciation rippled through the group of adult students. Addressing a new class was akin to opening night at the theater. The success of her initial performance determined the long-term impact of her entire body of work.

"Over the next few weeks, we will be examining the lives of some of the most infamous women in both history and legend. Women with stories that have left an indelible imprint on the evolution of modern society and thought; women who have been dramatically misunderstood and poorly represented by those individuals who have established the history of the Western world by committing their *opinions* to paper."

She was on a roll and unwilling to stop for questions so early on, but a young male student had been waving his hand at her from the front row since she started talking. He looked like he was about to climb out of his skin, but other than that there was nothing very remarkable about his appearance. Friend or foe? Fan or fundamentalist? That was always the question. Maureen called on him, knowing that he would distract her until she dealt with it.

"Would you consider this a feminist view of history?"

Was that it? Maureen relaxed a little as she answered the familiar question. "I consider it an honest view of history. I didn't approach this with any agenda other than getting to the truth."

She wasn't off the hook yet.

"Well, it seems a lot like man-bashing to me."

"Not at all. I love men. I think every woman should own one." Maureen paused to allow the female students their chuckle.

"I'm *kidding*. My goal is to bring things back into balance by looking at history with modern eyes. Do you live your life in the same way that people lived sixteen hundred years ago? No. So why should laws, beliefs, and historical interpretations dictated in the Dark Ages govern the way we live in the twenty-first century? It just doesn't make sense."

The student responded. "But that's why I'm here, to find out what it's all really about."

"Good. Then I applaud you for being here, and I ask only that you keep an open mind. In fact, I want you all to stop what you're doing, raise you right hands in the air, and take the following vow."

The group of night-school students murmured again and looked around the room, smiling and shrugging at each other, to determine if she was indeed serious. Their teacher, a best-selling author and respected journalist, stood before them with her right hand raised and an expectant look on her face.

"Come on," she prodded. "Hands up, and repeat after me."

The class followed along, raising their hands and waiting for her cue.

"I solemnly vow, as a serious student of history . . ." Maureen paused as the students responded obediently, "to remember at all times that all words committed to paper have been written by human beings."

Another pause for student response. "And, as all human beings are ruled by their emotions, opinions, and political and religious affiliations, subsequently all history is comprised of as much opinion as fact and, in many cases, has been entirely fabricated for the furthering of the author's personal ambitions or secret agenda.

"I solemnly vow to keep my mind open during every moment that I sit in this room. Here is our battle cry: History is *not* what happened. History is what was written down."

She lifted a hardcover book from the podium in front of her and displayed it to the class.

"Has everyone had a chance to pick up a copy of this book?" A general nodding of heads and a muttering of assent followed the query. The book in Maureen's raised hand was her own controversial work, *HerStory: A Defense of History's Most Hated Heroines.* It was the reason she filled night-school classrooms and lecture halls to capacity each time she elected to teach.

"Tonight, we will begin with a discussion of the women of the Old Testament, female ancestors of the Christian and Jewish traditions. Next week we will transition to the New Testament, spending the majority of the session on one woman—Mary Magdalene. We will examine the different sources and references to her life, both as a woman and as a disciple of Christ. Please read the corresponding chapters in preparation for next week's discussion.

"We will also have a special guest lecture by Dr. Peter Healy, whom some of you may know from our extension program for the humanities. For those of you who have not yet been fortunate enough to attend one of the good doctor's classes, he is also Father Healy, a Jesuit scholar and internationally acclaimed expert on Biblical studies."

The persistent student in the front row raised his hand again, not waiting for Maureen to call on him before asking, "Aren't you and Doctor Healy related?"

Maureen nodded. "Doctor Healy is my cousin.

"He will give us the Church perspective on Mary Magdalene's relationship to Christ and reveal how perceptions have evolved over two thousand years," Maureen continued, anxious to get back on track and finish on time. "It will be a good night, so try not to miss it.

"But tonight, we will begin with one of our ancestral mothers. When we first meet Bathsheba, she is 'purifying herself from her uncleanness . . . ' "

Maureen rushed out of the classroom, exclaiming her apologies and swearing over her shoulder that she would stay after class the following week. She would normally have spent at least another half an hour in the room, speaking with the group that inevitably remained after each session. She loved this time with her students, possibly even more than the lectures themselves, as the lingering few were inevitably her kindred spirits. These were the students who kept her teaching. She certainly didn't need the pittance that extension teaching provided. Maureen taught because she loved the contact and the stimulation of sharing her theories with others who were excited and open-minded.

Heels clicking in rhythm on the walkway, Maureen picked up her pace, walking swiftly through the tree-lined avenues of the north campus. She didn't want to miss Peter, not tonight. Maureen cursed her fashion sense, wishing she had worn more sensible shoes for the near sprint required to reach his office before he left. She was, as always, impeccably dressed, taking the same meticulous care with her clothing as she did with all the details in her life. The perfectly cut designer suit fit her petite figure flawlessly, and its forest color accentuated her green eyes. A pair of rather daring Manolo Blahnik heels added some dash to the otherwise conservative outfit—and some necessary height to her five-foot-nothing frame. It was precisely that pair of Manolos that were the source of her current frustration. She briefly considered hurling them across the quad.

*Please don't leave. Please be there.* She called out to Peter in her mind as she rushed. They had been strangely connected, even as kids, and she hoped now that somehow he could sense how badly she needed to speak to him. Maureen had tried to call him via more conventional means earlier, but to no avail. Peter hated cell phones and wouldn't carry one despite her multiple pleas over the years, and he generally refused to pick up the extension in his office if he was immersed in his work.

She ripped off the offending spiked heels and stuffed them into her leather tote bag as she ran the final length to her destination. Holding her breath as she rounded the corner, Maureen looked up at the second-story windows and counted from the left. She let out her breath in a relieved sigh when she saw the light in the fourth window. He was still here.

Maureen climbed the steps deliberately, allowing time to catch her breath. She turned left down the corridor, stopping when she reached the fourth door on her right. Peter was there, peering intently through a magnifying glass at a yellowed manuscript. He felt rather than saw her in the doorway, and when he looked up, his kind face broke into a welcoming smile.

"Maureen! What a wonderful surprise. I didn't expect to see you tonight."

"Hi, Pete," she responded with equal warmth, coming around the desk to give him a quick hug. "I'm so glad you're here—I was afraid you would have left by now, and I desperately needed to see you."

Father Peter Healy raised an eyebrow and considered for a long moment before responding. "You know, under normal circumstances I would have left hours ago. I was compelled to work late tonight, for some reason I didn't entirely understand—until now."

Then he shrugged off his comment with a slight, knowing smile. Maureen returned the expression. She had never been able to account for the connection she had with her older cousin on any logical level. But from the day she had arrived in Ireland as a young girl they had been as close as twins, sharing an uncanny ability to communicate without words.

Maureen reached into her tote bag and pulled out a blue plastic grocery sack, the type used by import shops the world over. It held a small rectangular box, which she handed to the priest.

"Ahh. Lyon's Gold Label. Beautiful choice. I still can't stomach American tea."

Maureen made a face and shuddered to indicate her shared distaste. "Bog water."

"I believe the kettle is full, so I'll just plug it in and we'll have a cuppa right here and now."

Maureen smiled as she watched Peter rise from the battered leather chair he had fought to obtain from the university. Upon acceptance of his position in the humanities extension department, the esteemed Dr. Peter Healy had been given a window office with modern furniture, which included a brand-new and very functional desk and chair. Peter hated functional when it came to his furniture, but he hated modern even more. Using his Gaelic charm as an irresistible force, he had managed to stir the usually unmovable staff into frenetic activity. He was a dead ringer for the Irish actor Gabriel Byrne, a likeness that never failed to inspire women, Roman collar or no. The staff had searched basements and scoured unused classrooms until they found exactly what he was looking for: a weathered and extremely comfortable leather high-backed chair, and a desk of aged wood that at least looked somewhat antique. The modern amenities in the office were of his choosing: the mini-refrigerator in the corner behind the desk, a small electric kettle for boiling water, and the generally ignored telephone.

Maureen was more relaxed now as she watched him, safe in the presence of a close relative and immersed in the entirely soothing and purely Irish art form of tea making.

Peter crossed back to his desk and leaned down to the refrigerator situated immediately behind him. He removed a small container of milk and placed it next to the pink and white box of sugar resting on top of the fridge. "There's a spoon here somewhere—wait—here we are."

The electric kettle was sputtering now, indicating that the water was on the boil.

"I'll do the honors," Maureen volunteered.

She stood up and took the box of tea from Peter's desk, opening the plastic seal with the edge of a manicured thumbnail. She removed two round bags and dropped them into mismatched, tea-stained mugs. The stereotypes about Irishmen and alcohol were dramatically overstated from Maureen's perspective; the real Irish addiction was to this stuff.

Maureen finished the preparations expertly and handed a steaming mug to her cousin as she sat down in the chair opposite his desk. Her own mug in hand, Maureen sipped quietly for a moment, feeling Peter's benevolent blue eyes on her. Now that she had hurried to see him, she was unsure of where to start. It was the priest who ultimately broke the silence.

"Is she back, then?" he asked softly.

Maureen sighed with relief. At those moments when she had thought herself truly on the distant edge of sanity, Peter was there for her: cousin, priest, friend.

"Yep," she replied, uncharacteristically inarticulate. "She's back."

Peter tossed restlessly in his bed, unable to sleep. The conversation with Maureen had disturbed him more than he let on to her. He was concerned about her, both as her closest living relative and as her spiritual counselor. He had known her dreams would come back with a vengeance, and had been biding his time, anticipating the day.

When Maureen first returned from the Holy Land, she had been disturbed by dreams of the regal, suffering woman in the red cloak, the woman she had seen in Jerusalem. Her dreams were always the same: she was immersed in the mob on the Via Dolorosa. Occasionally, a dream might contain minor variations or a stray additional detail, but they always featured the intense sense of desperation. It was this vivid intensity that disturbed Peter, the authenticity in Maureen's descriptions. It was intangible, something that was triggered by the Holy Land itself, a feeling Peter had first encountered himself while studying in Jerusalem. It was a sense of getting very close to the ancient—and the divine.

After her return from the Holy Land, Maureen spent many long-distance telephone hours speaking with Peter, who at the time was teaching in Ireland. His confident and independent cousin was beginning to question her own sanity, and the intensity and frequency of the dreams was beginning to trouble Peter. He applied for a transfer to Loyola, knowing it would be granted immediately, and boarded a plane for Los Angeles to be closer to his cousin.

Four years later, he wrestled with his thoughts and with his conscience, unsure of the best way to help Maureen now. He wanted to take her to see some of his superiors in the Church, but he knew she would never consent to that. Peter was the last link she allowed herself to her once-Catholic background. She trusted him only because he was family—and because he was the only person in her life who had never let her down.

Peter sat up, giving in to the understanding that sleep would elude him this night—and he was trying not to think about the pack of Marlboro's in the drawer of the nightstand. He had tried to stave off this particular bad habit—indeed, it was one of the reasons he chose to live alone in an apartment and not in Jesuit housing. But the stress was too much for him, and he yielded to this spot of sin. Lighting a cigarette, he exhaled deeply and contemplated the issues facing Maureen.

There had always been something special about his petite, feisty American cousin. When she had first arrived in Ireland with her mother she was a scared and lonely seven-year-old with a bayou drawl. Eight years her senior, Peter took Maureen under his wing, introducing her to the local children in the village—and providing black eyes for anyone who dared make fun of the newcomer with the funny accent.

But it didn't take long for Maureen to assimilate into her new environment. She healed rapidly from the traumas of her past in Louisiana as the mists of Ireland enveloped her in welcome. She found refuge in the countryside. Peter and his sisters took her on long walks, showing off the beauty of the river and warning her of the pitfalls in the bogs. They all spent long summer days picking the blackberries that grew wild on the family farm and playing soccer until the sun went down. In time, the local kids accepted her as she became more comfortable with her surroundings and allowed her true personality to emerge.

Peter had often wondered about the definition of the word "charisma" as it was used in the supernatural context of the early church: *charism, a divinely bestowed gift or power.* Perhaps it applied to Maureen more literally and profoundly than any of them had ever dreamed. He kept a journal of his discussions with her, had done so since those first long-distance phone calls, where he logged his own insights on the meaning of the dreams. And he prayed daily for guidance—if Maureen had been chosen by God to perform some task related to the time of the passion, which he was increasingly certain she was witnessing in her dreams, he would indeed require maximum guidance from his Creator. And his Church.

*Château des Pommes Bleues*
*The Languedoc region of France*
*October 2004*

" 'MARIE DE NEGRE shall choose when the time is come for The Expected One. She who is born of the paschal lamb when the day and night are equal, she who is a child of the resurrection. She who carries the Sangre-el will be granted the key upon viewing the Black Day of the Skull. She will become the new Shepherdess and show us The Way.' "

Lord Bérenger Sinclair paced the polished floors of his library. Flames from an enormous stone fireplace cast golden light upon an ancestral collection of priceless books and manuscripts. A tattered banner hung in a protective glass case that stretched across the full length of the enormous hearth. Once white, the yellowed fabric was emblazoned with faded gold fleurs-de-lis. The conjoined name *Jhesus-Maria* was embroidered on the buckram, but was visible only to the rare few who had the opportunity to get close to this particular relic.

Sinclair recited the prophecy aloud and by rote, his slight Scottish accent rolling the "r"s in the sentence. Berenger knew the words of the foretelling by heart; he had learned them while sitting on his grandfather's knee as a little boy. He didn't comprehend the meaning of those lines back then. It was merely a memorization game he played with his grandfather when he spent the summers here on the family's vast French estate.

He paused in his pacing to stand before an elaborate lineage, a family tree spanning the centuries that was painted floor to ceiling on the wide far wall. It was a massive mural that displayed the history of Bérenger's flamboyant ancestors.

This branch of the Sinclair family was one of the oldest in Europe. Originally called Saint Clair, they had been driven from the Continent to take refuge in Scotland in the thirteenth century, when the surname was subsequently anglicized to its current form. Bérenger's ancestors were some of the most illustrious in British history, including James the First of England and that king's infamous mother, Mary, Queen of Scots.

The influential and savvy Sinclair family managed to survive civil wars and political upheaval within Scotland, playing both sides of the crown through the country's tumultuous history. A captain of industry in the twentieth century, Bérenger's grandfather had established one of the greatest fortunes in Europe with the founding of a North Sea oil corporation. A billionaire several times over and a British peer with a seat in the House of Lords, Alistair Sinclair had everything any man could ask for. But he remained restless and unsatisfied, a seeker after something his fortune could not buy.

Grandfather Alistair became obsessed with France, buying an enormous château outside the village of Arques in the rugged and mysterious southwestern region known as the Languedoc. He called his new home Château des Pommes Bleues—House of the Blue Apples—for reasons known only to an initiated few.

The Languedoc was a mountainous land filled with mysticism. Local legends of buried treasure and mysterious knights dated back hundreds, even thousands, of years. Alistair Sinclair had become increasingly fixated on the Languedoc folklore, buying as much land in the region as he could acquire and searching with increasing urgency for treasure he believed was buried in the region. The cache he sought had little to do with gold or riches, items Alistair already possessed in overabundance. It was something far more valuable to him, to his family, and to the world. He spent less and less time in Scotland as he grew older, happy only when he was here in the wild, red mountains of the Languedoc. Alistair insisted that his grandson accompany him during the summers, and he ultimately instilled his passion for the mythic region—indeed, his obsession—in the young Bérenger.

Now in his forties, Bérenger Sinclair paused once more in his circuit around the great library, this time before a painting of his grandfather. Seeing the sharp, angular features, the curling dark hair, and intense eyes was like looking into a mirror.

"You look so much like him, Monsieur. You are more like him every day, in many ways."

Sinclair turned to answer his hulking manservant, Roland. For such an enormous man, he had uncommon stealth and often seemed to appear out of the air.

"Is that a good thing?" Bérenger asked wryly.

"Of course. Monsieur Alistair was a fine man, much loved by the people of the villages. And by my father, and myself."

Sinclair nodded with a small smile. Roland would say so, of course. The French giant was a son of the Languedoc. His own father was from a local family with deep roots in its legendary soil and had been Alistair's majordomo at the château. Roland was raised on the château grounds and understood the Sinclair family and their eccentric obsessions. When his father passed away suddenly, Roland stepped into his shoes as the caretaker of Château des Pommes Bleues. He was one of the very few people on earth whom Bérenger Sinclair trusted.

"If you do not mind me saying so, we were working across the hall and heard you—myself and Jean-Claude. We heard you speak the words of the prophecy." He looked at Sinclair quizzically. "Is something wrong?"

Sinclair crossed the room to where an enormous mahogany desk dominated the far wall. "No, Roland. Nothing is wrong. In fact, I think things may finally be very, very right."

He picked up a hardcover book that rested on the desk, showing the cover to his servant. It was a modern, nonfiction book cover, with a title that announced: *HerStory.* A subtitle read: *A Defense of History's Most Hated Heroines.*

Roland looked at the book, puzzled. "I don't understand."

"No, no. Turn it over. Look at this. Look at *her.*"

Roland turned the book over to reveal a back-cover photo of the author with the caption *Author Maureen Paschal.*

The author was an attractive, red-haired woman in her thirties. She was posed for the photograph with her hands resting on the chair in front of her. Sinclair ran his hand over the cover, stopping to point out the author's hands. Small, but visible on the right ring finger, was the ancient copper ring from Jerusalem, with its planetary pattern.

Roland looked up from the book with a start. "Sacre bleu."

"Indeed," Sinclair replied. "Or perhaps, more accurately, Sacre rouge."

Both men were interrupted by a presence in the doorway. Jean-Claude de la Motte, an elite and trusted member of the Pommes Bleues inner sanctum, looked at his comrades questioningly. "What has happened?"

Sinclair gestured for Jean-Claude to enter. "Nothing yet. But see what you think of this."

Roland handed the book to Jean-Claude and pointed out the ring on the author's hand in the back-cover photograph.

Jean-Claude removed reading glasses from his pocket and scrutinized the photo for a moment before asking in a near whisper, "*L'attendue?* The Expected One?"

Sinclair chuckled. "Yes, my friends. After all these years I think we may have finally found our Shepherdess."

. . . *I have known Peter since my earliest memories, as his father and mine were friends, and as he was very close to my brother. The temple at Capernaeum was near to the home of Simon-Peter's father and it was a place we visited often as children. I remember playing a game there, along the shore. I was far younger than the boys and I often played alone, but the sound of their laughter as they wrestled with each other is something I can still remember.*

*Peter was always the more serious of the boys, his brother Andrew having a lighter heart. And yet there was humor in both of them when they were young. Peter and Andrew lost that lightness entirely after Easa was gone, and they had little patience for those of us who clung to it for survival.*

*Peter was much like my own brother in that he took his family responsibilities very seriously, and as he grew into manhood, he transferred that sense of responsibility to the teachings of The Way. He had a strength and singleness of purpose that was unmatched by any but the teachers themselves—this is why he was trusted so highly. Yet as much as Easa taught him, Peter struggled against his own nature more ferociously than most people would ever know. I believe that he gave up more than the others to follow The Way as it was taught—it required more of himself, more internal change. Peter will be misunderstood and there are those who bear him ill. But I do not.*

*I loved Peter and trusted him. Even with my oldest son.*

THE ARQUES GOSPEL OF MARY MAGDALENE,
THE BOOK OF DISCIPLES

# Chapter Three

*McLean, Virginia*
*March 2005*

*M*cLean, Virginia, is an eclectic place, an odd mixture of politics and suburbia. Off the Beltway, it's a short drive past CIA headquarters to Tysons Corner, one of the largest and most prestigious shopping centers in America. McLean is not known as a suburban center for spirituality. At least, not to most people.

Maureen Paschal was not concerned in the least with sacred matters as she drove her rented Ford Taurus into the long driveway of the McLean Ritz-Carlton. Tomorrow morning's schedule was packed: up early for a breakfast meeting with the Eastern League of Women Writers, followed by an appearance and book signing at a behemoth retailer in Tysons Corner.

That would give Maureen most of Saturday afternoon to herself. Perfect. She would go exploring, as she always did when she was in a new town. It didn't matter how small or rural the place was; if Maureen had never been there, it held fascination. She never failed to find the jewel in the crown, the special feature of every place she visited that made it unique in her memory. Tomorrow, she would find McLean's.

Check-in was a breeze; her publisher had handled all the arrangements, and Maureen had only to sign a form and grab her key. Then it was up the elevator and into her beautifully appointed room, where she indulged her need for order by unpacking immediately and assessing the wrinkle damage to her clothing.

Maureen loved luxury hotels; everyone did, she supposed, but she was like a child when she stayed in one. She thoroughly inspected the amenities, scoped out the contents of the mini-bar, checked for the sumptuous crested robe behind the bathroom door, and smiled at the extension phone next to the toilet.

She vowed she would never be so jaded that she ceased to enjoy these little perks. Perhaps those years of scraping, eating Top Ramen, Pop Tarts, and peanut butter sandwiches while her research devoured what was left of her savings had been good for her, after all. Those early experiences helped her to appreciate the finer things that life was beginning to bestow.

She looked around the spacious room and felt a brief pang of regret—for all of her recent success, there was no one to share her accomplishments with. She was alone, she had always been alone, and perhaps she always would be . . .

Maureen banished the self-pity as immediately as it came, and turned to the greatest of distractions to take her mind off such troubling thoughts. Some of the most tantalizing shopping in America was waiting right outside her door. Picking up her bag, Maureen double-checked that she had her credit cards and ventured out to celebrate the culture of Tysons Corner.

The Eastern League of Women Writers held their breakfast in a conference hall of the McLean Ritz-Carlton. Maureen wore her public uniform—a conservative designer suit with high heels and a spritz of Chanel No. 5. Arriving in the hall precisely at 9:00 A.M., she declined food and requested a pot of Irish breakfast tea. Eating before a question-and-answer session was never a good idea for Maureen. It made her queasy.

Maureen was less nervous than usual this morning as the event's moderator was an ally, a lovely woman named Jenna Rosenberg with whom she had been in touch for several weeks in preparation for the event. First and foremost, Jenna was a fan of Maureen's work and was able to quote from it extensively. That alone won Maureen over. In addition, the event was set up in an intimate setting of small tables clustered together so that Maureen didn't need a microphone.

Jenna began the Q-and-A session herself, with an obvious but important query.

"What inspired you to write this book?"

Maureen put down her teacup and replied.

"I read once that early British historical texts were translated by a sect of monks who didn't believe that women had souls. They felt that the source of all evil came from women. These monks were the first to alter the legends of King Arthur and what we think of as Camelot. Guinevere became a scheming adulteress rather than a powerful warrior queen. Morgan le Fey became Arthur's evil sister who deceives him into incest, rather than the spiritual leader of an entire nation, which is what she was in the earliest versions of the legend.

"That understanding shocked me and made me ask the question: had other portrayals of women in history been written from such an extreme bias? Obviously, this perspective extends throughout history. I started thinking of the many women it might have applied to, and my research went from there."

Jenna allowed the questions to rotate around the tables. After some discussion of feminist literature and issues of equality in the publishing industry, a question came from a young woman wearing a small gold cross over her silk blouse.

"For those of us who were raised in a traditional environment, the chapter on Mary Magdalene was very eye-opening. You present a very different woman than that of the repentant prostitute, the fallen woman. But I'm still not sure I can buy into it."

Maureen nodded her understanding before launching into her response. "Even the Vatican has conceded that Mary Magdalene wasn't a prostitute and that we should no longer be teaching that particular lie in Sunday school. It has been more than thirty years since the Vatican formally proclaimed that Mary was *not* the fallen woman of Luke's gospel, and that Pope Gregory the Great had created that story to further his own purposes in the Dark Ages. But two millennia of public opinion is hard to erase. The Vatican's admission of error in the 1960s hasn't really been any more effective than a retraction buried on the last page of a newspaper. So essentially, Mary Magdalene becomes the godmother of misunderstood females, the first woman of major importance to be intentionally and completely altered and maligned by the writers of history. She was a close follower of Christ, arguably an apostle in her own right. And yet she's been excised almost entirely from the Gospels."

Jenna interjected, obviously excited about the subject. "But there is so much speculation now about Mary Magdalene, like that she may have had an intimate relationship with Christ."

The cross-wearing woman flinched, but Jenna continued. "You didn't address any of those issues in your book, and I was wondering how you felt about those theories."

"I don't address them because I don't believe there is any evidence to back up those claims—a lot of colorful and possibly wishful thinking, but no proof. Theologians agree on this across the board. There is certainly nothing that I, as a self-respecting journalist, could feel comfortable supporting as fact and publishing with my name on it. However, I might go so far as to say that there are authenticated documents that hint at a possibly intimate relationship between Jesus and Mary Magdalene. A gospel discovered in Egypt in 1945 says 'the companion of the Savior is Mary Magdalene. He loved her more than all the disciples, and used to kiss her often on her mouth.'

"Of course, these gospels have been questioned by Church authorities and may have been the first-century version of the *National Enquirer*, for all we know. I think it's important to tread carefully here, so I wrote what I was certain of. And I am certain that Mary Magdalene was not a prostitute and that she was an important follower of Jesus.

Perhaps she was even the most important, as she is the first person whom the risen Lord chose to bless with His appearance. Beyond that, I am not willing to speculate about her role in His life. It would be irresponsible."

Maureen answered the question safely, as she usually did. But she had always speculated that perhaps Magdalene's downfall came because she was too close to the Master, therefore inspiring jealousy in the male disciples who later attempted to discredit her. Saint Peter was openly disdainful of Mary Magdalene and berated her, based on those second-century documents that were discovered in Egypt. And the later writings of Saint Paul appeared to methodically eliminate all reference to the importance of women in Christ's life.

Maureen had spent a fair amount of research time ripping apart Pauline doctrine as a result. Paul, the persecutor turned apostle, had shaped Christian thought with his observations, despite his philosophical and literal distance from Jesus and the Savior's own chosen followers and family. He had no firsthand knowledge of Christ's teachings. Such a misogynistic and politically manipulative "disciple" was hardly going to immortalize Mary Magdalene as Christ's most devoted servant.

Maureen was determined to avenge Mary, viewing her as the archetype of the reviled woman in history, the mother of the misunderstood. Her story was, in essence if not in form, repeated in the lives of the other women Maureen had chosen to defend in *HerStory*. But it had been essential for Maureen to keep the Magdalene chapters as close to provable academic theory as possible. Any hint of a "new age" or otherwise unsubstantiated hypothesis about Mary's relationship with Jesus would potentially invalidate the rest of the research and damage her credibility. She was far too careful in her life and work to take such a chance. Despite her instincts, Maureen had rejected all alternative theories on Mary Magdalene, making the choice to hold to the most indisputable facts.

Shortly after she made that decision, the dreams had come in earnest.

Her right hand was cramping ferociously and her face was in immediate danger of cracking from a nonstop smile, but Maureen continued to work. Her bookstore appearance had been scheduled for a two-hour slot, which was to include a twenty-minute break. She was now well into the third hour, with no break taken, and was determined to continue signing until the last customer was satisfied. Maureen would never turn away a potential reader. She would not scorn the book-buying public that had turned her dream into a reality.

She was gratified to see a reasonably large number of men in the crowd today. The subject matter of her book suggested a predominantly female audience, but she hoped that it was written in a way that would appeal to everyone with an open mind and some common sense. Although her primary goal had been to avenge the wrongs endured by powerful women as victims of male historians, her research had revealed that the motivation behind committing history to paper in such a selective fashion was overwhelmingly political and religious. Gender was a secondary factor.

She had explained this during a recent television appearance, citing Marie Antoinette as perhaps the clearest example of that sociopolitical theory because *the dominant accounts of the French Revolution were written by revolutionaries.* Whereas the beleaguered queen was widely blamed for the excesses of the French monarchy, she really had had nothing to do with the creation of such traditions. Marie Antoinette had, in fact, inherited the practices of the French aristocracy when she came from Austria as the betrothed of the young dauphin, the future Louis XVI. Although she herself was the daughter of the great Maria Theresa, that Austrian empress had not been a practitioner of royal excess and indulgence. If anything, she was remarkably dour and thrifty for a woman of her position, raising her many daughters, including little Antoinette, with a very strict hand. The young dauphine would have been forced as a matter of pure survival to adapt to French custom as quickly as possible.

The palace of Versailles, the great monument to French extravagance, had been built decades before Marie Antoinette was born, yet it became an essential monument to *her* legendary greed. The famous retort to "The peasants are starving—they have no bread to eat" was actually uttered by a royal courtesan, a woman long dead before the young Austrienne had arrived in France. Yet to this day "Let them eat cake" is cited as a stimulus to revolution. With that one quote, the Reign of Terror and all of the bloodshed and violence that followed the fall of the Bastille have been justified.

And the tragically doomed Marie Antoinette never uttered the bloody phrase.

Maureen felt extraordinary sympathy for the ill-fated queen of France. Hated as a foreigner from the day of her arrival, Marie Antoinette was a victim of vicious and pointed racism. It was entirely convenient for the radically ethnocentric French nobility of the eighteenth century to attribute any and all negative political and social circumstances to their Austrian-born queen. Maureen had been stunned by this prevailing attitude during her research visit to France; the English-speaking tour guides at Versailles still spoke of the decapitated monarch with no small degree of venom, ignoring the historical evidence that exonerated Marie Antoinette from many heinous deeds she was said to have perpetrated. And all this despite the fact that the poor woman had been brutally mutilated two hundred years ago.

The first trip to Versailles had spurred Maureen on in her research. She had read numerous books, from the most academic descriptions of eighteenth-century France to elaborate historical novels that offered perspectives on the queen. The overall picture varied, but not too dramatically, from the accepted caricature: she was shallow, self-indulgent, not terribly bright. Maureen rejected this portrait. What about Marie Antoinette as a mother—a grieving woman who mourned a dead infant daughter and later lost her beloved son as well? Then there was Marie the wife, traded like an object on the proverbial political chessboard, a fourteen-year-old girl married to a foreigner in a strange land and subsequently rejected by his family, and later by his subjects. Finally, there was Marie the scapegoat, a woman who waited in captivity while the people she loved most were butchered in her name. Marie's closest friend, the Princess Lamballe, was literally torn to pieces by a mob; chunks of her body and various limbs were stuck on pikes and paraded past Marie's cell window.

Maureen had been determined to paint a sympathetic yet entirely realistic portrait of one of history's most despised monarchs. The result was powerful, one of the sections in *HerStory* that had received a tremendous amount of attention and engendered much debate.

But for all of Marie's controversy, she would always be first runner-up to Mary Magdalene.

It was the supernatural pull of Mary Magdalene that Maureen was currently discussing with the animated blonde standing before her.

"Did you know that McLean is considered a sacred spot to the followers of Mary Magdalene?" the woman asked suddenly.

Maureen opened her mouth to speak and then closed it again before managing to stammer, "No, I didn't know anything about that." There it was again, that electrical pulse that ripped through her every time something strange was on the horizon. She could feel it coming again, even here under the fluorescent lights of an American über-mall. Maureen gathered her composure with a deep breath. "Okay, I give up. In what way is McLean, Virginia, relevant to Mary Magdalene?"

The woman held out a business card to Maureen. "I don't know if you will have any free time while you are here, but if you do, please come and see me." The business card was for The Sacred Light bookstore, Rachel Martel, proprietor.

"It's nothing like this, of course," the woman who Maureen assumed must be Rachel said, indicating the huge bookstore where they were talking. "But I think we have a few books that you may find very interesting. Written by local people and self-published. They're about Mary. Our Mary."

Maureen gulped again, verified that the woman was indeed Rachel Martel, and then asked for directions to The Sacred Light.

There was a discreet cough to Maureen's left, and she looked up to see the bookstore manager gesturing emphatically that she needed to keep the line moving. Maureen gave him a look before returning to Rachel.

"Will you be there this afternoon by any chance? It's the only free time I have."

"I sure will. And I'm just a few miles down the main road. McLean isn't all that big. It's very easy to find. Call before you leave if you need better directions. Thanks for the autograph, and I hope to see you later."

As Maureen watched the woman retreat from the table, she glanced up at the store manager. "I think I may need a break after all," she said softly.

*Paris (First Arrondissement)*
*Caveau des Mousquetaires*
*March 2005*

THE WINDOWLESS, STONE BASEMENT in the antiquated building had been known as the Caveau des Mousquetaires for as long as anyone remembered. Its proximity to the Louvre in the days when the great museum had been the residence of the kings of France gave it strategic importance, one that was no less valid in modern times. The hidden space was named for the men made famous by Alexandre Dumas in his most celebrated work. Dumas had based the swashbucklers in his novel on real men with a real mission. This room was one of the secret meeting places of the queen's guard after the villainous Cardinal Richelieu drove them underground. In reality, it was not King Louis XIII of France whom the Musketeers were sworn to protect, but rather his queen. Anne of Austria was the daughter of a bloodline far more ancient and royal than that of her husband.

Dumas would undoubtedly shudder in his grave if he knew that this once-sacred space had fallen into enemy hands. On this night, the cave was the meeting site of another secret brotherhood. The occupying organization not only predated the Musketeers by 1,500 years, but also opposed their mission with an oath sworn in blood.

Illuminated by two-dozen candles, shadows danced off the walls to reveal the group of robed men in shades and silhouettes. They stood around a battered rectangular table, all faces cast in an interplay of dark and light. While none of their features were discernable in the half-light, the peculiar emblem of their Guild was visible on each of them—a blood-red cord tied tightly around the neck.

Hushed voices carried a variety of accents: English, French, Italian, and American. All fell silent as their leader took his place at the head of the table. Before him, a polished human skull, resting on a gold-filigreed platter, glowed in the candlelight. On one side of the skull was a chalice, decorated with golden spirals and encrusted with jewels that matched those on the platter. On the other side of the skull, a hand-carved wooden crucifix lay on the table, the image of Christ facedown.

The leader touched the skull reverently before raising the golden chalice filled with rich red liquid. He spoke in Oxford-accented English.

"The blood of the Teacher of Righteousness."

He drank slowly before passing the chalice to the brother on his left. The man took it with a nod, repeating the motto in his native French and taking his drink. Each member of the Guild repeated this rite, speaking in his native tongue, until the chalice returned to the head of the table.

The leader placed the cup gently before him. Next, he raised the platter and kissed the skull reverently on the brow bone. As with the chalice, he passed the skull to the left and each member of the brotherhood repeated his actions. This part of the ritual was performed in absolute silence, as if it was far too sacred to be diminished by words.

The skull completed the full cycle of worshipers, ending at the leader. He raised the platter high in the air before returning it to the table with a flourish and the words, "The first. The only."

The leader paused for a moment, then picked up the wooden crucifix. Turning it around so that the crucified image was facing him, he raised the cross to eye level—and spat viciously in the face of Jesus Christ.

*. . . Sarah-Tamar comes often and reads my memories while I write. She has reminded me that I have not yet explained about Peter and what is known as his denial.*

*There are some who judged him harshly and would call him Peter in Gallicantu—Peter in Denial—but that is unfair. What those who pass judgment cannot know is that Peter did nothing but fulfill Easa's wishes. I am told that some of the followers now say that Peter fulfilled a prophecy made by Easa, that Easa said to Peter, "You will deny me," and Peter said, "No, I will not."*

*This is the truth. Easa instructed Peter to deny him. It was not a prophecy. It was a command. Easa knew that if the worst happened, he would need Peter, of all his trusted disciples, to remain safe. Through Peter's determination, the teachings would continue to spread across the world as Easa had always dreamed. And so Easa told him, "You will deny me," but Peter in his torment said, "No, I cannot."*

*But Easa continued, "You must deny me so that you will be safe and the teachings of The Way will continue."*

*This is the truth of Peter's "denial." It was never a denial since he followed the orders of his teacher. Of this I am certain, for I was there and I witnessed.*

THE ARQUES GOSPEL OF MARY MAGDALENE,
THE BOOK OF DISCIPLES

# CHAPTER FOUR

*McLean, Virginia*
*March 2005*

aureen's pulse beat abnormally fast as she drove the main highway through McLean. She had been totally unprepared for Rachel Martel's odd invitation, but at the same time she was very excited by it. It had always been like this; hers was a life, connected by odd and often intense events, extraordinary coincidences that would influence her forever after. Would this be another one of those supernatural occurrences? She was particularly curious about any revelation that might pertain to Mary. Curious? Not nearly a strong enough word. Obsessed? More accurate.

Her connection to the Mary Magdalene legend had been a dominant force in her life since the early days of research for *HerStory*. Ever since that first vision in Jerusalem, Maureen had a solid sense of Mary Magdalene as a flesh-and-blood woman, almost as a friend. When she was working on the final draft of her book, she felt as though she were defending a friend who had been maligned by the press. Her relationship to Mary was very real. Or, perhaps more accurately, it was surreal.

The Sacred Light bookstore was small, although it was fronted by a large bay window that displayed angels of every description and in virtually every medium. There were books on angels, angel figurines, and lots of glittering crystals surrounded by artwork depicting the trendy cherubim. Maureen thought that Rachel herself was angelic in appearance: slightly plump with very blond curls surrounding a sweet face. She had even been wearing a two-piece outfit of flowing white gauze at the book signing earlier in the day.

The melodic tinkle of chimes announced Maureen's arrival as she pushed open the door and stepped into an expanded version of the window display. Rachel Martel was bent down behind the counter, fishing through the attached display case to locate a specific piece of jewelry for a customer. "This one?" she was asking the young woman, who was perhaps eighteen or nineteen.

"Yeah—that's the one." The girl was reaching out to examine the crystal point, a lavender stone set in silver. "It's amethyst, right?"

"Actually it's ametrine," Rachel corrected. She had just noticed that Maureen was the one who had sounded her door chime and flashed a quick, I'll-be-right-with-you smile before continuing the conversation with her customer. "Ametrine is amethyst that contains a piece of citrine inside of it. Here, if you hold it up to the light, you'll be able to see the beautiful gold center."

The teenage customer was squinting at the crystal in the light. "It's so pretty," she exclaimed. "But I was told that I needed amethyst. Will this do the same thing?"

"Yes, and more." Rachel smiled patiently. "Amethyst is believed to expand your spiritual nature, and citrine is good for balancing emotions in the physical body. All in all, it's quite a potent combination. But I have pure amethyst just over here, if you prefer."

Maureen was only half listening to the exchange. She was infinitely more curious about the books Rachel had told her about. The bookshelves appeared to be categorized by subject, and she scanned them quickly. There were volumes on Native American topics, a Celtic section where a less driven Maureen would have lingered on a different day, and the ubiquitous angel section.

To the right of the angels were some books on Christian thought. *Aha, I must be getting warmer.* She kept looking and stopped abruptly.

There was a large white volume with heavy black letters—MAGDA-LENE.

"I see you're finding everything just fine without me!"

Maureen jumped half a foot; she hadn't heard Rachel walk up behind her. The young customer was tinkling the door chimes as she exited the shop, clutching a small blue and white bag with her chosen crystal.

"This is one of the books I was telling you about. The rest are really more like booklets. Here, I think you should look at this one."

Rachel removed a thin booklet, not much more than a pamphlet, from the eye-level shelf. It was pink and looked like it had been printed on a home computer. *Mary in McLean,* it declared in 24-point Times New Roman.

"Which Mary is it?" Maureen asked. While writing the book, she had followed up a number of interesting research leads, only to find that they pertained to the Virgin, and not to the Magdalene.

"*Your* Mary," Rachel said with a knowing smile.

Maureen gave the woman a half smile in return. *My Mary, indeed.* She was beginning to feel that way.

"It doesn't need to specify, because it was written by a local person. The spiritual community in McLean knows it's Mary Magdalene. As I told you earlier, she has her own following here."

Rachel went on to explain that for many generations, residents of this small Virginia town had reported spiritual visions. "Jesus has been seen here on nearly a hundred documented occasions in the last century. The odd thing is that He's often seen standing on the side of the road—the main road—the one you took to get here, in fact. A few of the visions have actually involved Christ on the cross, also seen from the main road. In some of the visions, Christ has been seen walking with a woman. She has been described repeatedly as a small figure with long hair."

Rachel leafed through the booklet, pointing out the various chapters. "The first vision of this type was documented early in the twentieth century; the woman who had the vision was one Gwendolyn Maddox, and it transpired in her back garden, of all places. She insisted that the woman with Christ was Mary Magdalene, while her parish priest was somewhat insistent that the vision had actually been of Christ and the *Virgin* Mary. I suppose you get more Vatican points if you see *Her*. But old Gwen was adamant. It was Mary *Magdalene*. She said that she didn't know how she knew, she just did. And Gwen also claimed that the vision had completely cured her of a particularly nasty case of rheumatoid arthritis. That's when she set up a shrine and opened her garden to the public. To this day, the local people pray to Mary Magdalene for healing.

"It's also fascinating to note that none of Gwen's descendants suffered from rheumatoid arthritis, which is, as far as I know, a hereditary condition. I am particularly thankful for this, as are my mother and my grandmother. I'm Gwendolyn's great-granddaughter."

Maureen looked down at the booklet in her hand. She had missed the small print at the bottom of the *Mary in McLean* pamphlet. *By Rachel Maddox Martel.*

Rachel handed the booklet to Maureen. "Here, it's a gift. It contains Gwen's story, and a few other details about the visions. Now this other book"—Rachel indicated the large white volume with the bold black MAGDALENE heading—"this is also written by a native of McLean. The author has spent a lot of time investigating local Mary sightings, but she has also done enormous amounts of general research. This book really runs the gamut on Magdalene theories, and I will say that some of them are a little far out, even for my taste. But it's fascinating reading, and you won't find it anywhere else because it's never been distributed."

"I'll take it, of course," Maureen said somewhat absently. Her mind was in several places at once. "Why McLean, do you think? I mean, of all the places in America, why does she come here?"

Rachel smiled and shrugged a little. "I don't have an answer for that. Maybe there are other places in America where this happens as well, and they just keep it to themselves. Or perhaps there is something special about the location. What I do know is this: people with a spiritual interest in the life of Mary Magdalene tend to end up in McLean, sooner or later. I can't tell you how many people come through this shop looking for specific books on her. And, like you, they had no previous conscious knowledge about the Magdalene connection in this town. It can't be just a coincidence, now, can it? I believe that Mary lures her faithful here, to McLean."

Maureen thought about it for a moment before responding. "You know . . . ," she began slowly, still composing the thought. "When I made my travel arrangements, I had every intention of staying in D.C. I have a good friend there, and it would have been easy to drive in to McLean for the book signing. D.C. made a lot more sense with the airline as well, but at the last minute, I decided that I had to stay here."

Rachel was grinning as she listened to Maureen explain her change of travel plans. "See. Mary brought you here. Just promise me, if you see her while you're driving around McLean, that you won't forget to call and tell me about it."

"Have you ever seen her?" Maureen had to know.

Rachel tapped the pink booklet in Maureen's hand with the tip of her fingernail. "Yes, and this is really an explanation of how the visions have been passed down in my family," she explained in a surprisingly matter-of-fact tone. "The first time, I was very young. Four or five, I think. It was in my grandmother's garden at the shrine. Mary was alone that first time I saw her. The second vision happened when I was a teenager. That was a 'roadside,' as we call it here, and it was Mary with Jesus. It was very strange; I was in a car full of girls and we were driving back from a school football game. It was a Friday night. Well, my older sister Judith was driving, and as we came around a bend in the road, we saw a man and a woman walking toward us. Judy slowed down to see if it was someone who needed help. That's when we realized what it was. They were just standing there, frozen in time, but there was a glow surrounding them.

"Well, Judy was very upset by this and started to cry. Then the girl next to her in the front seat starting asking what was wrong and why were we stopped. That's when I realized that the other girls didn't see them. Only my sister and I saw them.

"I've wondered for a long time if genetics had anything to do with the visions. My family had experienced so many of them, and I had real proof that we were able to see visions that had remained hidden to others. I still don't know, really. Certainly, there have been people here in McLean who are no relation to me who have had the visions as well."

"Were all of the visions seen by women?"

"Oh, yes, I forgot that part. Anytime Mary has been seen alone that I know of, it has been by another woman. When she appears with Jesus, it has been to both sexes. But still, very rarely are the apparitions seen by men. Or maybe they are, but I think men are less likely to talk about it in public."

"I see." Maureen was nodding. "Rachel, how clearly did you see Mary? I mean, could you describe her face in any detail?"

Rachel continued to smile in that beatifically knowing way that Maureen found strangely comforting. Speaking with someone about visions as if it were the most natural thing in the world made Maureen feel surprisingly safe. At least if she did turn out to be completely nuts, she was in pleasant enough company.

"I can do better than describe her face. Come over here."

Rachel took Maureen gently by the arm and led her to the back of the shop. She pointed to the wall behind the cash register, but Maureen's eyes had already found the portrait. It was an oil painting; the subject was an auburn-haired woman with an exquisitely beautiful face and the most extraordinary hazel eyes.

Rachel was watching Maureen's reaction closely, and waiting for her to speak. It would be a long wait. Maureen was speechless.

Rachel offered quietly, "I see you two have already met."

As stunned as Maureen had been by the face in the frame, she was even more shaken by what followed. After the initial moment of shock, she began to tremble just before the sob burst through her body.

She stood there and cried for what must have been a minute, maybe two, sobs wracking her small frame for the first few seconds before waning into a softer cry. She felt such terrible sorrow, a deep and aching pain, but she wasn't entirely sure that the sadness was her own. It was as if she were experiencing the pain of the woman in the portrait. But then it changed; after the initial outburst, Maureen's crying felt more like relief, and she surrendered to it. The oil painting represented a type of validation; it made the dream woman real.

The dream woman, who just happened to be Mary Magdalene.

Rachel was kind enough to brew some herbal tea in the back room of the shop. She allowed Maureen to sit in the small stockroom for some privacy. A young couple looking for astrology books had entered the store, and Rachel glided off to help them. Maureen sat at a small desk in the back, sipping chamomile and hoping that the claim on the tea box, "soothes the nerves," was not just advertising hype.

When Rachel had finished her transaction at the front of the store, she came back to check on Maureen. "You okay?"

Maureen nodded and took another sip. "Fine now, thanks. Rachel, I'm really sorry about the outburst, I just, well . . . did you paint that?"

Rachel nodded. "Artistic ability runs in my family. My grandmother is a sculptor; she has done several versions of Mary in clay. I have often wondered if that's the reason Mary appears to us—because we have the ability to express her somehow."

"Or maybe it's because artistic people are more open," Maureen was thinking out loud. "Sort of a right-brain thing?"

"Possibly. I think it's a combination of the two, at least. But I'll tell you something else. I believe with all my heart that Mary wants to be heard. Her apparitions have increased here in McLean over the last decade. She was all but haunting me over the last year, and I knew that I had to paint her in order to find any degree of peace. Once the portrait was finished and displayed, I was able to sleep again. In fact, I haven't seen her since."

Back in her hotel room later that night, Maureen swirled the red wine in her glass and gazed absently at it. She glanced up at the television, tuned to a cable channel, trying hard not to let the ultra-conservative talk show host get to her. Despite her outward appearance of strength, Maureen hated confrontation. Even the possibility that they might be discussing her work was painful. It was like watching a devastating car accident—she couldn't tear her eyes away, no matter how unpleasant the sight before her.

The overzealous host introduced his esteemed guest, following with the question, "Isn't this just another in a long line of attacks against the Church?"

The identifying title *Bishop Magnus O'Connor* appeared under the aging face of an irate cleric as he responded in an unmistakable Irish accent. "Of course. For centuries, we have endured the slander of misguided individuals who would attempt to damage the faith of millions for their own personal gain. These feminist extremists need to accept the fact that all of the recognized apostles were men."

Maureen surrendered. She just wasn't up to this tonight—it had been too long and emotional a day. With a touch of the remote control button, she silenced the churchman, wishing it were that easy in real life.

"Bite me, your holiness," she grumbled, as she took herself off to bed.

A beam from the lights outside Maureen's hotel room shone on the bedside table, illuminating her sleeping potions: a half-empty glass of red wine and a box of an over-the-counter sleep aid. A small crystal ashtray adjacent to a table lamp held the ancient copper ring from Jerusalem.

Maureen tossed restlessly, despite her self-medicating attempt at achieving undisturbed sleep. The dream came, as relentless as it was unbidden.

It started as it always did—the commotion, the sweat, the crowd. But when Maureen reached the part of the dream where she first spotted the woman, everything went black. She was plunged into a void for an unknowable amount of time.

And then, the dream changed.

*On an idyllic day along the shores of the Sea of Galilee, a little boy ran ahead of his lovely mother. He did not share her startling hazel eyes and rich copper hair, as his little sister did. He had a different look, dark and intense, surprisingly brooding for such a small boy. Running to the shore, he picked up an interesting rock that caught his eye and held it up to glitter in the sun.*

*His mother called a warning to him not to go too far into the water. She was without her formal veil today, and her long, loose hair billowed around her face as she grabbed the hand of the little girl, who was a perfect miniature version of herself.*

*The voice of a man expressed a similar but good-natured warning to the tiny girl who had broken away from her mother's grasp and now ran to join her brother. The child looked rebellious, but her mother laughed, glancing over a shoulder to smile intimately at the man who walked behind her. On this casual walk with his young family, his garment was unbleached and unbelted, not the pristine white robe he wore in public. He brushed long strands of chestnut-colored hair from his eyes and returned her smile with his own, an expression filled with love and contentment.*

Maureen was thrust violently back into a waking state as if she had been thrown physically from the dream and propelled into her hotel room. She was shaking. The dreams always disturbed her, but this was even more disconcerting, this feeling of hurtling through time and space. She was breathing quickly, and made a concerted effort to regain her balance and breathe in a more relaxed fashion.

Maureen was just beginning to regain her bearings when she became aware of a movement across her room, in the doorway. She was sure of a rustle, yet sensed rather than saw the figure that appeared in the doorway of her room. What she actually did see was indefinable—a shape, a figure, a movement. It didn't matter. Maureen knew who it was just as surely as she knew she was no longer dreaming. It was *Her*. She was here, in Maureen's room.

Maureen swallowed. Her mouth was dry with shock and more than a little fear. She knew the figure in the doorway was not of the physical world, but she wasn't sure if that was exactly comforting. She summoned all of her courage and managed to whisper to the shape in the doorway.

"What . . . tell me how I can help you. Please."

There was a light rustle in reply, the swishing of a veil or the blowing of springtime leaves, and then nothing. The apparition vanished as quickly as it had appeared.

Maureen jumped out of bed and switched on the light—4:10 A.M., according to the digital clock. It was three hours earlier in Los Angeles. *Forgive me, Father,* she thought as she grabbed the phone from her nightstand and dialed as fast as her shaking fingers would allow. She needed her best friend—and maybe, just maybe, she needed a priest.

Peter's insistent voice, with its comforting Irish lilt, brought Maureen back to earth.

"It is incredibly important that you keep track of these . . . well, . . . visions. I hope you are writing them down?"

"Visions? Please don't go all Vatican on me, Pete." Maureen groaned loudly. "I would die before becoming some weird cause célèbre for the Roman inquisition."

"Pah, Maureen, I would never do such a thing to you. But what if these *are* visions? You can't discount the potential importance of what you have been shown."

"First of all, there have just been two so-called visions. The rest have been dreams. Very vivid and intense dreams, but dreams nonetheless. Maybe it's the genetic madness setting in. Runs in the family, you know." Maureen exhaled hard. "Damn, this is scaring me. You're supposed to be helping me to calm down, remember?"

"Sorry. You're right, and I do want to help you. But promise me you'll write down the dates and the times of your vis—er, dreams. Just for our purposes. You're a historian and a journalist. You of all people know that documenting your data is critical."

Maureen allowed herself a little laugh at this. "Oh, yes, and this is certainly historical data." She sighed across the telephone line. "Okay, I'll do that. Maybe it will help me to make sense of it all someday. I just feel like there's so much happening below the surface, and it's all so completely out of my control."

*. . . I must write more now of Nathaneal, who we called Bartolome, for I have been so moved by his devotion. Bartolome was little more than a youth when he first joined us in Galilee. And while he had been expelled from the house of his noble father, Tolma of Canae, it was clear upon meeting him that there was nothing of the incorrigible within him—surely, a cruel and unwise patriarch had misjudged the beauty and promise of such a precious and special soul, a beautiful son. Easa saw this as well, and as immediately.*

*Bartolome could be understood with a glance into his eyes. Outside of Easa and my daughter, I have never seen such purity and goodness through the eyes. His cleanliness was revealed within them—a soul that is pure and pristine. On the day he arrived in my house at Magdala, my tiny son climbed into his lap and stayed there for the remainder of the evening. Children are the greatest judges, and Easa and I smiled at each other across the table as we watched little John with his newest friend. John confirmed for us what we both knew upon looking at Bartolome—he was part of our family, and would be for eternity.*

THE ARQUES GOSPEL OF MARY MAGDALENE,
THE BOOK OF DISCIPLES

# CHAPTER FIVE

*Los Angeles*
*April 2005*

$\mathcal{M}$ aureen was exhausted as she drove up to the valet parking area outside her upscale condominium building on Wilshire Boulevard. She allowed Andre, the attendant on duty, to park the car for her and asked him to bring up her bag. The delayed flight out of Dulles, combined with her inability to sleep the night before, had left her nerves in a delicate state.

The last thing she expected or needed was a surprise, but that's exactly what was waiting for her as she entered the lobby.

"Miss Paschal, good evening. Excuse me." Laurence was the front-desk manager for the building. A diminutive and exacting man, he fussed as he came out from behind his desk to address Maureen. "Forgive me, I had to enter your unit this afternoon. The delivery was too large to keep here in the lobby. You should let us know in advance when you are expecting something of that size."

"Delivery? What delivery? I wasn't expecting anything."

"Well, it is unmistakably for you. You must have quite an admirer."

Puzzled, Maureen thanked Laurence and took the elevator to the eleventh floor. As the elevator door opened, she was hit with the heady scent of flowers. The perfume increased tenfold as she opened the door to her condo and gasped. She could not see her living room through the flowers. Elaborate floral arrangements were everywhere, some tall and on pillars, others in crystal vases placed on tables. They all held a variation of the same theme—rich red roses, calla lilies, and lush, white Casablanca lilies. The lilies, in full flower, were the source of the intoxicating scent in the room.

Maureen didn't have to look for a card. It was present, against the far wall of her living room, in an enormous gilt-framed painting that depicted a classical, pastoral scene. Three shepherds, toga-clad and laurel-crowned, were gathered around a large stone object that appeared to be a freestanding tomb. They were pointing to an inscription. The focal point of the painting was a woman, a red-haired shepherdess who appeared to be their leader.

Her face had been painted to bear an uncanny resemblance to Maureen's.

*Les Bergers d'Arcadie.* Peter read the inscription on a brass plaque at the base of the frame, impressed with the excellent copy that stood in Maureen's living room. "By Nicolas Poussin, the French Baroque master. I've seen the original of this painting; it's in the Louvre."

Maureen listened as Peter continued, relieved that he had come over so quickly. "The English translation of the title is *The Shepherds of Arcadia.*"

"I'm not sure if I should be wildly flattered or completely creeped out. Please tell me that in the original, the shepherdess doesn't look like I modeled for her."

Peter laughed a little. "No, no. That appears to be an addition made by the reproduction artist, or the sender. Who is . . . ? "

Maureen shook her head and handed a large envelope to Peter. "It was sent by someone named . . . Sinclair, something. No idea who he is."

"A fan? A fanatic? A nutcase crawling from the woodwork after reading your book?"

Maureen laughed a little nervously. "Could be. My publisher has forwarded some pretty weird letters to me in the last few months."

"Fan mail or hate mail?"

"Both."

Peter removed a letter from a large envelope. It was written in an elaborate hand on elegant vellum stationery. A prominent, engraved fleur-de-lis, the symbol of European royalty for centuries, adorned the parchment. Gilded letters at the bottom of the page announced the author as Bérenger Sinclair. Peter unfolded his reading glasses and read aloud:

*My Dear Ms. Paschal:*

> *Please forgive the intrusion.*
>
> *But I believe I have the answers you have been looking for—and you have some that I have been looking for. If you have the courage to stand behind your beliefs and to take part in an amazing expedition to uncover the truth, I hope you will join me in Paris on the summer solstice. The Magdalene herself requests your presence. Do not disappoint her. Perhaps this painting will serve to stimulate your subconscious. Think of it as a map of sorts—a map to your future and perhaps to your past. I am confident that you will do honor to the great Paschal name, as your father tried to.*

*Yours most sincerely,*
*Bérenger Sinclair*

"The great Paschal name? Your father?" Peter queried. "What do you suppose that's about, then?"

"No clue." Maureen was trying to take it all in. The mention of her father had unsettled her, but she didn't want Peter to know that. Her reply was flip.

"You know about my father's family. From the backwoods and

swamps of Louisiana. Nothing exalted about them, unless insanity equals greatness."

Peter said nothing and waited for her to continue. Maureen rarely spoke of her father, and he was curious to see if she would elaborate. He was slightly disappointed when she shrugged it off.

Maureen took the letter from Peter and read it again. "Weird. What answers do you suppose he's talking about? He couldn't possibly know about my dreams. Nobody does but you and me." She ran her finger along the letter as she mused.

Peter looked around the room at the opulent display of flowers and the towering piece of art. "Whoever he is, this whole scenario smacks of two things—fanaticism and big money. In my experience, that's a bad combination."

Maureen was only half listening.

"Look at the quality of this stationery, it's gorgeous. Very French. And this design embossed along the edges here . . . what are they? Grapes?" Something about the pattern on the stationery was ringing bells in her brain. "Blue apples?"

Adjusting the glasses on his nose, Peter peered at the bottom of the letter. "Blue apples? Hmm, I think you may be right. Look at this; there appears to be an address here at the bottom of the page. Le Château des Pommes Bleues."

"My French isn't flawless by any means, but isn't that something about blue apples?"

Peter nodded. "Castle—or house—of the Blue Apples. Does that mean something to you?"

Maureen nodded slowly, thinking. "Damn, I can't put my finger on it. I know I came across references to blue apples in my research. It's a code of some kind, I think. It had something to do with the religious groups in France who worshiped Mary Magdalene."

"The ones who believed that she went to France after the crucifixion?"

Maureen nodded. "The Church persecuted them as heretics because they claimed their teachings came directly from Christ. They were forced underground and evolved into secret societies, one of which was symbolized by blue apples."

"Okay, but what is the specific significance of blue apples?"

"I don't remember the answer to that." Maureen was thinking hard, but couldn't come up with it. "But I know somebody who will."

*Marina del Rey, California*
*April 2005*

MAUREEN STROLLED along the harbor in Marina del Rey. Luxury sailing craft, the perks of the Hollywood overprivileged, gleamed in the southern California sun. A surfer wearing a ripped T-shirt and the motto "Just Another Shitty Day in Paradise" waved to her from the deck of a small yacht. His skin was suntanned and his hair bleached by the relentless rays. Maureen didn't know him, but the beatific smile combined with the beer bottle in his hand indicated that he was in a friendly mood.

Maureen waved back and walked on, headed for a complex of restaurants and touristy boutiques. She turned in to El Burrito, a Mexican restaurant with a patio on the water.

"Reenie! I'm over here!"

Maureen heard Tammy before she saw her, which was most often the case. She turned in the direction of the voice and found her friend sipping a mango margarita at an outdoor table.

Tamara Wisdom was a study in contrast to Maureen Paschal. Statuesque and olive-skinned, she was beautiful in an exotic way. She wore straight black hair to her waist, and streaked it with various vibrant colors that were determined by her mood. Today it was laced with shiny violet highlights. Her nose was pierced and decorated with a surprisingly large diamond—the gift of a former boyfriend, who happened to be a successful independent film director. Her ears were stacked with multiple piercings, and she wore several amulets of esoteric design over her black lace tank top. She was nearly forty but looked a full ten years younger.

Tammy was flamboyant where Maureen was conservative, loud and opinionated where Maureen was discreet and careful. They could not have been more different in their lives and work, yet they had found a ground of mutual respect that had made them fast friends.

"Thanks for seeing me on such short notice, Tammy." Maureen sat down and ordered iced tea. Tammy rolled her eyes, but was too excited by the reason for their meeting to berate Maureen for her conservative beverage choice.

"Are you kidding? Bérenger Sinclair is stalking you and you think I wouldn't want to hear every juicy detail?"

"Well, you were very coy with me on the phone, so you'd better own up. I can't believe you know this guy."

"I can't believe you don't. How in God's name—literally—did you publish a book that includes Mary Magdalene without going to France for research? And you call yourself a journalist."

"I *do* call myself a journalist, which is precisely why I didn't go to France. I have no interest in all that secret society stuff. That's your department, not mine. I went to Israel to do serious research on the first century."

The good-natured ribbing was integral to their friendship. Maureen had first met Tammy during her research; a mutual friend had introduced them after learning that Maureen was investigating Mary Magdalene's life for her book. Tammy had published several alternative books on secret societies and alchemy, and a documentary she made about underground spiritual traditions featuring Magdalene worship had received critical acclaim on the festival circuit. Maureen had been shocked by what a close-knit network esoteric researchers maintained, because it seemed that Tammy knew everyone. And while Maureen quickly realized that Tammy's alternative approach was far from what she was looking for in terms of respectable source material, she also recognized the sharp mind behind the heavy eye makeup, the substance beneath the show. Maureen admired Tammy's raw courage and brutal honesty, even when she was on the receiving end of her needling.

Tammy reached into her neon orange tote bag to pull out an elegant envelope. She waved it tantalizingly in front of Maureen's nose before sliding it across the table at her. "Here, I wanted to show this to you in person."

Maureen raised an eyebrow at her friend as she saw the now-familiar fleur-de-lis design combined with the odd blue apples patterned on the envelope. She removed an engraved invitation and began to read.

"It's an invitation to Sinclair's very exclusive annual costume ball. Looks like I finally made the big time. Did he send you one of these, too?"

Maureen shook her head. "No. Just the weird message about meeting him on the summer solstice. How did you get this invitation?"

"I met him during *my* research in France," she said pointedly. "I'm petitioning him for funding to finish my new documentary. He's interested in creating one of his own, so we're negotiating—you know, I'll scratch his back if he scratches mine."

"You're working on a new film? Why didn't you tell me?"

"You haven't exactly been around lately, have you?"

Maureen looked sheepish. She had neglected her friends terribly during the career craziness of the past months. "Sorry. And stop looking so bloody pleased with yourself. What else aren't you telling me? Did you know about this Sinclair thing? About him . . . stalking me?"

"No, no. Not at all. I've only met him once but damn, I wish he wanted to stalk *me*. Worth a billion—that's billion with a B—and gorgeous to boot. You know, Reenie, this could be really good for you. For Chrissakes, let your hair down and go have a great adventure. When was the last time you were even on a date?"

"Not the point."

"Maybe it is."

Maureen waved off the question, trying to withhold her exasperation. "I don't have time for a relationship. Nor did I get the impression that I was being asked out on a date."

"More's the pity. There is no more romantic place on the planet."

"So that's why you've been spending so much time in France lately?"

Tammy laughed. "No, no. It's just that France is the focal point of Western esoterica and the melting pot of heresy. I could write a hundred books on the subject or make as many films and still just scratch the surface."

Maureen was finding it hard to concentrate. "What do you think Sinclair wants from me?"

"Who knows? He has a reputation for the eccentric and the outrageous. Too much time on his hands and too much money to waste. I'm guessing something in your book got his attention and he wants to add you to his collection. But I have no idea what that would be. You're work isn't exactly his thing."

"Meaning what?" Maureen was feeling a little defensive. "Why isn't it his thing?"

"Too mainstream and too academic. Come on, Maureen. When you wrote that chapter on Mary Magdalene you were so careful, so politically correct. Mary Magdalene *may* have had a relationship with Jesus but there's no proof, blah, blah . . . blech. You just played it so safe. Believe me, there is nothing safe about what Sinclair believes. That's why I like him."

Maureen shot back a comment that was a little more sharp than she intended. "You're in the business of revising history based on your personal beliefs. I am not."

Tammy was touching a nerve today, but in her usual style she refused to back down and kept after Maureen.

"And what are your beliefs? Sounds to me like you don't even know. Look, you're a good friend and I'm not disrespecting you, so don't get mad. But you know as well as I do that there is evidence that Mary Magdalene was in a relationship with Jesus and that they had children. Why are you so afraid of that possibility? You're not even religious. It shouldn't threaten you."

"It doesn't threaten me. I just didn't want to go down that path. I was afraid it would taint the rest of my work. Your standards for 'evidence' and mine are clearly not the same. I spent most of my adult life researching that book and I wasn't going to throw it away on some half-baked and unsubstantiated theory that I'm not the least bit invested in."

Tammy shot back. "That half-baked theory is about divine union—the idea that two people honoring each other in a sacred relationship is the greatest expression of God that there is on earth. Maybe you should consider getting invested in it."

Maureen cut her off, changing the subject abruptly. "You promised to tell me what you know about blue apples."

"Well, if you'll excuse my half-baked and unsubstantiated theories . . . ," she began.

"Sorry." Maureen looked sincerely contrite, which made Tammy laugh.

"Forget it. I've been called much worse. Okay, here is what I know about blue apples. They're a symbol of the bloodline—yes, *that* bloodline, the one you and your academic friends want to pretend doesn't exist. The bloodline of Jesus Christ and Mary Magdalene as established through their descendants. Various secret societies have used different symbols to represent the bloodline."

"And why blue apples?"

"That's been debated, but it's generally believed that it's a reference to grapes. The wine-producing regions in the south of France are famous for their large grapes, which could be symbolized by blue apples. Make the leap with me here: the children of Jesus equal the fruit of the vine, which are grapes, which are blue apples."

Maureen nodded. "So therefore Sinclair is involved with one of these secret societies?"

"Sinclair is his own secret society." Tammy laughed. "He's like the godfather down there. Nothing happens without his knowledge or approval. And he's the bankbook for a lot of research. Including mine." Tammy raised her glass in a mock toast to Sinclair's generosity.

Maureen took a sip of her tea and contemplated the envelope in her hand. "But you don't think Sinclair is dangerous?"

"Oh, Lord, no. He's too high profile for that—although he certainly has the money and influence to hide the bodies. That was a joke, so stop turning green. And he's probably the foremost expert on Mary Magdalene in the world. Could be a very interesting contact for you should you choose to open your mind a little."

"So I take it you're going to this party of his?"

"Are you nuts? Of course I am. I already have my ticket. And the party is on June twenty-fourth, so that's three days after the summer solstice. Hmmm . . ."

"What?"

"He's up to something, but I don't know what it is. He wants you in Paris on the twenty-first of June, and his party is on the twenty-fourth—that's midsummer on the ancient calendar, but it's also the feast day of John the Baptist. This is getting very interesting. I don't believe for a minute that these dates are a coincidence. Where does he want you to meet him?"

Maureen removed the letter from her bag, along with a map of France that had been included with it. She handed both to Tammy.

"See," Maureen pointed out. "There's a red line drawn here from Paris down to the south of France."

"That's the Paris Meridian, my dear. Runs straight through the heart of Mary Magdalene territory—and Sinclair's estate, for that matter."

Tammy turned the map over to reveal another, this one of Paris. She followed the map with a crimson fingernail, laughing uproariously when she spotted the Left Bank landmark, circled in red.

"Oh, my. What are you up to, Sinclair?" Tammy indicated the map of Paris. "The church of Saint-Sulpice. Is this where he is asking you to meet him?"

Maureen nodded. "You know it?"

"Of course. Huge church, second largest in Paris after Notre-Dame, sometimes called the Cathedral of the Left Bank. It's been the site of secret society activity since at least the sixteen hundreds. I wish I had known this sooner, I would have scheduled my flight into Paris to arrive a few days earlier. I'd give a lot to witness this meeting of yours with the godfather."

"I haven't said I'm going yet. It just all seems so crazy. I don't have any contact information for him—no phone number, no e-mail. He didn't even ask me to RSVP. It just seems that he assumes I'll be there."

"He's a man who is very used to getting what he wants. And for some reason that I can't quite fathom, he seems to want you. But you have to stop playing by the rules of normal society if you get involved with these people. They're not dangerous, but they can be very eccentric. Puzzles are all a part of their game, and you will have to solve a few to prove yourself worthy of their inner circle."

"I'm not sure I want to be worthy of their inner circle."

Tammy threw back the rest of her margarita. "It's your choice, sister. Personally, I wouldn't miss out on an invitation like this for anything. I think it's the chance of a lifetime for you. Go as a journalist, go to investigate. But just remember, once you step into this mystery, it's like walking through the looking glass and falling down the rabbit hole.

"So just be careful. And hold on to your reality, my conservative little Alice."

*Los Angeles*
*April 2005*

THE ARGUMENT with Peter had been more heated than she had anticipated. Maureen knew he would oppose her decision to meet Sinclair in France, but she was unprepared for how vehemently he defended his position.

"Tamara Wisdom is a crackpot, and I can't believe you allowed her to talk you into this. She is hardly a credible character witness for this Sinclair."

The debate had raged over most of dinner—Peter playing the elder brother and protector, concerned for her safety, Maureen trying to make him understand her decision.

"Pete, you know I've never been a big risk-taker. I like order and control in my life, and I'd be lying if I didn't tell you that this terrifies me."

"Then why do it?"

"Because the dreams and the coincidences terrify me even more. I have no control over them, and it's getting worse as they become more frequent and intense. I feel like I have to follow this path and see where it takes me. Maybe Sinclair does have the answers I'm looking for, as he claims. If he is the foremost expert on Mary Magdalene in the world, maybe some of this will make sense to him. There's only one way I'll ever find out, isn't there?"

At the end of an exhausting discussion, Peter finally conceded with one condition. "I'm going with you," he declared.

And that was the end of it.

Maureen hit the speed dial on her cell phone for Peter's number as she exited the Westwood Travel Agency the following Saturday morning. She hadn't told Peter everything yet. Sometimes he treated her like she was still a child and he was her protector. Although she appreciated his concern, she was a grown woman who needed to make some important choices at this crossroads in her life. Now, with the decision made and the tickets in her hands, it was time to let him know.

"Hi. We're all set, and I have the tickets. Listen, I made a spur of the moment decision to fly into New Orleans before we leave for France."

Peter was silent for a moment, surprised. "New Orleans? All right. Then are we flying to Paris from there?"

This was the hard part. "No. I'm going to New Orleans alone." She rushed forward into the next sentence before he could interrupt. "This is something I have to do by myself, Pete. I'll meet you at JFK the next day and we'll fly to Paris together from there."

Peter paused very briefly before accepting with a simple, "Okay."

Maureen was feeling guilty about the deception. "Listen, I'm in

Westwood, just leaving the travel agency. Can you meet me for lunch? Your choice. I'll buy."

"I can't. I'm holding refresher seminars for finals at Loyola today."

"Come on, you can't get someone else to teach Latin for a few hours?"

"Latin, yes. But I'm the only Greek teacher here, so it's all on me today."

"Okay. Maybe one day you'll tell me why twenty-first-century teenagers need to learn dead languages."

Peter knew Maureen was joking. Her respect for Peter's education and linguistic abilities was immense.

"For the same reason I needed to learn dead languages, and my grandfather needed to. It served us very well, now, didn't it?"

Maureen couldn't argue with that, even in jest. Peter's grandfather, the esteemed Dr. Cormac Healy, had been on a committee in Jerusalem that had studied and provided translations for some of the extraordinary Nag Hammadi library. Peter's passion for ancient manuscripts had flourished as a teenager when he spent the summer in Israel with his grandfather. As part of an internship, Peter had participated in an excavation at the Scriptorium in Qumran, where the Dead Sea Scrolls were written. For years, he kept a tiny piece of brick from the Scriptorium wall in a museum case next to his desk. But when his cousin showed true passion and calling for her work as a writer, he felt it was appropriate for her to have it as inspiration. Maureen wore the brick fragment in a leather pouch around her neck every time she sat down to write in earnest.

It was during his summer in Israel that the young Peter found his calling, both as a scholar and as a priest. He had visited the sacred sites of Christianity with a group of Jesuits, and the experience had a profound impact on the idealistic Irishman. The Jesuit order proved a perfect fit for his combined religious and scholastic passions.

Maureen made plans to meet him later in the week. As she flipped her cell phone closed, she realized that she felt lighter than she had in months.

The same would not prove true for Father Peter Healy.

The West Coast of the United States has a rich vein of historical buildings in the California missions. Founded by the industrious Franciscan monk Father Junípero Serra in the eighteenth century, these
remnants of Spanish architecture are generally blessed with beautiful
gardens or are located in sites of natural beauty.

Peter had a strong affinity for the Franciscan order, and he had
made it his personal goal to visit all of the California mission locations since his arrival in the state. The missions blended history with
faith, a combination that resonated in Peter's heart and soul. When he
needed time and space to think, he often escaped to one of the mission locations easily accessible to southern California. Each had a
unique charm and represented an oasis of calm, a welcome respite
from his hectic lifestyle in Los Angeles.

He chose the San Fernando Mission today because of its proximity to his friend Father Brian Rourke, who lived nearby and was a
leader of the Jesuit order based in the suburban San Fernando Valley.
Peter's history with Father Brian dated back to his early years in the
seminary when the older man had served as a mentor. Now Peter
needed a trusted friend; he was in search of sanctuary—even from the
church he loved and obeyed. Father Brian had agreed to meet him on
short notice, sensing the mild panic in Peter's tone.

"Your cousin, is she a practicing Catholic?" The elder priest
walked through the gardens of the mission with Peter. The afternoon
sun was blaring in the valley, and Peter wiped a bead of sweat with the
back of his hand.

"Lapsed. But she was very devout as a child. We both were."

Father Rourke nodded. "Anything happen to turn her from the
Church?"

Peter hesitated for a moment. "Family issues. I'd rather not elaborate on those." He already felt that disclosing Maureen's visions without
her knowledge was something of a betrayal. He didn't want to go into
all of her family secrets as well. At least, not yet. But he was at something

of a loss about what action to take next, and he needed sound advice from someone he could trust within the structure of the Church.

The elder priest nodded his understanding of the confidentiality issues. "It's very rare that these things ever turn out to be credited, divine visions. Sometimes they're dreams, sometimes delusions from childhood. Probably nothing to worry about. You're going to accompany her to France?"

"Yes. I've always been her spiritual adviser, and I'm probably the only person she really trusts."

"That's good, that's good. You can keep an eye on her then. Please call immediately if you feel this girl is becoming dangerous to herself in any way. We'll help you through it."

"I'm sure it won't come to that." Peter smiled and thanked his friend. The conversation dissolved into a discussion of the fierce heat in California versus the mild summers in their native Ireland. They chatted amicably about old friends and discussed the whereabouts of their former teacher and countryman who was now a bishop somewhere in the Deep South. When it was time to take his leave, Peter assured his old friend that he felt better after their discussion.

He lied.

Father Brian Rourke returned to his office that afternoon with a heavy heart and an embattled conscience. He sat for a long time, gazing at the crucifix hanging on the wall over his desk. Breathing a sigh of resignation, he picked up the phone and dialed the Louisiana area code. He didn't have to look up the number.

*New Orleans*
*June 2005*

MAUREEN DROVE her rented car through the outskirts of New Orleans, a map of the area spread on the vacant passenger's seat. She slowed and moved to the side of the road, glancing at the map to be sure she was still on track. Satisfied, she eased back into the street. As she rounded the next bend, the aboveground, sarcophagus-style tombs and monuments for which New Orleans cemeteries are renowned came into view.

Maureen parked in the lot, and reached into the backseat to grab her large handbag and the flowers she had purchased from a street vendor. She stepped out of the car, careful to avoid the muddy puddles that were the remnants of an early, pre-summer thunderstorm, and took in the landscape of manicured graves. Elaborate markers and floral wreaths stretched for acres. Taking a deep breath, Maureen walked toward the cemetery gates, carrying her own flowers. She stopped at the main entrance and looked up, but turned sharply to the left without entering the cemetery.

Maureen walked outside the gates, around the cemetery's perimeter, until she arrived at another set of burial plots. These graves were overgrown with moss and weeds, neglected and pathetic. This was the misfit burial ground.

She walked slowly, carefully, and reverently. She fought back tears as she climbed over forgotten graves of individuals who had been abandoned even in death. Next time she would bring more flowers, flowers for all of them.

Kneeling, she pushed aside the weeds that covered a battered grave marker. The name revealed was *Edouard Paul Paschal*.

Using her hands, Maureen began to rip at the offending growth with a vengeance. Debris flew as she cleared the area, oblivious to the dirt and mud that accumulated under her fingernails and splattered her clothing. She smoothed the area with her hands and rubbed the grave marker to give more definition to the letters of the occupant's name.

When she was satisfied that she had cleaned the area as well as she could, Maureen set the flowers on the grave. She removed the picture frame from her handbag and looked at the photograph for a moment, allowing the tears to come. The image showed Maureen as a child, no more than five or six years old, sitting on the knee of a man who was reading to her from a storybook. The two were smiling happily at each other, oblivious of the camera.

"Hi, Daddy," she whispered softly to the photo, before placing it against the headstone.

Maureen lingered for a moment, eyes closed, lost in her attempt to recall her father in any kind of detail. Outside of this photograph, she had very little to prompt memories of him. After his death, her mother had forbidden any discussion of the man or his role in their lives. He simply ceased to exist for them, as did his family. Maureen and her mother had moved to Ireland very soon after that. Her past in Louisiana was relegated to the dim memories of a traumatized and grieving child.

Earlier that morning, Maureen had thumbed through a New Orleans phone book looking for residents named Paschal. There were a number of them, some that may have been familiar. But she had closed the book quickly, never really intending to make any contact with potential relatives, not after all this time and certainly not now. It had been more of an exercise in remembering.

Maureen touched the photograph in farewell, then wiped the tears away with a muddy hand that smeared grime across her face. She didn't care. She rose and retraced her steps without looking back, stopping outside the main entrance gates. Inside the cemetery proper, a pristine white chapel crowned with a polished brass cross gleamed in the southern sunshine.

Maureen stared at the church through the bars, an outsider looking in.

She shielded her eyes from the glare of the light shining from the brass cross, then turned her back on the church and walked away.

*Vatican City, Rome*
*June 2005*

TOMAS CARDINAL DECARO stood up from his desk and looked out the window onto the piazza. His aging eyes weren't the only thing that needed a break from the stack of yellowed papers on his desk. His mind and his conscience needed to rest and ruminate on the information he had received this morning. There was an earthquake coming, that much was certain. What he wasn't sure about was just how much damage this particular cataclysm was going to inflict—and who its victims would be.

He opened his top desk drawer to look at the item that gave him strength at such times. It was a portrait of the Blessed Pope John XXIII under the heading *Vatican Secundum—Vatican II*. Beneath the image was a quote from this great and visionary leader who risked much to bring his beloved Church into the contemporary world. While DeCaro knew these words by rote, it fortified him to read them:

"It is not that the gospel has changed. It is that we have begun to understand it better. The moment has come to discern the signs of the times, to seize the opportunity and look far ahead."

Outside, summer was approaching, and it was promising to be a beautiful day in Rome. DeCaro decided to play truant for a few hours and take a long stroll through his beloved Eternal City.

He needed to walk, he needed to think, and above all he needed to pray for guidance. Perhaps the guiding spirit of the good Pope John would help him to find his way through the coming crisis.

*. . . Bartolome came to us through Philip, another of our tribe to be misjudged—and I will confess here that I was the first to misjudge him. He was long a follower of John, the Baptizer, and I knew of him from that association. Because of this, it took some time before I learned to trust Philip.*

*Philip was an enigma as a man—practical and educated. I was able to speak to him in the language of the Hellenists, in which I was also schooled. He came from nobility, having been born in Bethsaida, yet he had long chosen to live a life of utmost simplicity, denying himself the trappings of noble life. This trait he learned first from John. Philip was difficult and quarrelsome on the surface, but beneath this he was light and goodness.*

*There was nothing in Philip that would harm another living thing. Indeed, he was most severe about his eating habits and would not consume food that caused the suffering of any animal. While the remainder of our tribe fed on fish, Philip would not hear of it. He was unable to bear the idea of the tender mouths being torn by hooks, or the agony he felt they must suffer when trapped in nets. He had many quarrels with Peter and Andrew on this dilemma! I have thought about it often. Perhaps he was right, and his commitment to this belief is just one of the reasons I admired him.*

*I sometimes felt that Philip was much like the animals he so revered, those that protect themselves with spines or armor on the exterior, so that nothing is able to pierce the soft creature underneath. Yet he took Bartolome into his protection when he found him on the road and without a home. He saw the goodness in Bartolome, and brought that goodness to us.*

*After the Time of Darkness, Philip and Bartolome were my greatest comfort. They made the initial preparations with Joseph to quickly take all of us to safety in Alexandria, away from our own land. Bartolome was as important to the children as were the women. Indeed, he was the greatest comfort for little John, who loves all the men. But Sarah-Tamar adored Bartolome as much.*

*Yes, these two men deserve a place in heaven that is filled with light and perfection for all eternity. Philip became concerned only about protecting us and seeing us safely to our destination. I think he would have stopped at nothing, no matter what I asked of him. Had I told Philip that our destination was the moon itself, he would have tried everything in his power to get us there.*

THE ARQUES GOSPEL OF MARY MAGDALENE,
THE BOOK OF DISCIPLES

# Chapter Six

*Paris*
*June 19, 2005*

*T*he sun sparkled on the Seine as Maureen and Peter walked along the river. Paris was bathed in the warm light of early summer, and the two were content to relax a little and enjoy the sights of the world's most beautiful city. There would be opportunity enough to worry about the meeting with Sinclair in two days' time.

They were enjoying ice cream cones, eating rapidly before the confections could drip in the sun and leave a sticky rainbow trail in their wake.

"Mmm, you were right, Pete. Berthillon just may be the best ice cream in the world. This is amazing."

"What flavor did you get?"

Maureen was practicing her French. "Poivre."

"Pepper?" Peter burst out laughing. "You got pepper-flavored ice cream?"

Maureen turned red with embarrassment but tried again. "Pauvre?"

"Poor? You got a poor flavor?"

"Okay, I surrender. Stop tormenting me. It's *pear*-flavored."

"Poire. Poire is pear. Sorry, I shouldn't make fun of you. Nice try."

"Well, it's obvious who got the linguistic talent in our family."

"That's not true. You speak beautiful English."

They both laughed, enjoying the lightness of the moment and the beauty of the day.

The Gothic magnificence of Notre-Dame dominated the Île de la Cité as it had for 800 years. As they approached the cathedral, Peter looked reverently at the looming exterior, with its mixture of saints and gargoyles.

"The first time I saw it I said, 'God lives here.' Want to go inside?"

"No, I'd rather stay outside with the gargoyles, where I belong."

"It's the most famous Gothic structure in the world and a symbol of Paris. You're obligated as a tourist to go inside. Besides, the stained glass is phenomenal, and you have to see the rose window in the mid-day sun."

Maureen hesitated, but Peter grabbed her arm and pulled her along behind him. "Come on. I promise the walls won't tumble down as you enter."

Sun streamed through the world-famous rose window, illuminating Peter and Maureen in azure light streaked with crimson. Peter wandered, face elevated to the windows, enjoying a perfect feeling of bliss. Maureen walked slowly beside him, trying her best to remind herself that this was a building of enormous historic and architectural significance, and not just another church.

A French priest walked past them, nodding a solemn greeting. Maureen stumbled slightly as he passed. The priest stopped and held out a hand to steady her, addressing her with mild concern in French. Maureen smiled and put her hand up, indicating that she was fine. Peter returned to her side as the French priest went on his way.

"You okay?"

"Yeah, just a little dizzy all of a sudden. Jet lag, maybe."

"You haven't had much sleep in the last few days."

"I'm sure that hasn't helped." Maureen pointed to one of the side pews that was in line with the rose window. "I'm just going to sit down here for a minute and enjoy the stained glass. You go look around."

Peter looked concerned, but Maureen waved him away. "I'm fine. Go. I'll be right here."

Peter nodded and went off to explore the cathedral. Maureen sat in the pew, steadying herself. She didn't want to admit to Peter just how unstable she was really feeling. It had come on so fast, and she knew that if she didn't sit down she would fall. But she hadn't wanted to tell Peter that. It probably was just a combination of jet lag and exhaustion.

Maureen wiped her hands over her face, trying to shake off the dizziness. Kaleidoscopic beams of colored light from the rose window shone on the altar, illuminating a large crucifix. Maureen blinked hard. The crucifix appeared to be growing, looming larger and larger in her sight.

She grabbed her head as the dizziness enveloped her and the vision took over.

*Lightning ripped through the unnaturally dark sky on that bleakest Friday afternoon. The woman in red stumbled up the hill as she scrambled to reach the crest. She was oblivious to the cuts and scrapes that were accumulating on her body and shredding her clothing. She had only one goal, and that was to reach Him.*

*The sound of a hammer striking a nail—metal pounding metal—rang with a sickening finality through the air. The woman finally lost her composure and wailed, a singular sound of unredeemable human despair.*

*The woman reached the foot of the cross just as the rain began. She looked up at Him, and drops of His blood splashed down on her distraught face, blending with the relentless rain.*

Lost in the vision, Maureen had no sense of where she was. Her wail, a perfect echo of Mary Magdalene's despair, rang through the cathedral of Notre-Dame, frightening the tourists and sending Peter toward her at a full run.

"Where are we?"

Maureen awoke on a couch in a wood-paneled room. Peter's grave face hovered over her as he answered. "In one of the offices of the cathedral." He nodded to the French priest they had encountered earlier, who entered from a concealed door at the back of the room, looking concerned.

"Father Marcel helped me to bring you in here. You weren't going anywhere of your own volition."

Father Marcel came forward and handed her a glass of water. She drank gratefully. "Merci," she said to the cleric, who nodded silently and retreated to the rear of the room to wait discreetly in case further assistance was required. "I'm sorry," she said lamely to Peter.

"Don't be. This is obviously out of your control. Do you want to tell me what you saw?"

Maureen recounted the vision. Peter's face grew whiter with each word. When she finished, he looked at her very seriously.

"Maureen, I know you don't want to hear this, but I think you're having divine visions."

"Think maybe I should talk to a priest?" she quipped.

"I'm serious. This is out of my sphere of experience, but I can find you someone who knows about these things. Just to talk, that's all. It might help."

"No way." Maureen was adamant as she sat up on the couch. "Just get me back to the hotel so I can get some rest. Once I've had some sleep, I'm sure I'll be fine."

Maureen was able to shake off the vision and walk on her own out of the cathedral quarters. She was relieved that she was able to use a side exit and wasn't required to traverse the interior of that great icon to Christianity once again.

Once Peter saw that she was safely settled in her room, he returned to his. He sat for a moment, contemplating the telephone. It was too early to call the States. He would go out for a while and come back when the hour was a little more decent.

Farther down the Seine, Father Marcel walked back through the candlelit interior of the world's most famous Gothic cathedral. He was followed by the Irish cleric Bishop O'Connor, who was attempting to ask questions in very bad French.

Father Marcel took him to the pew where Maureen had had her vision and gave his explanation slowly, attempting to bridge the language barrier. Though it was a sincere effort to communicate with the Irishman, the French priest sounded as if he were speaking to an idiot. O'Connor dismissed him with an impatient wave, settled into the pew, and looked up at the crucifix over the altar, deep in concentration.

*Paris*
*June 19, 2005*

THE CAVE OF THE MUSKETEERS was less ominous by day, lit as it was by an unforgiving fluorescent bulb. The occupants were dressed in their street clothes and without the strange red cords that identified them as the Guild of the Righteous tied around their necks.

A replica of Leonardo da Vinci's portrait of John the Baptist hung on the rear wall, a mere block away from where the priceless original resided in the Louvre. In this renowned painting, John looks out from the canvas with a knowing smile on his face. His hand is raised, right index finger and thumb pointing toward heaven. Leonardo painted John in this pose, often referred to as the "Remember John" gesture, on several occasions. The meaning of that hand position had been debated for centuries.

The Englishman sat at the head of the table as usual, his back to the painting. An American and a Frenchman sat on either side of him.

"I just don't understand what he is up to," the Englishman snapped. He picked up a hardcover book from the table and shook it at the two men. "I've read it twice. There's nothing new here, nothing at all that could be of interest to us. Or to him. So what is it? Do either of you have any thoughts on this at all? Or am I talking to myself?"

The Englishman tossed the book onto the table with obvious disdain. The American picked it up and thumbed through it absently.

The American stopped at the inside cover and looked at the photograph of the author. "She's cute. Maybe that's all it is."

The Englishman scoffed. *Typical ridiculous Yank, missing the point.* He had always objected to American members in the Guild, but this idiot was from a wealthy family connected to their legacy and they were stuck with him.

"With Sinclair's money and power, he has far more than 'cute' at his beck and call, twenty-four hours a day. His playboy exploits are legendary in Britain and the Continent. No, there is something other than a romp going on with this girl, and I expect the two of you to figure it out. Fast."

"I'm almost certain he believes she's the Shepherdess, but I'll know soon enough," asserted the Frenchman. "I'm traveling to the Languedoc this weekend."

"This weekend is too late," snapped the Englishman. "Leave no later than tomorrow. Today would be preferable. There is a time element here, as you well know."

"She has red hair," observed the American.

The Englishman growled. "Any tart with twenty euros and an inclination can have red hair. Get in there and find out why she matters. Fast. Because if Sinclair finds what he is looking for before we do . . ."

He didn't finish his sentence; he didn't have to. The others knew exactly what would happen then, knew what had happened the last time someone from the wrong side got too close. The American man was particularly squeamish, and the thought of the red-haired author without her head made him very uncomfortable.

The American picked up the copy of Maureen's book from the table, tucked it under his arm, and followed his French companion out into the glaring Paris sunlight.

When his underlings were gone, the Englishman, who had been baptized with the name John Simon Cromwell, rose from the table and walked to the rear of the basement. Around the corner and out of view from the main room was a shallow alcove. Within the space was a heavy cabinet made of dark wood; a small altar sat to the right of the fixture. A single kneeler made room for one supplicant before the altar.

There were wrought-iron fixtures on the doors of the cabinet, and the lower compartment was protected by an oppressive-looking lock. The Englishman reached into his shirt to find the key he wore around his neck. Kneeling, he applied the key to the weighty lock and opened the lower cabinet.

He extracted two items. First, he took out a bottle of what appeared to be holy water, which he poured into a golden font that rested on the altar. Next, he removed a small but ornate reliquary.

Cromwell placed the reliquary gently on the altar and dipped his hands into the water. He rubbed the water into his neck with both palms and said an invocation as he did so. Then he held the reliquary at eye level. Through a tiny window in the otherwise solid gold box, a glint of what looked like ivory was visible. Long, narrow, and notched, the human bone rattled in its casket as the Englishman peered at it. He clutched the bone to his chest and said a fervent prayer.

"O great Teacher of Righteousness, know that I will not fail you.

But we beseech that you help us. Help us who seek the truth. Help us who live only to serve your exalted name.

"Most of all, help us to keep the whore in her place."

The American, alone now, walked down the rue de Rivoli and shouted over the noise of Paris traffic into his cell phone.

"We can't wait any longer. He's a complete renegade, totally out of control."

The voice on the other end echoed his American accent— polished, northeastern, and equally angry.

"Stick to the plan. It accomplishes our goal in a methodical and complete way. And it was created by those far wiser than you," clipped the elder voice across the miles.

"Those wiser than me aren't here," the younger man spat into the phone. "They don't see what I see. Goddamit, Dad, when are you going to give me some credit?"

"When you earn it. In the meantime, I forbid you to do anything idiotic."

The younger American flipped his cell phone shut abruptly, swearing as he did so. He had rounded the corner in front of the Hotel Regina, cutting through the place des Pyramides. Looking up, he stopped just in time to avoid a collision with the famous gilded statue of Joan of Arc, sculpted by the great Frémiet.

"Bitch," he grumbled at the female savior of France, pausing just long enough to spit on her, and not caring who saw him do it.

*Paris*
*June 20, 2005*

I. M. PEI'S GLASS PYRAMID gleamed in the morning rays of the French summer sun. Maureen and Peter, both refreshed after a real night of sleep, waited in line with the other tourists to enter the Louvre.

Peter looked around at the patrons waiting in the long queue, clutching their guidebooks. "All this fuss over the *Mona Lisa*. I'll never understand it. The most overrated painting on the planet."

"Agreed. But while they trip over each other to view it, we'll have the Richelieu wing all to ourselves."

Maureen and Peter purchased their tickets and double-checked the Louvre floor plan. "Where are we going first?"

Maureen replied, "Nicolas Poussin. I want to see *The Shepherds of Arcadia* in person before we do anything else."

They moved through the wing that contained the French masters, scanning the walls for the enigmatic Poussin masterpiece.

Maureen explained, "Tammy told me that this painting has been the center of controversy for several hundred years. Louis XIV fought to obtain it for two decades. When he finally got it, he locked it up in a basement in Versailles where no one else could see it. Strange, isn't it? Why do you think the king of France would fight so hard to obtain an important piece of art and then hide it from the world?"

"It's just another in a mounting series of mysteries." Peter was checking numbers on the guide as he listened. "According to this, that painting should be right about . . ."

"Here!" Maureen exclaimed. Peter came up behind her and they both stared at the painting for a minute. Maureen broke the silence, turning to Peter.

"I feel so silly. Like I'm waiting for the painting to tell me something." She turned back to the painting. "Are you trying to tell me something, Shepherdess?"

Peter was struck by a thought. "I can't believe I didn't think of this before."

"Think of what?"

"The idea of a shepherdess. Jesus is the Good Shepherd. Maybe Poussin—or at least Sinclair—was indicating the Good *Shepherdess*?"

"Yes!" Maureen shouted, a little too loud in her excitement over the idea. "Maybe Poussin was showing us Mary Magdalene as the Shepherdess, the leader of the flock. The leader of her own church!"

Peter cringed. "Well, I didn't exactly say that . . ."

"You didn't have to. But look, there's a Latin inscription on the tomb in this painting."

"Et in Arcadia ego," Peter read aloud. "Hmm. Doesn't make sense."

"How does it translate?"

"It doesn't. It's a grammatical mess."

"Give me your best guess."

"It's either very bad Latin or it's some kind of code. The literal translation is an incomplete phrase, roughly 'And in Arcadia I . . . ' It doesn't really mean anything."

Maureen attempted to listen, but a woman's voice began calling out with urgency across the museum, distracting her.

"Sandro! Sandro!"

She looked around for the source of the voice before apologizing to Peter. "Sorry, but that woman is so distracting."

The voice called out again, louder this time, annoying Maureen. "Who is that?"

Peter looked at her, puzzled. "Who is what?"

"That woman calling . . ."

"Sandro! Sandro!"

Maureen looked at Peter as the voice grew louder. He clearly didn't hear it. She turned to watch the other tourists and students who were absorbed in the priceless artwork on the walls. No one else appeared to be aware of the urgent voice calling across the Louvre.

"Oh, God. You don't hear it, do you? No one else hears it but me."

Peter looked helpless. "Hear what?"

"There's a woman's voice calling across the museum. 'Sandro! Sandro!' Come on."

Maureen grabbed Peter by the sleeve and hurried off in the direction of the voice.

"Where are we going?"

"We're following that voice. It's coming from this direction."

They hurried through the museum corridors, Maureen apologizing over her shoulder as she bumped into various museum patrons. The voice had turned into an urgent whisper, but it was leading her somewhere, and she was determined to follow. They ran back through the Richelieu wing, ignoring the glare of an irritated museum guard, then down some steps and through another corridor, passing the signs that indicated the Denon wing.

"Sandro . . . Sandro . . . Sandro . . . !"

The voice stopped suddenly as Maureen and Peter came up the grand staircase to pass the iconic statue of the goddess Nike in all her winged victory. As they turned the corner to the right at the top of the stairs, they came face-to-face with two of the lesser-known masterpieces of the Italian Renaissance. Peter made the first observation.

"Botticelli frescoes."

The realization struck them simultaneously. "*Sandro*. Alessandro Botticelli."

Peter looked at the frescoes and then back at Maureen. "Wow, how did you do that?"

Maureen shivered. "I didn't do anything. I just listened and followed."

They turned their attention to the nearly life-size figures in the frescoes that stood side by side. Peter translated the plaques for Maureen. "This first fresco is called *Venus and the Three Graces presenting gifts to a young woman.* The second is called *A Young Man is presented by Venus? to the Liberal Arts.* Fresco painted for the wedding of Lorenzo Tornabuoni and Giovanna Albizzi."

"Yes, but why is there a question mark after Venus?" Maureen wondered.

Peter shook his head. "They must not be sure that she is the subject."

The painting was an elegant yet odd depiction of a young man holding the hand of a woman draped in a red cloak. They were facing seven women, three of whom held unusual and incongruous-looking objects; one clutched an enormous and somewhat menacing black scorpion, while the woman next to her held an archer's bow. Another held an architect's tool at an awkward angle.

Peter was thinking out loud. "The seven liberal arts. The realms of higher learning. Is it telling us that this was a very educated young man?"

"What are the seven liberal arts?"

Closing his eyes to recall his classical studies, Peter recited, "The trivium, or first three roads of study, are grammar, rhetoric, and logic. The final four, the quadrivium, are mathematics, geometry, music, and cosmology, and they're inspired by Pythagoras and his perspective that all numbers represented the study of patterns in time and space."

Maureen smiled at him. "Very impressive. Now what?"

Peter shrugged. "I don't know how any of it fits into our ever-expanding puzzle."

Maureen pointed to the scorpion. "Why would a wedding painting depict a woman holding a huge, venomous insect? Which of the liberal arts could that represent?"

"I'm not certain." Peter had stepped in as near to the fresco as the Louvre barricades would allow and leaned in. "But look closer. The scorpion is darker and more vivid than the rest of the painting. All of the objects the women are holding are. It almost looks like . . ."

Maureen finished his sentence for him. "Like it was added later."

"But by whom? By Sandro himself? Or was somebody messing with the master's frescoes?"

Maureen shook her head, bewildered by the entire encounter.

Over a café crème at the Louvre coffee shop, Maureen went through her purchases with Peter. She had picked up prints of the paintings they had examined, as well as a book on the life and work of Botticelli.

"I'm hoping to find out more about the origins of that fresco."

"I'm more interested in finding out about the origins of the voice that led you to the fresco."

Maureen took a sip of her coffee before answering. "But what was it? My subconscious? Divine guidance? Insanity? Ghosts in the Louvre?"

"I wish I could answer that, but I can't."

"Some spiritual adviser you are," Maureen quipped, then turned her attention to the print of the Botticelli as she removed it from its wrapping. As the refracted light of the glass pyramid struck the print, Maureen had an epiphany.

"Wait a minute. Didn't you say cosmology was one of the liberal arts?" Maureen looked down at the copper ring she wore.

Peter nodded. "Astronomy, cosmology. Study of the stars. Why?"

"My ring. The man in Jerusalem who gave it to me said it was the ring of a cosmologist."

Peter ran his hands over his face as if doing so would direct his brain toward a solution. "So what is the connection? That we should be looking to the stars for an answer?"

Maureen placed her finger over the enigmatic woman holding the huge black insect, then nearly jumped out of her seat as she shouted, "Scorpio!"

"Sorry?"

"It's the symbol of the astrological sign Scorpio. And the woman next to her is holding an archer's bow. The symbol of Sagittarius. Scorpio and Sagittarius are right next to each other in the zodiac."

"So you think there is some kind of code in the fresco that deals with astronomy?"

Maureen nodded slowly. "At the very least, it may give us a place to start."

The lights of Paris shone through the window of Maureen's hotel room, striking the items that lay next to her on the bed. She had fallen asleep reading the Botticelli book, and the Poussin print was faceup, on her other side.

Maureen was unaware of either of these things. She was once again absorbed in a dream.

*In a stone-walled room, illuminated dimly by oil lanterns, an ancient woman crouched over a table. The woman wore a faded red shawl over her long, gray hair. Her arthritic hand carefully moved a quill pen across the page.*

*A large wooden chest was the only other ornament in the chamber. The crone stopped writing, rose from her chair, and moved slowly to the chest. She knelt carefully on brittle joints and opened the heavy lid. Looking back over her shoulder, a smile of serenity and knowing crept across her face. She turned to Maureen and beckoned her to come forward.*

*Paris*
*June 21, 2005*

IN A CHARMING TRIBUTE to Gallic eccentricity, the oldest bridge in Paris, the Pont Neuf, is often referred to as the "New Bridge." It is a main artery of Parisian life, crossing the Seine to link the fashionable First Arrondissement with the heart of the Left Bank.

Peter and Maureen passed the statue of Henri IV, one of France's most beloved kings, on the bridge that was completed during his tolerant reign in 1606. It was a beautiful morning in Paris, filled with the sparkling majesty that is specific to the incomparable City of Light. Despite the perfect setting, Maureen was nervous.

"What time is it?"

"Five minutes later than the last time you asked," replied Peter, smiling.

"Sorry. I'm starting to get very jumpy about all of this."

"His letter said to be in the church at midday. It's just eleven now. We have plenty of time."

They crossed the Seine and followed a map, toward the winding streets of the Left Bank. From the Pont Neuf they entered the rue Dauphine, walked past the Odeon metro station to the rue Saint-Sulpice, and ended up in the picturesque square of the same name.

The enormous, mismatched bell towers of the church dominated the square, casting shadows over the celebrated fountain built by Vis-

conti in 1844. As Maureen and Peter approached the oversized entrance doors, he felt her hesitate.

"I won't leave you this time." Peter put his hand reassuringly on
her arm and opened the doors to the cavernous church.

They entered quietly, spotting a group of tourists in the first chapel on
the right side. They were British art students, apparently. Their
teacher was lecturing in hushed tones on the three Delacroix masterpieces that decorated that area of the church: *Jacob Wrestling with the
Angel, Heliodorus Driven from the Temple,* and *Saint Michael Van-
quishing the Devil.* On another day, Maureen would have been inclined to view the famous artwork and eavesdrop on a lecture given in
English, but she had other things on her mind today.

They moved past the British students and into the belly of the
building, both gazing up in awe at the massive, historic structure. Almost instinctively, Maureen approached the altar, which was flanked
by a pair of huge paintings. Each was easily thirty feet high. The first
was a scene featuring two women—one cloaked in blue, the other in
red.

"Mary Magdalene with the Virgin?" Maureen ventured.

"From the clothing colors I would say so. The Vatican decreed that
Our Lady only be depicted wearing blue or white."

"And my lady is always in red."

Maureen crossed to the companion painting on the opposite side
of the altar. "Look at this . . ."

The painting showed Jesus laid out in his tomb, while Mary Magdalene appeared to prepare His body for burial. The Virgin Mary and
two other women wept at the edge of the painting.

"Mary Magdalene prepares Christ's body for burial? That's not
specifically in the Gospels though, is it?"

"Mark fifteen and sixteen mention that she and other women
brought spices to the sepulcher that they might anoint Him, but it
does not specifically describe the anointing of the body."

"Hmm," Maureen mused aloud. "And here is Mary Magdalene, doing just that. Yet in Hebrew tradition, wasn't the anointing of the body for burial reserved exclusively for . . ."

"The wife," answered an aristocratic male voice with a smooth hint of Scottish burr.

Maureen and Peter turned sharply to the man who had come up behind them with such stealth. His was an arresting presence. He was darkly handsome and impeccably dressed, yet while his clothes and carriage screamed of breeding, there was nothing stuffy about him. In fact, everything about Bérenger Sinclair was just the slightest bit offbeat, totally individual. His hair was perfectly cut, yet too long to ever be accepted in the House of Lords. His silk shirt was Versace rather than Savile Row. The natural arrogance that comes with extreme privilege was tempered by humor—a crooked and almost boyish smile threatened to reveal itself as he spoke. Maureen was instantly fascinated, rooted in place as she listened to him continue with his explanation.

"Only the wife was allowed to prepare her man for burial. Unless he died unmarried, in which case the honor went to his mother. As you'll see in this painting, the mother of Jesus is present, yet clearly not performing that task. Which can lead to only one conclusion."

Maureen looked up at the painting, then back at the charismatic man standing in front of her.

"That Mary Magdalene was His wife," Maureen finished.

"Bravo, Miss Paschal." The Scotsman bowed theatrically. "But forgive me, I have completely forgotten my manners. Lord Bérenger Sinclair, at your service."

Maureen stepped forward to take his hand, but Sinclair surprised her by holding on to it for a long moment. He didn't release it immediately; rather he turned her smaller hand over in his larger one, and ran his finger lightly over the ring. He flashed the smile at her again, a tiny bit wicked, and winked.

Maureen was completely disconcerted. In truth, she had wondered many times what this Lord Sinclair would be like in person. Whatever she had been expecting, it wasn't this. She tried not to sound completely tongue-tied as she spoke.

"You already know who I am." She turned to introduce Peter. "This is . . ."

Sinclair cut her off. "Father Peter Healy, of course. Your cousin, if I'm not mistaken? And a very learned man. Welcome to Paris, Father Healy. Of course, you've been here before." He glanced at his fashionable and outrageously expensive Swiss watch. "We have a few minutes. Come, there are things to see here that I think you will find very interesting."

Sinclair spoke over his shoulder as he hurried across the church. "Incidentally, don't bother with the guidebook they sell here. Fifty pages that completely ignore the presence of Mary Magdalene. As if by ignoring her she will just go away."

Maureen and Peter followed his quick pace, stopping beside him at another small side altar. "And as you will see, she is depicted repeatedly in this church, yet pointedly ignored. Here's a wonderful example."

Sinclair had led them to a large and elegant marble statue, a Pietà, the classical sculpture of the Virgin Mother holding the broken body of Christ. To the right of the Virgin, Mary Magdalene cradled her head on the Virgin's shoulder.

"The guidebook simply refers to this as 'Pietà, eighteenth-century Italian.' Of course, a traditional Pietà shows the Virgin cradling her son after the crucifixion. The inclusion of Mary Magdalene in this piece is highly unorthodox, yet . . . deliberately ignored." Sinclair heaved a dramatic sigh and shook his head with the injustice of it all.

"So what is your theory?" Peter asked, a little more sharply than he had intended. Something about Sinclair's arrogance was getting under his skin. "That there's some Church conspiracy to exclude mention of Mary Magdalene?"

"Draw your own conclusions, Father. But I'll tell you this—there are more churches dedicated to Mary Magdalene in France than to any other saint, including the Holy Mother. There is an entire region in Paris named after her—you've been to the Madeleine, I presume?"

Maureen was struck by the realization. "It never occurred to me until now, but Madeleine is Magdalene in French, isn't it?"

"Quite. Have you been to her church there in the Madeleine? An enormous structure, ostensibly dedicated to her, and yet within all of the art and decoration there were originally no images of Mary Magdalene inside. Not one. Odd, isn't it? They added the Marochetti sculpture above the altar, which I am told was originally titled *The Assumption of the Virgin*, and changed it to *The Assumption of Mary Magdalene* because of pressure put upon them by . . . well, by those who cared about the truth."

"I suppose you're now going to tell me that Marcel Proust also named his cookies after her," Peter cracked. In contrast to Maureen's instant fascination, he was irritated by Sinclair's offhand assuredness.

"Well, they're shaped like scallop shells for a reason." Sinclair shrugged, leaving Peter to contemplate the riddle while he joined Maureen near the Pietà.

"It is almost as if they tried to erase her," Maureen commented.

"Indeed, my dear Miss Paschal. Many have tried to make us forget the Magdalene's legacy, but her presence is too strong. And as you have no doubt noticed, she will not be ignored, particularly . . ."

Church bells began to chime the midday hour, interrupting Sinclair's reply. Instead, he hurried them across the church yet again. He pointed out a narrow bronze meridian line embedded in the church floor, running directly across the north–south transept. The line ended at a marble obelisk, fashioned in the Egyptian style, with a golden globe and a cross at the top.

"Come, quickly. It is now midday and you must see this. It happens only once a year."

Maureen pointed to the bronze line. "What does it signify?"

"The Paris Meridian. It divides France in a most interesting way. But watch, look up there."

Sinclair pointed to a window above them across the church. As they turned to look, a beam of sunlight shone through the window and shot down to illuminate the bronze line embedded in the stone. They watched as the light danced across the floor of the church, following the brass. The light moved up the obelisk until it reached the globe, perfectly illuminating the golden cross in a shower of light.

"Beautiful, isn't it? This church is aligned to mark the solstice perfectly."

"It is beautiful," Peter conceded. "And I hate to burst your bubble, Lord Sinclair, but there's a legitimate religious reason for that. Easter is marked as the Sunday after the full moon following the vernal equinox. It was not uncommon for churches to devise a means of identifying the equinoxes and solstices."

Sinclair shrugged and turned to Maureen. "He's quite right, you know."

"But there's more to this Paris Meridian, isn't there?"

"Some refer to it as the Magdalene Line. It's similar to the line on the map that I sent to you, the one that begins in Amiens and ends in Montserrat. If you'd like to find out why, meet me at my home in the Languedoc in two days and I will show you the reason for this, and much more. Oh, I almost forgot."

Sinclair removed one of his luxe vellum envelopes from an interior pocket.

"I understand you are acquainted with the delightful filmmaker Tamara Wisdom. She will be attending our costume ball later in the week. I hope the two of you will join her. And I insist that you stay with me as guests of the château as well."

Maureen looked at Peter to gauge his reaction. They hadn't expected this.

"Lord Sinclair," Peter began, "Maureen has traveled a great distance to make this appointment. In your letter you promised her some answers . . ."

Sinclair cut him off. "Father Healy, people have been trying to understand this mystery for two thousand years. You can't expect to know everything in one day. True knowledge must be earned, no? Now, I'm late for an appointment, and I must rush off."

Maureen put her hand on Sinclair's arm to stop him. "Lord Sinclair, in your letter you mentioned my father. I was hoping you would at least tell me what you know about him."

Sinclair looked at Maureen and softened. "My dear," he said kindly, "I have a letter written by your father that I think you will find very interesting. It's not here, of course, it's back at the château. That's one of the reasons you must come and stay with me. And Father Healy, of course."

Maureen was floored. "A letter? Are you sure it was written by my father?"

"Was your father's name Edouard Paul Paschal, spelled the French way? And did he reside in Louisiana?"

"Yes," Maureen answered in barely more than a whisper.

"Then the letter is most certainly from him. I found it in our family archives."

"But what does it say?"

"Miss Paschal, it would be a terrible injustice for me to try to tell you here as my memory is simply abominable. I will gladly show it to you when you arrive in the Languedoc. Now, I really must go. I'm late as it is. If you need anything before then, ring the number on the invitation and ask for Roland. He will help you with anything you need. Absolutely anything, just name it."

Sinclair rushed off without saying good-bye. He threw his parting shot over his shoulder. "Oh, and I believe you already have a map. Just follow the Magdalene Line."

The Scotsman's footsteps echoed through the cavernous church as he strode out of the building, leaving Maureen and Peter to look at each other helplessly.

Maureen and Peter reviewed their strange meeting with Sinclair over a lunch at a Left Bank café. They were of decidedly different opinions about him. Peter was suspicious to the edge of irritation. Maureen was fascinated to the point of enthralled.

They decided to walk off the meal with a stroll through the Jardin du Luxembourg.

A family with a gaggle of raucous children was enjoying a picnic on the grass as the pair passed. Two of the younger kids were chasing a soccer ball, and each other, as the elder children and the parents cheered them on. Peter stopped to watch them, his expression wistful.

"What's wrong?" Maureen noticed.

"Nothing, nothing. I was just thinking about everyone back home. My sisters, their kids. You know, I haven't been back to Ireland in two years. I won't mention how long it's been since you went back."

"It's just a little over an hour away by plane from here."

"I know. Believe me, I've been thinking about it. We'll see how things go here. If I have time, I may hop over there for a few days."

"Pete, I'm a big girl and perfectly capable of handling this by myself. Why don't you take advantage of being here and go home?"

"And leave you alone in the hands of Sinclair? Are you out of your mind?"

The soccer ball, now in the control of the older kids, flew toward Peter. He handled it deftly with his feet, kicking it back to the children. With a little wave to the cheering kids, Peter continued his walk with Maureen.

"Do you ever regret your decision?"

"What decision? To come here with you?"

"No. To become a priest."

Peter stopped suddenly, shocked by the question. "What on earth caused you to ask that?"

"Watching you just now. You love kids. You would have made a great dad."

Peter resumed the walk as he explained. "No regrets. I had a vocation and I followed it. I still have that vocation and I think I always will. I know that's always been hard for you to understand."

"It still is."

"Hmm. You know what's ironic about that?"

"What?"

"You're one of the reasons I became a priest."

It was Maureen's turn to stop in her tracks. "Me? How? Why?"

"Outmoded laws of the church turned you against your faith. It happens all the time, and it doesn't have to. And now there are orders—younger, scholarly, progressive orders—trying to bring spirituality into the twenty-first century and make it accessible to youth. I found that with the Jesuits I first encountered in Israel. They were trying to change the very things that drove you away. I wanted to be part of that. I wanted to help you find your faith again. You, and others like you."

Maureen was staring at him, fighting the unexpected tears that welled behind her eyes.

"I can't believe you never told me this before."

Peter shrugged. "You never asked."

*. . . Easa's final suffering was pure torment for all of us, but it took a large part of Philip's being to cope with it. He cried out in his sleep often and would not tell me why or allow me to help him. Finally the truth came to me from Bartolome, who advised that Philip didn't want to harm me with such terrible memories. But Philip was haunted each night by the thought of Easa's agony, by the way his wounds had been described.*

*The men give me honor as I am the only one of us who witnessed Easa's passion.*

*During our time in Egypt, Bartolome became my most dedicated student. He wanted to know as much as possible and as quickly as possible. He was eager, hungry for it, like a man starving for bread. It was as if Easa's sacrifice had created a hole in Bartolome that could only be filled by the teachings of The Way. I knew then that he had a special calling, that he would take the words of Love and Light out into the world, and that others would be changed by him. So each night when the children and the others slept, I taught Bartolome the secrets. He would be ready when the time came.*

*But I did not know if I would be. I had grown to love him as much as my own blood, and I feared for him—because his beauty and purity would not be understood by others the way it was understood by those who loved him best. He was a man without guile.*

THE ARQUES GOSPEL OF MARY MAGDALENE,
THE BOOK OF DISCIPLES

# CHAPTER SEVEN

*The Languedoc region of France*
*June 22, 2005*

*T*he greenery of the French countryside flew past the windows of the high-speed train. Maureen and Peter were far from focused on the scenery; their attention was totally absorbed by the assortment of maps, books, and papers laid out before them.

"Et in Arcadia ego," Peter mumbled, scribbling on a yellow legal pad. "Et . . . in . . . Arca-di-a . . . e-go . . ."

He was engrossed in the map of France, the one with the red line drawn down the center. He pointed to the line. "See how the Paris Meridian runs down to the Languedoc, down here to this town. Arques. Very interesting name."

Peter pronounced the name of the town, which sounded similar to "Ark."

"As in Noah's Ark or Ark of the Covenant?" Maureen was very interested in where this could be leading them.

"Exactly. Ark is a versatile word in Latin—it generally means container, but it can also mean tomb. Wait a minute, let's look at this."

Peter picked up the legal pad again, and his pen. He began doodling the letters of *Et in Arcadia ego*. He scrawled ARK across the top of the page in black capitals. Below it, he wrote ARC in the same lettering.

Maureen had an idea. "Okay, what about this? ARC. ARC — ADIA. Maybe it's not a reference to the mythical place of Arcadia; maybe it's several words run together? Does that make any sense in Latin?"

Peter wrote it out in capitals: ARC A DIA.

"Well?" Maureen was dying to know. "Does it mean anything?"

"Looking at it this way, it could mean 'Ark of God.' With just a little imagination, the phrase could mean 'and in the Ark of God I am.' "

Peter pointed to the town of Arques on the map. "I don't suppose you know anything about the history of Arques? If the town had a sacred legend attached to it, this could mean 'and in the village of God I am.' I know it's a stretch, but that's the best I can come up with."

"Sinclair's estate is just outside Arques."

"Yes, but that doesn't tell us why Nicolas Poussin may have been painting it four hundred years ago, does it? Or why you heard voices in the Louvre when you were looking at this painting. I think we have to look at these things that have been happening to you as separate from Sinclair for a minute."

Peter was intent on diminishing Sinclair's importance in Maureen's experience. She had been having Magdalene visions for several years, long before she had ever heard of Bérenger Sinclair.

Maureen nodded her agreement. "So let's say that if Arques was known as sacred ground for some reason, was 'the village of God,' Poussin was telling us that something important is there, in Arques? Is that the theory? 'And in the village of God I am?' "

Peter nodded, thoughtful. "Just a guess. But I think the area surrounding Arques may be worth a visit, don't you?"

It was market day in the village of Quillan, and the town at the foot of the French Pyrenees bustled with the activity of the weekly event. Residents of the inland Languedoc region hurried from stall to stall, stocking up on fresh produce and fish brought in from the Mediterranean.

Maureen and Peter moved through the marketplace. In Maureen's hand was the print of *The Shepherds of Arcadia.* A fruit peddler recognized it and laughed, pointing at the print.

"Ah, Poussin!"

He began to give them directions in rapid French. Peter asked him to slow down, taking in the instructions. The merchant's ten-year-old son watched Maureen's confusion as his father spoke to Peter in French and decided to try out his broken but intrepid English.

"You want go to tomb of Poussin?"

Maureen nodded with excitement. She didn't even know that the tomb in the painting actually existed, until now. "Yes. Oui!"

"Okay. Go to main road and down. When you see the church, left. Tomb of Poussin is on the hill."

Maureen thanked the boy, then reached into her bag and pulled out a five-euro note. "Merci, merci beaucoup," she said to the boy as she slid the note into his hand. The child smiled broadly.

"De rien, Madame! Bon chance," the fruit peddler called out as Maureen and Peter retreated from the marketplace.

His son had the last word. "Et in Arcadia ego!" The boy laughed, then scampered off to spend his newly earned euros on sweets.

Between them, they managed to piece together the directions of the father and son, which ultimately took them to the correct road. Peter drove slowly as Maureen scanned the region through the passenger window.

"There! Is that it? Up on the hill there?"

Peter pulled over beside a gentle slope topped by scrub trees and bushes. Behind the cluster of shrubbery, they could see the upper edges of a rectangular stone tomb.

"I saw this same style of freestanding tomb in the Holy Land. There are several of them in the Galilee region," Peter explained. He stopped for a moment as a thought struck him.

"What is it?" Maureen asked.

"It just occurred to me that there is one of these on the road to Magdala. It looks very much like this one. It may even be identical."

They skirted the side of the road, looking for a path that would lead up to the tomb. They found one that was overgrown. Maureen stopped at the base of the path and kneeled down.

"Look at this, the overgrowth. It's not living vegetation."

Peter knelt beside her and picked up some sticks and brush that had been placed over the entrance to the path. "You're right."

"Looks like someone has deliberately tried to conceal the path," Maureen observed.

"That may just be the landowner's work. Maybe he's tired of people like us stomping through his land. Four hundred years of tourism would make anyone cranky."

They moved carefully, stepping over the growth and following the path to the top of the hillock. When the rectangular, granite tomb was immediately ahead of them, Maureen took out the print of Poussin's painting and compared it to the landscape. The rocky outcropping located behind the tomb was mirrored in the painting.

"It's identical."

Peter approached the structure and ran his hand over the face of the tomb. "Except the tomb is smooth," he observed. "There's no inscription."

"So was the inscription Poussin's invention?" Maureen let the question hang in the air as she circled the sarcophagus. Noting that the rear of the tomb was covered by brush and overgrowth, Maureen tried to move the obstructions. A clear view of the back of the tomb caused her to cry out for Peter.

"Come here! You have to see this!"

Peter came around to her side, helping to hold back the overgrowth. When he saw the source of Maureen's excitement, he shook his head in disbelief.

Inscribed on the back of the tomb was a pattern of nine circles surrounding a central disk.

It was identical to the design on Maureen's ancient ring.

Maureen and Peter spent the night in a small hotel in Couiza, a few miles from Arques. Tammy had chosen the location for them because of its proximity to an enigmatic place called Rennes-le-Château, known in esoteric circles as the Village of Mystery. She was flying into the Languedoc late in the evening, and the three of them had agreed to meet in the breakfast room the following morning.

Tammy bounced into the breakfast room, where Maureen and Peter were having coffee while waiting for her.

"Sorry I'm late. My flight into Carcassonne was delayed, and by the time I arrived it was after midnight. Took me forever to fall asleep and then I couldn't get up."

"I was worried when I didn't hear from you last night," Maureen said. "Did you drive in from Carcassonne?"

"No. I have other friends coming in for Sinclair's bash tomorrow night and I traveled with them. One of them is a local and he picked us up."

A basket of flaky croissants was deposited on the table and the waiter took Tammy's beverage order. Tammy waited for the server to retreat to the kitchen before continuing. "Now, we need to check out this morning."

Maureen and Peter looked puzzled. "Why?" they asked in unison.

"Sinclair is raging that we stayed in a hotel. He left a message for me last night. He has rooms at the château for all of us."

Peter looked wary. "I don't like that idea." He turned to plead his case to Maureen. "I'd prefer to remain here; I think it's safer for you. The hotel is neutral territory, a place we can retreat to if something happens that makes you uncomfortable."

Tammy looked annoyed. "Listen, do you know how many people would kill for this invitation? The château is fantastic; it's like a living museum. You really do run the risk of offending Sinclair if you refuse, and you may not want to do that. He has too much to offer you."

Maureen was stuck. She looked back and forth at the two of them.

Peter was right—the hotel provided them with neutral territory. But her imagination was sparked by the idea of staying in the château and observing the enigmatic Bérenger Sinclair at a closer proximity.

Tammy sensed Maureen's dilemma. "I've told you that Sinclair isn't dangerous. In fact, I think he's a wonderful man." She looked at Peter. "But if you feel differently, look at it this way: it's like taking the approach of 'Keep your friends close but your enemies closer.' "

By the end of breakfast, Tammy had convinced them to check out of the hotel. Peter watched her carefully as they dined, noting to himself that she was a very persuasive woman.

*Rennes-le-Château, France*
*June 23, 2005*

"YOU'D NEVER FIND THIS PLACE for the first time unless somebody showed you how to get here." Tammy gave directions from the backseat. "Turn right up here—see that little lane there? It leads up the hill to Rennes-le-Château."

The narrow road was roughly paved as it twisted upward in a steep series of switchbacks. At the top of the hill, a utilitarian sign partially obscured by scrub announced the name of the tiny hamlet.

"You can park over here." Tammy directed them to a small, dusty clearing at the entrance to the village.

As they exited the car, Maureen looked down at her watch. She did a double take before commenting, "How strange. My watch has stopped and I just put a new battery in it before we left the States."

Tammy laughed. "See, the fun is starting already. Time takes on a new meaning up here on the magic mountain. I guarantee your watch will return to normal when we leave this area."

Peter and Maureen looked at each other, following where Tammy led them. She didn't bother to explain, just kept walking as she tossed a quip behind her at the pair of them. "Ladies and gentlemen, you are now entering the Twilight Zone."

The village did give an eerie impression of a land that time had forgotten. It was surprisingly small and appeared strangely deserted.

Peter asked, "Does anybody live here?"

"Oh, yeah. It's a fully functional village. The population is less than two hundred, but it's a population all the same."

"It's uncannily quiet," Maureen noted.

"It's always like this," Tammy explained, "until a tour bus unloads." As they entered the village, to their right was what remained of a château, a near ruin of the house that gave the village its name.

"That's the Château Hautpol. It was a stronghold of the Knights Templar during the Crusades. See the tower?" She pointed to a decrepit turret. "Don't be fooled by this backwater location and its worn condition. The Tower of Alchemy is one of the most important esoteric landmarks in France. Maybe in the world."

"I assume you're going to tell us why?" Peter was finding his annoyance increasing. He was tired of games wrapped in mysteries; he just wanted somebody to give him some answers that made sense.

"I'll tell you, but not yet. Only because it won't mean anything to you until you know the story of the village. We'll leave that for last. I'll tell you on the way out."

They passed a small bookshop on the left. It was closed, but volumes featuring occult symbolism graced the windows.

"Not your average Catholic farming village?" Maureen whispered to Peter as Tammy walked ahead.

"Apparently not," Peter agreed, looking at the strange inventory of books and the pentagram jewelry in the window.

Another oddity on the opposite wall of the narrow street caught Maureen's attention as they followed Tammy through the ancient stone streets of the odd little village. Engraved on the side of a house at eye level was what appeared to be a sundial. The metal centerpiece had long since fallen out, leaving a weathered hole in the center. Closer inspection showed that there was nothing ordinary about the markings. They began with the number nine and continued through the number seventeen, with half hours marked in between. But scratched above the numbers were a series of arcane-looking symbols.

Peter looked over Maureen's shoulder as she pointed out the strange glyphs. "What do you think these mean?" she asked him.

Tammy was walking back toward them, smiling like the cat who ate the cream. "I see you've found the first of our important oddities here in RLC," she said.

"RLC?"

"Rennes-le-Château. It's what everyone calls it as the full name is too damn long. Gotta start learning the local lingo so you fit in at the party tomorrow night."

Maureen turned back to the engraving on the wall. Peter was inspecting it closely.

"I recognize these symbols, the planets. That's the moon, and Mercury. Is that the sun?" He pointed to a circle with a dot in the center.

"Sure is," Tammy answered. "And that's Saturn. The rest of the symbols deal with astrology. Here is Libra, Virgo, Leo, Cancer, and this is Gemini."

Maureen had a thought. "Is Scorpio on there anywhere? Or Sagittarius?"

Tammy shook her head, but pointed to the left side of the sundial, which would have been the seven o'clock position on a normal clockface.

"No. See here where the markings stop? That's the planet Saturn. If the markings continued in a counterclockwise direction, you'd have Scorpio following Libra and then Sagittarius after that."

"Why does it stop in such an odd place?" Maureen asked.

"And what does it mean?" Peter was far more interested in an answer.

Tammy raised her palms in an I-can't-help-you gesture. "It's a reference to a planetary alignment, we think. Other than that, we really don't know."

Maureen continued to stare at it. She was thinking about Sandro's fresco in the Louvre, trying to determine if there was a connection to the scorpion in the painting. She wanted to understand the possible use of such a strange sundial, if that's what it was. "Is it like a 'when the moon is in the seventh house and Jupiter aligns with Mars' kind of thing?"

"If you two start singing 'The Age of Aquarius,' I'm leaving," Peter announced.

They all laughed as Tammy explained. "She's right, though. It's probably a reference to a specific planetary alignment. And since it was placed here on the front of a prominent home, we have to assume that it was important for every person in the village to know about it."

Tammy led them away from the sundial and resumed her tour, pointing to the villa up ahead. "The focal point of the village is the museum and the entire villa area. It's up there, just ahead of us."

At the end of the narrow street ahead of them stood a residential building, a quaint stone villa. An oddly shaped stone tower rose in the distance behind it, clinging to the side of the mountain.

"The mystery of this village centers on a very strange story about a famous—rather, infamous—priest who lived here in the late eighteen hundreds. Abbé Bérenger Saunière."

"Bérenger? Isn't that Sinclair's first name?" Peter asked.

Tammy nodded. "Yes, and it's not a coincidence. Sinclair's grandfather hoped that if his grandson had the same name, perhaps he would inherit some of the qualities of his namesake—Saunière was fearless in his protection of the local histories and mysteries, and absolutely devoted to Mary Magdalene's legacy.

"Anyway, there are various legends about what the Abbé found here when he set out to restore the church. Some believe he found the lost treasure of the Temple of Jerusalem. Because the adjacent château was associated with the Templar Knights, it's possible they used this remote outpost to hide their spoils from the Holy Land. Who would look for anything valuable up here? And some say Saunière discovered priceless documents. Whatever it was, he became a very wealthy man, suddenly and mysteriously. He spent millions in his lifetime, yet he made the equivalent of about twenty-five bucks a year in salary as a local priest. So where did all that cash come from?

"Back in the 1980s a trio of British researchers wrote a book about

Saunière and his mysterious wealth that became a bestseller. It was called *Holy Blood, Holy Grail* in the States, and is considered a classic in esoteric circles. The bad news is that the same book created a treasure-hunting craze in this area. The natural resources were exploited, and local landmarks were vandalized by religious fanatics and souvenir hunters. Sinclair even had to put armed guards on his land to protect the tomb."

"Poussin's tomb?" Maureen asked.

Tammy nodded. "Of course. That's the centerpiece for the whole mystery, thanks to the Shepherds of Arcadia."

"We went to see the tomb yesterday. I didn't see any guards," Peter said.

Tammy laughed in her rich, throaty way. "That's because you're welcome on Sinclair's land. Believe me, if you were there, he knows about it. And if he didn't want you there, you'd know about it."

They arrived at the large building that dominated the village. A sign announced "Villa Bethania—Residence of Bérenger Saunière."

As they entered the museum doors, Tammy smiled and nodded to the woman at the front desk, who waved them through.

"Don't we need to buy tickets?" Maureen asked as they passed the sign displaying ticket prices.

Tammy shook her head. "Nah, they know me here. I am using this as a setting for a documentary on the history of alchemy."

She led them past glass cases displaying priestly vestments worn by the Abbé Saunière in the nineteenth century. Peter paused to look at these as Tammy walked on to the end of the hallway. She stopped at an ancient stone pillar engraved with a cross.

"It's called the Knights' Pillar, and is believed to have been carved by the Visigoths in the eighth century. It used to make up part of the altar in the old church. When Abbé Saunière moved the pillar during the villa's restoration, he discovered some mysterious, encoded parchments, or so they say."

The display of the parchments had been enlarged by the museum curators to make the code more obvious. Scattered letters stood out in bold print, but upon closer inspection there was nothing random about the placement. Maureen pointed to the phrase ET IN ARCADIA EGO as it appeared within the darkened capital letters.

"There it is again," Maureen said to Peter. She turned to Tammy. "So what does it mean? It's a code of some sort?"

"There are at least fifty different theories I have heard on the meaning of that phrase. It's spurred a cottage industry almost by it-self."

"Peter came up with an interesting theory in the train on the way down here," Maureen chimed in. "He thought it pertained to the vil-lage of Arques. 'In Arques, the village of God, I am.' "

Tammy appeared impressed. "Good guess, Padre. The most com-mon belief is the Latin anagram explanation. If you rearrange the let-ters it reads " 'I tego arcana Dei.' "

Peter translated. "I conceal God's secrets."

"Yep. Not much help, is it?" Tammy laughed. "Come on, I want you to see the house from the outside."

Peter was still thinking about Poussin's tomb. "Wait a minute. Wouldn't that imply that something was hidden inside the tomb? If you put it all together it's something like 'In Arques, the village of God, I conceal the secrets.' "

Maureen and Peter waited for Tammy to answer. She paused to think for a moment. "It's as good a theory as any other I've heard. Un-fortunately, the tomb has been opened and searched many times. Sin-clair's grandfather excavated every inch of that property for a square mile surrounding the tomb, and Bérenger brought in every type of technology imaginable to search for buried treasure—ultrasound, radar, you name it."

"And they never found anything?" Maureen asked.

"Not a thing."

"Maybe somebody got to it first," Peter offered. "What about this priest Saunière? Could that be what made him so wealthy? Some trea-sure he found?"

"That's what a lot of people believe. But you know what's funny? After decades of research by very determined men and women, no-body knows what Saunière's secret was, even today." Tammy was leading them through a lovely courtyard dominated by a stone and marble fountain.

"Very impressive for a simple parish priest in the nineteenth century," Peter observed.

"Isn't it? And here's the stranger thing. While Abbé Saunière spent a fortune building this place, he never lived here. In fact, he refused to. Ultimately, he left it to his . . . housekeeper."

"You paused there," Peter observed, "paused before you said 'housekeeper.' "

"Well, there are many who believe that she was more than Saunière's housekeeper, that she was his life partner."

"But wasn't he a Catholic priest?"

"Judge not, Padre. That's my motto and always has been."

Maureen had wandered out of earshot, her attention captured by a weathered sculpture in the garden. "Who is the statue?"

"Joan of Arc," Tammy answered.

Peter moved to look closer at the statue. "Oh, right. There's her sword and her banner. But she seems out of place here," he commented.

"Why?" Maureen asked him.

"She just seems . . . very traditional. A classic symbol of French Catholicism. Yet there doesn't seem to be anything else here that is even remotely conventional."

"Joanie? Conventional?" Tammy burst out laughing again. "Not in these parts. But that's a major history lesson that we'll tackle later. You wanna see something really unorthodox? You've got to see the church."

Even in the warmth and sunlight of midsummer, Rennes-le-Château was a place of strangeness and shadows. Maureen had the disconcerting sense of being followed, of a silhouette creeping up on her at every turn of the gardens. She found herself spinning quickly around on several occasions, only to find that there was no one there when she did. The village made her jumpy—this strange place where her watch wouldn't work and she constantly felt that someone was creeping up on her. Fascinating as it was, she would be happy to get out of there, sooner rather than later.

Tammy took them out of the gardens and around the house. Through another courtyard they saw the entrance of an aged stone church.

"This is the parish church for the village of RLC. There has been a church dedicated to Mary Magdalene on this site for a thousand years. Saunière started to renovate it somewhere around 1891, which is about the time he supposedly found the mysterious documents. He took them to Paris, and the next thing we know, he's a millionaire. He used his money to make some very unusual additions to the church."

As they moved toward the church, Peter stopped to read a Latin inscription on the lintel above the door. "Terribilis est locus iste."

"Terribilis?" Maureen questioned.

"This place is terrible," Peter explained.

"Recognize it, Padre?" Tammy asked.

Peter nodded. "Of course." If Tammy wanted to test his Biblical knowledge, she was going to have to work much harder than this. "Genesis, chapter twenty-eight. Jacob says it after dreaming about the ladder to heaven."

"Why would a priest choose that to inscribe above his church?" Maureen asked, looking to both Peter and Tammy for an answer.

"Maybe you should look inside the church before you try to answer that question." This was Tammy's suggestion. Peter followed it and entered.

"It's pitch dark in here," he called back to them.

"Oh, wait a minute," Tammy said as she fished in her bag for a coin. "The lights are coin-operated." She slipped the euro into a box near the door and the fluorescent lights flickered on. "The first time I came here, I tried to view the church in the dark. I brought a flashlight with me the second time. It was then that one of the caretakers showed me the coin box. This way the tourists can give something back to the church. It gives us about twenty minutes of light."

"What is that?" Peter exclaimed. As Tammy was explaining the light situation, Peter had turned to see the statue of a hideous demon crouched at the entrance of the church.

"Oh, that's Rex. Hi, Rex." Tammy patted the statue playfully on the head. "He's like the official mascot of Rennes-le-Château. As with everything else here, there are tons of theories about him. Some say that he is the demon Asmodeus, the guardian of secrets and hidden treasures. Others say that he is the Rex Mundi of Cathar tradition, which is my personal belief."

"Rex Mundi. The King of the World?" Peter was translating.

Tammy nodded and explained to Maureen. "The Cathars dominated this area in the Middle Ages. Remember, there's been a church here since 1059, when Catharism was at its peak. They believed that a lesser being was guardian of the earth plane, a demon they called Rex Mundi—the King of the World. Our souls are in a constant struggle to defeat Rex and achieve the kingdom of God, the realm of the spirit. Rex represents all earthly and physical temptations."

"But what is he doing in a consecrated Catholic church?" Peter asked.

"Being vanquished by angels, of course. Look above him." Statuary of four angels making the sign of the cross stood on top of the demon's back, perched on a holy-water font shaped like a giant scallop shell.

Peter read the inscription aloud, then translated it into English. "Par ce signe tu le vaincrais. By this sign I conquer him."

"Good defeats evil. Spirit conquers matter. Angels over demons. Unorthodox, yes, but très Saunière." Tammy ran her hand across the demon's neck. "See this? A few years ago someone broke into the church and cut off Rex's head. This is a replacement. No one knows if it was a souvenir hunter or an angry Catholic who objected to such a dualist symbol on consecrated ground. To my knowledge, he is the only demon statue in a Catholic church. Is that right, Padre?"

Peter nodded. "I would have to say that I don't know of anything like this in a Roman Catholic church. It's essentially blasphemous."

"The Cathars were dualists. They believed in two opposing divine forces, one that worked for good and was concerned with purifying the essence of the spirit, and one that worked for evil and was shackled to the corrupted material world," Tammy explained. "Look at the floor here."

She directed their attention to the tiles that made up the church floor. They were ebony and stark white, laid out like a checkerboard. "Another of Saunière's concessions to duality—black and white, good and evil. More eccentric design touches. But I think Saunière was crazy like a fox. He was born just a few miles from here and understood the local mentality. He knew his congregation was descended from Cathar blood and they had good reason to mistrust Rome, even centuries later. No offense, Padre."

"None taken," Peter answered. He was getting used to Tammy's ribbing. It seemed good-natured overall, and he really didn't mind. Tammy's quirkiness was actually beginning to grow on him. "The Church dealt with the Cathar heresy in a harsh manner. I can understand why it would still be offensive to the local people."

Tammy turned to Maureen. "The only official Crusade in history where Christians killed other Christians. The Pope's army massacred the Cathars, and no one here has ever forgotten it. So by adding overtly Cathar and Gnostic elements to his church, Saunière created an environment where his flock would feel comfortable and therefore increased church attendance and loyalty. It worked. The local people loved him to the point of worship."

Peter walked through the church, taking it all in. Every element of the décor was bizarre. It was garish, overblown, and certainly unconventional. There were painted plaster statues of unlikely saints, like the obscure Saint Roche raising his tunic to reveal a wounded leg or Saint Germaine, depicted in plaster as a young shepherdess carrying a lamb. In every piece of artwork in the church, something was irregular or unusual. Most notably, an almost life-size sculpture of the baptism of Jesus showed John towering over him—dressed incongruously in a full Roman tunic and cape.

"Why would anyone put John the Baptist in the clothes of a Roman?" Peter asked.

A shadow crossed Tammy's face for the briefest instant, but she didn't answer. Instead, she continued her commentary as she led them toward the altar.

"Local legend said Saunière painted some of the sculptures himself. We are pretty sure he was responsible for at least a part of the altarpiece. He was obsessed with your Mary." Maureen followed Tammy to where a bas-relief of Mary Magdalene constituted the focal point at the altar. Her usual icons surrounded her—the skull at her feet, the book beside her. She stared intently at a cross that appeared to be made from a living tree.

Peter was fixated on the relief plaques depicting the Stations of the Cross. Like the statues, every piece of art contained a strange detail or idiosyncrasy that was contrary to Church tradition.

They examined the bizarre elements within the church, each a new building block of the growing mystery around them.

Without warning, a sharp click shook the church and they were plunged into pitch blackness.

Maureen panicked in the absolute darkness. The shadows that had followed her even in the sunlight were suffocating in here.

She screamed for Peter.

"I'm right here," he yelled back. "Where are you?" The acoustics in the church caused the sound to bounce through the building, making it impossible to track anyone.

"I'm by the altar," Maureen yelled.

"It's okay," Tammy yelled. "Don't panic. Our meter has just run out."

Tammy hurried to the door and let the daylight in, allowing Peter and Maureen to find each other. She grabbed him and ran out the front door of the church, deliberately looking to the left to avoid seeing the statue of the demon again.

"I know it was a matter of mechanics, but that was creepy. The whole church is just so . . . weird." Maureen was shivering in spite of the Languedoc sun that was rising toward midday. This other-worldly village that time had forgotten was utterly disturbing, completely out of her realm of experience. There was a sense of chaos under the surface here. While the village itself was nearly deserted, there was a deafening quality to the silence of this place. Maureen glanced down at her wrist and was reminded that her watch had been completely immobilized since she arrived here, a fact that reinforced her unease.

Peter had questions for Tammy as she led them back through the garden and around the Villa Bethania. "I can't imagine that Saunière did all of this without getting into trouble with the Church."

"Oh, he was in trouble quite a lot," Tammy explained. "They even tried to de-frock him once and replaced him with another priest, but it didn't work. The local people simply wouldn't accept anyone but Saunière, because he was one of them. He was groomed to take over this position, contrary to what you'll read in most of the books. It's so funny to me that so-called authorities on RLC talk about Saunière coming here as some kind of random occurrence. Believe me, nothing that happens in this region is a coincidence. There are too many powerful forces at work."

"Do you mean powerful human forces or powerful supernatural forces?"

"Both." Tammy gestured for them to follow her. She walked toward a stone tower at the far west of the property, perched at the very edge of a cliff.

"Come on, you have to see the pièce de résistance. The Tour Magdala."

"Tour Magdala?" Maureen was intrigued by the name.

"The Tower of the Magdalene. This was Saunière's private library. But it's the view that is worth the effort."

They followed Tammy through the interior of the turret, looking briefly at some of Saunière's personal items entombed in glass cases before scaling the twenty-two stairs to the turret deck. The view of the Languedoc was breathtaking.

Tammy pointed to a hill in the distance. "Can you see that out there? That's Arques. And across the valley is the legendary village of Coustaussa, where another priest, a friend of Saunière's named Antoine Gélis, was brutally murdered in his home. His place was ransacked, and it is believed that whoever killed the old man was looking for something bigger than money. They left gold coins sitting on the table, but stole everything that looked like a document. Poor old guy—he was in his seventies and was found lying in his own blood, killed with fireplace tongs and an axe."

"That's horrible." Maureen shuddered, reacting to the story as Tammy told it, but also to the setting they were in. As fascinated as she was by this place, she was also repelled by it.

"People are willing to kill over these mysteries." Peter stated it simply.

"Well, that was a hundred years ago. I like to think we've become more civilized about it these days."

"What happened to Saunière?" Maureen brought her focus back to the story of the strange priest and his mysterious millions.

"It gets weirder. He had a stroke within days of ordering his own casket. Local legend says that a priest who was a stranger to these parts was brought in to administer last rites, but refused to do so after hearing Saunière's final confession. The poor man left Rennes-le-Château in a deep depression and was said to have never smiled again."

"Wow. I wonder what Saunière told him?"

"No one knew exactly, except for the arguably euphemistic house-keeper, Marie Dénarnaud, to whom Saunière left all his wealth—and secrets. She died mysteriously herself some years later and was unable to speak in the last days of her life, so no one will ever know for sure.

"That's why this village has given birth to an industry. A hundred thousand tourists a year visit this little backwater now. Some come out of curiosity; some come determined to find Saunière's treasure."

Tammy walked to the edge of the turret deck and looked over at the expansive valley below them. "And we don't know for sure why he built the tower here, but you can bet he was looking for something. Don't you think, Padre?" She winked at Peter, then turned to retreat down the stairs.

As the three of them made their way toward the car, Maureen insisted that Tammy keep her earlier promise to explain the Tower of Alchemy, the once-majestic turret of the now-crumbling Château Hautpol. Tammy paused, unsure of where to begin. There were volumes written about this area and she had done years of research, so coming up with the condensed version was always tough.

"There has been something in this region that has attracted people here for thousands of years," she began. "It has to be indigenous, something in the land itself. How else can we account for the fact that it has a universal appeal that reaches across over two thousand years of history and such varied religious beliefs?

"Like everything else in this area, there are countless theories. It's always fun to start with the real wackos, of course—those who swear it's all connected to aliens and sea monsters."

"Sea monsters?" Peter laughed with Maureen as she asked the question. "I'd almost expect aliens, but sea monsters?"

"I kid you not. Sea monsters show up in the local mysteries here all the time. Pretty funny for such a landlocked area, but not nearly as bizarre as some of the UFO stuff. I'm telling you, there is something about this area that makes people almost literally crazy.

"Then there's the time element. Is your watch still stopped?"

Maureen knew the answer, but looked down for confirmation, to where it had been 9:33 for more than an hour. She nodded.

"It probably will be until we get off the mountain," Tammy continued. "There is something here that affects clocks and watches as well as electronics, which may be one of the reasons that so many people here still use sundials, even in the twenty-first century. It doesn't happen to everybody, but I can't tell you how many weird encounters I've had personally."

She began to tell them one of her many stories about the inexplicable time elements in the Rennes-le-Château area.

"I was driving up here with some friends one day and checked the clock in the car at the base of the hill. When we reached the top, the car clock indicated that it had taken almost half an hour to get up to the top. Now you just drove it—how long did it take, even driving as slowly as we did? Five minutes?"

She was asking Peter, who nodded in agreement. "Not much more than that."

"It's not very far, maybe two miles. So, we thought the clock was just wrong in the car, until we all looked at our watches. Half an hour had actually passed. Now, we all knew we hadn't been on that road for half an hour, but somehow thirty full minutes had passed as we drove up here. Can I explain it? No. It was like some kind of time warp, and I've since talked to a number of people who have experienced the same thing. The locals don't even bother to worry about it because they're so used to it. Ask them and they just shrug it off like it's the most normal thing in the world.

"But people have experienced similar phenomena around the Great Pyramid and within some of the sacred sites in Britain and Ireland. So what is it? Is it a magnetic force of some kind? Or is it something less tangible and therefore impossible for our feeble human brains to grasp?"

Tammy elaborated on the various theories that had been explored by local and international research teams, rattling off a laundry list of possibilities: ley lines, vortexes, hollow earth, star gates. "Salvador Dali said that the train station in Perpignan was the center of the universe because it was where these magnetic power points intersected."

"How far is Perpignan from here?" This came from Maureen.

"Forty miles or so. Close enough to make it interesting, certainly. I wish I had a definitive answer to it all, but I don't. Nobody does. That's why I'm addicted to this place and keep coming back. Remember the meridian that Sinclair showed you in the church of Saint-Sulpice in Paris?"

Maureen was nodding, trying to keep up. "The Magdalene Line."

"Exactly. And it runs from Paris straight through this area. Why? Because there is something about this region that transcends time and space, and I think that is why it has attracted alchemists from all over Europe for as long as anyone can remember."

"I was wondering when we were going to get back to alchemy," Peter remarked.

"Sorry, Padre. I tend to get long-winded, but then again, none of these explanations are simple. So that tower up there, called the Tower of Alchemy, is apparently built over the legendary power point and the Magdalene Line runs through it. The tower has been the site of countless experiments in alchemy."

"So when you say alchemy, you mean the medieval belief system of turning sulfur into gold?" This was Maureen's question.

"In some cases, yes. But what is the true definition of alchemy? If you ever want to start a great fight, ask that question at a convention of esoteric thinkers. The room will be torn down before a definitive answer is ever reached."

Tammy rattled off the different kinds of alchemy. "There are the scientific alchemists, those who physically attempt to change base materials into gold. Some of these scientific alchemists came here believing that the magic in the land itself was the magical x-factor they were looking for to complete their experiments. Then there are the philosophers, who believe that alchemy is a spiritual transformation, that it is about turning the base elements of the human spirit into a golden self; there are the esoterics who pursue the idea that alchemical processes can be used to achieve immortality and somehow impact the nature of time. Then there are sexual alchemists, who believe that sexual energy creates a type of transformation when two bodies are blended using a certain combination of physical and metaphysical methods."

Maureen listened closely; she wanted to know more about Tammy's personal perspective. "And what theory do you favor?"

"I'm a big fan of sexual alchemy, personally. But I think they're all true. I really do. I think alchemy is actually a term for the most ancient set of principles we have on earth. Once upon a time I think those rules were understood by the ancients, like the architects of the Great Pyramid of Giza."

The next question came from Peter. "So what does all of this have to do with Mary Magdalene?"

"Well, for starters we believe she lived here, or at least spent some time here. Which leads to this question: why here? It's remote even now, with modern transportation. Can you even imagine what it must have been like trying to get through these mountains in the first century? The terrain was totally inhospitable. So why did she choose this place? Why have so many chosen this place? Because there's something special about the land itself.

"Oh, and I forgot to mention the other kind of alchemy that happens here, and it's something that I have just recently dubbed Gnostic alchemy."

"Sounds like an interesting title for a new religion," Maureen said, weighing it.

"Or for an old one. But there is a belief here that extends to the Cathars and maybe beyond, a belief that this region was the center of duality: that the King of the World, old Rex Mundi himself, lives here. The earthly balance of light and dark, good and evil, takes place in this strange little village and its immediate environs. And on some level, those two elements are at war with each other all the time, right here under our feet. You think it's eerie here during the day? You couldn't pay me to walk these streets in the middle of the night. There is something very important about this place, and it isn't all good."

Maureen nodded at Tammy. "I feel that, too. So maybe Dali was off by about forty miles. Maybe Rennes-le-Château is actually the center of the universe?"

Peter chimed in, more seriously. "Well, that would have made sense for the medieval people of France as this *was* their universe. But do people really believe this still?"

"All I can tell you is that there are strange occurrences here that no one can explain, and they happen all the time. Here, in Arques, and in the surrounding areas where the châteaux were built. Some say that the Cathars built their castles as stone fortresses against the energies of darkness. They chose to build on top of vortexes or power points where they could conduct holy ceremonies to control or defeat the forces of darkness. And all of the châteaux have towers, which is significant."

Peter was listening carefully. "But wouldn't towers be strategic, built for defensive purposes?"

"Sure." Tammy nodded emphatically. "But that doesn't explain why each of these châteaux has legends involving alchemy within their towers. The towers are renowned for being places where some kind of magic or transformation occurred. It relates directly to the alchemical motto 'As above, so below.' Towers represent earth, because they're grounded, but they also represent heaven because they reach to the sky, making them appropriate locations for conducting alchemical experiments. And like Saunière's tower, they were all built with twenty-two stairs."

"Why twenty-two?" Maureen asked, her interest piqued.

"Twenty-two is a master number, and numerological elements are critical in alchemy. The master numbers are eleven, twenty-two, and thirty-three. But twenty-two is the pattern you will see most frequently in this area as it pertains to divine female energy. You'll note that Mary Magdalene's feast day on the church calendar . . ."

"Is the twenty-second of July," Peter and Maureen interrupted simultaneously.

"Bingo. So to finally answer your question, maybe that's why Mary Magdalene came here, because she knew of the natural power elements or understood something about the struggle between light and dark as it happens here. This region wasn't unknown to the people of Palestine, you know. The Herod family owned retreats not all that far from here. There is even a tradition that says Mary Magdalene's mother was originally of Languedoc stock. So maybe she was coming home in some way."

Tammy looked up at the crumbling tower of the Château Hautpol. "What I wouldn't give to have been an immortal fly on the wall in that place."

*The Languedoc*
*June 23, 2005*

THEY DROPPED TAMMY OFF IN COUIZA, where she was meeting some friends for a late lunch. Maureen was disappointed that Tammy wouldn't be joining them until later; she was nervous about approaching Sinclair's home without a mutual friend to make things less awkward. And she could feel Peter's tension. He was doing his best to hide it, but it was there in the tightening of his arms on the steering wheel. Perhaps staying at Sinclair's was a mistake after all.

But they had already committed to doing so, and to change their minds now would appear rude and insulting to their host. Maureen didn't want to risk that. Sinclair was too important a piece of her puzzle.

Peter eased the rental car from the road and through the enormous iron gates. Maureen noted as they passed that the gates were decorated with large gold fleurs-de-lis intertwined with vines of grapes—or, perhaps, blue apples. The winding driveway curved uphill, through the sprawling and sumptuous estate that was the Château des Pommes Bleues.

They stopped in front of the château, both speechless for a moment at the sheer size and grandeur of the property, a perfectly restored castle built in the sixteenth century. As Peter and Maureen stepped out of the car, Sinclair's imposing majordomo, the giant Roland, emerged from the front door. Two liveried servants scurried around the car to gather luggage and otherwise respond to Roland's commands.

"Bonjour, Mademoiselle Paschal, Abbé Healy. Bienvenue." Roland smiled suddenly and the expression softened his face, causing both Maureen and Peter to release their collective indrawn breaths. "Welcome to Château des Pommes Bleues. Monsieur Sinclair is most delighted that you are here!"

Maureen and Peter were left to wait in the lavish entry hall as Roland went in search of his master. It wasn't a hardship—the room was filled with valuable art and priceless antiques, the equal of those in many a museum in France.

Maureen stopped at a glass case that served as a focal point for the room, and Peter followed. A massive and ornate silver chalice occupied the case, and a human skull rested in a place of honor in the reliquary. The skull was bleached by time, yet a distinct split could be seen across the cranial bone. A lock of hair—faded, yet still carrying an obvious red pigment—was placed alongside the skull within the chalice.

"The ancients believed that red hair was a source of great magic." Bérenger Sinclair had arrived behind them. Maureen jumped a little at his unexpected voice, then turned to respond.

"The ancients never had to attend public school in Louisiana."

Sinclair laughed, a rich Celtic sound, and reached out to run a finger playfully through Maureen's hair. "Were there no boys at your school?"

Maureen smiled, but returned her attention to the relic in the case quickly before he could see her blush. She read aloud from the placard within the case.

"The skull of King Dagobert the Second."

"One of my more colorful ancestors," Sinclair replied.

Peter was fascinated and a little incredulous. "*Saint* Dagobert the Second? The last Merovingian king? You're a descendant of his?"

"Yes. And your grasp of history is as fine as your Latin. Well done, Father."

"Refresh my memory." Maureen looked sheepish. "Sorry, but my real grasp of French history doesn't start until Louis Quatorze. Who were the Merovingians again?"

Peter answered, "An early line of kings in what is now France and Germany. Ruled from about the fifth to the eighth centuries. The line died out with the death of this Dagobert."

Maureen pointed to the jagged split in the skull. "Something tells me he didn't die of natural causes."

Sinclair answered. "Not exactly. His godson shoved a lance into his brain through an eye socket while he slept."

"So much for family loyalty," Maureen replied.

"Sadly, he chose religious duty over family loyalty, a dilemma that has plagued many throughout history. Isn't that right, Father Healy?"

Peter frowned at the perceived implication. "What is that supposed to mean?"

Sinclair gestured grandly to a heraldic shield on the wall: a cross surrounded by roses over which a Latin inscription read

ELIGE MAGISTRUM.

"My family motto. Elige magistrum."

Maureen looked to Peter for clarification. Something was happening between the two men that was starting to make her nervous. "Which means?"

"Choose a master," Peter translated.

Sinclair elaborated. "King Dagobert was murdered on orders from Rome, as the Pope was uncomfortable with his version of Christianity. Dagobert's godson was challenged to choose a master, and he chose Rome, thus becoming an assassin for the Church."

"And why was Dagobert's version of Christianity so disturbing?" Maureen questioned.

"He believed that Mary Magdalene was a queen and the lawful wife of Jesus Christ, and that he was descended from them both, therefore giving him the divine right of kings in a way that outmatched all other earthly power. The Pope at the time found it terribly threatening for a king to believe such a thing."

Maureen cringed and made an attempt at keeping the discussion light. She nudged Peter. "Promise you won't shove any lances in my eye socket while I sleep?"

Peter gave her a sidelong glance. "I'm afraid I can't make any promises. Elige magistrum and all that."

Maureen glared at him in mock horror and returned to studying the heavy silver reliquary, which was decorated with an elaborate fleur-de-lis pattern.

"For someone who isn't French, you're very partial to that symbol."

"The fleur-de-lis? Of course. Don't forget that the Scots and the French have been allied for hundreds of years. But my reason for using it is different. It's the symbol of . . ."

Peter finished his sentence. "The trinity."

Sinclair smiled at them. "Yes, yes, it is. But I wonder, Father Healy, if it is the symbol of your trinity . . . or of mine?"

Before Maureen or Peter could ask for an explanation, Roland entered the room and addressed Sinclair rapidly in a language that resembled French combined with more Mediterranean tones. Sinclair turned to his guests.

"Roland will show you to your rooms so you may rest and refresh yourselves before dinner."

He bowed elaborately, with a quick wink at Maureen, and swept out of the room.

Maureen entered the bedroom and her jaw dropped in awe. The suite was magnificent. As enormous, canopied four-poster bed, draped in red velvet hangings embroidered with the ubiquitous golden fleurs-de-lis, dominated the space. The rest of the furniture was obviously antique, all of it gilded.

A portrait titled *Mary Magdalene in the Desert,* by the Spanish master Ribera, covered one wall of the room. Mary Magdalene's eyes lifted up toward the heavens. Heavy Baccarat crystal vases filled with red roses and white lilies were scattered throughout the room, reminiscent of the flower arrangements Sinclair had sent to Maureen's home in Los Angeles.

"A girl could get used to this," she said to herself, as the servants knocked on the door and began to unpack her bag.

Peter's room was smaller than Maureen's, yet still ornate and fit for royalty. His own suitcase had not arrived yet, but he had his carry-on, which was sufficient for his immediate purposes. He removed his leather-bound Bible and crystal rosary beads from the black bag.

Peter clutched the beads and dropped onto the bed. He was tired—worn-out from the journey and exhausted by the weighty responsibility he felt for Maureen's welfare, physically and spiritually. Now he was in uncharted territory, and it made him nervous. He didn't trust Sinclair. Worse, he didn't trust his cousin's reaction to Sinclair. The man's money and physical appearance obviously created a mystique that held an attraction for women.

At least he knew that Maureen wasn't someone to be swept away easily. In fact, Peter knew of very few relationships she had ever had with men. Maureen's perspective on romance had been damaged by her mother's hatred of her father. That their toxic marriage had ended in tragedy was Maureen's reason for staying away from anything that resembled a relationship.

Still, she was female and she was human. And she was very vulnerable where her visions were concerned. Peter intended to make it his business to see that Sinclair did not use Maureen's vulnerability to manipulate her. He wasn't sure how much Sinclair knew yet—or how he knew it—but he was determined to find out as soon as possible.

Peter closed his eyes and began to pray for guidance, but his silent prayers were interrupted by an insistent humming sound. He tried to ignore the vibration at first but gave in to it finally. Crossing the room to where his traveling bag rested, Peter reached inside and answered the cell phone.

Thankfully, Peter's room was just down the hallway from Maureen's, otherwise they might have never found each other in the vast Sinclair mansion. Maureen was entranced with the house, absorbing every detail of art and architecture as they passed from one wing to the next.

They were on their way to investigate the exterior of the château together as it would be several hours until dinner. Both were too fascinated by their surroundings to leave them unexplored. They entered a broad hallway that was illuminated with natural light from a leaded crystal window. An enormous and unusual mural depicting a somewhat abstract crucifixion scene adorned the length of the hall.

Maureen stopped to admire the work. Beside the crucified Christ, a woman in a red veil held up three fingers as a tear slid down her face. She stood beside a body of water—a river?—from which three small fish, one red and two blue, leaped into the air. Both the pattern of the three fish and the woman's raised finger echoed the fleur-de-lis pattern in an abstract way.

There were countless details in the elaborate and obviously modern work of art. Maureen was sure they were all symbolic, but it would take hours to view every one of them—and probably years to understand them.

Peter stood back to view the crucifixion scene, which was beautiful in its simplicity. The sky above the cross was darkened by what appeared to be a black sun, and a bolt of lightning ripped through the sky.

"It resembles Picasso's style, doesn't it?" Peter said.

Their host appeared at the end of the hallway. "It's by Jean Cocteau, France's most prolific artist and one of my personal heroes. He painted it here while a guest of my grandfather."

Maureen was dumbfounded. "Cocteau stayed here? Wow. This house must be a national treasure for France. All of the artwork is phenomenal. The painting in my room . . ."

"The Ribera? It's my personal favorite Magdalene portrait. It captures her beauty and divine grace more than any other. Exquisite."

Peter was incredulous. "But you can't be saying it's an original. I've seen it in the Prado."

"Oh, but it is original. Ribera painted it at the request of the king of Aragon. He painted two, actually. And you're quite right, the smaller of them is in the Prado. The Spanish king gave this to another of my ancestors, a member of the Stuart family, as a peace offering. As you will see, fine art has a strong association with Our Lady. I will show you further examples of this over dinner later. But if you don't mind my asking, where are you going now?"

Maureen answered him. "We were just going to take a walk before dinner. I saw some ruins up on the hill as we drove in and wanted to take a closer look."

"Yes, of course. But I would be most honored to act as your tour guide. If that is acceptable with Father Healy, of course?"

"Of course." Peter smiled, but Maureen noticed the tightness at the edges of his mouth as Sinclair took her arm.

*Rome*
*June 23, 2005*

THE SUN SHONE MORE BRIGHTLY in Rome than anywhere else in the world, or at least that was how Bishop Magnus O'Connor felt as he strode across the hallowed stones of St. Peter's Basilica. He all but swooned with the honor of having access to the private chapel.

As he entered the hallowed ground, he paused before the marble statue of Peter holding the keys to the church and kissed the saint's bare feet. Then he waddled to the front of the church, settling into the first pew. He gave thanks to his Lord for bringing him to this holy place. He prayed for himself, he prayed for his bishopric, and he prayed for the future of Holy Mother Church.

When he had completed his devotions, Magnus O'Connor entered the office of Tomas Cardinal DeCaro carrying the red file folders that had been his ticket to the Vatican.

"They're all here, Your Grace."

The Cardinal thanked him. If O'Connor had expected an invitation to join the Cardinal in any prolonged discussion, he was to be highly disappointed. Cardinal DeCaro excused him with a curt nod of his head, and not another word.

DeCaro was anxious to see the contents of the folders, but he preferred to do so for the first time without an audience.

He opened the first of the file folders, all of which were labeled in bold black: EDOUARD PAUL PASCHAL.

*. . . I have not written yet about the Great Mother, the Great Mary. I have waited this long for I have often wondered if I had the words that would do justice to her goodness, her wisdom, and her strength. In the life of every woman, there will always be the influence and teachings of one woman who stands supreme. For me this could only be the Great Mary, the mother of Easa.*

*My own mother died when I was very small. I do not remember her. And while Martha always cared for me and attended to my worldly needs as a sister, it was Easa's mother who provided my spiritual instruction. She nurtured my soul and taught me the many lessons of compassion and forgiveness. She showed me what it was to be a queen and schooled me in the behaviors appropriate to a woman of our charted destiny.*

*When the time came for me to step into the red veil and become a true Mary, I was prepared. Because of her, and all that she gave me.*

*The Great Mary was a model of obedience, but hers was an obedience only to the Lord. She heard the messages of God with utter clarity. Her son had this same ability, and it is why they were set apart from others who had also come from noble birth. Yes, Easa was a child of the Lion, the heir to the throne of David, and his mother descended from the great priestly caste of Aaron. She was born a queen and Easa a king. But it was not mere blood that set them apart from all others; it was their spirit and the strength of their faith in God's message to us.*

*Had I done nothing but walk in her shadow for all of my days, I would have been blessed to do so.*

*The Great Mary was the first woman in memory to be so gifted with clear knowledge of the divine. This was a challenge to the high priests, who did not know how to accept a woman of such power. But nor could they condemn her. The Great Mary had a blood lineage that was untainted, and her heart and spirit were beyond reproach. Her unblemished reputation was known across many lands.*

*Men of power feared her, for they could not control her. She answered only to God.*

THE ARQUES GOSPEL OF MARY MAGDALENE,
THE BOOK OF DISCIPLES

# CHAPTER EIGHT

Sinclair lead Maureen and Peter out on a cobbled path that led away from the vast house. The rugged foothills of rich red rock surrounded them, crowned by the ruins of a craggy castle on a nearby hill.

Maureen was enthralled by the breathtaking scenery. "This place is stunning. It has such a mystical feel to it."

"We're in the heart of Cathar country. This entire region was once dominated by the Cathars. The Pure Ones."

"How did they get that title?"

"Their teachings came in a pure, unbroken line from Jesus Christ. Through Mary Magdalene. She was the founder of Catharism."

Peter looked wildly skeptical, but it was Maureen who voiced the doubt. "Why have I never read that anywhere?"

Bérenger Sinclair just laughed, not the least bit concerned about whether or not they found him credible. He was a man so comfortable with his beliefs and so confident in himself that the opinions of others held no validity for him.

"No, and you won't read it either. The real history of the Cathars isn't in any history books, and you can't research it with any authenticity anywhere but here. The truth of the Cathar people lies in the red rocks of the Languedoc and nowhere else."

"I'd love to read about them," Maureen said. "Can you recommend any books that you feel are authentic?"

Sinclair shrugged and shook his head. "Very few, and virtually none that I find credible have been translated into English. The majority of books on Cathar history are based on confessions extracted during torture. Virtually all medieval accounts of the Cathar people were written by their enemies. How accurate do you think those are? Maureen, I would expect you to understand that principle based on your own re-examining of history. No authentic Cathar practice has ever been committed to writing. Their traditions have been passed down by families in this area for two thousand years, but they are fiercely protected oral traditions."

"Didn't Tammy say there was an official Crusade against them?" Maureen asked as they continued on the winding path into the red hills.

Sinclair nodded. "A savage act of genocide, killing over a million people and launched by the ironically named Pope Innocent III. Have you ever heard the phrase 'Kill them all and let God sort them out'?"

Maureen cringed. "Yes, of course. It's a barbaric sentiment."

"It was first uttered in the thirteenth century, by the papal troops who butchered the Cathars at Béziers. To be precise, they said, 'Neca eos omnes. Deus suos agnoset,' which translates as 'Kill them all. God will recognize his own.' "

He turned to Peter abruptly. "Recognize it?"

Peter shook his head, not sure where Sinclair was going with this, but unwilling to fall into an intellectual trap.

"It's borrowed from your Saint Paul. From Second Timothy, chapter two, verse nineteen. 'The Lord knoweth them that are his.' "

Peter put up his hand to stop Sinclair. "You can hardly blame Paul for the fact that his words were corrupted."

"Can't I? I believe I just did. Paul sticks in my craw, to be sure. And it's no accident that our enemies have used his words against us for many centuries. That is only the beginning."

Maureen attempted to diffuse the increasing tension between the two men, bringing Sinclair back to the local history.

"What happened at Béziers?"

"Neca eos omnes. Kill them all," Sinclair repeated. "And that is precisely what the Crusaders did in our beautiful town of Béziers. They put every soul to the sword—from the most elderly to the tiniest infant. Not one person was spared by the butchers. Perhaps as many as a hundred thousand were murdered in that siege alone. Legend says that our hills are red to this day in mourning for the slaughtered innocents."

They walked in silence for a few moments, out of respect for the departed souls of this ancient land. The massacres had occurred almost eight centuries prior, yet there was a sense of these lost spirits all around, a presence that hung on every breeze that blew across the foothills of the Pyrenees. This was and would always be Cathar country.

Sinclair resumed his lecture. "Of course, a number of Cathars escaped, taking refuge in Spain, Germany, and Italy. They preserved their secrets and their teachings, but no one knows what became of their greatest treasure."

"What treasure was that?" Peter asked.

Sinclair looked around him, his inextricable connection to the land evident in his expression. This place and its history were etched into his soul. No matter how many times he related these stories, each telling revealed his unparalleled passion.

"There are a great many legends about what the Cathar treasures actually consisted of. Some say it was the Holy Grail, others claim it was the real shroud of Christ or the crown of thorns. But the true treasure was one of the two most sacred books ever written. The Cathars were the custodians of the Book of Love, the one—the only—true gospel."

He paused for emphasis, before adding the exclamation point.

"The Book of Love was the one true gospel because it was written entirely in the hand of Jesus Christ himself."

Peter stopped dead in his tracks at this revelation. He stared at Sinclair.

"What's the matter, Father Healy? They didn't teach you about the Book of Love in the seminary?"

Maureen looked equally incredulous. "Do you think such a thing really ever existed?"

"Oh, it existed. It was brought from the Holy Land by Mary Magdalene and passed down with extreme caution by her descendants. It's highly likely that the Book of Love was the true purpose behind the Crusades against the Cathars. The officials of the Church were desperate to get their hands on that book, but not to protect and treasure it, I can assure you."

"The Church would never damage something so priceless and sacred," Peter scoffed.

"No? And what if such a document could be authenticated? And what if that authenticated document disputed not only many of the tenets, but the very authority of the Church itself? In Christ's own hand? What then, Father?"

"That's pure speculation."

"You are entitled to your opinion, as I am to mine. However, mine is based in the knowledge of highly protected facts. But to continue with my . . . speculation, the Church was successful in its quest on some level. After the open persecution of the Cathars, the Pure Ones were forced underground and the Book of Love disappeared forever. Very few people today even realize it ever existed. Quite a task, to eliminate the existence of something so powerful from history."

Peter had been deep in concentration during Sinclair's speech. He spoke after another contemplative minute. "You said the true treasure was *one of the two* most sacred books ever written. If a gospel written in Jesus' own hand is one, what could the other possibly be?"

Bérenger Sinclair stopped and closed his eyes. The summer winds, similar to the mistrals farther east in Provence, were brewing, blowing his hair around his face. He took a deep breath, then opened his eyes and looked straight into Maureen's as he answered.

"The other is the Gospel of Mary Magdalene, a pure and perfect account of her life with Jesus Christ."

Maureen was frozen. She stared back at Sinclair, trapped by his expression of passion.

Peter broke the spell. "Did the Cathars claim to have that in their possession as well?"

Sinclair looked away from Maureen after another second, then shook his head as he answered Peter. "No, they didn't. Unlike the Book of Love, which had historical witnesses, no one has ever seen Magdalene's gospel. Probably because it has never been found. It is believed that it may have been hidden near the village of Rennes-le-Château, where you visited earlier. Did Tammy show you the Tower of Alchemy?"

Maureen nodded. Peter was too busy trying to discern how Sinclair knew so much about their movements. Maureen was beyond caring, too caught up in the living history—and in Sinclair's unabashed love of it. "She did, but I still don't really understand why it's so important."

"It's important for many reasons, but for our purposes here and now, it is believed by some that Mary Magdalene lived and wrote her gospel on the site where the tower now stands. She hid the documents, then sealed them in a cave somewhere, where they would remain until the time was right to reveal her version of events."

Sinclair pointed to a series of large holes resembling caverns in the mountains around them. "See those craters in the mountain? They're scars made by treasure seekers over the last hundred years."

"They're looking for these gospels?"

Sinclair's laugh was a small, wry sound. "Ironically, most of them don't even know what they're looking for. Utterly clueless. They know the legend of the Cathar treasure, or they've read one of the many books on Saunière and his mysterious wealth. But most don't know what it is. Some think it's the Holy Grail or the Ark of the Covenant, while others are sure it's the looted treasure from the Temple of Jerusalem or a hoard of Visigoth gold in a hidden tomb.

"Utter the word 'treasure' and otherwise rational human beings become instant savages. People have traveled here from all over the world for centuries to solve the mysteries of the Languedoc. Believe me, I've seen it many times. Treasure hunters used dynamite to create those caves up there. Without my permission, I might add."

Sinclair pointed out more ragged caverns in the mountainside, then continued with his explanation.

"Protecting the nature of the treasure became as important as the treasure itself to the Cathars, which is why so few people in this modern age even know these gospels existed. Look at the devastation wrought here even based on speculation. You can imagine what they would do to our land if people were to discover the priceless and sacred nature of the true treasure trove."

Sinclair regaled them with further local legends of treasure, as well as the more sordid stories of unscrupulous seekers who had ravaged the natural resources of the area. He told them how the Nazis had sent teams here during the war in an effort to uncover occult artifacts that they believed to be buried in the region. As far as anyone knew, Hitler's troops were unsuccessful in their search and ultimately left the area empty-handed—and lost the war shortly thereafter.

Peter was subdued and quiet, content to hang back and allow the vast amount of information to settle in. Later, he would sort through the details and determine how much was potentially true and how much was Sinclair's Languedoc romanticism. It would be easy to get caught up in legends of the Grail and of lost holy manuscripts in such a raw and mystical place as this. Yet even Peter felt his pulse quicken at the very idea of the existence of such artifacts.

Maureen walked with Sinclair, listening carefully. Peter wasn't sure if it was Maureen the journalist and author or Maureen the single woman who was hanging on Sinclair's every word. But she was rapt, her attention utterly focused on the charismatic Scot.

As they rounded a corner at the top of a small hill, a stone tower resembling a castle turret appeared to spring out of the side of the slope. It stood several stories tall, singular and incongruous in the rocky landscape.

"This looks like Saunière's tower!" Maureen exclaimed.

"We call it Sinclair's Folly. Built by my grandfather. And yes, he modeled it after Saunière's. Our view isn't quite as dramatic as the one from Rennes-le-Château because we're lower in elevation, but it's still quite lovely. Care to see it?"

Maureen looked over at a preoccupied Peter to see if he wanted to explore the tower. He shook his head. "I'll stay down here. You go on up."

Sinclair removed a key from his pocket and unlocked the door to the tower. He entered first, leading Maureen up a steep set of spiral stairs. He opened a door onto a rooftop deck and gestured for Maureen to go ahead of him.

The view of Cathar country and the ruined and ancient châteaux in the distance was magnificent. Maureen savored the vista for a moment before asking Sinclair, "Why did he build it?"

"Same reason Saunière built his. Bird's-eye view. They believed you could glimpse many secrets from above."

Maureen leaned on the rampart and groaned with frustration. "Why is everything a riddle? You promised answers, but so far you've only given me more questions."

"Why don't you ask the voices in your head? Or better still, the woman in your visions? She's the one who brought you here."

Maureen was stunned. "How do you know about her?"

Sinclair's smile was knowing, but not smug.

"You're a female of the Paschal blood. It's to be expected. Do you know about the origins of your family name?"

"Paschal? My father was born in Louisiana of French descent, like everyone else in the bayou."

"Cajun?"

Maureen nodded. "From what I understand. He died when I was young. I don't remember much about him."

"Do you know where the word 'Cajun' comes from? 'Arcadian.' The French who settled in Louisiana were called Arcadians, which evolved via local dialect into 'Acadian' and then to 'Cajun.' Tell me, have you ever looked up the word 'paschal' in an English dictionary?"

Maureen was watching him now, curious but increasingly cautious. "No, I can't say I ever have."

"It surprises me that someone of your research capabilities knows so little about her own family name."

Maureen turned away from him when she spoke about her past. "When my father died, my mother took me to live with her people in Ireland. I had no contact with my father's family after that."

"Still, one of your parents must have had a premonition of your destiny."

"Why do you say that?"

"Your name. Maureen. You do know what that means?"

The warm wind blew through again, ruffling Maureen's red hair. "Of course. It's Irish for 'little Mary.' Peter calls me that all the time."

Sinclair shrugged as if he had made his point and gazed out at the Languedoc. Maureen followed his line of sight to where a series of massive rocks were scattered across the sprawling grassy plain.

The summer sun struck something in the distance. The reflection caused Maureen to do a quick double take, as if she saw something out in the field.

Sinclair appeared keenly interested in Maureen's line of vision. "What is it?"

"Nothing." Maureen shook her head. "Just . . . the sun in my eyes."

Sinclair wasn't ready to let it go. "Are you sure?"

Maureen hesitated for a long moment as she looked to the field again. She nodded, before asking the question that was heavy on her mind. "All this talk about my family name. When will you show me the letter from my father?"

"I think you will have more of an understanding when this evening is over."

Maureen returned to her lavish bedroom at the château to bathe and change for dinner. As she emerged from the bathroom, she noticed something she had not seen upon first entering the room. On her bed was a large hardcover book—an English dictionary—opened to the letter "p" pages.

The word "Paschal" was circled in red pen. Maureen read the definition.

"Paschal—Any symbolic representation of Christ. The Paschal Lamb is the symbol of Christ and of Easter."

*. . . I am told by many of this man who was called Paul. He caused great turmoil among the elect, and some journeyed the long distance from Rome as well as Ephesus to consult me on this man and his words.*

*It is not for me to judge, nor can I say what was in his soul as I did not encounter him in the flesh and did not look into his eyes. But I can say with certainty that this man Paul never met Easa and that I was most distressed to hear that he would speak for him and all that he taught of the light and goodness that is The Way.*

*There were many things about this man that I believed to be dangerous. He was once allied with the harshest followers of John, all men who held Easa in great contempt. They opposed the teachings of The Way as it was given to us by him. I am told that he was once known as Saul of Tarsus and was a man who persecuted the elect. He stood by while a young follower of Easa, a beautiful young man called Stephen who had a heart filled with love, was crushed with stones. Some tell that this Saul encouraged the stoning of Stephen. That man was the first after Easa to die for his faith in The Way. But he would be far from the last. Because of men like Saul of Tarsus.*

*There was much to beware of there.*

THE ARQUES GOSPEL OF MARY MAGDALENE,
THE BOOK OF DISCIPLES

CHAPTER NINE

*Château des Pommes Bleues*
*June 23, 2005*

The dining room Sinclair had chosen for this evening was his private one, less formal than the cavernous main dining salon of the château. The room was adorned with excellent replicas of Botticelli's most famous paintings. Both versions of the masterworks known as *Lamentation* covered most of one wall, showing the crucified Jesus in the Pietà position across his mother's lap. In the first version, his head is cradled by a weeping Mary Magdalene; in the second, she holds his feet. Three of the Renaissance master's madonna paintings, *Madonna with Pomegranate, Madonna with the Book,* and *Madonna of the Magnificat* hung in costly gilded frames on two other walls.

Maureen and Peter were distracted from the artwork only when they saw that a traditional Languedoc feast was in store for them. Bubbling tureens of cassoulet, the hearty white bean stew flavored with duck confit and sausage, were brought to the table by serving women, while crusty bread filled baskets on the table. Rich red wine from the Corbières waited to be poured.

"Welcome to the Botticelli room," Sinclair announced as he entered. "I understand you have recently developed quite an affinity for our Sandro."

Maureen and Peter stared at him.

"Did you have us followed?" Peter asked.

"Of course," Sinclair replied matter-of-factly. "And I'm delighted that I did because I was immensely impressed that you ended up at the wedding frescoes. Our Sandro was entirely devoted to the Magdalene, which becomes obvious in his most famous works. Like this one."

Sinclair pointed to a replica of Botticelli's *Birth of Venus,* the now-iconic painting that depicts the naked goddess rising out of the waves standing on a scallop shell.

"This represents Mary Magdalene's arrival on the shores of France. She is shown as the Goddess of Love often in Renaissance painting and has a strong association with the planet Venus."

"I've seen that painting a hundred times, at least," Maureen commented. "I had no idea it was Mary Magdalene."

"Few people do. Our Sandro was instrumental in a Tuscan organization that was dedicated to preserving her name and memory, the Confraternity of Mary Magdalene. Did you understand the symbolism of the frescoes you saw in the Louvre?"

Maureen hesitated. "I'm not sure."

"Take your best guess."

"My first thought was astrology, or at least astronomy. The scorpion represented the constellation of Scorpio, and the archer's bow was representative of Sagittarius."

"Bravo. I believe that to be quite right. Have you ever heard of the Languedoc Zodiac?"

"No, but I have heard of the Glastonbury Zodiac in England. Are they similar?"

"Yes. If you lay a map of the constellations over this region, you will find that the cities fall within certain constellations. The same is true of Glastonbury."

Peter spoke his confusion. "Sorry, but I'm not following this at all."

Maureen filled him in. "This was a common theme for the ancients, starting with the Egyptians. Sacred locations on earth are built to mirror the heavens. For example, the pyramids in Giza are laid out to mirror the constellation of Orion. Entire cities were planned to match the pattern of the stars. It fulfilled the alchemical philosophy of 'As above, so below.' "

"The wedding fresco is a map," Sinclair explained. "Sandro was telling us where to look."

"Wait a minute. You're saying that one of the greatest painters in history was in on this Magdalene conspiracy theory?" Peter was tired and feeling far less diplomatic than usual as a result.

"Actually, Father Healy, I'm saying that *many* of the greatest painters in history were in on it. We have the Magdalene to thank for so many things, including a wealth of artistic treasures from great masters."

"Like Leonardo da Vinci?" Maureen asked.

Sinclair's face darkened so quickly that Maureen was taken aback.

"No! Leonardo is not included in that list for good reason."

"But he painted Mary Magdalene in his fresco *The Last Supper*. And there is so much popular speculation that he was a leader of a secret society that revered her and the divine feminine." Leonardo was the one artist Maureen had heard about over and over again while researching Mary Magdalene. She was shocked and confused by Sinclair's unexpected distaste for the subject.

Sinclair took a sip of his wine, setting the glass down very deliberately. When he spoke, it was with an edge. "My dear, we will not spoil this evening with talk of that man or his work. You will find no references to Leonardo da Vinci in my house, nor in the homes of anyone in this area. For now, that explanation will have to suffice." He smiled to lighten the mood a bit. "Besides, we have so many other wonderful artists to choose from, like our Sandro, Poussin, Ribera, El Greco, Moreau, Cocteau, Dali . . ."

"But why?" Peter asked. "Why are all of these artists involved in what is essentially a heresy?"

"Heresy is in the eyes of the beholder. But to answer your question, these great artists painted for wealthy patrons who supported them and their work, and the majority of those noble patrons were related to the sacred bloodline and were descendants of Mary Magdalene. Take these Botticelli wedding frescoes, for example. The groom, Lorenzo Tornabuoni, was from one strand of the bloodline. His bride, Giovanna Albizzi, was from an even more exalted noble lineage. You will notice in the fresco that she wears red to symbolize her relationship with the Magdalene line. That was a very important wedding because it merged two very powerful dynastic families who had been at war for a very long time."

Neither Maureen nor Peter spoke, waiting to see what other details Sinclair would choose to share.

"It has even been speculated that all of these artists were bloodline themselves and that their great talent came from divine genetics. This is entirely possible, probable in Sandro's case. And we are certain it is true of several French masters, like Georges de la Tour, who painted his muse and ancestor over and over again."

Maureen was excited that she recognized this reference. "I saw one of de la Tour's paintings during my research. *The Penitent Magdalene* is in Los Angeles." She had been very moved by the beautiful painting's use of light and shadow. Mary Magdalene, her hand on the skull of penitence, stares into the flickering light of a candle that reflects in a mirror.

"You saw *one* of the *Penitent Magdalenes*," Sinclair clarified. "He painted many with subtle variations. Several have been lost. One was stolen from a museum in my grandfather's day."

"How do you know that Georges de la Tour was related to the bloodline?"

"His name is the first clue. De la Tour means 'of the tower.' It's a bit of a pun, actually. The name Magdala comes from the word 'migdal,' which means tower. So she is literally Mary from the place of the tower. As you already know, some argue that Magdalene is a title, meaning the Mary *was* the tower, or the leader of her tribe.

"When the Cathars were persecuted, the survivors were forced to change their names to protect their identities, as Cathar names were highly recognizable. They hid their heritage in plain sight, using names like de la Tour and . . ."—he paused here for dramatic effect—"de Paschal."

Maureen's eyes widened at this. "De Paschal?"

"Of course. The Paschal name was used to shield one of the most noble of Cathar families. Again, hiding in plain sight. They called themselves de Paschal in French and di Pasquale in Italian. Children of the paschal lamb."

Sinclair continued. "And I further know that Georges de la Tour was bloodline because he was the Grand Master of an organization dedicated to preserving the traditions of pure Christianity as brought to Europe by Mary Magdalene."

It was Peter's turn to ask. "And what organization is that?"

Sinclair gestured for them to look around. "The Society of Blue Apples. You are dining in the official headquarters of an organization that has existed on this land for over a thousand years."

Sinclair declined to discuss the society any further, brushing it off with the efficiency of a master manipulator. They spent the rest of the meal discussing their day at Rennes-le-Château and learning more about the enigmatic priest Bérenger Saunière. Sinclair was fiercely proud of his namesake. "The Abbé baptized my grandfather in that church," Sinclair explained. "It's no wonder old Alistair was so dedicated to this land."

"He obviously passed that dedication on to you," Maureen observed.

"Yes. When he named me after Bérenger Saunière, my grandfather laid a particular blessing on my head. My father objected, but Alistair was made of steel, and no one opposed him for very long, certainly not my father."

Sinclair declined further explanation, and Maureen and Peter didn't push for any on what was obviously a personal and sensitive subject. When he was satisfied that the meal was over, Sinclair herded Maureen and Peter out of the dining room. "Come, I want to get back to this issue of Sandro and your marvelous discovery in the Louvre. This way."

He ushered them into an incongruously modern room filled with state-of-the-art home theater equipment and several computers. Roland was stationed at one of the monitors and offered a genial "bonsoir" as they entered. The French servant punched some keys on a keyboard and then leaned over to press a button on a console. A projection screen dropped from the far wall.

A map of the local area appeared on the screen ahead of them, and Sinclair pointed out several landmarks. "You'll notice familiar villages: Rennes-le-Château is right over here, and of course, here we are in Arques. The tomb of Poussin that you saw yesterday is here."

"And that is on your property?" Maureen asked.

Sinclair nodded. "We are certain that one of the most precious treasures in human history is located on these grounds."

He gestured to Roland, who dropped a grid of the constellations to overlay the local map. The constellations were labeled, with Scorpio falling directly atop the village of Rennes-le-Château. Arques rested between Scorpio and Sagittarius.

"Sandro has drawn us a map. That was his real wedding gift to the noble couple. In fact, what he created was so dangerously accurate that it had to be destroyed immediately. The frescoes were on walls that were part of the Tornabuoni property, so they couldn't demolish them. Instead, they whitewashed over the painting. They remained hidden until the latter part of the eighteen hundreds, when they were uncovered quite by accident."

The dawning of realization came over Maureen. "That's why you live here. In Arques. You think Mary Magdalene buried her gospel here?"

"I'm certain of it. And now you see that Sandro knew it as well. Look at the fresco again. Roland, if you please."

Roland punched keys that brought up the fresco from the Louvre. Sinclair pointed out the elements. "See, the woman with the scorpion is here. Then moving to the right, there is a woman next to her who is not holding a symbol of any kind. Sitting above them on a throne is the woman with the archer's bow. But look closely. This woman is draped in red, Mary Magdalene robes, and she is offering the sign of benediction directly over the head of the woman who sits between her and the scorpion woman. That's the X that marks the spot on the map, between Scorpio and Sagittarius.

"Sandro Botticelli knew the location of the treasure, and Nicolas Poussin certainly did as well. And they were kind enough to leave us clues to find it."

It wasn't making sense to Peter. "But why would these artists make maps for public display to reveal the location of such a priceless treasure?"

"Because this treasure has to be earned. It cannot be uncovered by just anyone. We can stand in the very place where the Magdalene buried her treasure every day of our lives, but we will never see it until she decides to show it to us. It was ostensibly hidden with an alchemical process, a lock that can only be opened by the appropriate . . . energetics, shall we say? The legend says the treasure will reveal itself at the proper time, when one chosen by the Magdalene herself comes to claim it. Sandro and Poussin both hoped it would be uncovered in their lifetimes and tried to assist the process.

"In Botticelli's case, Giovanna Albizzi was believed to have the potential to find the treasure. She was by all accounts an astonishingly virtuous and spiritual woman, as well as a brilliant and educated one. In Ghirlandaio's portrait of her, he included an epigram that read 'Would that art could represent character and mind, there would be no more beautiful painting on earth.' Do you remember the other fresco in the Louvre? The one they call *Venus and the Three Graces presenting gifts to a young woman*? Well, the young woman, dressed entirely in red, is Giovanna Albizzi. You will note that she is wearing the same bloodline necklace in Botticelli's fresco that she wears in Ghirlandaio's portrait. It was a very valuable piece of jewelry made for her to celebrate peace between these very powerful families. There were high hopes for the exalted Giovanna.

"Sadly, it was not to be. Poor, lovely Giovanna died in childbirth just two years after the wedding."

Maureen was taking it all in, trying to process the Italian story with what she had seen earlier in the day at Rennes-le-Château. She was struck by a thought.

"Do you think that Saunière could have found Magdalene's gospel? Is that what made him so wealthy?"

"No. Absolutely not." Sinclair was emphatic on this point. "Saunière was definitely looking for it, however. Locals say he would walk for miles in the area, examining rocks and caverns, looking for clues."

"How can you be so sure he didn't find it?" Peter wanted to know.

"Because if he had found it, my family would have known. Besides, it can only be found by a woman, a woman of the bloodline who has been chosen by Magdalene herself."

Peter could no longer hold in his suspicions. "And you think Maureen is the chosen one."

Sinclair stopped for a moment to consider, then replied with his customary candor. "I admire your directness, Father. And to answer in kind . . . Yes, I do think Maureen is the chosen one. No one else has succeeded, and thousands have tried. We know the treasure is here, yet even the most intrepid have failed in their attempts to uncover it. Myself included."

When he turned to Maureen, his expression and tone both softened. "My dear, I hope this is not frightening to you. I know it must all sound strange and even shocking. All I ask is that you hear me out. You will never be asked to do anything that is against your will. Your presence here is entirely voluntary, and I hope you will choose to continue your stay."

Maureen nodded at him, but said nothing yet. She didn't know what to say, how to respond to such a revelation. She wasn't even sure how she felt about it all. Was it an honor to be thought of in this way? A privilege? Or was it just plain scary? Maybe she was nothing more than the pawn of an eccentric and his cult. It seemed impossible that all of this could be not only true, but also connected to her. But there was something about Sinclair's manner that felt ultimately sincere to her. For all of his extreme opinions and eccentricities, Maureen didn't find him erratic.

Finally, she responded simply, "Go on."

Peter pressed for more details. "What makes you think that Maureen is the one?"

Sinclair nodded to Roland. "*Primavera*, please."

Roland punched more keys until a full-screen version of Botticelli's masterpiece, *Primavera*, appeared in glorious color.

"More from our boy Sandro. You know it, of course."

"Yes." Maureen's reply was barely audible. She wasn't sure where this was going, but her stomach was clenched in a tangled knot.

Peter replied. "Of course. It's one of the most famous paintings in the world."

"*The Allegory of Spring.* Few people know the truth behind this painting, but once again Sandro is paying tribute to our lady. The central figure here is the pregnant Mary Magdalene—note the red cape. Do you know why our Mary represents spring?"

Peter was trying to follow Sinclair's thinking as closely as possible. "Because of Easter?"

"Because the first Easter fell on the vernal equinox. Christ was crucified on the twentieth of March and rose on the twenty-second of March. An esoteric legend here in the region indicates that Magdalene was born on the twenty-second of March as well. The first degree of the first zodiac sign, Aries the ram. It is the date of new beginnings and resurrection, and it carries the added blessing of the master spiritual number twenty-two, the number of the divine feminine. March twenty-second. Does that date mean anything to you, Maureen, my dear?"

Peter had already discerned the connection and turned to see how Maureen was handling this revelation. She was speechless for a long moment. When her reply came, it was hoarse, whispered.

"It's my birthday."

Sinclair turned to Peter. "Born on the day of resurrection, born to the bloodline of the Shepherdess. Born under the sign of the ram on the first full day of spring and rebirth."

He delivered the final decree to Maureen. "My dear, you *are* the paschal lamb."

Maureen had excused herself immediately from the room, needing time to think and to process all of the information and Sinclair's implications. She reclined on the bed and closed her eyes.

The knock on the door was inevitable, but it came sooner than she had hoped. She was thankful it was Peter's voice on the other side of the threshold.

"Maureen, it's me. May I come in?"

Maureen rose from the bed and moved across the room to open the door.

"How are you feeling?"

"Overwhelmed. Come in."

Maureen motioned for him to sit in one of the rich, red leather armchairs that flanked the fireplace in her sitting area. Peter shook his head. He was too wound up to settle in a chair.

"Maureen, listen to me. I want to get you out of here before this gets any weirder."

Maureen sighed and took the seat herself. "But I'm just starting to get the answers that I came for. That *we* came for."

"I can't say that I care much for Sinclair's answers. And I think you're at great risk here."

"From Sinclair?"

"Yes."

Maureen gave him an exasperated look. "Oh, please. Why would he want to harm me if he sees me as the answer to his lifelong goal?"

"Because his goal is a delusion, wrapped in centuries of superstition and legend. This is very dangerous, Maureen. We're talking about religious cults here. Fanatics. What worries me is what he'll do to you once he realizes that you're not his savior."

Maureen was silent for a moment. Her next question was surprisingly calm.

"How do you know I'm not?"

Peter was stunned by the question. "You're buying into all of this?"

"Can you account for all of the coincidences, Pete? The voices, the visions? Because outside of Sinclair's explanation, I can't."

Peter's tone was firm, as though he were speaking to a child. "We're leaving in the morning. We can catch a flight from Toulouse to Paris. We can even fly from Carcassonne to London . . ."

Maureen held her ground, inflexible. "I'm not leaving, Peter. I'm not going anywhere until I have the answers I came for."

Peter's escalating agitation was getting the best of him. "Maureen, I swore to your mother before she passed away that I would always look after you, that I wouldn't let what happened to your father . . ." Peter stopped himself, but not before the damage had been inflicted.

Maureen looked like she had been slapped. Peter backpedaled quickly. "I'm sorry, Maureen, I . . ."

She cut him off cold. "My father. Thank you for reminding me of yet another reason I need to stay here. To find out what Sinclair knows about my father. I spent most of my life wondering about him, when all my mother would tell me was that he was criminally insane. I suppose that's what she told you, too. But in my memories of him, as dim as they are, I simply know that isn't true. If anyone else can give me a larger picture of him, I'll do whatever it takes to see that. I owe it to him. And to myself."

Peter started to say something, but thought better of it. Instead he turned to leave the room, looking tormented. Maureen watched him for a moment, softened, and called out after him.

"Please, try to be patient with me. I have to figure this out. How will we ever know if these visions mean anything if I don't follow this through? What if—just what if—even a fraction of what Sinclair presented tonight is the truth? I have to know the answer to that, Pete. If I leave now, I will regret it until I die, and I don't want to live like that. I've been running all my life, running from everything. As a child, I ran from Louisiana—ran so far and so fast that I don't even remember any of it. After my mother died, I ran from Ireland and came back to the U.S., running to a city where there were no memories, to a place where everyone becomes someone different than what they were born to originally. Los Angeles is a place where everyone is like me, everyone is on the run from what they once were. But I don't want to be that anymore."

She crossed the room to meet him face-to-face. "Now for the first time in my life I feel like I may be running *toward* something. Yes, it's terrifying, but I know I can't stop. And I'd rather not face this without you, but I can—and I will—if you choose to leave in the morning."

Peter listened attentively to her outburst. When she was finished, he nodded to her and turned to go. Standing quietly with his hand on the door for a moment, he turned back to her before leaving.

"I'm not going anywhere. But please don't make me regret this for the rest of my life. Or yours."

Peter went back to his room and spent the remainder of the night praying. He found himself ruminating long and hard on the teachings of Ignatius Loyola, the founder of the Jesuit order. One passage in particular, written by the saint in 1556, haunted him.

> As the devil showed great skill in tempting men to perdition, equal skill ought to be shown in saving them. The devil studied the nature of each man, seized upon the traits of his soul, adjusted himself to them, and insinuated himself gradually into his victim's confidence— suggesting splendors to the ambitious, gain to the covetous, delight to the sensuous, and a false appearance of piety to the pious—and a winner of souls ought to act in the same cautious and skillful way.

Sleep was elusive as the words of the founder of his order ran through his heart as well as his mind.

*Rome*
*June 23, 2005*

BISHOP MAGNUS O'CONNOR wiped the drop of sweat from his brow. The Vatican Council chamber was air-conditioned, but that was of no help to him at the moment. He sat in the center of a large, oval-shaped table, surrounded by officials of his Church. The red folders he had delivered the previous day were in the hands of the intense and intimidating Cardinal DeCaro, who was acting as interrogator.

"And how do you know these photographs are authentic?" The Cardinal placed the folders on the table, but did not open them yet to reveal the contents to the others.

"I was present when they were taken." Magnus was trying hard to conquer his stammer, which emerged in stressful situations. "The subject was referred to me by his parish priest."

Cardinal DeCaro now removed a series of 8 x 10 photographs from the folder. They were taken in black-and-white and had yellowed with time, but this did not diminish the impact of the images as they were passed around the table.

The first to circulate, labeled "Exhibit I," was a deeply gruesome photograph of a man's arms, placed side by side and turned palms up. They were inflicted with gaping, bloody wounds in the wrists.

"Exhibit II" showed the man's feet, both damaged with similarly gruesome, bleeding holes.

The third photo, "Exhibit III," showed a shirtless man. A jagged and bleeding gash ran underneath his rib cage on the lower right side.

The Cardinal waited for the shocking photographs to make their rounds before returning them to the folders and addressing the members of the Council. The faces around the table were grave as he verified what they all suspected.

"We are looking at authenticated stigmata. All five points and accurate as to the wrists."

*Château des Pommes Bleues*
*June 24, 2005*

SINCLAIR WAS NOWHERE TO BE FOUND the next morning. Maureen and Peter were greeted by Roland, who escorted them to breakfast. Peter wasn't sure if the extraordinary attention they were receiving was a sign of impeccable hospitality or something more akin to house arrest. Clearly, Sinclair was being very careful not to leave Maureen and Peter on their own.

"Monsieur Sinclair asked me to assure you that you have been provided with excellent costumes for the ball this evening. He is busy with the final preparations for the fête, but has put the chauffeur at your disposal if you would like to tour the local area today. He thought perhaps you would enjoy viewing the Cathar castles in the region. I would be honored to attend you as your guide."

They accepted the offer and were accompanied through the area by the giant Roland, who provided them with excellent commentary. He showed them the magnificent ruins of the once-mighty Cathar strongholds, describing how the wealthy counts of Toulouse had at one time rivaled the kings of France in terms of power and privilege. The Toulouse nobles were all of Cathar stock, or at the very least highly sympathetic to the Cathar ideals. It was one of the reasons that the vicious Crusades against the Pure Ones had been welcomed by the French king—he was able to confiscate what had once belonged to Toulouse, enlarging his own French holdings and increasing his net worth while diminishing the influence of his rivals.

Roland spoke with pride of his homeland and of their native dialect, called Oc, which gave this region its name. The *langue* (language) *of Oc* became known more simply as the Languedoc. When Peter referred to Roland as a Frenchman during a point of conversation, Roland asserted instantly that he was not French. He was Occitan.

Roland recounted in detail the numerous atrocities that had scarred his land and his people in the thirteenth century. He was passionate about his history.

"Many people outside of France don't even know about the Cathars, or if they do, they think of a small and unimportant cult tucked away here in the mountains. People don't realize that the Cathars were the dominant race and culture in a large and prosperous area of Europe. What happened here was nothing less than genocide. Close to a million people were slaughtered by the papal forces."

He looked at Peter somewhat sympathetically. "I hold no grudges against modern clergy for the sins of the medieval church, Abbé Healy. You are a priest because you have a calling to God, anyone can see that."

Roland led them in silence after that, as Maureen and Peter marveled at the enormous castles that had been built on jagged mountain peaks almost a thousand years ago. These fortresses were essentially impenetrable, given their location in the mountains, but they were equally unfathomable in terms of architecture. The two visitors wondered about the resources of a culture that was capable of building such immense fortification in a relentless and forbidding landscape without benefit of modern technology.

Over lunch in the village of Limoux, Maureen felt comfortable enough in the company of Roland to ask about his relationship with Sinclair. The sat companionably in a café overlooking the River Aude, the body of water for which the surrounding area was named. The hulking manservant turned out to be surprisingly warm and affable, even humorous, belying his intimidating appearance.

"I grew up at the Château des Pommes Bleues, Mademoiselle," he explained. "My mother died when I was a baby. My father was in service with both Monsieur Alistair and Monsieur Bérenger, and we lived on the estate. When my father died, I insisted on taking over his position at the château. It is my home, and the Sinclairs are my family."

Roland's imposing stature seemed to soften as he spoke of the loss of his parents and his loyalty to the Sinclair family.

"It must have been very hard for you, losing both parents," Maureen said sympathetically.

Roland stiffened, his spine straightening as he answered. "Yes, Mademoiselle Paschal. As I say, my mother died when I was a baby of a disease that could not be contained. I have accepted that as God's will. But my father's death is another matter . . . my father was murdered senselessly, just a few years ago."

Maureen gasped. "My God. I'm so sorry, Roland." She didn't want to push him for details.

Peter, however, felt that the need to know outweighed his normal inclination to sensitivity and asked the question. "What happened?"

Roland got up from the table to signal the end of the meal and the conversation. "There are bitter rivalries in our land, Abbé Healy. They reach back many years through time and know no reason. This place . . . it is filled with the most beautiful light. But that light sometimes attracts the most terrible darkness. We fight the darkness as best we can. But as with our ancestors, we do not always win.

"However, one thing is certain. No attempt at genocide has ever been successful here. We are still Cathars, we have always been Cathars, and we will always be Cathars. We may practice our faith quietly and in private, but it is as much a part of our lives today as it has always been. Do not let any history book or scholar tell you otherwise."

When Maureen returned to the château that afternoon, one of the chambermaids was waiting for her in her room. "The coiffeur will be here soon, Mademoiselle. And your costume has arrived. Please, if there is anything I can get for you . . ."

"No, merci." Maureen thanked the maid and closed the door. She wanted to rest before the party. It had been a beautiful day, filled with some of the most extraordinary sights Maureen had ever seen in her travels. But it had exhausted her as well, and she was left more than a little unsettled by Roland's enigmatic revelations about his father's murder.

She saw an extra-large garment bag lying across the bed as she crossed the room. Assuming it was the costume for the ball, she unzipped the heavy plastic casing and removed the dress. It took her a moment to realize what it was, then she gasped in recognition.

Holding the dress up to the Ribera painting, she saw that the gown was identical to the voluminous, crimson-skirted confection worn by Mary Magdalene in the Spanish artist's rendering.

Peter wasn't thrilled about wearing a costume. He had not planned to attend the ball initially, finding it potentially unseemly for him to do so. However, with the escalated intrigues of Sinclair—and Maureen's reaction to them—he was determined to keep her within sight. This meant wearing the elaborate thirteenth-century tunic and leggings that had been set out for him.

"Bollocks," Peter grumbled, as he removed the costume from its wrap and attempted to figure out where his head went.

Peter knocked on Maureen's door, adjusting his costume awkwardly as he waited in the hallway. The hat might have to go. It was heavy and sat on his head at an uncomfortable angle, a constant reminder that he looked ridiculous.

The door opened, and a transformed Maureen emerged from her room. The Ribera dress fit as if it had been made for her—the lace, off-the-shoulder bodice giving way to a sea of the richest crimson taffeta. Maureen's long red hair had been coiffed in a way that added fullness and volume, falling around her shoulders in a glossy curtain. But it was the new and surprising air of calm confidence radiating from her that was most noticeable to Peter. It was as if she had stepped into a role that suited her to perfection.

"What do you think? Is it too much?"

"Definitely. But you look . . . like a vision."

"Interesting choice of words. Pun intended?"

Peter winked and nodded, happy that they were joking again and that their relationship hadn't suffered too much from their argument the night before. The excursion through the extraordinary Cathar country had been restorative for both of them.

Peter escorted her down the winding halls of the château, in search of the ballroom in a distant wing. Maureen laughed as he complained about his costume.

"You look very noble and dashing," she assured him.

"I feel like an absolute eejit," he replied.

*Carcassonne*
*June 24, 2005*

IN AN ANCIENT STONE CHURCH outside the walled city of Carcassonne, preparation for an event of another kind was taking place. The expanded membership of the Guild of the Righteous was gathered in solemn earnest. More than two hundred formally robed men attended the service, wearing the heavy red cords of their order tied at their necks.

There were no women in the group. No female had ever profaned the Guild's halls or their private chapels. Engraved plaques citing Saint Paul's perspective on women were posted in every Guild location. One was a verse from First Corinthians:

> *Let your women keep silence in the churches: for it is not permitted unto them to speak. They are commanded to be under obedience, as also saith the law. And if they will learn anything, let them ask their husbands at home. It is shame for women to speak in the church.*

The second was from First Timothy:

> *Suffer not a woman to teach, nor to usurp authority to teach, nor to usurp authority over the man, but to be in silence.*

Yet while the Guild revered these words of Paul, he was not their messiah.

The relics of their ancestral master were displayed on velvet cushions above the altar—the skull gleamed in the candlelight, and the bony remnants of his right index finger had been removed from their reliquary for this annual display. Following the formal service and the presentation by the Guild Master, each member would be allowed to touch the relics. This was a privilege normally reserved only for members of the Guild council after they swore an oath in blood to uphold the teachings of righteousness. But the annual feast day was a pilgrimage attended by Guild members the world over, and on this night all of the faithful were allowed the honor of touching the relics.

Their leader stepped to the pulpit to begin his introductory speech. John Simon Cromwell's aristocratic English accent rang out within the ancient stone walls of the church.

"My brothers, tonight, not far from here, the spawn of the whore and the wicked priest have gathered. They celebrate their hereditary uncleanness with debauchery. They intentionally choose to defile this sacred night to flaunt their lascivious evils and show us their perceived strength.

"But we are not cowed by them. We will take our revenge on them soon, a vengeance that has waited two thousand years to see the full light of righteousness. We struck down their wicked shepherd then, and we will strike his descendants now. We will destroy their Grand Master and his puppets. We will eliminate the woman they call their shepherdess and see that this harlot queen is cast into hell before she can spread the lies of the witch she descends from.

"We do this in the name of the First, of the One True Messiah, for he has spoken to me and this is his wish. We do this in the name of the Teacher of Righteousness and with the blessings of the Lord our God."

Cromwell began the procession of the relics, touching the skull first, and then lingering on the finger bone, reverently. He whispered aloud as he did so.

"Neca eos omnes."

Kill them all.

*. . . Those who informed me of Paul said that he spoke out against the role of women in The Way. This is the most certain proof that such a man cannot have known the truth of Easa's teachings or the essence of Easa himself. Easa's great reverence for women is well known to the elect, and I have served as proof of this.*

*No one can change that, save that they erase me from history completely.*

*I am told further that this Paul revered the means of Easa's death, rather than the words that Easa spoke. This saddens me as a great loss of understanding.*

*This man Paul was imprisoned by Nero for a long period of time. I am told that he composed many letters to his faithful, giving teachings he claimed were from Easa. But those who came to me say he was not one to speak for The Way, that his teachings were false to our path.*

*I mourn for any man who was tortured and murdered in the dark realm of that monster Nero. And yet it fills me with fear. I fear that this man Paul will be seen as a great martyr for The Way, and that many will believe his false teachings to be those of Easa.*

*They are not.*

THE ARQUES GOSPEL OF MARY MAGDALENE,
THE BOOK OF DISCIPLES

# Chapter Ten

*Château des Pommes Bleues*
*June 24, 2005*

Maureen and Peter followed the melodious sound of madrigals as they drifted through the halls. Approaching the entrance to the ballroom, they received their first glimpse of Sinclair's elaborate and sumptuous affair.

Maureen felt as if she had been transported to another time. The cavernous ballroom had been draped in velvet hangings, and flowers and candles adorned the halls by the thousands. Elaborately wigged and costumed servants moved quietly and efficiently through the room, providing food and drink and cleaning up discreetly after the more rambunctious revelers.

But it was the guests themselves who were the bijoux for this luxurious jewelry box. Their costumes were elaborate and extravagant, period outfits from various eras throughout French and Occitan history, or costumes representing elements of the mystery traditions. An invitation to Sinclair's event was coveted by the esoteric elite across the globe; delighted recipients went to enormous lengths of time and expense to develop appropriate attire. There was a contest for the most original costume, as well as for the most beautiful and the most humorous. Sinclair was the sole judge and jury, and the prizes he awarded were often worth a small fortune. More important, a win guaranteed a coveted spot on the guest list for next year's event.

The music, the laughter, the clanking of crystal wineglasses stopped abruptly as Maureen and Peter entered the room.

A liveried man with a trumpet blew a heraldic note as Roland stepped forward, dressed in a simple Cathar robe, to announce their arrival. Maureen was surprised to see Roland dressed as a reveler rather than an employee on this night, but she had little time to contemplate this as she was swept into the entrance.

"It is my privilege to announce our honored guests, Mademoiselle Maureen de Paschal and the Abbé Peter Healy."

The crowd froze like wax mannequins in their places, staring at the new arrivals. Roland quickly indicated that the band should resume playing to cover the awkward moment. He put his arm out for Maureen and escorted her into the ballroom. The gaping continued, but not as obviously. Those more skilled in decorum had covered their shock with feigned disinterest.

"Do not mind them, Mademoiselle. You are a new face, and a new mystery to be discovered. But now," he said pointedly, "they will accept you quickly. They have little choice."

Maureen didn't have time to think about Roland's meaning as he swept her out to the dance floor, leaving Peter behind to watch with growing interest.

"Reenie!" Tamara Wisdom's American accent was incongruous in this European setting. She swept across the ballroom floor where Maureen had just completed a dance with Roland. Tammy looked wildly exotic in a gypsy costume. Her extraordinary hair was dyed a shiny raven's wing black and hung to her waist. Gold bangles covered her arms. Roland winked at Tamara—somewhat flirtatiously, Maureen noticed—before bowing to Maureen and excusing himself.

Maureen hugged Tammy, delighted to see another familiar face in this increasingly strange land. "You look gorgeous! Who are you dressed as?"

Tammy twirled gracefully, ebony hair flying behind her. "Sarah the Egyptian, also know as the Gypsy Queen. She was Mary Magdalene's handmaiden."

Tammy lifted the red taffeta of Maureen's skirt with one finger. "And I don't have to ask who you are. Did Berry give you this?"

*"Berry?"*

Tammy laughed. "That's what Sinclair's friends call him."

"I didn't realize the two of you were that close." Maureen hoped the disappointment wasn't obvious in her voice.

Tammy didn't have a chance to respond. They were interrupted by a young woman, not much older than a teenager, dressed in a simple Cathar robe. The girl carried a single calla lily and handed it to Maureen.

"Marie de Negre," she said, then bowed deeply and scampered off.

Maureen turned to Tammy for an explanation. "What was that about?"

"You. You're all the gossip tonight. There's only one rule for this annual soiree, and it's that no one has ever been allowed to dress as *Her*. And then you appear, the portrait version of Mary Magdalene. Sinclair is announcing you to the world. This is your coming-out party."

"Lovely. It would have been nice if I had been informed of this little detail. What did that girl just call me?"

"Marie de Negre. Black Mary. It's a local slang for Mary Magdalene, the Black Madonna. In every generation, a woman of the bloodline is given that name as an official title and holds it until death. Congratulations, it's a very serious honor here. It's as though she just said, 'Your Majesty.'"

Maureen had little time to contemplate the chaos that swirled around her. The room was filled to capacity with elaborate distractions: too much music, too many eccentric and interesting revelers. Sinclair was nowhere to be found; she had asked Roland about him during their dance, but the Languedoc giant had shrugged and answered as vaguely and enigmatically as always.

Maureen was looking around the room as Tammy spoke.

"Looking for your watchdog?" Tammy asked.

Maureen gave her a look, but nodded, willing to let Tammy think her concern was only for Peter's whereabouts. Tammy indicated that Peter was walking toward them, coming up from behind Maureen.

"Behave yourself, please," Maureen hissed at her friend.

Tammy ignored her. She had already stepped up to welcome Peter. "Welcome to Babylon, Padre."

Peter laughed. "Thank you. I think."

"You're just in time. I was about to give Our Lady here a tour of the freak show. Wanna join us?"

Peter nodded, and smiled helplessly at Maureen, tagging along as Tammy led them at her rapid pace across the ballroom.

Tammy led Maureen and Peter through the party, whispering conspiratorially at the various small groupings as they passed. She made introductions as appropriate when she saw friends or acquaintances in the crowd. Maureen was acutely aware that she was the center of scrutiny as they moved through the room.

The trio passed a small grouping of scantily clad men and women. Tammy nudged Maureen.

"That's the sex cult. They believe that Mary Magdalene was the high priestess in a bizarre set of sexual rituals that evolved from ancient Egypt."

Maureen and Peter both looked scandalized.

"Don't shoot the messenger, I just call them as I see them. But wait, don't answer yet. Look over there . . ."

The most bizarre group so far, dressed in elaborate alien garb replete with antennae, stood in the back of the room.

"Rennes-le-Château is a star gate, with direct access to other galaxies."

Maureen burst out laughing, while Peter shook his head in disbelief. "You weren't kidding about the freak show part."

"And you thought I made this stuff up."

They stopped to observe a huddled group of people who were listening intently to a rotund little man with a goatee. He appeared to be speaking in rhyme as his admirers tried to take in every word.

"Who's that?" Maureen whispered.

"Nostradumbass," Tammy quipped.

Maureen stifled her laughter as Tammy continued.

"Claims to be the reincarnation of you-know-who. Speaks only in quatrains. Tedious as hell. Remind me later to tell you why I hate the whole Nostradamus cult." She shuddered dramatically. "Charlatans. Might as well be selling snake oil."

Tammy kept them moving across the room. "Thankfully, they're not all freaks here. Some of the people are amazing, and I see two of them right now. Come on."

They approached a group of men dressed in costumes of the seventeenth- and eighteenth-century nobility. A patrician Englishman broke into a huge grin as they approached.

"Tamara Wisdom! It is a pleasure to see you again, my dear. You're looking marvelous."

Tammy gave the Englishman a European double-cheek air kiss. "Where's your apple?"

The man laughed. "I left it in England. Please introduce us to your friends."

Tammy made the introductions, referring to the Englishman only as Sir Isaac. He explained his choice of costume for them. "There is far more to Sir Isaac Newton than the apple," he said. "His discovery of the laws of gravity was a by-product of his greater work. Isaac Newton was arguably one of the most gifted alchemists in history."

At the end of Sir Isaac's speech, the group was approached by a young American man, tall and looking somewhat uncomfortable in his Thomas Jefferson costume and his powdered wig. "Tammy, baby!"

His embrace of Tammy was an all-American bear hug, which he

followed with a dramatic dip and a kiss on the lips. Tammy laughed and explained to Maureen.

"This is Derek Wainwright. He was my first guide through France when I started researching this madness. Speaks flawless French, which saved my life more times than I can tell you."

Derek bowed low to Maureen. His accent was pure Cape Cod, full of Massachusetts broad vowels. "Thomas Jefferson at your service, ma'am." He nodded to Peter. "Father."

Derek was the first member of the group to even acknowledge Peter's presence. Maureen noticed, but didn't have much time to consider it as Peter asked a question.

"So what is Thomas Jefferson's association with . . . all this?"

"Our great country was founded by Freemasons. Every American president from George Washington to George W. Bush has been a descendant of the bloodline—one way or another."

Maureen was taken aback by this. "Really?"

Tammy answered. "Really. Derek can prove it on paper. Too much free time in boarding school."

Isaac stepped forward to pat Derek on the shoulder. He announced grandly, "Paul was the first corrupter of the doctrines of Jesus, isn't that right, Tammy?"

Peter shot him a look. "Excuse me?"

"It's one of Jefferson's more controversial quotes," the Englishman explained.

It was Maureen's turn to look surprised. "Jefferson said that?"

Derek nodded, but appeared to be only half listening. He was glancing around, checking out the party as Tammy talked. "Hey, where's Draco? I thought Maureen might enjoy meeting him."

Three of them laughed hard at this. Isaac answered. "I offended him, and he stomped off to find the other Red Dragons. I'm sure they're holed up in a corner somewhere with their concealed spy cameras, taking notes on everyone. They're in their colors tonight, so you won't be able to miss them."

Maureen's curiosity was piqued. "Who are they?"

"The Knights of the Red Dragon," Derek answered with feigned dramatic emphasis.

"Creepy." Tammy elaborated, wrinkling her nose in distaste. "They wear these outfits that look like Ku Klux Klan uniforms, only in bright red satin. They told me I could learn the secrets of their esteemed club if I would donate my menstrual blood to their alchemical experiments. Of course, I jumped at that offer."

"Who wouldn't?" Maureen's reply was dry before she burst out laughing. "Where are these guys? I've got to get a look at them." She looked around the room but didn't see anyone who met Tammy's bizarre description.

"I saw them go outside," Newton answered helpfully. "But I don't know if I would expose Maureen to them just yet. She may not be ready."

Tammy explained. "Very secret society stuff, and they all claim to be descended from somebody royal and famous. Leader is a guy they call Draco Ormus."

"Why does that sound familiar?" Maureen asked.

"He's a writer. We have the same esoteric publisher in the U.K., which is why I know him. You may have run across one of his books in your travels through Magdalene territory. The ironic thing about him is that he writes about the importance of goddess worship and the female principle, yet they won't allow women into their boys' club."

"How very British," Derek said, nudging Sir Isaac, who looked perturbed.

"Don't include me in that lunatic's company, cowboy. All Brits are not created equal."

"Isaac here is one of the good ones," Tammy explained. "Of course, there are a number of bona-fide geniuses in the U.K., and some of them are my great friends. But in my experience, a lot of the English esoterics are snobs. They all think they hold the secret of the universe and that the rest of us—particularly the Americans—are new age idiots who do shoddy research. They think that because they can write three hundred pages about the sacred geometry of the Languedoc and create another two hundred pages of mostly fictional family trees, they have it all figured out. But if they would put their compasses down for a minute and allow themselves to feel something, they'd discover that there is a lot more to the treasure here than can be quantified on paper."

Tammy nodded to a group dressed in Elizabethan-era costumes across the room. "There are some of them now, as a matter of fact. I call them the Protractor Crowd. They've spent lifetimes analyzing the sacred geometry of survey maps. You want an opinion on the meaning of 'Et in Arcadia ego'? They can give you anagrams in twelve different languages and translate those into mathematical equations."

She pointed out an attractive but arrogant-looking woman in an elaborate Tudor-style costume. A gold letter "M" with a baroque pearl hung from a chain on her neck. The protractor crowd gathered around her appeared to be fawning.

"The woman in the center claims to be descended from Mary, Queen of Scots."

As if sensing that they were speaking about her, the woman turned to stare in their direction. She fixed her gaze on Maureen, looking her up and down with pure disdain before returning to her minions.

"Haughty bitch," Tammy snapped. "She's at the center of a not-so-secret society that wants to restore the Stuart dynasty to the British crown. With her on the throne, of course."

Maureen was fascinated by the sheer breadth of belief systems that were represented in the room, not to mention the extreme, individual personalities.

Peter leaned over and quipped, "Freud would have a field day in this place."

Maureen laughed, but returned her attention to the British group across the room. "How does Sinclair feel about *her*? He's a Scot, and isn't he related to the Stuarts?" she asked. Her curiosity about Sinclair was increasing—and the Mary, Queen of Scots woman was certainly beautiful.

"Oh, he knows she's a nut job. And don't underestimate Berry. He's obsessive, but he's not stupid."

"Check it out," Derek interrupted in his somewhat juvenile, limited-attention-span way. "There goes Hans, and his band of renown. I hear Sinclair almost banned them this year."

"Why?" Maureen was becoming increasingly fascinated by the Languedoc and the strange, esoteric subculture it had produced.

"They're treasure hunters in the most literal sense," Sir Isaac offered. "Rumor has it that they're the most recent group to use dynamite in Sinclair's mountains."

Maureen looked at the group of large, boisterous Germans. Their image wasn't improved by their costumes—they were all dressed as barbarians.

"Who are they supposed to be dressed as?"

"Visigoths," Isaac answered. "This part of France was their territory in the seventh and eighth centuries. The Germans believe that the treasures of a Visigoth king are hidden in the area."

Tammy continued. "It would be the European equivalent of discovering the tomb of Tutankhamen. Gold, jewels, priceless artifacts. Standard treasure stuff."

A particularly raucous group of revelers ran through the room, directly past them, jostling Peter and Tammy. Five robed men chased a woman dressed in colorful Middle Eastern veils. She carried a grotesque human head on a platter. The men called after her, apparently addressing the severed head. "Speak to us, Baphomet, speak to us!"

Tammy shrugged and explained simply as they passed, "Baptists."

"Not real ones, of course," Derek chimed in.

"No. Not real ones."

Peter was intrigued by this religious angle. "What do you mean, not real ones?"

Tammy turned to him. "I'm sure you know what day this is on the Christian calendar, Father?"

Peter nodded. "It's the feast day of Saint John the Baptist."

"True followers of John the Baptist would never attend a party like this on his feast day," Derek continued. "It would be blasphemy."

Tammy finished up the explanation. "They're a very conservative group, at least the European branch is." She nodded in the direction of the woman with the head. "They're a parody. A rather brutal one, I might add. Not that it isn't warranted."

Revelers around the ballroom watched the antics with varying degrees of amusement. Some laughed outright; some shook their heads; others looked scandalized.

Derek interrupted, seemingly unable to stick to one topic for very long. "I need a drink. Who wants something from the bar?"

Peter had taken Derek's departure as an opportunity to excuse himself temporarily. His costume was behaving badly, and he was desperately uncomfortable for more than sartorial reasons. He told Maureen he was going in search of a restroom. In truth, he made a beeline for the patio. He was in France, after all—there was sure to be someone out there who would give him a cigarette.

A Frenchman, incredibly elegant despite his simple Cathar robe, approached Maureen and Tammy. He nodded to Tammy and bowed before Maureen.

"Bienvenue, Marie de Negre."

Uncomfortable with the attention, Maureen laughed. "I'm sorry, my French is terrible."

The Frenchman spoke in flawless, if accented, English. "I said, 'That color suits you.' "

A voice across the room was yelling for Tammy. Maureen glanced over, thinking it sounded like Derek, then back at Tammy, who was beaming.

"Aha! Looks like Derek has one of my potential investors cornered at the bar. Can you excuse me for a minute?"

Tammy was gone in a split second, leaving Maureen with the mysterious Frenchman. He kissed her right hand, hesitating just for a moment to look at the pattern on her ring, then introduced himself formally.

"I am Jean-Claude de la Motte. Bérenger tells me that we are related, you and I. My grandmother's name was also Paschal."

"Really?" Maureen was excited by the connection.

"Yes. There are still a few Paschals here in the Languedoc. You are aware of our history, no?"

"Not really. I'm ashamed to tell you that anything I know I've learned from Lord Sinclair these last few days. I'd love to hear more about my family."

Costumed dancers in the garb of eighteenth-century Versailles whirled past them as Jean-Claude spoke.

"The Paschal name is one of the oldest in France. It was a name taken by one of the great Cathar families, the direct descendants of Jesus and Mary Magdalene. Most of the family was eliminated in the Crusade against our people. At the massacre of Montsegur, those who remained were burned alive as heretics. But some escaped, later becoming advisers to the kings and queens of France."

Jean-Claude gestured at the couple dressed elaborately as Marie Antoinette and Louis XVI on the dance floor.

"Marie Antoinette and Louis?" Maureen was surprised.

"Oui. Marie Antoinette was a Hapsburg and Louis was a Bourbon—both bloodline descendants through different streams. They united two strands of the blood, which is why people were so afraid of them. The Revolution was caused in part by the fear of the two families joining together to form the most powerful dynasty in the world. Have you been to Versailles, Mademoiselle?"

"Yes, I was there during my research on Marie Antoinette."

"Then you know the hamlet?"

"Of course." The hamlet had been Maureen's favorite part of the vast palace grounds of Versailles. She had an overwhelming feeling of sympathy for the queen as she toured the halls of the royal residence. Each of Marie Antoinette's daily activities, from sitting on the toilet to preparing for bed, was witnessed by noble watchdogs. Her children were born to audiences of nobles crowded into her bed-chamber.

Marie the Queen had rebelled against the suffocating traditions of French royalty and invented an escape from her gilded prison. She built a private hamlet, a tiny Disneyland of a village surrounding a duck pond with rowboats. A miniature mill and a small farmhouse were the settings for pastoral parties with small groups of trusted friends.

"Then you also know that Marie was very fond of dressing as the Shepherdess. In all of her private gatherings, she alone wore that costume."

Maureen shook her head in amazement as pieces fell into place. "Marie Antoinette always dressed as the Shepherdess. I knew that when I went to Versailles, but I didn't know then about all of this." She gestured to the wild scene surrounding them.

"That's why the hamlet was built away from the palace and with very strict security," Jean-Claude continued. "It was Marie's way of celebrating the bloodline traditions in privacy. But, of course, others knew about it, as nothing was a secret in that palace. Too many spies, too much power at stake. It would be one of the factors that led to Marie's demise—and to the revolution.

"The Paschals were loyal to the royal family, of course, and were often invited to Marie's private fêtes. But the family was forced to flee France during the Reign of Terror."

Maureen could feel the goose bumps running down her arms. The story of the tragic Austrian queen of France had always been a source of intense fascination for her and had become a major motivating factor behind her book. Jean-Claude continued.

"Most settled in the States, many in Louisiana."

Maureen snapped back to attention at this. "That's where my father was from."

"But of course. Anyone with eyes to see would know that you are of that strain of the royal bloodline. You have the visions, no?"

Maureen hesitated. She was reluctant to speak of her visions even with those closest to her, and this was a complete stranger. But there was something immensely liberating about being in the company of others like her—others who felt that it was perfectly natural to have such visions. She answered simply. "Yes."

"Many bloodline women have visions of the Magdalene. Sometimes even the men, like Bérenger Sinclair. He has had them since he was a child. It's very common."

*It certainly doesn't feel common,* Maureen thought. But she was very curious about this new revelation. "Sinclair has visions?" He certainly hadn't mentioned this to her.

But she would have the opportunity to ask the man himself, as Sinclair was gliding across the floor, dressed impeccably as the last Count of Toulouse.

"Jean-Claude, I see you've found your long-lost cousin."

"Oui. And she is a credit to the family name."

"Quite. May I steal her from you for a moment?"

"Only if you will allow me to take her out for a drive tomorrow. I would like to show her some of the landmarks that pertain to the Paschal name. You have not been to Montsegur, have you, cherie?"

"No. Roland took us out today, but we didn't go as far as Montsegur."

"It is sacred ground for a Paschal. Do you mind, Bérenger?"

"Not at all, but Maureen is perfectly capable of making her own decisions."

"Will you do me the honor? I can show you Montsegur, and then take you to a traditional restaurant. They serve only food that has been prepared in the authentic Cathar manner."

Maureen couldn't see a graceful way to say no, even if she had wanted to. But the combination of French charm and an insight into more of her family history proved irresistible.

"I'd be delighted," she replied.

"Then I will see you tomorrow, cousine. Eleven o'clock?"

Jean-Claude kissed her hand again as she agreed, then said his farewell to Bérenger. "I shall take my leave now, as I have plans to make for the morning."

Maureen and Sinclair smiled at him as he departed.

"You made quite an impression on Jean-Claude, I see. Not surprising. You look marvelous in that dress, as I knew you would."

"Thank you, for everything." Maureen knew she was blushing, completely unused to so much concentrated male attention. She steered the conversation back toward Jean-Claude.

"He seems very nice."

"He's a brilliant scholar, an absolute expert in French and Occitan history. Worked for years in the Bibliothèque Nationale, where he had access to the most astonishing research materials. He has helped me and Roland immensely."

"Roland?" Maureen was surprised at the deferential way in which Sinclair spoke of his manservant. It did not seem to be typical behavior for an aristocrat.

Sinclair shrugged. "Roland is a loyal son of the Languedoc. He has a great interest in the history of his people." He took Maureen's arm and began to guide her through the room. "Come, I want to show you something."

He led her up a flight of stairs and into a small sitting room with a private terrace. A large balcony overlooked the patio and the enormous gardens that stretched beyond. The gardens, with their gilded fleur-de-lis gates, were locked, and protected on both sides by guards.

"Why are there so many guards at the gate?"

"That is my most private domain, sacred ground. I call them the Trinity Gardens and I allow very few visitors inside—and believe me, many of the guests here tonight would pay dearly to get behind those gates."

Sinclair elaborated. "The costume ball is a tradition—my annual gathering for certain people who share a common interest." He gestured to the revelers below them on the patio. "Some I respect—even revere, some I call friend, others . . . others are amusing to me. But all of them I watch closely. Some very closely.

"I thought you might find it interesting to see how people come from all over the world to investigate the mysteries of the Languedoc."

Maureen watched the scene over the balcony, enjoying the silky breeze carrying the scent of the nearby rose garden on the early summer air. She noticed Tammy looking very chummy with Derek—and Derek looking like he was all hands on the sultry gypsy queen. She squinted at someone who might have been Peter, but decided it couldn't be. The man in her line of vision was smoking. Peter hadn't smoked since he was a teenager.

She turned to Sinclair suddenly and asked, "How did you find me?"

He lifted her right hand gently. "The ring."

"The ring?"

"You're wearing it in the photo, on the jacket of your book."

Maureen nodded the beginning of understanding. "You know what the pattern means?"

"I have a theory on the pattern, which is why I brought you to this particular balcony. Come."

Sinclair took Maureen gently by the arm and led her back inside to where a piece of artwork encased in glass was mounted on the wall. The piece was small, not much larger than an 8 x 10 photograph, but its central placement and the careful lighting showed it to its best advantage.

"It's a medieval engraving," he explained. "It represents philosophy. And the seven liberal arts."

"Like the Botticelli fresco."

"Exactly. You see, it comes from the classical perspective that if you embrace all seven of the liberal arts, you may attain the title of philosopher. That's why this female figure in the center is depicted here as the goddess, Philosophia, and the liberal arts are at her feet, in service to her. But here is what I thought you would find most interesting."

He started at the left, naming the liberal arts as he traced them with his fingers. He stopped at the seventh and final.

"Here we are. Cosmology. See anything there that looks familiar?"

Maureen gasped with excitement. "My ring!"

The figure representing cosmology held a disk decorated with the pattern on Maureen's ring. She counted the stars and held her hand up to the image.

"It's identical, right down to the off-center spacing of some of the circles." She was quiet for a moment, taking it all in, before turning back to Sinclair.

"But what does it all mean? How does it all apply to Mary Magdalene? And to me?"

"There are spiritual and alchemical applications. In terms of the Magdalene's mysteries, I believe this symbol shows up so frequently as a clue, a reminder that we need to pay attention to the critical relationship between the earth and the stars. The ancients knew that, but we have forgotten it in our modern age. As above, so below. The stars remind us every night that we have the opportunity to create heaven on earth. I believe that is what they wanted to teach us. It was their ultimate gift to us, their message of love."

"They?"

"Jesus Christ and Mary Magdalene. Our ancestors."

And as if a cosmic timer had been set to punctuate his sentence, the fireworks began their light show over the garden as the revelers watched in delight. Sinclair eased Maureen back outside to watch bursts of color rain over the château grounds. When he put his arm around her she allowed it, feeling strangely comfortable there in the warm embrace of his strength.

Below on the patio, Father Peter Healy wasn't watching the fireworks. At least, not those in the sky. His attention was focused on Bérenger Sinclair, who stood on the balcony with an arm placed firmly and possessively around the waist of Peter's red-haired cousin. In contrast to Maureen, he was feeling anything but comfortable—about Sinclair, about these people, and about their plans.

There were other sets of eyes watching the evolution of Sinclair and Maureen's chemistry that night. Derek watched from below, looking up from his place on the opposite end of the patio. Scanning the balcony, he noticed his French colleague was well positioned upstairs, perhaps even close enough to eavesdrop on the conversation between their host and the woman dressed as Mary Magdalene.

Derek Wainwright patted his body discreetly, to be sure that the blood-red ceremonial cord of the Guild was tucked safely away in the folds of his Thomas Jefferson costume. He would need it later tonight, when he returned to Carcassonne.

*. . . Perhaps I am the sole defender of the princess called Salome, but it is my duty to be so. I regret that I have left it so late, for she did not deserve her terrible fate. There was a time when it was death to speak of her and of her actions, and I could not defend her without risking the followers of Easa and the higher path of The Way. But like so many of us, she was judged by those who did not know the truth, or even an echo of it.*

*First, I will say this: Salome loved me, and she loved Easa even more. Given a chance, another time or place, or another set of circumstances, the girl could have been a true disciple, a sincere follower of The Way of Light. Thus, I include her in his Book of Disciples, for what she could have been. Like Judas and Peter and the others, Salome had a role carved out for her, and little chance to escape that role. Her name was etched in the stones of Israel, etched in John's blood, and perhaps in some of Easa's.*

*If hers were the rash, childish actions of youth—of a young person who does not think things through before she speaks—then she is indeed guilty of that. But to be remembered as she is—reviled and despised as a harlot who ordered John the Baptizer's death—I think it is one of the greatest of all the injustices that I can remember.*

*On the Day of Judgment, perhaps she will forgive me.*

*And perhaps John will forgive us all.*

The Arques Gospel of Mary Magdalene,
The Book of Disciples

# CHAPTER ELEVEN

*Château des Pommes Bleues*
*June 24, 2005*

*M*aureen retired to bed shortly after the fireworks display. Peter had appeared as she descended the stairs with Sinclair, offering to escort her back to her room. She took him up on the offer, more than ready to escape into some much-needed solitude. It had been an overwhelming twenty-four hours and her head was throbbing.

Later that night Maureen was awakened by voices in the hallway. She thought she recognized Tammy, speaking in a whisper. A man's muffled voice whispered back. Then the throaty laughter came, a trait that was as specific to Tammy as her fingerprints. Maureen listened, amused that her friend was enjoying the party.

She smiled as she drifted back to sleep, with the slightest, sleepy notion that the male voice she heard whispering intimately to Tammy was definitely not American.

*Carcassonne*
*June 25, 2005*

DEREK WAINWRIGHT GROANED as the morning sun blared relentlessly through his hotel room window. There were two things he didn't want to deal with today—his hangover and the eight new messages on his cell phone.

Rising slowly to gauge the extremity of his headache, he shuffled over to his Italian leather traveling bag and extracted a prescription bottle. He opened it to reveal an assortment of pills. Picking through them, he found what he wanted and threw back a Vicodin before chasing it with three Tylenol tablets for good measure. Thus fortified, he glanced at his phone on the nightstand. He had turned it off late last night when he came back to the hotel; he couldn't deal with the incessant beeping, and he certainly didn't want to listen to the messages.

Derek had spent most of his life escaping responsibility in much the same way. A trust-fund baby from a supremely wealthy and influential East Coast family, the youngest of real estate mogul Eli Wainwright's boys had been given a very generous ticket to ride. He breezed into Yale on his father and elder brothers' legacies, and later, despite his mediocre academic performance, secured an executive position in a top-notch investment firm. Derek left that job after less than a year when he determined that the hours were not compatible with his party boy lifestyle. Not that he needed to work. His family trust was large enough to carry him for life, and for the lives of his children and grandchildren—if he ever settled down enough to have any.

Eli Wainwright had been surprisingly patient with his youngest son's deficiencies. Derek lacked the scholastic drive and aptitude of his siblings, but he had shown the most interest in a vital element of the family's life and success—membership in the Guild of the Righteous. Baptized first as an infant and then again at fifteen, as was tradition in their organization, Derek seemed to have a natural affinity for the society and its teachings. His father selected Derek to follow in his shoes as one of the top American members of the Guild, an organization that stretched across not only the Western world but into parts of Asia and the Middle East. The Guild of the Righteous counted among its members some extremely influential men from the arenas of big business and international politics.

Membership was limited strictly to blood legacies, and baptized men were expected to marry into the Daughters of Righteousness, female children of the Guild who were raised within a strict code of decorum. Girls were given special training in the appropriate behavior for a wife and mother, taking their lessons from an ancient document known as *The True Book of the Holy Grail* that had been handed down for centuries. Some of the largest debutante balls and cotillions on the Eastern seaboard, into the South, and throughout Texas were in essence "coming-out parties" for Daughters of Righteousness, announcing their readiness to enter the world as the obedient and proper wives of Guild members.

Eli's older sons had all married Daughters of Righteousness and were well ensconced in perfect upper-crust lives. Pressure was coming to bear on the youngest Wainwright, now well into his thirties, to settle down in a similar fashion. Derek wasn't interested, although he didn't dare say so to his father. He found the Daughters immensely boring in all of their pristine virginity. The idea of bedding one of those perfectly bred ice princesses each night made him shudder. Sure, he could do what his brothers and all the other Guild members did—marry the approved and appropriate mother for your children and find a tantalizing trollop to keep things interesting on the side. But why settle for that at this stage? He was still young and terrifyingly rich, and he had few responsibilities. And as long as there were exotic, sensual women like Tamara Wisdom to entice him, he wasn't going to shackle himself to some tedious prize broodmare who reminded him too much of his mother. If his father remained convinced that he was interested only in carrying out Guild business, Derek could get away with shirking his other responsibilities for at least a few more years.

What Eli Wainwright did not see with the blind eyes of a father who chooses not to view the flaws in his son was that Derek's affinity wasn't for the Guild's philosophy. It was for the mystique of an outlawed society, the rituals, the sense of elitism that came with knowing secrets that had been handed down for centuries and protected in blood. The true attraction came from the understanding that virtually any unsavory act of a member could be cleaned up and swiftly concealed due to the Guild's global network of influence. Derek reveled in these things, and in the way he was treated because of his father's wealth and influence everywhere he went. Or at least he had previously, until the former Teacher of Righteousness died somewhat mysteriously and was replaced with this new one, the fanatical Englishman who ruled the Guild with an iron fist.

Their new leader had changed everything. He flaunted his hereditary connection to Oliver Cromwell while studying his ancestor's ruthless and often gruesome tactics for dealing with opposition. Upon ascending to the title of Teacher of Righteousness, John Simon Cromwell made his first dramatic statement via an ugly execution. True, the murdered man was an enemy of the Guild and the leader of an organization that had opposed it for hundreds of years. But the message was clear: I will eliminate anyone who challenges me, and I will do it in an ugly way. Beheading the man with a sword and severing his right index finger carried the dramatic and literal touch of their new leader's unstoppable fanaticism.

Derek attempted to block that specific image from his cloudy mind as he picked up the cell phone and switched it on, dialing into his voice mail. It was time to face the music. He had a mission to complete and he was committed to it, determined to show that British bastard once and for all what he was made of. He was sick of being ridiculed by him and the Frenchman. They treated him like an idiot, and no one had ever been allowed to do that before.

As the messages began to play, Derek steeled himself against the Oxford accent that grew progressively more menacing with each message. By the final words of the eighth voice mail, Derek knew what had to be done.

*Château des Pommes Bleues*
*June 25, 2005*

TAMARA WISDOM BRUSHED HER GLOSSY BLACK HAIR while looking into the gargantuan gilded mirror. Vibrant morning sunlight illuminated her room, which was every inch as palatial as Maureen's. Roses in shades of cream and lavender were clustered in crystal vases on every table. Purple velvets and heavy brocades draped her enormous bed, a place that she rarely occupied alone.

She smiled, allowing herself to bask briefly in the warmth of memories from the night before. The heat of his body had left an impression on her skin long after he had taken his leave of her just before dawn. In her wild and experiential attitude toward life she had known many great passions, but none had ever been quite like this. She finally understood what the alchemists meant when they spoke of the Great Work, the perfect union of a man and a woman—a joining of body, mind, and spirit.

Her smile faded as she came back to the reality of what must be done today.

It had all been so much fun at first, like a great game of chess played across two continents. She had grown to care about Maureen very quickly. They all had. Even the priest had not turned out to be the meddlesome creature they had feared. He was a mystic in his own way, a far cry from the rigid dogmatist they had anticipated.

Then there was the question of her own deepening involvement. The Mata Hari element had been amusing at first, but now it was becoming repellent. She would have to balance this very carefully today in order to obtain the information she needed, yet not lose herself in the deal. She had several goals to accomplish today, for herself, for the Society, and for Roland. *Keep the big picture in mind, Tammy,* she reminded herself. *There is everything to gain if you are successful, and everything to lose if you fail.*

The game had changed. And it was becoming far more perilous than any of them had anticipated.

Tammy set the brush down and splashed a heady floral fragrance on her pulse points and her throat, making preparations for what was to come. As she turned to leave the room, she stopped before the astonishing painting that graced her wall. It was by the French symbolist Gustave Moreau, and it depicted the princess Salome, draped in her seven veils and holding the head of John the Baptist on a platter.

"That's my girl," Tammy whispered to herself as she departed on her latest and most crucial piece of intrigue.

Maureen dined alone in the breakfast room. Roland, walking through the adjoining hallway, noticed and entered.

"Bonjour, Mademoiselle Paschal. You are alone?"

"Good morning, Roland. Yes. Peter was still asleep, and I didn't want to disturb him."

Roland nodded. "I have a message for you from your friend Miss Wisdom. She is now staying here at the château and would like to join you here for dinner tonight."

"That would be great." Maureen was anxious to catch up with Tammy and recap the party. "Where is she?"

Roland shrugged. "She left early this morning for Carcassonne. Something to do with the film she is making. She gave me only this message for you. Now, Mademoiselle, I will go and find Monsieur Bérenger as he would be most distressed to find you dining alone."

Sinclair interrupted Maureen's thoughts, arriving very quickly in the breakfast room following Roland's departure.

"Did you get some sleep?"

"How can you help it in that bed? It's like sleeping on clouds." Maureen had noted the first night that there was a massive feather mattress beneath the expensive Egyptian cotton sheets.

"Superb. Have you plans this morning?"

"Not until eleven. I'm meeting Jean-Claude today, remember?"

"Yes, of course. He's taking you to Montsegur. Astonishing place. My only regret is that I won't be the one to show it to you for the first time."

"Would you like to join us?"

Sinclair laughed. "My dear, Jean-Claude would have me hung,

drawn, and quartered if I tagged along with you today. You're the star of the region now, after your big debut last night. Everyone wants to know more about you. You will raise Jean-Claude's stock in the region by one hundred points once he is seen squiring you around.

"But I shall not begrudge him that. I have something of my own to show you, once you have finished your breakfast, something that I am sure you will find entirely memorable."

They were standing on the same balcony where they had watched the fireworks the night before. The extraordinary château gardens fanned out before them.

"The gardens are much easier to see and appreciate in the daylight," Sinclair said proudly, pointing out that there were three separated sections. "See how they form a fleur-de-lis pattern?"

"They're magnificent." Maureen was entirely honest. The gardens were stunning in their sculptural beauty as seen from above.

"They can tell the story of our ancestors far better than I can on my own. It would be my honor to show them to you. Shall we?"

Maureen took his arm as he led her down the stairs and through the atrium. She noticed that the house was spotless, despite several hundred revelers having traipsed through the previous night. Servants must have worked nonstop to clean up the debris. There was no sign of anything other than sparkling order in the château.

They moved through the huge French doors and out to the marbled patio, following the perfectly meticulous path toward the ornate golden gates. Sinclair removed a key from his pocket and slipped it into the solid padlock. He loosened the chain and pushed on the gilded bars, allowing them to enter his inner sanctum.

A gleaming fountain of pink marble gurgled before them, the centerpiece of the garden entrance. Sun glittered off the water droplets as they fell across the shoulders of a life-size sculpture of Mary Magdalene, carved in ivory-colored marble. In her left hand, the icon held a rose; perched on her outstretched right hand was a dove. The base of the fountain was carved with the omnipresent fleurs-de-lis.

"You met a lot of people last night. All of them have theories about this region and the mysterious treasure. I'm sure you heard many, from the sublime to the ridiculous."

Maureen laughed. "Mostly ridiculous, but yes."

Sinclair smiled at her. "All of them have their theories, and all of them believe—or shall I say know—that Mary Magdalene is our queen here in the south of France. That is, in fact, the only thing that everyone in that room last night does agree upon."

Maureen was listening carefully. Sinclair's voice had an air of excitement, anticipation. It was contagious.

"And they all know that there is a bloodline. A royal lineage that stems from Mary Magdalene and her children. But very few of them know the whole truth. The entire story is reserved for those who are true followers of The Way. The Way as it was taught by our Magdalene, The Way as it was taught by Jesus Christ Himself."

Maureen stopped him, a little hesitant. "I don't know if it's appropriate for me to ask this or not, but is this the goal of your Society of Blue Apples?"

"The Society of Blue Apples is ancient and complex. I will tell you more about it in time. But for now, suffice it to say that the Society exists to defend and preserve the truth.

"And the truth is that Mary Magdalene was the mother of three children."

Maureen was stunned. *"Three?"*

Sinclair nodded. "Very few people know the story in its entirety, because the details were intentionally obscured for the protection of the descendants. Three children. A trinity. And each founded a line of royal blood that would change the face of Europe, and ultimately the world. These gardens celebrate the dynasty established by each child. My grandfather created all of this. I expanded it and have committed myself to preserving it."

Three separate archways branched off from the main garden.

"Come, we will begin with our own ancestor."

He steered an overwhelmed Maureen through the center gate. "What is it? Are you surprised that we're related? Very distantly, no doubt, but we come from the same bloodline originally."

"I'm just taking it all in. This is common knowledge for you, but it's shocking to me. I can't imagine how the rest of the world would feel about it."

They entered a rose garden of extraordinary lushness. Surrounding another statue, several species of lily were planted in a circle. This combination created the magnificent scent Maureen had experienced the night before.

A white dove cooed and flew over the exquisite, intertwining roses as Sinclair and Maureen walked together in silence. Maureen paused to inhale deeply from a rich red rose in full bloom.

"Roses. Symbolic for all females of the bloodline. And lilies. The lily is a specific symbol of Mary Magdalene. The rose can refer to any woman who is descended, but in our tradition, no one is allowed the lily but her."

He steered Maureen toward the dominant statue, a depiction of a willowy-looking young woman with flowing hair.

Maureen was having difficulty finding her voice. Her question was little more than a whisper. "This is the daughter?"

"May I introduce you to Sarah-Tamar, the only daughter of Jesus Christ and Mary Magdalene. The founder of the French royal dynasties. And our mutual great-grandmother, nineteen hundred years removed."

Maureen stared at the statue before turning to Sinclair. "It's all so incredible. And yet, I'm not finding it at all difficult to accept. So strange and yet it just seems . . . right."

"That's because your soul recognizes the truth."

A dove cooed in agreement from the rose bushes.

"You hear the doves? They are the symbol of Sarah-Tamar, emblems of her pure heart. They later became the symbol of her descendants—the Cathars."

"And this is why the Cathars were wiped out as heretics by the Church?"

"Yes, in part. Because they could prove through certain objects and documents in their possession that they were descendants of Jesus and Mary, and that made their very existence a threat to Rome. Men, women, children. The Church tried to exterminate them all to keep the secret. But there's more to it. Come."

Sinclair led Maureen in a semicircle through the roses, giving her an opportunity to experience the beauty of the garden in the summer sunshine of a golden Languedoc morning. He took her hand and she allowed it, feeling surprisingly comfortable with this eccentric stranger. She followed as he led her gently back through the archway and around the fountain of Mary Magdalene.

"Time to meet little brother." Maureen could sense his excitement building again and wondered how it must feel to keep a secret of this magnitude. She thought briefly and with a pang of trepidation that she would soon know firsthand.

Sinclair moved them through the far right archway, into a more precise and manicured garden. "This looks very English," Maureen observed.

"Very well done, my dear. And now I shall show you why."

A statue of a long-haired young man holding a chalice aloft was the focal point of the large and central fountain in this section. Crystal-clear water poured from the chalice.

"Yeshua-David, the youngest child of Jesus and Mary. He never knew his father as the Magdalene was pregnant with him at the crucifixion. He was born in Alexandria, in Egypt, where his mother and her entourage took refuge before setting sail for France."

Maureen stopped cold. Unconsciously, she put her hand to her belly.

"What's wrong?"

"She was pregnant. I saw it. She was pregnant on the Via Dolorosa and . . . at the crucifixion."

Sinclair began to nod in his matter-of-fact way, then stopped abruptly. Now it was Maureen's turn to ask.

"What is it?"

"Did you say the crucifixion? Did you have a vision of the crucifixion?"

Maureen was beginning to feel a lump in her throat and tears burning the back of her eyes. She was afraid to speak for a moment, fearful that her voice would crack. Sinclair saw it and spoke with increased gentleness.

"Maureen, love, you can trust me. Tell me, please. Did you have a vision of the Magdalene at the crucifixion?"

The tears came unbidden, yet Maureen didn't feel the need to stifle them. There was release, if not safety, in sharing this with someone who understood. "Yes," she whispered. "It happened at Notre-Dame."

Sinclair reached up and brushed the tear from her face. "My dear, my dear Maureen. Do you know how extraordinary that is?"

Maureen shook her head. Sinclair continued softly. "In all of the local history, hundreds of descendants have had dreams and visions of Our Lady, myself included. But the visions stop before Good Friday. To my knowledge, no one else has ever had a complete vision of her at the crucifixion."

"And why is that so important?"

"The prophecy."

Maureen waited for the explanation she knew would come.

"There is a prophecy that has been handed down for as long as anyone here can remember. Legend says that it was part of a larger book of prophecies and revelations that once existed in writing, in Greek. The book was attributed to Sarah-Tamar, so it would have been a gospel in its own right. We know that an important bloodline princess, Mathilda of Tuscany, the duchess of Lorraine, possessed the original book when she built the Abbey of Orval in the eleventh century.

"Where is Orval?"

"On what is now the Belgian border. There are several very important religious settlements in Belgium that pertain to our story, but Orval is where Sarah-Tamar's prophecies were secured for a number of years. We know that the original of her book was later in the possession of the Languedoc Cathars for some time after that. Sadly, it disappeared from history, and very little is known about what happened to it. Our only insight into its contents comes from Nostradamus."

"Nostradamus?" Maureen's head was spinning. She thought she would never cease to be shocked at all the threads and how they connected.

Sinclair rolled his eyes. "Yes, yes. He gets all the credit for his astonishing vision and clairvoyance, but they weren't his prophecies at all. They were Sarah-Tamar's. Apparently Nostradamus had access to a hand-copied version of the original when he visited Orval. That copy disappeared shortly thereafter, so draw your own conclusions about its fate."

Maureen laughed. "No wonder Tammy speaks of him so disparagingly. Nostradamus was a plagiarist."

"And a very clever one. We have to credit him with creating the quatrains. Those were entirely his invention. He just rewrote Sarah-Tamar's prophecies in a way that would disguise the original source and have maximum impact in his own time. Old Michel was quite brilliant, actually. And his extensive understanding of alchemy gave him the ability to decode what must have been a very complicated document.

"But we have little left of our Sarah-Tamar, outside of the Nostradamus work and the single prophecy that is ingrained into some of us down here."

"And what does that prophecy say?"

Sinclair looked up at the water splashing from the chalice. He closed his eyes then and recited a portion of the prophecy.

" 'Marie de Negre shall choose when the time is come for The Expected One. She who is born of the paschal lamb when the day and night are equal, she who is a child of the resurrection. She who carries the Sangre-El will be granted the key upon viewing the Black Day of the Skull. She will become the new Shepherdess of The Way.' "

Maureen was numb. Sinclair took her hand again. "The Black Day of the Skull. Golgotha, the hill of the crucifixion, translates to 'the place of the skull' and the Black Day is what we now call Good Friday. The prophecy indicates that the bloodline daughter who has a vision of the crucifixion will then subsequently have the key."

"The key to what?" Maureen was still unclear. Her head was swimming with the information.

"The key to unlock Mary Magdalene's secret. Her gospel. A first-person account of her life and times. She hid it using a type of alchemy, you know. It can only be found when certain spiritual criteria have been met."

He gestured to the statue of the young man in the fountain and specifically to the chalice he was holding. "That is what so many have searched for, for such a long time."

Maureen was trying to think and order the myriad thoughts running across her mind. The chalice. It clicked. "The chalice he's holding—is it the Holy Grail?"

"Yes. The word 'grail' comes from an ancient term, Sangre-El, meaning the Blood of God. Symbolic of the divine bloodline, of course. But they weren't just searching for the general children of the bloodline. Most of the Grail knights were of the blood themselves, and they were well aware of what that legacy meant. No, they were searching for a specific descendant: a Grail princess who is also known as The Expected One. She is the daughter who held the key that they all wanted."

"Wait a minute. You're telling me that the quest for the Holy Grail was the search for the woman of your prophecy?"

"In part, absolutely. This youngest child, Yeshua-David, went to Glastonbury in England with his great-uncle, the man known to history as Joseph of Arimathea. Together, they founded the first Christian settlement in Britain. From there, the Grail legends were born."

Sinclair gestured to another statue within the same garden structure, but in the distance. It appeared to be a king wielding an enormous sword.

"Why do you think King Arthur was known as the Once and Future King? Because of his blood descent from Yeshua-David. There is

British nobility descended from him to this day. Much of it in Scotland."

"Including you."

"Yes, on my mother's side. But I'm also descended from the Sarah-Tamar line on my father's side, as you are."

An incongruous beeping interrupted him. He cursed and picked up the cell phone, speaking rapidly in French, then clicking it off.

"That was Roland. Jean-Claude has arrived to take you away from me."

Maureen could not mask her disappointment. She wasn't ready to leave all of this yet. "But I haven't seen the third branch of the garden."

Sinclair's face seemed to darken. It was hardly perceptible, but it was there.

"Perhaps that's for the best," he said. "It's such a beautiful day. And that," he indicated with a nod of his head, "is the garden of the Magdalene's eldest son."

He answered Maureen's unspoken question in the enigmatic and vague way of which the natives of this region seemed infuriatingly fond.

"And while it is beautiful in its own way, that garden is too filled with shadows for a day such as this."

As Sinclair led Maureen back out of the garden, he stopped at the gilded gates.

"The day you arrived here, you asked why I was so partial to the fleur-de-lis. This is why. Fleur-de-lis means 'flower of the lily,' and as you now know, the lily is symbolic of Mary Magdalene. The 'flower of the lily' represents her offspring. There are three of them, therefore the three petals on the flower."

He demostrated by tracing the three branches with his finger.

"The first branch, her eldest son John-Joseph, is a very complex character about whom I will tell you more when the time is right. But suffice it to say that his heirs flourished in Italy. The central petal represents the daughter, Sarah-Tamar, and this third leaf is the youngest child, the boy Yeshua-David.

"That's the well-kept secret of the fleur-de-lis. The reason it represents both Italian and French nobility. The reason you see it in British heraldry. It was first used by those who were descended of Mary Magdalene through her trinity of children. It was once a very protected, arcane symbol, so that only those initiated into these truths could recognize each other as they traveled across Europe."

Maureen marveled at this revelation. "And now it's one of the most common symbols in the world. It's on jewelry, clothing, furniture. Hiding in plain sight all this time. And people have no idea what it symbolizes."

*The Languedoc*
*June 25, 2005*

MAUREEN SAT IN THE PASSENGER SEAT of Jean-Claude's Renault sports car as they waited for the electronic gates of the château to open out onto the main road. Out of the corner of her eye, she saw a man moving strangely along the perimeter fence.

"What's wrong?" Jean-Claude asked as he observed Maureen's facial expression.

"There's a man over there by the fence. You can't see him now, but he was there just a moment ago."

Jean-Claude shrugged in his classically Gallic, unconcerned way. "A gardener, perhaps? Or one of Bérenger's security guards. Who knows? His staff is extensive."

"Are there security guards on duty all the time here?" Maureen was curious about the château and its extraordinary contents, including the owner.

"Ah, oui. You rarely see them because it is their job to not be seen. Perhaps that was one of them."

But Maureen wasn't given an opportunity to consider the mundane aspects of running the château. Jean-Claude was launching into the legend of the Paschal family as he knew it.

"Your English is flawless," Maureen noted as he related some of the more complicated historical elements.

"Thank you. I spent two years at Oxford perfecting it."

Maureen was fascinated, hanging on every word while the esteemed French historian drove through the dramatic red foothills. Their destination was Montsegur, the majestic and tragic emblem of the Cathars' last stand.

There are locations on earth that exude a powerful aura of both mystery and tragedy. Steeped in rivers of blood and centuries of history, these rare places can haunt the spirit for many years, long after the visitor has returned to his or her place of security in the modern world. Maureen had seen some of these places in her travels. During her years in Ireland she had experienced this feeling in historical towns like that of Drogheda, where Oliver Cromwell had once slaughtered the entire population, as well as in villages that had been ravaged by the Great Famine in the 1840s. While in Israel, Maureen had climbed the mountain at Masada to watch the sun rise over the Dead Sea. She had been moved beyond both words and tears as she walked through the ruins of the palace where several hundred Jews in the first century had taken their own lives rather than submit to Roman oppressors and certain slavery.

As Jean-Claude maneuvered the Renault into the parking lot at the foot of the hill where Montsegur rests, Maureen had an overwhelming feeling that this was another of those extraordinary locations. Even on this bright summer day, the area seemed shrouded in the mists of time. She stared up at the mountain ahead of them as Jean-Claude guided her toward the hiking trail.

"A long way up, oui? This is why I told you to wear comfortable shoes."

Maureen was thankful that she always traveled with solid athletic shoes, as walking and hiking were her favorite forms of exercise. They began the long, circuitous climb up the mountain, Maureen reflecting that her recent schedule hadn't left much time for working out and cursing that she wasn't in her usual good shape. But Jean-Claude wasn't in a hurry, and they walked at a leisurely pace as he talked more about the mysterious Cathars and answered Maureen's questions.

"How much do we know about their practices? I mean, accurately. Lord Sinclair says that so much of what has been written about them is speculation."

"That is true. Their enemies wrote many of the details that have been ascribed to them, to make them look more heretical and outrageous. You see, the world does not mind if you slaughter outcasts. But if you massacre fellow Christians who are arguably closer to Christ than you are yourself, you may have a problem. So, many stories were invented about Cathar practices by the historians of their time, and after. But you know what we are certain is true? The cornerstone of the Cathar faith was the Lord's Prayer."

Maureen stopped at this, to catch her breath and ask more questions. "Really? The same Lord's Prayer that we say today?"

He nodded. "Oui, the same, but recited in Occitan, of course. When you went to Jerusalem, did you go to the Pater Noster Church on the Mount of Olives?"

"Yes!" Maureen knew exactly the location. There was a church on the eastern side of Jerusalem built over a cave that was reputed to be the location where Jesus first taught the Lord's Prayer. A beautiful exterior cloister displayed the prayer in mosaic-tiled panels representing more than sixty languages. Maureen had photographed the panel that showed the prayer in an ancient form of Irish Gaelic to give to Peter.

"The prayer is displayed there in Occitan," Jean-Claude explained. "Every Cathar recited it upon rising in the morning. Not by rote, as many say it today, but as an act of meditation and true prayer. Each line was a sacred law for them."

Maureen thought about this as they walked, and Jean-Claude continued. "So you see, here were people who lived in peace and taught what they called The Way, a life centered on teachings of love. They were a culture that recognized the Lord's Prayer as their most holy scripture."

Maureen saw where he was leading. "So if you're the Church and you want to eliminate these people, you can't very well let it be known that they're good Christians."

"Exactly. Bizarre rituals and accusations were made against the Cathars to make it acceptable to butcher them."

Jean-Claude stopped now as they reached a monument in the middle of the trail. It was a large granite slab topped with a version of the equal-armed cross of the Languedoc.

"This is the martyr's monument," he explained. "It is placed here because this is where the pyre stood."

Maureen shivered. That same haunting, yet strangely exhilarating feeling overtook her, a sense of standing in a terrible place of history. She listened as Jean-Claude recited the story of the Cathars' last stand here on the mountain.

By the end of 1243 the Cathars had suffered almost half a century of persecution by the armies of the Pope. Entire cities had been put to the sword, and the streets of towns like Béziers had literally run with the blood of innocents. The Church was determined to eradicate this "heresy" at any cost, and the king of France was happy to assist with his own troops as each victory over the once-wealthy Cathar nobles added land to French territories. The counts of Toulouse had threatened one too many times to create their own independent state. If using the wrath of the Church was convenient for stopping them, the king was all for that solution, which he hoped would take away some of the blame from his legacy in history.

The remaining heads of Cathar society made a last stand at the fortress of Montsegur in March of 1244. Like the Jews at Masada more than a thousand years earlier, they came together to pray as a community for their salvation from the oppressor, and they vowed never to surrender their faith. Indeed, there was some speculation that the Cathars had taken strength from the legacy of the Masada martyrs during their final confinement. And like the Roman armies who were their own ancestors, the papal forces attempted to starve their quarry out by cutting off their access to water and food. This proved as difficult at Montsegur as it had been at Masada, as both were perched precariously on hilltops that were almost impossible to secure from all angles. The rebels from both cultures found ways to thwart and confound their oppressors.

After several months of siege, the papal forces determined that they were finished with the standoff. They delivered an ultimatum to the Cathar leadership. If they would confess and repent as heretics in surrender to the Inquisition, they would be spared. But if they did not, they would all be burned at the stake for their insult to the Holy Roman Church. They were given two weeks to make a decision.

On the final day, the leaders of the Pope's army lit the funeral pyre and called for an answer. They were met with a reply that has never been forgotten in the Languedoc. Two hundred Cathars emerged from the keep of Montsegur, dressed in their simple robes and holding hands. In perfect unison, they sang the Lord's Prayer in Occitan as they walked into the funeral pyre en masse. They died as they had lived, in perfect harmony with their faith in God.

The legends surrounding the final days of the Cathars were abundant, and each was more dramatic than the next. The most memorable was of the French envoys who were sent to speak with the Cathars on behalf of the king's troops. The envoys, hardened mercenaries, were invited to stay within the walls of Montsegur and witness the Cathar teachings for themselves. What they saw in those final days was reportedly so miraculous, so stunning, that the French soldiers asked to be admitted to the faith of these Pure Ones. Knowing that only death could await them, the Frenchmen took the ultimate Cathar sacrament known as the consolamentum and marched into the flames with their newfound brothers and sisters.

Maureen pushed a tear from her face as she gazed up at the mountain and then back at the cross. "What do you think it was? What did the Frenchmen see that was enough for them to pledge to die with these people? Does anyone know?"

"No." Jean-Claude shook his head. "There is only speculation. Some say that the Holy Ghost appeared during Cathar rituals and showed that the kingdom of heaven awaited them. Others say it was something else, the infamous Cathar treasure that they possessed."

The legend of Montsegur continued to unfold before Maureen as they resumed their climb up the arduous trail. On the penultimate day of the Cathars' last stand, four members of their group were lowered down the most precarious wall of the castle and escaped to safety. It was believed that they were aided by intelligence from the French envoys who converted to Catharism and died with the rest a day later.

"They carried with them the legendary treasure of the Cathars. But what that actually was is still a matter of speculation. It had to be portable as two of those chosen to escape were young women and presumably small. Also, they would have all been frail after months of captivity and rationed food and water. Some say they carried the Holy Grail, or the crown of thorns, or even the most valuable treasure on earth, the Book of Love."

"That's the gospel written by Jesus Himself?"

Jean-Claude nodded. "All legends of it certainly disappeared from history around that time."

The historian and journalist in Maureen was on overload. "Are there books you can recommend? Documents I can research while I'm here in France that provide more information about this?"

The Frenchman laughed a little and shrugged. "Madamoiselle Paschal, they are folklorists here in the Languedoc. They protect their secrets and their legends by *not* committing them to paper. I know that is hard for many to understand. But look around you, cherie. Who needs books when you have all of this to tell the story?"

They had reached the rise of the hill, and the ruins of the once-great fortress lay ahead of them. In the presence of these massive stone walls that seemed to radiate the history of their surroundings, Maureen understood Jean-Claude's point perfectly. Still, she was torn between her senses and her journalist's need to authenticate all of her findings. "That's a strange sentiment for a man who calls himself a historian," she observed.

Now he laughed outright, a sound that echoed through the

green valley below them. "I consider myself a historian, but not an academic. There's a difference, particularly in a place like this. The academic approach doesn't apply everywhere, Mademoiselle Paschal."

Maureen's expression must have given away that she wasn't following him completely. He elaborated.

"You see, in order to hold the most prestigious titles in the academic world, you simply have to read all the right books and write the proper papers. When I was on a lecture tour in Boston, I met an American woman who had a doctorate in French history with an emphasis on the medieval heresies. She is now considered one of the great experts in the subject and has even written a university textbook or two. And do you know something funny? She has never been to France, not once. Not even to Paris, much less the Languedoc. Worse, she doesn't feel it is necessary. In true academic form, she believes everything she needs is in books or documents available on university databases. The woman's understanding of Catharism is about as realistic as reading a comic book, and twice as laughable. Yet she would be recognized publicly as a greater authority than any of us here because of the degrees she holds and the initials after her name."

Maureen was listening as they stepped through the rocks and moved among the magnificent ruins. Jean-Claude's point hit her hard. She had always thought of herself as an academic, yet her reporter's experience had also driven her to seek out stories in their native environment. She couldn't imagine writing about Mary Magdalene without visiting the Holy Land, and had insisted on touring Versailles and the revolutionary prison of the Conciergerie while researching Marie Antoinette. Now, even in the few days that she had spent surrounded by the living history of the Languedoc, she recognized that this was a culture that required experiential understanding.

Jean-Claude wasn't finished. "Let me give you an example. You can read one of fifty versions of the tragedy here at Montsegur as written by historians. But look around. If you have never climbed this mountain or seen the place where the fire burned or observed how impenetrable these walls are, how would you ever understand it? Come, let me show you something."

Maureen followed the Frenchman to the edge of a cliff, where the walls of the once-impenetrable fortress had crumbled. He pointed to a sheer and excruciatingly steep drop thousands of feet down the mountainside. The warm winds were rising, blowing her hair as Maureen tried to put herself in the position of a young Cathar girl in the thirteenth century.

"This spot is where the four escaped," he explained. "Imagine it now as you stand here. In the dead of night, carrying the most precious relics of your people strapped to your body, weak after months of stress and starvation. You are young and terrified and know that while you may survive, every person you love in the world will be burned alive. With all of this on your mind, you are lowered down a wall into the bitter cold and nothingness of midnight, and there's a strong possibility you will fall to your death."

Maureen sighed heavily. It was a heady experience to stand here where the legends were alive and very real all around her.

Jean-Claude interrupted her thoughts. "Now imagine only reading about this account in a library in New Haven. It is a different experience, no?"

Nodding in agreement, Maureen answered, "Most definitely."

"Oh, and one thing I forgot to mention. The youngest girl who escaped that night? She was quite possibly your ancestor. The one who later took the name of Paschal. In fact, they referred to her as La Paschalina until she died."

Maureen was numb with the knowledge of yet another phenomenal Paschal ancestor. "How much do you know about her?"

"Just a little. She died at the monastery of Montserrat on the Spanish border as a very old woman, and some records of her life remain there. We know she married another Cathar refugee in Spain and had a number of children. It is written that she brought with her a priceless gift to the monastery, but the nature of that gift has never been revealed publicly."

Maureen reached down and picked one of the wildflowers that grew in the crevices of the ruined walls. She walked to the edge of the cliff where the Cathar girl who would later take the name of La Paschalina had courageously descended the mountain as the last hope of her people. Tossing the tiny purple flower over the edge of the cliff, Maureen said a small prayer for the woman who may or may not have been her ancestor. It almost didn't matter. With the story of these beautiful people and the gift of the land itself, this day had already changed her irrevocably.

"Thank you," she said to Jean-Claude in little more than a whisper. He left her alone then, to contemplate how her past and her future were intertwined with this most ancient and enigmatic place.

Maureen and Jean-Claude had lunch in the tiny village at the base of Montsegur. As he had promised, the restaurant served food in the Cathar style. The menu was simple fare consisting primarily of fish and fresh vegetables.

"There is a misconception that the Cathars were strict vegetarians, but they did eat fish," Jean-Claude explained. "They were very literal about certain elements in the life of Jesus. And as Jesus fed the multitudes with loaves and fishes, they believed that this meant they should include fish in their diet."

Maureen found the food remarkably hearty and was enjoying herself immensely. Sinclair was right: Jean-Claude was a brilliant historian. Maureen had thrown countless questions at him as they walked down the mountain, and he responded to all of them patiently and with amazing insight. By the time they sat down to eat, she was happy to answer the questions he had for her.

Jean-Claude began to make inquiries about Maureen's dreams and visions. Previously, this would have made her very uncomfortable, but these last days in the Languedoc had opened her mind on the issue. Here, visions like hers were treated as commonplace; they were simply a fact of life. It was a relief to talk about them with these accepting people.

"Did you have these visions as a child?" Jean-Claude wanted to know.

Maureen shook her head in the negative.

"Are you sure?"

"If I did, I have no memory of it. I didn't have them until I went to Jerusalem. Why do you ask?"

"Just curious. Please, go on."

Maureen went into some detail, and Jean-Claude appeared to listen very closely, asking questions at intervals. His interest became concentrated as she described the crucifixion vision at Notre-Dame.

Maureen noticed. "Lord Sinclair also thought that vision was significant."

"It is." Jean-Claude nodded. "He told you about the prophecy?"

"Yes, it's fascinating. But it concerns me a little that he seems to think I'm The Expected One of the prophecy. Talk about performance anxiety."

The Frenchman laughed. "No, no. These things cannot be forced. You either are or you are not, and if you are, it will be revealed very soon. How long are you staying in the Languedoc?"

"We had allocated four days before going back to Paris for a few more nights. But I'm not sure now. There's so much to see and learn down here. I'm playing it by ear."

Jean-Claude looked somewhat pensive as he listened to her. "Did anything strange happen last night after the party? Anything out of the ordinary for you? Any new dreams?"

Maureen shook her head. "No, nothing. I was exhausted and I slept very well. Why?"

Jean-Claude shrugged as he called for the check. When he spoke, it was almost to himself. "Well, that narrows the field."

"Narrows what field?"

"Oh, just that if you're planning to leave us soon, we will have to see what we can do to determine if you are the ancestral daughter of

La Paschalina—if you are indeed The Expected One who will lead us to the great secret treasure."

He winked at Maureen playfully as he held out her chair and they prepared to leave the sacred ground that was Montsegur. "I'd better get you back before Bérenger has my head."

... *How does one begin to write about a time that changes the world?*

*I have waited so long to begin because I have always feared that this day would come and I would have to live it all again. I have seen it in my sleep these many years, over and over again, but it comes without leave to torment me. To bring it back with intention, has never been my choice. For while I have forgiven everyone who played a part in Easa's suffering, forgiveness does not bring forgetting.*

*But that is as it should be, for I am the only one left who can tell what really came to pass during the days of darkness.*

*There are those who say Easa planned it, from the very first. This is not the truth. It was planned for Easa, and he lived it in his strength and his obedience to God. He drank from the cup that was handed to him with a courage and grace that has never been seen before or since, save in the form of his mother. Only His mother, the Great Mary, heard the call of the Lord with the same clarity, and only His mother answered that call with the same courage.*

*The rest of us were humbled to learn from their grace.*

THE ARQUES GOSPEL OF MARY MAGDALENE,
THE BOOK OF THE TIME OF DARKNESS

## Chapter Twelve

*Carcassonne*
*June 25, 2005*

*T*amara Wisdom and Derek Wainwright appeared as any typical American tourist couple outside the walled fortress city of Carcassonne. When they met in the lobby of Derek's hotel, he kissed Tammy passionately. Her smile was coy as she pushed him away gently.

"There will be plenty of time for that later, Derek."

"Promise?"

"Of course." She ran her hand along his back to affirm her pledge. "But you know what a workaholic I am. Once I get that out of my system, we'll have the rest of the day to . . . play."

"Right, let's go. I'd better drive."

Derek took Tammy's hand and led her to the parking lot and his rented car. He eased out onto the perimeter street and drove around the walled city, turning onto a road that led deeper into the hills.

"You're sure this is safe?" she asked him.

Derek nodded. "They all left for Paris this morning. All but . . ."

"But what?"

He looked as though he were about to tell her but reconsidered. "Nothing. There is one left here in the Languedoc, but he's preoccupied today and there's no chance he'll walk in on us."

"Care to elaborate?"

Derek laughed. "Not yet. It's bad enough that I'm taking this chance at all. Do you know what the penalty is if I get caught?"

Tammy shook her head. "No, what? Double secret probation?"

He gave her a sidelong look. "Joke all you want, but these guys don't play." He drew his right index finger across his throat in a slashing motion.

"You're not serious."

"I am. The penalty for revealing Guild secrets to a non-Guild member is death."

"Has it ever happened? Or is that just the bogeyman they create to increase the secret society mystique and control their members?"

"There's a new Teacher of Righteousness—that's what we call our leader—and this guy is extreme."

Tammy thought about this seriously for a moment. Derek had confessed his Guild membership to her a few years ago in a drunken indiscretion, but then clammed up and refused to talk about it. She had wheedled more out of him last night at the party. Ultimately, the combination of alcohol and his long-frustrated desire for her had caused him to reveal that their headquarters were just outside Carcassonne. Or at least that's what she thought had prompted Derek's loose lips. He had even offered to show her the inner sanctum today. But if he was serious about the dire consequences of discovery, that was something Tammy did not want on her conscience.

"Listen, Derek, if this really is so dangerous, I don't want to push you to do it. Really. I can use you as an anonymous source if I decide to mention the Guild in my projects. Let's just go back to Carcassonne and have lunch. You can spill some beans to me there in the safety of a café in broad daylight."

There. She had given him an easy exit. He surprised her by not accepting it.

"Oh, no. I want to show this to you. In fact, now I can't wait to show this to you."

Tammy was uneasy about the enthusiasm in his answer. "Why?"

"You'll see."

Derek parked behind a hedge, several hundred yards from the entrance to the grounds. They walked carefully along the road, veering off to a narrow and unpaved lane. They walked it for another hundred yards until the stone chapel came into view, the same church where Guild members had held religious services the night before.

"That's the church. We'll go in there afterward if you want to see it."

Tammy nodded, content to follow and see where he was leading. She had known Derek for years, but it had always been as a casual acquaintance. She realized now that she honestly didn't know him well enough to gauge what his true motives were. She thought originally that they were basic, primal male impulses, and those she could handle. But there was a determination in him suddenly, something else that she had never seen. It scared her. Thank God both Sinclair and Roland knew where she was.

He led her to a long bungalow behind the church, removed a key from his pocket, and opened the door. The unremarkable exterior of the building did not prepare Tammy for the sheer size and ornate interior of the Guild Hall. It was plush and gilded, every square foot of wall space was covered with artwork—and each was a copy of a Leonardo da Vinci painting. On the opposite wall, the first space seen upon entering the room, copies of two versions of Leonardo's *Saint John the Baptist* hung side by side.

"My God," Tammy whispered. "So it is true. Leonardo was a Johannite. A total heretic."

Derek laughed. "By what standards? As far as the Guild is concerned, 'Christians' who follow Christ are the true heretics. We like to call him 'The Usurper,' and 'The Wicked Priest.' " Derek made a 360-degree gesture in the direction of the artwork and spoke grandly, in a manner Tammy had never heard from him. "Leonardo da Vinci was the Teacher of Righteousness in his time, the leader of our Guild. He believed that John the Baptist was the only true messiah and that Jesus stole his position through the manipulation of women."

"The manipulation of women?"

Derek nodded. "That's a foundation of our tradition. Salome and Mary Magdalene plotted the death of our messiah in order to place their own false prophet on the throne. The Guild refers to both of them as whores. Always has, always will."

Tammy looked at him incredulously. "Do you believe that? Damn, Derek, how invested are you in this philosophy? And how have you kept this a secret from me?"

Derek shrugged. "Secrets are our business. As for the philosophy, I was raised to believe it and studied the secret texts for years. It's very convincing, you know."

"What is?"

"The material we have. We call it *The True Book of the Holy Grail*. It's been passed down since Roman times from original followers of the Baptist. It describes the events around John's death in detail. You'd find it fascinating."

"Can I see it?"

"I'll get you a copy. I have one back in my hotel room." There was more than a touch of insinuation in his latter statement.

Tammy made a mental note and tried not to cringe outwardly. She could certainly guess what Derek might expect in exchange for that particularly valuable document. She turned away from him, moving slowly through the room to look at the paintings.

"Notice what they all have in common?" Derek asked her.

"Other than they're all by Leonardo?" Tammy shook her head. She wasn't seeing the connection outside of the obvious one. "No. At first I thought they all depicted John the Baptist, but they don't. That looks like a detail of *The Last Supper* over there, but that doesn't make sense based on what you just told me. Why would you have that here if the Guild despises Jesus as a usurper and blames Mary Magdalene for John's death?"

"This is why," Derek said, holding his right hand in front of his face in a specific gesture. His index finger pointed toward the sky and his thumb curled upward, the other three fingers folded tightly down. Tammy looked and realized that one of the apostles in Leonardo's famous fresco was making the same motion with his hand—and doing it in an almost threatening way in Jesus' face.

"What does that mean?" Tammy asked. "I've seen it before, in the *John the Baptist* painting in the Louvre." Tammy pointed to the copy on the wall. "That one there. I assumed it was a reference to heaven, pointing to the sky."

Derek clucked at her in mock disappointment. "Come, come, Tammy. You should know that Leonardo was never obvious. We call this the 'Remember John' gesture, and it has multiple meanings. First, if you look closely, the fingers form a letter J, for John. The right index finger held up also represents the number one. So the total gesture means 'John is the first messiah.' Oh, and there's one more important thing about the 'Remember John' gesture, and that is the relic."

"You have a John relic?"

Derek's grin was sly. "I wish they were here so I could show them to you, but the Teacher of Righteousness never lets them out of his possession. We have the bones of John's right index finger, the same finger used to make the gesture that has been our password in public for a thousand years. It enabled knights and nobles to recognize each other discreetly in the middle ages, and we still use it today. John's finger is used in our initiation ceremonies. And so is his head."

This grabbed Tammy's attention. "You have John's *head*?"

Now Derek did laugh. "Yep. The Teacher of Righteousness shines it up every day. It's at the center of all Guild rituals."

"How do you know it's really his? I thought his head was in Amiens, at the cathedral there."

"Do you have any idea how many places have claimed Baptist remains? Trust me, we know that ours is the authentic relic. It's been passed down from a long line. There's a great story behind it, but I'll let you read it in *The True Book of the Holy Grail*. Look, here's more of the index finger. It shows up in each of these paintings."

Even when discussing such an important subject, Tammy noted that Derek's attention span seemed limited, and he skipped around from subject to subject. Was it intentional? Did he have an agenda? She hadn't previously given him much credit for intelligence, but now she had a creeping feeling that she had underestimated him. Her mind was racing as she tried to remain cool. Was this guy a fanatic? How had she not noticed how entrenched he was? Tammy was trying not to be swamped with the sick notion that she was about to be in over her pretty raven head.

Derek led her through the paintings, pointing out the 'Remember John' gesture in each one. In the portraits of John, the Baptist himself was making the gesture. In *The Last Supper*, it was one of the apostles, a clearly agitated Thomas.

"Several of the apostles were followers of John long before Jesus came along," Derek informed her. "What's important about this version of *The Last Supper* is that Jesus is announcing that one of them will betray him. Thomas here is affirming that, and telling him why with the 'Remember John' gesture—this is in memory of John. John's fate will become your fate. That's what he's saying with the index finger in the false prophet's face. You'll be martyred just as John was, and it's payback."

Tammy was shocked at this new and startling interpretation of one of the world's most famous images. She couldn't resist her next question.

"So you probably don't believe that's Mary Magdalene seated next to Christ in *The Last Supper*."

Derek spat on the floor in reply. "That's what I think of that theory, and of everyone who believes in it."

Derek waved off *The Last Supper*, but he wasn't nearly finished with Tammy's art history lesson. He led her to the long wall that held two versions of Leonardo's famous *Madonna of the Rocks* paintings and pointed first to the canvas on the right.

"Leo was commissioned to do a painting of the virgin and child for the Feast of the Immaculate Conception. Apparently, this wasn't what the Confraternity of the Immaculate Conception wanted. They rejected it. But it has become a classic of our Guild, and we all have a version of this in our homes."

The painting centered on a madonna with her right arm around an infant and her left hand over another baby that sat below her. An angel observed the scene. "Everyone thinks that's Mary, but they're wrong. The original title of the painting was *Madonna of the Rocks,* not *Virgin of the Rocks,* as it is sometimes now called. Look closely. That's Elisabeth, the mother of John the Baptist."

Tammy wasn't convinced. "What makes you think so?"

"Guild tradition, first of all. We know it is." The answer was arrogant in its certainty. "But there's art history to back us up. Leonardo was in a huge fight with the Confraternity over payment for this painting, so he got back at them by making them think he was delivering the traditional scene they ordered. But in reality he painted a version of our entire philosophy to slap them in the face. He was wicked funny that way. A lot of Leonardo's art was his way of taunting the Church and getting away with it because he was so much smarter than the idiot papists in Rome."

Tammy tried not to show her surprise at Derek's overt bigotry. She had never seen this side of him before, and it was making her increasingly uncomfortable. She felt in her pocket for the security of her cell phone. She considered putting out an SOS call if the situation got any creepier. But she was torn. As an author and a filmmaker she was being handed solid gold here—did she dare use it?

Derek was on a roll about his idol, Leonardo. "Did you know that the *Mona Lisa* is actually a self-portrait? Leonardo sketched himself and then turned it into the painting as we know it today. It was all a big joke for him. And see, the joke's on us now as people wait in line for hours to see that painting. He hated women because of his mother, you know. He even increased the restrictions on females in the Guild as his way of punishing women for his own miserable childhood. That's in an amendment to *The True Book of the Holy Grail.* You'll see it."

Derek elaborated with a brief history of Leonardo—that the artist was abandoned by his natural mother and had a confusing childhood with a difficult stepmother. In fact, all of Leonardo's documented relationships with women were negative or otherwise traumatic. His aversion to women had been well researched by historians who also reported that the artist had been arrested and jailed for sodomy. But the most damning stain on his reputation came when Leonardo adopted a ten-year-old boy as his apprentice and kept him as his companion for many years. While Leonardo's personal life was often scandalous, he kept himself out of trouble with authorities through painting for the Church and relying on other wealthy patrons who called in favors on his behalf.

"Anytime he was forced to paint a woman, like Mona Lisa, he turned it into some kind of a joke, mostly to amuse himself. That's how he dealt with being forced to paint subjects that didn't appeal to him."

Derek turned back to the *Madonna of the Rocks*. "The only female we know he respected was Elisabeth, the perfect woman and mother. The real madonna. See, here she is with her arm around this child— her child. It's clearly John."

Tammy nodded. The infant sheltered in the woman's arms was undoubtedly John the Baptist.

"Now look at Elisabeth's left hand. She is pushing the Christ child away, showing that he is lower than her child. Leonardo has even placed Jesus physically below John to show you his inferiority. And finally, look at the angel Uriel's eyes. Who is he looking at with adoration? See in the first painting? He is pointing at John, but he is also making our 'Remember John' symbol.

"The Immaculate Conception crowd were unhappy with the original painting and its obvious Johannite message. They made Leo do a second one, insisting that this time Mary and Jesus have haloes and that the angel not point at John. So look over here and you will see that they got what they asked for, sort of. Mary and Jesus have a halo, but so does John. He also gave John a baptismal staff, to make it even more clear just who he is and to give him more authority. In both paintings, Jesus is bestowing his blessing on John. So, looking at these now, who do you think Leonardo revered as the true messiah and prophet?"

Tammy answered honestly. "John the Baptist. Clearly."

"Of course. The archangel Uriel is affirming the Baptist's superiority, and so is John's mother. In our tradition, we worship Elisabeth in the same way that deluded Christians worship the mother of Jesus. Our girls are raised in Elisabeth's image, to be Daughters of Righteousness."

Tammy raised an eyebrow. "What exactly does that mean?"

Derek smiled slyly at her and moved closer. "That women should know their place, and their place is to be obedient and subservient to the men in their lives. But you know, it's not as bad as it sounds. Once they become the mother of a son, they earn the title of 'An Elisabeth' and are treated like queens. You should see the diamonds my mother was given for each one of us. Believe me, if you saw what her overprivileged life was like you would not feel any sympathy for her."

"And you support this idea of women as subservient?" Tammy held her ground, not showing her increasing nervousness.

"As I said, I was raised with it. Works for me." He shrugged.

Tammy shook her head, then started to laugh, half with irony and half with increasing nerves.

"What?" Derek asked.

"I was just thinking about this room, with all of the da Vinci heresy, as opposed to Sinclair's room, with all of the Botticelli heresy. It's like 'Renaissance Death Match. Leonardo versus Sandro.' "

Derek didn't laugh. "It would be funny if it wasn't so damn serious. The rivalry between John's descendants and Jesus' descendants has caused a lot of bloodshed. It's still causing a lot of trouble now, more than you'd ever believe."

Tammy looked at Derek with feigned confusion. She knew exactly what he was getting at but couldn't allow him to know that. She asked innocently, "John's descendants?"

Derek looked taken aback. "Of course. Don't tell me you didn't know that?"

Tammy kept up the front, shaking her head. "No, I didn't." Her expression implored him to continue.

"Come on, you didn't know that John had a son? That's how the Guild was founded, by the descendants of John. Well, it's a long story because half of them eventually sold out to the papists and the Christ followers, like the Medicis." He made a distasteful face at the mention of Italy's historic first family.

"Even Leonardo ended up in the service of the enemy at the end of his life, although we think he was held captive in France against his will. But the others, the hard core, formed our Guild. In fact, you're looking at a great-grandson, about two thousand years removed, of John the Baptist."

Tammy dreaded the inevitable—that she would end up in Derek's hotel room, and worse. But there was no getting around it. She had to get her hands on this so-called *True Book of the Holy Grail* and find out just what these John boys were all about. She had the opportunity to be the first person outside the Guild to obtain this rare information, and she wasn't going to blow it. This went so much deeper than any of them had imagined, and there was no way she was leaving without that book. She would do it for her future film, she would do it for her friends in Blue Apples, and most of all she would do it for Roland. Of course, Roland could never know to what lengths Tammy went to obtain the documents. She would have to devise a credible version of events for his ears. She was thankful that the chauffeur from the Château des Pommes Bleues was picking her up later in the afternoon, so she would have time on the drive back to Arques to consider her story.

Tammy insisted on lunch before they returned to Derek's hotel, and proceeded to order copious amounts of ruby-colored Pays d'Oc wine. She had watched him throw back a handful of prescription drugs in deference to his hangover, and she had the smallest glimmer of hope that the mixture of the pills and the wine might buy her a more docile Derek, if not an unconscious one.

Derek confessed over the meal that he was telling Tammy secrets of the Guild because he wanted her to expose them in print and on film. While he could never go on record—he had an agenda, but he wasn't crazy—he wanted someone to reveal the truth about the Guild.

"But why?" Tammy had asked. It didn't make sense to her. Derek was immersed in the Guild and obviously deeply influenced by its teachings. The Guild was partially responsible for the wealth his family had accumulated. Why would Derek turn on them?

"Listen, Tammy," he leaned across the table and whispered to her, "I'm willing to tell you a lot of stuff—things that deal with serious crimes. Even murder. But you can't ever let anyone know that it was me or I'm dead."

"I still don't understand," Tammy replied. "Why are you turning your coat here on an organization that is so important to you and your family?"

"The new Teacher of Righteousness," Derek spat. "Cromwell. He's a crazy bastard and he will take us all down with him. I'm actually being loyal, not disloyal. The only hope we have to save the Guild is to see him taken out before he does permanent damage. I want you to expose *him*, not the Guild. Make him look like a loose cannon, a crazy fanatic."

"Why are you trusting me with this?" Tammy was becoming increasingly uncomfortable. This was far bigger than she had anticipated, and far murkier than she desired.

Derek looked smug as he ran his fingers up one of her arms. "Because you're ambitious and you'll love having the exclusive on this information for a book and a film. And because my trust fund is equal to the gross national product of several independent nations and you know I'll write you whatever checks you need for funding. Am I right?"

Tammy smiled at him sweetly and placed her hand over his, trying not to be sick. She had to play this out, she simply had to. "But of course."

What Derek hadn't revealed in this conversation was that the American delegation was planning a coup within the Guild. First, they needed to tidy up some loose ends in Europe by eliminating the power players there. His father, Eli Wainwright, was poised to become the next Teacher of Righteousness—with Derek as his eventual successor—if they could neutralize the European power structure.

Derek Wainwright smiled then, the cunning expression of a predator. He had been using Tammy for this purpose all along. If she thought she had duped him into spilling Guild secrets by using her feminine wiles, then she was just a stupid tramp who deserved to be used in exactly the way he intended. Still, it would be a pleasant enough way to end the afternoon. And hadn't the little slut teased him quite long enough?

Tammy tried not to wake Derek as she gathered her belongings. She needed to get the hell out of there, couldn't wait to get back to the safety of the château to take a very long shower. Tammy wondered briefly how long it would take to scrub the stench of these Guild fanatics from her skin.

She was grateful that the worst possible outcome had been avoided. She had calculated accurately—Derek's consumption of prescription drugs, combined with the wine and his exhaustion, had caused him to pass out when they got back to the hotel room.

It had been dodgy at first. Derek was all hands when they got to his room, but Tammy rerouted him skillfully toward his obvious obsession: bringing down his rival, John Simon Cromwell. She emphasized that she needed as much information as possible if she was going to be his partner in such a dangerous game. Derek delivered on what he promised and more—documents, secrets, and the shockingly graphic description of a particularly brutal murder in Marseille a few years earlier.

It had taken every ounce of control that Tammy possessed not to be sick at Derek's account of the execution of the Languedoc man. He had been decapitated and mutilated, his right index finger severed as a symbol of the Guild's revenge. The knowledge of such an act would have been abhorrent to Tammy under any circumstances. But the dead man was known to her; he was the former Grand Master of the Society of Blue Apples. She could not allow Derek to see that she recognized the crime as he described it. She had been very careful to keep her face as expressionless as possible.

Tammy was scrambling to find everything and make her way out of Derek's room when she knocked over a table lamp with a loud *thud.* She heard Derek stir at this and cursed to herself.

"Hey," he grumbled, groggy, "where ya goin'?"

"Sinclair's car is here to take me back to Arques. I have to get back for a dinner there tonight with Maureen."

He tried to sit up, grabbed his head, and groaned. He collapsed on his back again but said as he did, "Oh, Maureen. Damn, I almost forgot to tell you."

Tammy froze. "What?"

"She may be in trouble today."

"How?"

"She's out with Jean-Claude de la Motte today, right?"

Tammy nodded, thinking as fast as she could, trying to figure it out. Derek rolled over and stretched languidly.

"Wake up, girl. Jean-Claude is one of us. Or maybe I should say one of *them.* He's the right arm of that nutcase Teacher of Righteousness and the head of our French chapter. Has been since he was a kid. His real name isn't even Jean-Claude, it's Jean-Baptiste." He paused to laugh at this little joke before continuing. "But he probably won't hurt her. Yet. They have too much interest in whether or not she can find the so-called treasure while she's here. And we both know there's a time limit on that possibility."

Tammy's head was spinning. She couldn't process Jean-Claude's treachery, not this quickly. He had been a friend of Sinclair and Roland's for years and they trusted him implicitly. How long had this infiltration been going on? But something else was bothering her, and she had to know. She prayed she didn't look as shaken as she was, and asked her question with a calm she didn't feel.

"Historically, The Expected One was eliminated before the treasure could be uncovered. Why would this be any different? If Jean . . . Baptiste and your leader believe Maureen is the prophesied one, why wouldn't they just get rid of her before she can fulfill that role? Like they did with Joan and Germaine?"

Derek yawned. "Because they want her to lead them to the Magdalene book once and for all so they can destroy it. After that, your friend will be history, too—before she has the chance to write about it."

"Why are you telling me this?" Tammy asked carefully.

"Because I want Jean-Baptiste to go down with his leader. And I figure that once your Grand Master Sinclair knows he's been duped, he'll eliminate that problematic frog for me."

Tammy wanted to scream at him then, wanted to tell him that Sinclair and the others in their organization weren't like Derek and the hate-mongers in his Guild. But she didn't dare say a word to tip her hand before she was safely out the door.

Derek wasn't finished. "Meanwhile, let's just say that if I were you I'd get that redhead the hell out of the Languedoc as soon as possible."

Tammy turned toward the door and then stopped. She had to ask one final question, had to know just how badly she had been duped by Derek all these years.

"How do *you* feel about all this?" she asked quietly.

"Don't care one way or the other, really," Derek replied, sounding supremely bored and more than ready to return to his wine-induced slumber. "Although your friend seems nice enough, she's still a Jesus spawn and that makes her my natural enemy. And that's just the way it is. Maybe you can't understand it, but our beliefs go back a long way.

As for the actual discovery of the whore's scrolls, everyone seems certain that it will happen this time because your girl fits all the points of the prophecy, and not just some of them. But I'm not worried about it. What's the big deal, anyway?"

He laughed for a second and rolled onto his side, raising himself up on one elbow to look at her. "See, here's the funny thing. *Nobody* wants what's in those scrolls. The Vatican won't want to recognize them because of the content, nor will any of the other mainstream Christians. Historians don't want them because it will make all the academics and Bible scholars look like idiots. So chances are that our own enemies will bury them before the public ever knows what's in there. Saves us the trouble of having to deal with it—that's how I look at it."

He yawned again as if the whole topic was too mundane to be dealt with further and rolled onto his back again as he added, "Of course, we despise it because we know it will contain lies about John the Baptist. And because it was written by a whore."

Tammy wanted to run from the hotel, get away from Derek and his hateful Guild philosophy as quickly as possible. She had a death grip on her cell phone and whipped it out of her pocket as soon as she was outside. There was no time to think, no time to do anything but find out where Maureen was now.

She hit the speed dial for Roland and wanted to cry when she heard his comforting Occitan accent. The connection was terrible, and she had to yell several times to be heard. "Maureen! Where is Maureen now, do you know?"

Damn it! She couldn't hear his reply. She yelled again. "What? I can't hear you. Yell, Roland. Yell so I can hear you."

Roland yelled. "Maureen. Is. Here."

"You're sure?"

"Yes. She was looking for you, she . . ."

And they were cut off. *That's just as well,* thought Tammy. *I don't want to explain anything to Roland until I've had time to think about it all.* As long as Maureen was safely in the Château des Pommes Bleues, there was time to regroup. She would meet with Sinclair before dinner to strategize.

Tammy checked the time on her cell phone. She was scheduled to meet the chauffeur in less than half an hour near the gates of the city. It wasn't a long walk from where she was, but she felt weak and wasn't sure she could trust her wobbly legs to get her there quickly. She began to walk, trying to breathe while considering all of the shocking things she had learned from and about Derek. As it all came back to her in vivid color, she felt her stomach turn. Noticing the garden of a small hotel just ahead, Tammy ran and reached the bushes just in time to vomit violently.

*Château des Pommes Bleues*
*June 25, 2005*

MAUREEN WAS FEELING WILDLY GUILTY about neglecting Peter. But when she returned from her outing with Jean-Claude, he was nowhere to be found.

"I have not seen the Abbé since this morning," Roland informed her. "He had a late breakfast, then I saw him leave shortly after in your hired car. But it is Sunday. Perhaps he went to church? We have many in the area."

Maureen nodded, not giving it too much more thought. Peter was wordly and spoke fluent French, so it was logical that he may have planned to go in search of a mass and then to take in more of the sights in this extraordinary region.

She was scheduled to have dinner in the château later with Tammy—something she was anxious to do, but not at the expense of hurting Peter's feelings. She asked Roland, "Do you have any way of contacting Tamara Wisdom? I forgot to ask if she has a cell phone with her."

"Oui, she does. And I can do that for you as I need to ask her something for Lord Bérenger. Is something wrong?"

"No, I was just wondering if she would mind if Peter joined us for dinner."

"I am sure it will not be a problem, Mademoiselle Paschal. In fact, I believe she is expecting the Abbé to attend. She requested that I set dinner for the four of you at eight o'clock."

Maureen thanked Roland and retreated to her room. She stopped first at Peter's door and knocked—no reply. She jiggled the gilded knob and pushed the door gently open, peeking her head in. Peter's things were laid out neatly by the side of the bed—his leather-bound Bible and his crystal rosary beads. But he was nowhere to be seen.

Maureen returned to her palatial suite and removed the larger of her Moleskine notebooks. She wanted to write about Montsegur while it was fresh in her mind. But as she slid the elastic strap off the notebook and opened the pages, she was surprised when another story of martyrdom came to her mind.

Maureen had climbed the rugged mountains of the Dead Sea region at sunrise on her visit to the Holy Land, hiking the rocky, serpentine trail alongside a handful of seekers. She was unsure just what drove her to undertake the arduous climb. Even so early, the heat was powerful. The others on the path that morning were all Jewish, and for them this was an obvious and emotional pilgrimage. Maureen could make no such claim of heritage or religion.

She paused many times on the way up to admire the almost painfully beautiful vistas of light and color as they played over the strange, lunar landscape and glittered off the salt crystals of the dormant water. The view inspired her, giving her the strength to push her screaming muscles farther up the mountain.

She listened to snippets of conversation from the other pilgrims as they climbed. She did not understand the Hebrew language, but their passion for their journey was unmistakable. She wondered if they were discussing the Masada martyrs who chose to die rather than live in bondage or subject their women and children to Roman slavery and debasement.

Reaching the summit, she explored the remains of what was once a great fortress, wandering through ruined rooms and crumbling walls. Because it was a surprisingly large space, she soon found herself alone, separated from the other pilgrims, who were exploring for their own reasons elsewhere on the sacred site. There was an absorbing stillness in this place, a calm silence that felt like a ruin unto itself, as tangible as the stones. She was immersed in that sensation as she stared almost absently at the ruins of a Roman mosaic. Then, she saw her.

It happened fast and came completely unbidden, like her other visions. She couldn't recall how she knew the child was there; she just knew that there was a presence in the room. About ten feet away, a child of no more than four or five was staring up at her with huge, dark eyes. Her clothes were torn and filthy; tears mixed with the mud that splashed across her face. She did not speak, but in that moment Maureen knew the child's name was Hannah—and that she had witnessed events that no child should ever endure.

Maureen also knew that somehow the child had survived the unspeakable tragedy of Masada. She had left this place and taken the stories of it with her. That was her legacy, to share the truth of what had occurred there to her people.

She did not know how long the child appeared before her. There was a sense of timelessness to her visions. Were they minutes? Seconds? Or eternities?

Later, Maureen spoke with one of the Israeli guides at Masada. He was young and open, and she surprised herself by telling him of the encounter. He shrugged and said he did not believe it was unnatural or uncommon to see such a thing in so emotional a place. He explained that there were legends of survivors from Masada, of a woman and several children who hid in a cave and ultimately escaped, taking the true story with them and preserving it in their way.

Maureen believed that little Hannah was one of those children.

She had wondered so many times since that day why she had seen that vision, why it had happened to her. She felt unworthy of it, undeserving of such a profound encounter with the sacred history of the Jewish people. But after her experience at Montsegur, it all began to come together in a beautiful pattern that Maureen was finally beginning to understand. Little Hannah and the Cathar girl known as La Paschalina were related, in spirit if not in blood. They were the children left to carry on and hold the stories within them, so that the truth would never be lost. It was their destiny to become humanity's most sacred teachers. These little girls, and what they grew to become, embodied the history and survival of the human race. Their experiences had no boundaries; these stores belonged to all people, regardless of ethnic identity or religious beliefs.

By grasping that connection, couldn't we all come together in the knowledge that we are all one tribe, ultimately?

Maureen thanked Hannah and La Paschalina in a whisper as she finished her journal entry.

Tammy ran into the château, hoping to avoid contact with anyone before she could take a shower. She was exhausted and felt that every inch of her body was dirty. But solitude was not to come so easily. She was intercepted by Roland as she reached the door of her room.

He opened it for her and stepped inside. "You are all right?" he asked with grave concern.

"I'm fine." She had practiced a speech in her head all the way home, but one look at the enormous Occitan and her heart melted. She was so relieved to be here, safe in the house and safe with him, that she threw herself against the massive strength of his body and cried.

Roland was stunned. He had never seen vulnerability in this woman before. "Tamara, what has happened? Did he hurt you? You must tell me."

Tammy tried to steady herself. She stopped crying and looked up at Roland. "No, he didn't hurt me. But . . ."

"But what, what has happened?"

She reached up and touched his face, the angular, masculine face that she was growing to love.

"Roland," she whispered. "Roland . . . you were right about who killed your father. And now I think we can prove it."

*. . . Easa was the child of the prophecy, this was something everyone knew. And the prophecy brought with it a destiny that had to be fulfilled in an exact way. Easa did this; not for any glory to himself, but to make his role as the messiah easier to understand and embrace for the children of Israel. The closer Easa's role came to fulfilling the exact nature of the prophecy, the stronger the people would be when he was gone.*

*But even for all of that, we did not expect it to happen the way that it did.*

*Easa entered Jerusalem on the back of an ass fulfilling the prophet Zechariah's words about the arrival of the anointed one. We followed him with palms and sang hosannas. A great crowd joined us as we entered Jerusalem, and there was a sense of joy and hope in the air. Many followed us in from Bethany, and we were met by Simon's compatriots, the Zealots. Even representatives of one reclusive Essene movement had left their desert dwelling to accompany us on this triumphant day.*

*The children of Israel rejoiced that this chosen one had come to liberate them from Rome and the yoke of oppression, poverty, and misery. This son of the prophecy had grown to be a man and a messiah. There was strength in our hearts, and in our numbers.*

THE ARQUES GOSPEL OF MARY MAGDALENE,
THE BOOK OF THE TIME OF DARKNESS

# CHAPTER THIRTEEN

*Château des Pommes Bleues*
*June 25, 2005*

Dinner at the château was always an elaborate affair when guests were present, and this night was no different. Bérenger Sinclair had spared neither his kitchen staff nor his wine cellar to present a Languedoc feast of medieval and decadent proportions. The conversation was equally robust. Tammy had pulled herself together with Oscar-worthy aplomb. Donning her trademark saucy attitude, she appeared to be fully herself once again.

Maureen enjoyed watching Sinclair and Tammy spar with Peter, secure in the knowledge that her cousin could hold his own in any theological debate. She certainly knew that from firsthand experience.

Sinclair started out on a soapbox. "We know historically that the New Testament as it exists now was shaped at the Council of Nicea. Emperor Constantine and his council had many gospels to choose from, and yet selected only four—four that were altered dramatically. It was an act of censorship that changed history."

"It can't help but make you wonder what he decided to conceal from us," Tammy chimed in.

Peter wasn't bothered in the least by an argument he had heard a hundred times. He surprised both of his would-be antagonists with his answer. "Don't stop there. Remember, we don't even know for sure who wrote those four Gospels. In fact, the only thing we're even moderately sure about is that they *weren't* written by Matthew, Mark, Luke, and John. They were probably attributed to the evangelists sometime in the second century, and some would say those aren't even very good guesses. And a further thing. Even with the staggering documentation available in the Vatican, we can't say with certainty what language the original Gospels were written in."

Tammy looked taken aback. "I thought they were written in Greek."

Peter shook his head. "The earliest versions we have are in Greek, but they are possibly translations from some earlier form. We simply can't be sure."

"Why does the original language matter?" Maureen asked. "I mean, other than translation errors."

"Because the original language is the first indication of the author's identity and location," Peter explained. "For example, if the original Gospels were written in Greek, that would indicate authors who were Hellenized—a Greek influence that would have been reserved for the elite, the worldly, and the educated. We don't traditionally think of the apostles in that way, so we would expect something else, a common vernacular like Aramaic or Hebrew. If we were certain the originals were written in Greek, we would have to take a close look at what that means about the original followers of Jesus."

"The Gnostic gospels found in Egypt were written in Coptic," Tammy added.

Peter corrected her gently. "There are Coptic texts, but many were written originally from Greek originals and then copied into Coptic."

"So what does that tell us?" Maureen asked.

"Well, we know none of the original followers were Egyptian, so it tells us that some took their earliest ministry to Egypt and that early Christianity flourished there. Thus, Coptic Christians."

"But then what do we know with certainty about the four Gospels?" Maureen was curious about the direction of the conversation. She hadn't had the luxury of time during her research to dig too deeply into issues surrounding the history of the New Testament. She had focused strictly on the passages relevant to Mary Magdalene.

Peter answered. "We know that Mark came first and that Matthew is nearly an exact copy of Mark, with almost six hundred identical passages. Luke is also very similar, although there the author gives us a few new insights that aren't found in Mark and Matthew. And the Gospel of John is the greatest mystery of the four, as it takes a very different position politically and socially from the other three."

"I do know that there are people who even believe Mary Magdalene wrote the fourth Gospel, the one attributed to John," Maureen added. "I interviewed a really brilliant scholar during my research who made that claim. I don't necessarily agree with him, but I found the idea fascinating."

Sinclair shook his head and replied vehemently. "No, I don't believe that. Mary's version is still out there, waiting to be discovered."

"The fourth Gospel is the great mystery of the New Testament," Peter said. "There are many theories, including the committee theory: that it was written by several people over a period of time in an attempt to convey the events of Jesus' life in a specific manner."

Tammy was listening to Peter with interest. "But it seems to me that so many traditional Christians want to just plug their ears and ignore these facts," she responded. She was passionate about this subject and had been involved in many arguments over the years. "They don't want to know this history; they just want to blindly believe what the Church tells them. Or what their clerics tell them."

Peter responded with passion. "No, no. You're missing the point. It's not blindness; it's faith. For people of faith the facts simply don't matter. But don't make the common mistake of confusing faith with ignorance."

Sinclair laughed, a derisive sound.

"I'm very serious," Peter continued. "People of faith believe that the New Testament was divinely inspired; therefore it doesn't matter who actually wrote the Gospels or what language they were written in. The authors were inspired by God to do so. And whoever made the decision to edit the Gospels at the Councils of Constantinople or Nicea, they must have been divinely inspired to do that as well. And so on, and so on. It's a matter of faith, and there's no room for history there. Nor can you debate it. Faith is something that can't be argued."

No one replied, waiting to see what else Peter was going to say. "You think I don't know the history of my own Church? I do, which is why Maureen's research and your opinions don't offend me in the least. By the way, do you realize that there are some scholars who even believe that the Gospel of Luke was written by a woman?"

It was Sinclair's turn to look surprised. "Really? I hadn't heard that. And that idea doesn't bother you?"

"Not at all," Peter replied. "The importance of women in the early church, as well as in the continuation of Christianity, is something we can't deny. Nor should we want to, when we consider great women like Clare of Assisi, who kept the Franciscan movement together after Francis died so young." Peter looked at the amazed faces of Sinclair and Tammy. "Sorry to spoil a perfectly good argument, but I agree with the idea that Mary Magdalene deserves the title Apostle of the Apostles."

"You do?" This was an incredulous Tammy.

"Absolutely. In *Acts,* Luke provides the specific requirements for becoming an apostle: one must have been a part of Jesus' ministry while He lived, one must have been a witness to His crucifixion and a witness to His resurrection. Now, to be entirely literal about this, there is only one person who fits all of these requirements—and that is Mary Magdalene. The male apostles didn't witness the crucifixion, which really is somewhat embarrassing. And Mary Magdalene is the first person to whom Jesus appears when He is risen."

Maureen was trying her hardest to keep from laughing at the expressions on the faces of Sinclair and Tammy. They were stunned by this show of Peter's intellect and personality.

Peter continued. "Arguably, the only other persons to technically fit the description of apostles are other Marys—the Virgin Mary, as well as Mary Salome and Mary Jacoby, both of whom are accounted for at the crucifixion and at the sepulcher on the day of resurrection."

When Peter caught Maureen's eye she could no longer hold it in. Her laughter rang through the room.

"What?" Peter asked mischievously.

"I'm sorry," Maureen apologized, hiding behind a quick sip of her wine for a moment. "It's just—well, Peter does tend to take people by surprise, and I always find it amusing to watch."

Sinclair nodded. "I concede that you are nothing like I anticipated, Father Healy."

"And what did you anticipate, Lord Sinclair?" Peter asked.

"Well, with all due apologies, I expected something of a Roman watchdog, I suppose. Someone immersed in dogma and doctrine."

Peter laughed. "Ah, but Lord Sinclair, you have forgotten a very important thing. I am not simply a priest; I'm a Jesuit. And an Irish one at that."

"Touché, Father Healy." Sinclair raised his glass in Peter's direction. Peter's order, the Society of Jesus, better known to the world as the Jesuits, focused on education and scholarly pursuits. While they were currently the single largest order in Catholicism, conservatives within the Roman Catholic Church traditionally have felt that the Jesuits were a law unto themselves and have been for several hundred years. They were nicknamed "footsoldiers of the Pope," yet there had been rumors for centuries that the Jesuits elected their own leader within the order and answered to the Roman pontiff only as a matter of formality and ceremony.

Tammy was curious now. "Do other priests in your order feel this way? I mean, about the role of women."

"It is always unwise to generalize," Peter answered. "As Maureen said, people tend to stereotype the clergy, assuming we all think with one brain, which is simply not true. Priests are people, and many of us are highly intelligent and educated as well as committed to our faith. Each man draws his own conclusions.

"But there is something we have discussed at length about Mary Magdalene and the accuracy of the four Gospels. The male apostles must have found it somewhat embarrassing that Jesus trusted His entire mission to this woman, whatever her position was in His life and

His ministry. She was still a female at a time when women were not considered equal to men. So the evangelists would have been forced to write that account of her because it was the truth, no matter how embarrassing that was for them. Because even if the authors of the Gospels played with other facts, they would not have altered this most important element of Jesus' resurrection—that He came first to Mary Magdalene. He didn't appear to the male apostles, He appeared to *her*. So I believe that the authors of the Gospels had no choice but to write this, because it's simply the truth."

Tammy's admiration for Peter was growing; it was visible on her expressive face. "So you're willing to explore the possibility that Mary Magdalene may have been the most important disciple? Or even that she may have been more than that?"

Peter looked directly at Tammy, this time very seriously. "I'm willing to explore anything that brings us closer to an honest understanding of the nature of Jesus Christ, our Lord and Savior."

It was a great evening for Maureen. Peter was her most trusted adviser, but she had grown to admire Sinclair and found him fascinating. For her cousin to find common ground with the eccentric Scotsman was a profound relief for her. Perhaps they could now all work together to explore the strange circumstances of Maureen's visions.

At the conclusion of the meal, Peter, who had spent the day exploring the region on his own, claimed exhaustion and excused himself. Tammy made a comment about getting back to some scripting on her documentary and did the same. This left Maureen with Sinclair on her own. Bolstered by the wine and conversation, she cornered Sinclair.

"I think it's time you kept your promise," she said.

"Which promise is that, my dear?"

"I want to see the letter from my father."

Sinclair seemed to consider this for a moment. After a slight hesitation, he conceded. "Very well. Come with me."

Sinclair led Maureen down a winding corridor to a locked room. Removing a sizable key ring from his pocket, he opened the door and ushered Maureen into his private study. He touched a switch on the right as they entered, which served to illuminate a huge painting on the far wall.

Maureen gasped, then squealed with delight. "Cowper! It's my painting!"

Sinclair laughed. *"Lucretia Borgia Reigns in the Vatican in the Absence of Pope Alexander VI.* I confess that I acquired it after reading your book. It took quite a bit of haggling to obtain it from the Tate, but I am a very determined man when I want something."

Maureen approached the painting with reverence, admiring the artistry and the color used by early twentieth-century British artist Frank Cadogan Cowper. The painting depicted Lucrezia Borgia enthroned on high in the Vatican, surrounded by a lavish sea of red-robed cardinals. She had first seen the painting at its former home, the Tate Britain museum in London. It had struck her like lightning. For Maureen, this single image had explained the hundreds of years of character assassination that this daughter of the Pope had endured. She had been called every distasteful name imaginable, murderess and incestuous whore among them. Lucrezia Borgia had been punished by male medieval historians because she had had the audacity to sit on the sacred throne of Saint Peter and issue papal instructions during her father's absences.

"Lucrezia was a driving force behind my book. Her story embodied the theme of the woman who was reviled and stripped of her true power in history," Maureen explained to Sinclair.

Maureen's research revealed that the devastating accusations of incest were devised by Lucrezia's first husband, a violent lout who had been ruined after their marriage was annulled. He started the rumors that Lucrezia wanted an annulment because she was sexually involved with her own father and brother. These vicious lies endured for centuries, perpetuated by the enemies of the much-envied Borgia family.

"They're bloodline, you know."

"The Borgias?" Maureen was incredulous. "How?"

"Through the Sarah-Tamar line. Their ancestors were Cathars who escaped into Spain. They sought refuge at the monastery in Montserrat and eventually assimilated into Aragon, where they adopted the name Borgia, before immigrating to Italy. But their choice of location was not an accident, nor was their legendary ambition. Rodrigo Borgia was determined to sit on the throne, to restore Rome to those he believed were its rightful rulers."

Maureen shook her head in amazement as Sinclair continued.

"The installation of his daughter on the throne was emblematic of his Cathar descent. Of course, women are equal to men in The Way, in all matters, including spiritual leadership. Cesare was making a statement, which would cause the downfall of his daughter. Sadly, history now remembers the Borgias only as evil and scheming."

Maureen agreed. "Some writers have even gone so far as to call them the first family of organized crime. It just seems brutally unfair."

"It is, not to mention totally inaccurate."

"This bloodline information . . ." Maureen was still absorbing it all. "It certainly adds a new layer to history."

"Feel a sequel coming on, my dear?" Sinclair joked.

"I feel about two decades of research coming on, at the very least. I'm fascinated. I can't wait to see where this takes me."

"Yes, but first I think it is time to look at a chapter in your own life."

Maureen stiffened. She had begged him for this moment, insisted on it. It was the reason she had come to France in the first place. But now, she wasn't sure she wanted to know.

"Are you all right?" Sinclair sounded sincerely worried.

She nodded. "I'm fine. It's just that now that I'm here . . . I'm nervous, that's all."

Sinclair gestured to a chair and Maureen sat, gratefully. He opened a built-in filing cabinet with yet another key and extracted a folder, explaining to Maureen as he walked.

"I discovered this letter in my grandfather's archives years ago. When I learned about your work and saw your photograph and the ring, alarm bells went off in my head. I knew of Paschal descendants here in France, but I also remembered that there was once an American named Paschal who was important. I couldn't remember why, until I found this letter."

Sinclair placed the folder gently in front of Maureen and opened it to reveal yellowed paper and faded ink. "Would you like me to leave you alone?"

Maureen looked up at him but saw only understanding and security in his face. "No. Please stay with me."

Sinclair nodded, patting her hand gently, then sat down across the table from her, silent. Maureen picked up the folder and began to read.

"My dear Monsieur Gélis," the letter began.

"Gélis?" Maureen asked. "I thought this was to your grandfather."

Sinclair shook his head. "No, it was in my grandfather's files, but it was written to a local man here from an old Cathar family called Gélis."

Maureen thought briefly that she had heard the name before but didn't spend much time on it. She was too concerned about the remaining elements of the letter.

*Dear Monsieur Gélis,*

*Please forgive me, but I have no one else to turn to. I hear tell that you have great knowledge in matters of the spirit. That you are a true Christian man. I hope this is so. For many months I have been tormented by nightmares and visions of Our Lord on the cross. I have been visited by him and he has given me his pain.*

*But I do not write for myself. I write for my little daughter, my Maureen. She screams in the night and tells me of the same nightmares. She is little more than a baby. How can this be happening to her? How can I stop this before she feels the pain that I have felt?*

*I cannot stand to see my child like this. Her mother blames me; she threatens to take away my baby forever. Please help me. Please tell me what I can do to save my little girl.*

*With all my thanks,*
*Edouard Paschal*

Maureen could not see through her tears as she replaced the letter and allowed herself to sob.

Sinclair offered to stay with Maureen, but she declined. She was shaken to her core by the letter, and needed to be alone. She briefly considered waking Peter, but decided against it. She needed to think about this first. And Peter's recent slip about "promising her mother not to let the same thing happen" made her suspicious and uncomfortable. Peter had always been her anchor, the safe male figure in her life. She trusted him implicitly and knew he would never do anything that he didn't feel was in the best interest of her safety. But what if Peter were operating on misinformation? Peter's understanding of Maureen's childhood, which he refused to speak of in any concrete terms, came solely from her mother.

Her mother. Maureen sat on the expansive bed, reclining slightly on the embroidered pillows. Bernadette Healy had been a hard and uncompromising woman, or that's how Maureen remembered her. The only clues that she may have had a different disposition earlier in her life came from photographs; Maureen had some snapshots of her mother in Louisiana, holding the baby Maureen. Bernadette beamed at the camera, every inch the proud new mother.

How often had Maureen wondered what changed Bernadette, turned her from the young and hopeful mother in the photos to the cold disciplinarian of her memory? When they moved to Ireland, Maureen was raised predominantly by her aunt and uncle—Peter's parents. Her mother deposited Maureen into the safety and anonymity of the remote farming community in the west of Ireland, while Bernadette herself returned to nursing in Galway city.

Maureen saw her mother rarely, when Bernadette would return to the farm out of a sense of duty or obligation. Those visits were strained as her mother became more and more of a stranger. Maureen embraced Peter's family as her own and was absorbed into the healing warmth of their large and boisterous brood. Auntie Ailish, Peter's mother, filled the maternal role. Maureen had developed her warmth and humor through the influence of Peter's family. A tendency toward restraint, order, and caution came from her mother.

On a few occasions, usually following one of Bernadette's disastrous and destructive visits, Ailish took her niece aside.

"You mustn't judge your mother too harshly, Maureen," she said in her patient way. "Bernadette loves you. Perhaps her downfall is that she loves you too much. But she has had a hard life, and it changed her. When you're older, you will understand."

Time and fate had removed any chance of Maureen ever growing to know or understand her mother better. Bernadette was struck with lymphoma when Maureen was in her teens; she died quickly. Peter had been summoned to Bernadette's deathbed and was the priest who administered last rites. He heard her final confession, and had carried the weight of his aunt's shocking revelations on his shoulders every day of his life. But he would not discuss any of this with Maureen, citing the seal of the confessional.

And now there was a new piece of the puzzle. Maureen had to attempt an interpretation of the meaning of her father's letter, a glimpse into the complex legacy he may have left for her. She would sleep on it tonight, then discuss it with Peter in the morning with a clearer head.

*Carcassonne*
*June 25, 2005*

DEREK WAINWRIGHT SLEPT HARD. The cocktail of prescription drugs and red wine had mixed with his exhaustion and stress to induce a state of oblivion.

Had he been more conscious, perhaps he would have been warned—by the footsteps, by the sound of his door opening, or by the whispered chanting of his attacker.

"Neca eos omnes. Neca eos omnes. Deus suos agnoset."

Kill them all. Kill them all. God will know his own.

But by the time the red cord was tied around his neck, it was too late for Derek Wainwright. Unlike Roger-Bernard Gélis, he did not have the good fortune of being dead by the time the ritual began.

*Château des Pommes Bleues*

MAUREEN CRINGED at the knock on her door. She wasn't up to Sinclair or Peter at the moment. She was relieved when the voice on the other side was female.

"Reenie? It's me."

Maureen opened the door to Tammy, who took one look at her and groaned. "You look wretched."

"Gee, thanks. I feel wonderful."

"Do you want to talk about it?"

"Not yet. I'm just processing some personal stuff."

Tammy hesitated. Maureen snapped to attention as she realized she was seeing something completely new: Tamara Wisdom was nervous.

"What's wrong, Tammy?"

Tammy sighed, running her hand through her long hair. "I hate to do this to you when you're already emotional, but I really need to talk to you."

Maureen gestured to the sitting area. "Come in and sit."

Tammy shook her head. "No, I need you to come with me. I have to show you something."

"Okay," Maureen said simply, and followed Tammy through the labyrinthine corridors of the Château des Pommes Bleues. After all that had happened, she didn't think there was much that could surprise her. She was wrong.

They entered the modern media room where Sinclair had first shown Maureen and Peter the maps of the local area compared to the constellations. Tammy pointed to a leather couch that was positioned before a large-screen television set. She picked up a remote control and sat next to Maureen. Taking a deep breath, she began her explanation.

"I want to show you some footage I've been working on for my next documentary. It's about the bloodline. Now, I need you to hear me out on this because it's very important, and it ultimately comes back to you and your part in this whole situation.

"As you know, the mystery of Jesus and Mary Magdalene has inspired a lot of secret societies and cloak-and-dagger groups. They whisper about the bloodline, perform super-secret rituals."

Tammy hit the remote and brought the monitor to life. A slow slide show filled the screen, one image at a time. The first images were paintings of Mary Magdalene by the masters of Renaissance and Baroque art.

"Some of these groups are made up of fanatics, but some are truly good and spiritual people. Sinclair is one of the good guys, so you're on safe ground here. Let me just be clear about that." She paused for a moment, gathering her thoughts.

"I wanted to make a film that showed the scope of this whole concept—how far the idea of a sacred bloodline really reaches in the Western world and our history. The idea here is to show a wide range of who Jesus and Mary Magdalene's descendants were—and are. From the famous to the infamous to the truly anonymous."

Familiar portraits of historical and religious figures filled the screen as Tammy continued.

"Some of them may surprise you. Charlemagne. King Arthur. Robert the Bruce. Saint Francis of Assisi."

"Wait a minute. Saint Francis of Assisi?"

Tammy nodded. "You bet. His mother, Lady Pica, was born in Tarascon. Pure Cathar stock of the Sarah-Tamar line, from the noble family Bourlemont. That's how he got his name, you know. He was born Giovanni, but his parents called him Francesco because he reminded them so much of his mother's French-Cathar side of the family. Have you ever been to Assisi?"

Maureen shook her head. Every new revelation was astonishing to her, overwhelming. She watched in fascination as images of the Italian village of Assisi, the home of the Franciscan movement, filled the screen.

"You need to see it; it's one of the most magical places on earth. And the spirit of Saint Francis and his partner, Saint Clare, is still very much alive there. I believe they were reliving the Jesus and Mary Magdalene roles. But look closely at the artwork in the Basilica of St. Francis. The Italian master Giotto dedicated an entire chapel of art to Mary Magdalene. It contains a mural of Mary Magdalene arriving on the shores of France following the crucifixion. He was definitely making a statement. And there is a lot of Cathar sentiment in what we think of as Franciscan thought."

She paused on Giotto's portrait of Saint Francis receiving the stigmata from heaven.

"Francis is the only saint on record to manifest all five points of the stigmata. Why? The bloodline. He is a descendant of Jesus Christ. I think there is an argument that any authenticated stigmatist is probably from the bloodline. But what's important about Francis is that he has all five. And no one else has ever had that."

Maureen was counting, trying to keep up with Tammy. "Both palms, both feet—that's four—and . . . ?"

"The right side. Where the centurion pierced Jesus with the spear. But I have to correct you. The truest authentic stigmata does not occur on the palms, but on the wrists. Contrary to popular belief, Christ wasn't nailed by his hands. He was nailed through the wrist bones. The hands aren't strong enough to support the weight of the body.

"So while stigmata have been authenticated in the hands, like with Saint Padre Pio, it is wrist stigmata that really cause the Church to snap to attention. That's what makes Francis here so important. Although artists like Giotto show the stigmata in the hands for dramatic effect, historical accounts tell us a different story. Francis had all five points, including the wrists."

Tammy released the pause button to reveal the next image, the golden statue of Joan of Arc in Paris. The footage cut to another Joan image, the statue in Saunière's garden that they had viewed two days prior.

"Remember when Peter asked me about this Joan statue? He said the world thinks of her as a symbol of conventional Catholicism. Well, here is why she is anything but that."

Tammy clicked to a portrait of Joan of Arc holding her trademark "Jhesus-Maria" banner.

"Christians have long believed that Joan's motto was a reference to Christ and his mother because her banner said "Jhesus-Maria." But it wasn't. It was a reference to Christ and Mary Magdalene, which is why she hyphenated the name, to show them joined together. Jesus and his wife, who were Joan's ancestors."

"But I thought she was a peasant. A . . . shepherdess." Maureen groaned out loud, the realization striking as she said the word.

"Exactly. A shepherdess. And what about her name? 'Of Arc' indicates she had some association with this region, Arques, yet she was born in Domrémy. Joan of Arques—it's a reference to her bloodline. And to her dangerous legacy. Berry told you about the prophecy, right? About The Expected One?"

Maureen nodded slowly. "I don't think the world is ready for this. I don't think I am ready for this."

Tammy hit pause and turned her full attention to Maureen. "I need you to listen to the rest of Joan's story, because it's important. How much do you know about her?"

"Probably what most people in the world know. She fought to restore the dauphin to the throne of France, she led battles against the English. She was burned at the stake as a witch although everyone knows that she wasn't . . ."

"She was burned at the stake because she had visions."

Maureen was weighing it all, trying to figure out where Tammy was going. She still wasn't quite following, so Tammy explained with emphasis.

"Joan had visions, divine visions. And she was bloodline. What does that mean to you?"

Tammy didn't wait for her answer. "Joan was The Expected One, and everybody knew it. She was going to fulfill the prophecy. She had visions that would have led her to the Magdalene Gospel. That's why they had to silence her permanently."

Maureen was flabbergasted. "But . . . was Joan's birth date the same as mine?"

"Yes, but you won't see it written that way historically. It's usually shown as sometime in January. It was deliberately obscured in an effort to protect her true identity, both as a royal bastard and as the long-awaited Grail princess."

"How do you know this? Is there documentation that backs it up?"

"Yes. But you have to stop thinking like an academic. You have to read between the lines because it's all there. And don't discount the local legends. You're Irish, you know the power of the oral traditions and how they are handed down. The Cathars were no different than the Celts; in fact, there is a ton of evidence that those two cultures blended throughout France and Spain. They protected their traditions by not writing them down and not leaving evidence for their enemies. But the legend of Joan as The Expected One is prevalent here when you scratch the surface."

"I thought the English forces executed Joan."

"Wrong. The English arrested Joan, but it was the French clergy who prosecuted her and insisted on her death. Joan's tormentor was a cleric called Cauchon. That's a big joke in these parts, as 'cochon' means 'pig' in French. Well, it was that swine who extracted Joan's confession and then twisted the evidence to force her martyrdom. Cauchon had to kill Joan before she was able to fulfill her role as The Expected One."

Maureen was silent, listening intently as Tammy continued. "And Joanie wasn't the last shepherdess to die. Do you remember the statue of the saint in Rennes-le-Château? The girl carrying a lamb?"

"Saint Germaine." Maureen nodded. "I had a dream about her that night."

"That's because she's another daughter of the vernal equinox and the resurrection. She is depicted with a paschal lamb for obvious reasons, but also with a young ram, representing her birth at the beginning of Aries."

Maureen remembered the statue well. She had been very moved by the solemn face of the young shepherdess.

"Her mother was of high rank in the bloodline, the Marie de Negre of her time. When Germaine was an infant, her mother died very mysteriously. Germaine was raised by an abusive foster family who murdered her in her sleep when she was in her late teens."

Tammy took Maureen's hand, suddenly very serious. "Listen to me, Maureen. For a thousand years there have been people who would kill to stop the discovery of Mary's gospel. Do you understand what I'm saying to you?"

The gravity of the situation began to impress itself upon Maureen. She suddenly felt very cold as Tammy drove the point home.

"There are still people who would kill to stop the fulfillment of that prophecy. If those people believe that you are The Expected One, you may be in serious danger."

Tammy had had the foresight to bring a bottle of fine local wine into the room with her. She re-filled Maureen's glass as the two women sat in silence for a moment.

Maureen finally spoke. She looked at Tammy, her tone somewhat accusatory. "You knew a lot more than you led me to believe back in L.A., didn't you?"

Tammy sighed and leaned back hard against the couch. "I'm really sorry, Maureen. I couldn't tell you everything I knew then."

*I still can't,* she thought dismally before continuing. "I didn't want to scare you off. You would have never made this trip and we couldn't take that chance."

"We? You mean you and Sinclair? Are you a member of his Blue Apples society?"

"It's not that simple. Look, Sinclair will do everything he can to protect you."

"Because he thinks I'm his golden girl?"

"Yes, but also because he truly cares about you. I can see that in him. But Berry also feels the responsibility. He led you to the slaughter, like your proverbial paschal lamb namesake, when he announced you in that damn dress. In his excitement, he didn't think it through."

Maureen took another sip of the rich red wine. "So what do you suggest I do? This is foreign territory to me, Tammy. Do I leave? Just forget any of this ever happened and go back to my life?" She gave an ironic little laugh. "Sure, no problem."

Tammy looked sympathetic. "Maybe you should, just for the sake of your physical safety. Berry can sneak you and Peter out of here tomorrow. It will kill him, but he'll do it if you ask."

"And then what? I go back to L.A. where I'm haunted for the rest of my life by nightmares and visions? Where my work suffers because I will never be able to look at history again in the same way, yet don't dare risk further investigation because of some shadowy henchmen who would harm me? And who are these dangerous people? Why do they want to stop the prophecy so much that they would kill for it?"

Tammy stood up and began to pace. "There are a number of factions who have a vested interest in keeping Mary Magdalene's views a secret. There's the traditional Church, of course. But they're not the dangerous ones."

"Then who is? Damn it, Tammy, I'm tired of riddles and I'm sick of games. Somebody owes me a complete explanation, and I want one fast."

Tammy nodded somberly. "And you will have one in the morning. But it's not my place to give it to you."

"Then where is Sinclair? I want to speak to him. Now."

Tammy shrugged helplessly. "I'm afraid that's not possible. He left shortly after your departure from his study. I'm not sure where he went, but he said he wouldn't be back until very, very late. He'll tell you everything in the morning, I promise you."

But by the time Bérenger Sinclair returned to Château des Pommes Bleues, the world had changed.

*. . . Easa's arrival was certainly noted by all of the authorities in Jerusalem, from the priests in the Temple to Pilate's guard. The Romans were concerned about Passover. They feared uprising or rioting could be incited by any surge of Jewish sentiment or nationalism. And because there were Zealots with us, Pilate had no choice but to take note.*

*There were those among our own who had brothers in the priestly caste. They informed us that the high priest Caiaphas, the son-in-law of Jonathan Annas, who so despised us, held a council on "this idea of the Nazarene turned messiah."*

*I have said my piece about this man Annas in the past, and here I will tell more of his deeds. But I do so with one warning:* **do not condemn many for the actions of one man.** *For the priestly caste is the same as all others—some are just and good in their hearts, some are not. There are those who followed the orders of Jonathan Annas in the dark days—priests and men. Some did so because they were obedient to the Temple, because they were good and righteous men, just as my own brother had been when he made that terrible choice.*

*Our people were misled by corrupt leaders, blinded to the truth by those who had a duty to give them something more. Some opposed us because they feared more Jewish bloodshed and wanted only to find peace for the people during Passover. I cannot fault anyone for that choice.*

*Should we condemn those who did not see the light? No. Easa taught us we must not shun them; we must forgive them.*

THE ARQUES GOSPEL OF MARY MAGDALENE,
THE BOOK OF THE TIME OF DARKNESS

# Chapter Fourteen

*Château des Pommes Bleues*
*June 25, 2005*

aureen returned to her room feeling heavy with dread and anxiety. She was in over her head and had no idea what to do about it. She dressed for bed slowly, trying to think with a brain muddled by overload and a little too much red wine. *This is an exercise in futility,* she thought to herself. *I'll never sleep tonight.*

But as she surrendered to the sumptuous comfort of the massive bed, sleep claimed her in a matter of minutes. And so did the dream.

*The petite woman in the red veil followed quietly in the darkness. Her heart beat in rapid rhythm as she tried to keep up with the two men and their long strides. This was all or nothing—a terrible risk for each of them, but the most important task of her life.*

*They ran quickly down the exterior stairs; this was the greatest risk of their journey. They would be exposed to the Jerusalem night and could only pray that the guards had been drawn away, as promised.*

*They looked at each other with relief as they approached the subterranean entrance. No guards. One man stayed on the outside to keep watch. The other man, who knew the way through the corridors of the prison, continued to lead the woman. He stopped before a heavy door, removing a key that had been concealed beneath the folds of his tunic.*

*He looked at the woman and said something to her emphatically. They all knew there was very little time before they risked discovery, she most of all.*

*The man turned the key in the lock and opened the door to admit her, closing it quickly behind her to provide privacy to the woman and the prisoner.*

*She did not know what she had expected, but it wasn't this. Her beautiful man had been treated cruelly, of that there was no doubt. His clothes were torn, and he had suffered bruises on his face. Yet for all of his injury, he had a smile of warmth and love for the woman as she threw herself into his arms.*

*He held her for only the briefest moment, as time was against them. Next he took her by the shoulders and began to issue instructions— emphatic, urgent directives. She nodded over and over again, assuring him she understood and that all of his wishes would be carried out. Finally, he placed his hand lightly on the swell of her belly and gave her one final instruction. When he was finished, she fell into his arms for a final time, trying valiantly to stifle the sound of the sobs that wracked her body.*

The same sobs shook Maureen. She cried uncontrollably, burying her face in the pillow so the others in the château would not hear her. Peter's room was closest, and she certainly didn't want to attract his attention.

This dream was the worst of all. It was too real, too vivid. She felt every second of strain and grief, felt the urgency of the directives that were being given. And she knew why. These were the final instructions given to Mary Magdalene by Jesus Christ on the eve of Good Friday.

And there was another urgent directive in the dream, this one given to Maureen. She had heard the man's voice in her ear—was it her ear? Or was it Mary's ear? She watched Mary from the outside, and yet she felt everything Mary experienced on the inside. And she heard the final instructions.

"Because it is time. Go, and be sure that our message lives on."

Maureen sat up in bed and tried to think. She was operating on instinct now and on something else—something indefinable and without logic or reason. It was something she had to trust with her heart and not overanalyze with her brain.

It was full night in the Languedoc, black and silky, and the beams of a bright moon shone into Maureen's room. Moonlight struck the lovely face of *Mary Magdalene in the Desert* as Ribera's framed madonna looked heavenward for divine direction. Maureen decided to follow Mary's direction. For the first time since she was eight years old, she began to pray for guidance.

Later, Maureen couldn't remember how long it had been before she heard the voice. Seconds? Minutes? It didn't matter. When she heard it, she knew. It was just like in the Louvre, the same insistent female whisper calling to her, leading her forward. This time it called her name.

"Maureen. Maureen . . . ," it whispered with growing urgency.

She threw on clothing and shoes, afraid to stall too long and lose contact with the ethereal guide who was directing her. She opened the door of her room carefully, praying that it wouldn't squeak and awaken anyone. As for Mary Magdalene in the dream, stealth was of the utmost importance here. She couldn't be seen, not yet. This was something she had to do on her own.

Maureen's heart thumped in her ears as she tiptoed quietly through the château. Sinclair was gone and everyone else was asleep. As she made her way to the front door, she froze as the thought struck her. The alarm. The front door was secured with a coded alarm. She had watched Roland release it one morning after breakfast, but didn't see the number. He had punched the keyboard in three rapid strokes—tap, tap, tap. Three numbers. The alarm code was three digits.

Standing before the panel, she tried to think like Sinclair. What code would he use? Then she hit on it. July 22 was the feast day of Mary Magdalene. She pressed the code into the panel just as she had seen Roland do it. 7–2–2. Nothing. A red light flashed and there was a loud beep that caused Maureen to jump half out of her skin. *Damn! Please, please, don't let that have been loud enough to wake anyone.*

Maureen gathered herself and thought about it again. She knew she didn't have too much room for error. The alarm was certain to trigger if she stood here pressing incorrect codes. She lifted her head and looked upward, whispering, "Please, help me." She didn't know what she expected—would the voice answer? Would it give her the number? Would the door magically open and let her out? She waited for a moment, but none of these things occurred.

*Don't be an idiot. Come on, Maureen, think.* And then she heard it. Not the ephemeral woman's voice, but one in her own head, from memory. It was Sinclair's, from their first night in the château.

"My dear, you are the paschal lamb."

Maureen turned to the panel and hit the numbers. 3–2–2. 322. Her birthday, the day of the resurrection.

Two short blips sounded as a green light flashed and a mechanical voice said something in French. Maureen didn't wait to see if this woke anyone. She opened the heavy door and dashed out to where the moonlight illuminated the cobbled drive outside the château.

Maureen knew exactly where she was going. She didn't know why and she didn't know how; she just knew what her destination had to be. The voice was no longer audible, but she didn't need it. Something else had taken over, some knowing inside her that she followed without question.

She walked quickly around the side of the house, the same route that Sinclair had taken when they toured the grounds. There was a path here, overgrown and difficult, that would have been impossible to follow during a dark moon. But the full lunar light illuminated her way. She followed it at a half run until she saw her goal in the distance. Sinclair's Folly. The tower Alistair Sinclair had build in the middle of his property for no apparent reason.

Only there *was* a reason and she knew it now. It was a watchtower, just as Bérenger Saunière's Tour Magdala in Rennes-le-Château was a watchtower. Both men were keeping a close eye on the region for the day when their Mary decided to reveal her secrets. Both towers over-looked the area that had been defined as the location of the treasure trove. Maureen headed toward the tower in anticipation, but her heart sank as she drew closer. She remembered that Sinclair kept it locked. He had used a key to open it when they were here.

But wait, what about when they left? Maureen combed her memory as she came closer to the tower. They had been deep in conversation, and she didn't remember Sinclair locking it behind them. Could it be that he was so caught up in the discussion that he forgot? Would he have come back later to repair his negligence? Or did it lock automatically?

She didn't have long to wait. As she rounded the tower to the entrance, she saw the door—hanging open on its hinges.

She exhaled, a breath of relief and gratitude. "Thank you," she said skyward. She didn't know if it was Sinclair's doing or divine intervention, but whatever it was, it was very welcome.

Maureen climbed the stairs cautiously. It was pitch-black inside the strange stone building, and she could see nothing. She swallowed her tendency toward claustrophobia and pushed through the fear. Tammy's voice in her head reminded her that both Sinclair and Saunière built their towers according to spiritual numerology. Counting carefully, she knew to reach out for the door ahead of her at the twenty-second step. The door opened, and moonlight flooded the turret stairs as Maureen walked out to the roof deck.

She stood there for a minute, taking in the eerie beauty of the warm night. Not knowing what she was looking for, Maureen merely waited. She had come this far; she had to keep faith that her journey wouldn't stop here. The moonlight flashed on something she had not noticed when she was here with Sinclair. Carved into the stone wall behind the door was a sundial similar to the one they had seen in Rennes-le-Château. Maureen ran her hand along the carving, but wasn't familiar enough with the symbols to be certain if it was identical or merely comparable to the other. She considered this as she returned to the more central lookout post—she thought she had seen something on the horizon for a moment. She waited, watching in the Languedoc night.

Then she saw it, first as a flash in her peripheral vision. She did a double take, as she had done the first time she stood here with Sinclair. Something intangible, a bit of light or movement drew her eye to a place on the horizon. She turned toward it and watched as the moonlight seemed to swell, focusing an intense beam on a region straight ahead of her in the distance. The light struck something—a stone? A building?

Then she knew. The tomb. The light was swelling in the region of Poussin's tomb.

Of course. Hiding in plain sight, just as everything had been so far.

The light continued to move and shift, growing more opaque, as if taking on an elongated human form. It was an iridescent shape now, alive and dancing, moving across the fields toward her, then away from her. It was beckoning her to follow, showing her the way. She watched in absolute fascination for as long as she dared before making the only possible decision—to follow it.

Maureen propped open the door so the moonlight would illuminate the path down the stairs. She ran now, down the steps and out of the tower. But when she arrived outside again, she stopped. Getting to the tomb was a logistical problem in the dark. There was no path as the crow flies, no way to just cut across from here to there. It was a rugged terrain filled with huge boulders and strangling scrub brush.

The only certain path Maureen could think of was to exit through the driveway and follow the main road around the château grounds to the tomb. This would require her to walk past the main entrance of the house and expose her position on the public road. Moving as quickly as she dared through the tangled path, Maureen saw the house ahead of her. It appeared dark and silent. So far, so good. She moved along the edge of the long driveway, running now on the cobbles until she reached the front gates.

She was relieved to discover that the front gates on this side had motion detectors, and they opened with a mechanical whisper as Maureen approached. She dashed through them, turning left to follow the main road. It was the middle of the night, so it was unlikely that there would be many cars in this remote area. The stillness of the region threatened to engulf her—it was eerily quiet, the kind of silence that is disconcerting. The château grounds were expansive, and there were no immediate neighbors. The only sound came from Maureen's heart as it pounded within her chest.

She tried to keep to the edge of the road and watched carefully as she walked.

Maureen's heart jumped in her throat and she tried not to panic as a sound shattered the silence. An engine. Which direction was it coming from? The acoustics in this mountainous region made it difficult to know. She didn't wait to find out. Instead, she threw herself to the ground and prayed the brush and the long grass would shelter her from any headlights. She lay perfectly still as a car flew past and bright headlights illuminated the area around her. But the driver must have had other things on his mind as he never slowed as he passed the red-haired woman lying prone in the brush on the side of the road.

When she was certain the car was well out of range, Maureen picked herself up and shook the brush off. She kept moving, following the road. She glanced up at the château, now in the distance—was that a light in an upstairs window? She squinted for a moment, trying to determine where that window would be, but the building was too huge and she didn't have time to stop and figure it out.

She picked up her pace again, heart beating in increased excitement as she rounded a bend that she recognized. Just ahead of her, up on the rise, Poussin's tomb gleamed in the moonlight. "Et in Arcadia ego," Maureen whispered to herself. "Here we are."

She looked for the path that she and Peter had discovered a few days earlier, the one that had been obviously concealed. Maureen found it through a mixture of luck and memory and perhaps something more, and climbed to the rise, where the tomb had stood for centuries in staunch and silent testimony to an ancient legacy that had yet to reveal its secrets.

Now what? Maureen looked around the immediate area, then walked over and stood beside the tomb, thinking and waiting. She felt a brief moment of doubt, hearing Tammy's voice in her memory again. "Alistair excavated every inch of that land, and Sinclair has used every type of technology imaginable."

Not only that, but thousands of treasure seekers had traversed this ground too, over and over again. No one had ever found anything. Why would she be any different? What made her think she had the right to expect more?

But then she heard it, the voice from her dream. His voice. "Because it is time."

A loud rustling in the bushes startled her so much that she jumped, lost her footing, and fell to the ground. Her right hand came down on a sharp rock, and she could feel it slice her palm. She didn't have the luxury of thinking about the pain; she was too afraid of the sound. What was it? Maureen waited, perfectly still. She couldn't breathe. Then the rustling sound came again, as two perfect white doves flew out from the bushes and up into the Languedoc night.

Maureen breathed again. She picked herself up and moved toward the tangle of bushes that concealed a large cluster of boulders fronting the mountain. She pushed around with her hands to see if there was anything behind them. Nothing but sheer rock. She pushed harder on the rock, but there was no movement, no give of any kind. She stopped to rest for a minute, trying to think. Her hand was throbbing where she had cut it; blood streamed down across the palm. As Maureen raised her right hand to evaluate the damage, the moonlight bounced off her ring, glinting on the circular pattern etched in ancient copper.

The ring. She always took her jewelry off before going to bed, but tonight she was too spent to follow her normal routine and had fallen asleep with it on her finger. The circular star pattern. *As above, so below.* There was a duplicate of the pattern on the back of the monument.

Maureen dashed around to the other side of the tomb, pushing aside brush to find the pattern she knew was there. She ran her hand along the pattern, and the blood from her palm stained the inside of the circle. She held her breath and became perfectly still, waiting for what would come.

Nothing happened. The stillness stretched into minutes until Maureen felt trapped in a vacuum—all of the air had been sucked out of the night. Then, in one shattering moment, a sound penetrated the air. Coming from an unknown distance, perhaps from atop the strange hill that is Rennes-le-Château, a church bell rang out. The deep, droning sound vibrated through Maureen's body. It was either the most holy sound she had ever experienced, or the most unholy. But the incongruent tolling of the church bell in the dead of night felt monumental.

The bell shattered the darkness around Maureen, but it was followed a breath later by a sharp and ominous crack. It was a loud and definite sound in the stone immediately behind her, the place from which the doves had flown. The strange lunar spotlight shone on the place now, but it had changed. Where a wall of brush and solid rock had stood, there was now an opening, a split in the side of the mountain, inviting Maureen to enter.

Maureen inched toward the newly opened cavern. She was shaking now, almost uncontrollably. But she continued forward. As she neared the opening, which was big enough for her to stand in, she saw a faint glow from within. She swallowed her fear at the entrance to the cavern, ducked, and walked into the mountain.

She caught her breath immediately upon entering, stunned. Sitting inside was an ancient and battered chest. Maureen had seen it in a dream in Paris. The old woman had shown it to her, had beckoned her toward it. She was sure it was the same one. A strange, otherworldly glow surrounded the chest. Maureen kneeled and put her hands on it reverently. There was no lock. As she edged her fingers under the lid to lift it she was so focused on her task that she didn't hear the footsteps behind her. Then she was aware of nothing other than the blinding pain that shot through the back of her skull right before the world went black.

*Rome*
*June 26, 2005*

IF BISHOP MAGNUS O'CONNOR had been expecting a hero's welcome from the Vatican Council, he was to be sorely disappointed. The faces of the stoic men sitting around the polished antique table were tight-lipped and unflinching. Cardinal DeCaro had turned into his chief inquisitor.

"Will you explain to the Council, please, why the first man to manifest five points of stigmata since Saint Francis of Assisi was not taken seriously?"

Bishop O'Connor was sweating profusely now. He clutched a handkerchief in his lap, which he used to wipe the accumulating beads from his face. Clearing his throat, the answer came out a little shakier than he had hoped.

"Your Grace, Edouard Paschal fell into disturbing trances. He would scream and cry and claim to have visions. It was determined that these were nothing more than the lunatic ravings of a disturbed mind."

"And who made these official determinations?"

"I did, Your Grace. But you have to understand that this man was common, a Cajun from the bayou . . ."

DeCaro was unsuccessful in controlling his annoyance. He no longer cared about the Bishop's explanation. There was too much at stake, and they would have to move very quickly. His questions became increasingly clipped, his tone harsh. "Describe his visions for those who haven't had the opportunity to read the files."

"He had visions of Our Lord with Mary Magdalene, very disturbing visions. He ranted about their . . . union and spoke of children. These ravings became more intense following . . . the stigmata."

The assembled Council members were growing increasingly unsettled. They shifted in their chairs and whispered as they consulted one another. DeCaro continued the relentless interrogation.

"And what happened to this man, Edouard Paschal?"

O'Connor took a deep breath before answering. "He grew so tormented by his delusions, that . . . he shot himself in the head."

"And following his death?"

"As a suicide, we could not allow him to be buried in sanctified ground. We sealed his records, and forgot about them. Until . . . until his daughter came to our attention."

Cardinal DeCaro nodded, picking up another red folder from the desk. He addressed the rest of the Council. "Ah, yes, that brings us to the issue of his daughter."

*. . . Many will find it shocking that I include the Roman woman Claudia Procula, the granddaughter of Augustus Caesar and the fosterling of Emperor Tiberius, among our followers. But it was not her status as a Roman that made her an unexpected member among us. It was that Claudia was the wife of Pontius Pilate, the same procurator who condemned Easa to the cross.*

*Of the many who came to our aid in the darkest days, Claudia Procula risked as much or more for Easa than anyone. Indeed, she had much more to lose than many.*

*But on that night when our lives crossed in Jerusalem, she and I became bonded in our hearts and in our spirits. We were linked from that day forward, as wives, as mothers, as women. I knew from her eyes that she would become a daughter of The Way when her time had come. I saw it there, the look of light that comes with conversion, when a man or woman sees God clearly for the first time.*

*And Claudia had a heart filled with love and forgiveness. That she stayed with Pontius Pilate through all that transpired is a sign of her faithfulness. Until his end, she suffered for him as only a woman who truly loves can do. This is something I know much about.*

*Claudia's story has not yet been told. I will hope to do it justice.*

THE ARQUES GOSPEL OF MARY MAGDALENE,
THE BOOK OF THE TIME OF DARKNESS

# Chapter Fifteen

*Château des Pommes Bleues*
*June 27, 2005*

Maureen's mouth was bone dry and her head felt like it weighed three tons. Where was she? She tried to turn. *Ouch.* The pain came from her head, but she was otherwise comfortable. Very comfortable. She was in bed, in the château. But how?

Fuzzy, nothing was clear. She had a brief thought that she may have been drugged as well as bludgeoned. By whom? Where was Peter?

Voices outside the door. Raised. Upset and worried. Angry? Men. Trying to identify accents. Occitan, for sure. Roland. The raised one was . . . Scottish? Irish. That was Peter. She tried to call out to him but emitted only a lame croak. Still, it was enough to attract attention and they ran into the room.

Peter had never been so relieved in his life as when he heard that noise come from Maureen's room. He pushed the giant Roland aside and overtook Sinclair to be the first to enter her room. The other two rushed in behind him. Her eyes were open and she looked dazed, but definitely conscious. Her head was wrapped where the doctor had stanched the blood, giving her the look of a war victim.

"Maureen, thank God. Can you hear me?" Peter grabbed her hand.

Maureen tried to nod. Bad idea. Her head swam and she lost her vision for a full minute.

Sinclair moved up behind Peter, leaving Roland to stand silently in the background. "Don't move if you can help it. The doctor said it's best if you stay as still as possible."

He knelt down beside Peter to get closer to Maureen. His face was etched with misery and concern.

Maureen blinked hard to indicate she understood. She wanted to speak but found she could not. She managed to whisper, "Water?"

Sinclair ventured to a crystal dish with a spoon on the nightstand. He made an effort at sounding chipper. "No water yet, doctor's orders. But you can have ice chips. If you do well with these, we'll graduate."

Together, Sinclair and Peter worked to nurse Maureen. Peter helped to raise her gently while Sinclair spooned the ice chips into her mouth.

Feeling the rehydration, Maureen attempted to talk again. "What . . . ?"

"What happened?" Peter offered. He looked at Sinclair and then back at Roland before continuing his explanation. "We'll tell you when you've had a little more rest. Roland here . . . well, he's your hero. And mine."

Maureen's eyes moved to Roland, who nodded solemnly at her. She had grown very fond of the big Occitan and was grateful for whatever it was he had done to bring her here. But her first concern was not herself. The answer she needed hadn't come yet. Sinclair fed her another spoonful of ice chips and she tried again.

"The . . . chest?"

Sinclair smiled for the first time in days. "Is safe. It was brought here with you and has been locked in my study."

"What . . . ?"

"What's inside? We don't know yet. We will not open it without you, my dear. It would be wrong. The trunk was given to you, and you must be present when the contents are revealed."

Maureen closed her eyes with relief and allowed the warm sleep of sedation to overtake her once again, safe in the knowledge that she had not failed.

When Maureen stirred for the second time, Tammy was sitting by her bed in one of the red leather armchairs.

"Good morning, gorgeous," she said, putting the book she had been reading aside. "Nurse Tammy at your service. What can I get ya? Margarita? Piña colada?"

Maureen wanted to smile at her but couldn't yet.

"Would ya settle for some ice chips? Ah, I see the international thumbs-up sign. Here we go."

Tammy collected the crystal dish and moved to Maureen's side. She spooned some chips into her mouth. "Delicious? I made them fresh this morning."

This time Maureen could smile a little. But it still hurt. After a few more spoonfuls she felt she could talk. Better yet, she could think. Her head throbbed, but the haziness was fading, and her memory was coming back.

"What happened to me?"

All humor drained from Tammy's face. She sat next to Maureen again, very serious. "We're hoping you can tell us the first half. Then we can give you the second. Not now, of course, whenever you're ready to speak. But the police . . ."

"Police?" Maureen croaked.

"Shh, don't get excited. I shouldn't have said that. It's all okay now. That's all you need to know."

"No, it's not." Maureen's voice was coming back, along with her strength. "I need to know what happened."

"Okay." Tammy nodded. "I'll get the boys."

The four of them filed into Maureen's room—Sinclair first, followed by Peter, then Roland with Tammy. Sinclair approached her bed and sat in the single chair next to it.

"Maureen, I cannot tell you how sorry I am. I brought you here and put you in this danger. But I never dreamed anything like this would happen to you. I was sure we could protect you on the château grounds. We hadn't anticipated that you would venture out alone and in the middle of the night as you did."

Tammy moved closer to Maureen. "Remember what I told you? That there were people who would want to stop you from finding the treasure?"

Maureen nodded, just enough to be seen, not enough to make her head swim. "Who are they?" she whispered.

Sinclair stepped forward again. "The Guild of the Righteous. A group of fanatics who have operated here in France for centuries. They have a complicated agenda that will be better explained when you are more fully recovered."

Maureen started to object. She wanted real answers. Surprisingly, it was Peter who came to Sinclair's assistance.

"He's right, Maureen. You're still in delicate health, so let's save the sordid details for when you're a little stronger."

"You were followed," Sinclair continued. "They've been monitoring your movements since you came to France."

"But how?"

Sinclair looked pale and exhausted as he leaned forward to explain. Maureen noted the purple shadows of sleeplessness beneath his eyes as he ran his hands over his face.

"This is where I failed you, my dear. We were infiltrated. I had no idea, but one of our own was a mole, a traitor, and has been for years."

The pain of this failure, and the shame of it, had taken its toll on Bérenger Sinclair. But as miserable as he looked, Roland, standing behind him, appeared positively murderous. Maureen directed her question at him.

"Who?"

The big man spat viciously on the floor. "De la Motte." He dissolved into his native tongue, not French but Occitan. Sinclair picked up where he left off.

"Jean-Claude," he explained. "But you don't have to feel betrayed by your own kin. He isn't really of Paschal blood. That, like everything else about him, was a lie. Damn the man to hell, I trusted him implicitly or I would have never allowed him near you. When he arrived to pick you up yesterday, he deposited his spy on my property."

Maureen was thinking about the charming Jean-Claude, who had been so deferential and kind on their outing. Was it possible that this man had been plotting to harm her all along? It was hard to fathom. There was another thing that didn't make sense. She attempted a complete question. "How could they know? The timing . . ."

Roland, Sinclair, and Tammy looked at one another with more than a little guilt on their faces. Tammy raised a hand in a mock volunteer gesture. "I'll tell her."

She knelt beside Maureen's bed, then looked up at Peter to include him in the explanation.

"It's part of the prophecy. Remember the strange sundial at Rennes-le-Château? It points to an astrological alignment spoken of in the prophecy, one that occurs roughly every twenty-two years or so, for a total period of about two and a half days."

Sinclair continued. "Every twenty-plus years when this alignment happens, local residents keep a constant watch on the area for any indication of unusual activity. It's what the towers were originally built for—Saunière's and my own. And it's where I was last night. In fact, I must have just missed you. I kept the watch in Sinclair's Folly for several hours before driving up to RLC and watching from there. That's the tradition in my family.

"From the Tour Magdala I saw a bright spot growing on the horizon in the area of Arques, and knew I would need to get back to my own land immediately. I rang for Roland on the mobile, but he was already out searching for you. You see, the land around the tomb is monitored by advanced security equipment and there are motion sensors that trigger alarms in Roland's quarters. Of course, he was watching these most carefully because of the alignment—and because Tammy had been tipped off that our adversaries may have been closer than we thought. Roland went out immediately when an alarm was triggered near the tomb, and arrived seconds after your attack. I wasn't too far behind him by car. I will say that your attacker . . . is not feeling as well today as you are. And when he is released from the hospital, he will nurse his broken bones in prison."

It was coming together for Maureen as she remembered that the tower had been unlocked and the door open—because Sinclair had just been there.

"Jean-Claude knew the timing as well as we did, because until yesterday he was a member of our most trusted inner circle." Sinclair continued. "When we discovered you and your work within two years of the alignment, we were almost certain that the time had come, if we could just get you here during the configuration."

Peter asked a question that was also roiling through Maureen's head. He looked at Tammy accusingly.

"Wait a minute. How long have you known this?"

It was Tammy's turn to look miserable. Her eyes were red with stress, sleeplessness, and unshed tears.

"Maureen," her voice cracked, but she went on, "I'm so sorry. I have been anything but honest with you. When I first met you in L.A. two years ago, I took one look at you and your ring and listened to the stories that you told me in your perfect innocence . . . well, I didn't take any action then, but I was careful to stay in your circle of acquaintances and watch your progress. Once your book came out, I sent a copy here to Berry. We've been close friends for years, and I knew what he was looking for. What we were all looking for."

Peter wasn't pleased with this latest revelation as he had grown to like Tammy. Now that he knew she had used Maureen, he felt differently.

"You've been lying to her all along."

Tammy let the tears come. "He's right. And I'm sorry. More sorry than I can tell either of you."

Roland put a protective arm around Tammy, but it was Sinclair who spoke in her defense.

"Don't judge her too harshly. You may not like what she did, but she had her reasons for doing it. And there is much more that Tammy has risked that you aren't yet aware of. She is selfless, and a true warrior for The Way."

Maureen was trying to put it all together—the lies, the deliberate deceit, the consummation of years of strange prophecies and dreams. It was all too much in her current state. Her agitation must have shown on her face, as Peter intervened quickly.

"That's enough of this for now. Once you recover, they can fill in the blanks for you."

Maureen paused for a moment. There was still a crucial question that needed to be answered. "When do we open the chest?"

She was sincerely surprised that they had not done so. These people had dedicated large portions of their lives to finding this treasure. In Sinclair's case, multiple generations had spent millions of dollars in pursuit of it. Although they regarded her as The Expected One, she hardly felt that she deserved to see it before they did. But Sinclair had insisted that no one even touch the chest until Maureen was ready, and Roland stood guard over it personally during the night, sleeping between the door and the chest.

"As soon as you are ready to make it downstairs," Sinclair responded.

Roland was fidgeting, an interesting spectacle for such a large man. Tammy noticed and asked with concern, "What is it, Roland?"

The Occitan hulk stepped closer to Maureen. "The chest. It is a holy relic, Mademoiselle. I think . . . I believe if you touch it, maybe it will heal your wounds?"

Maureen was touched deeply by his faith. She reached out and took his hand. "You may be right. Let's see if I can get up . . ."

Peter was worried. "Are you sure you're ready to try this so soon?

It's a long walk down these corridors, and there are several flights of stairs."

Roland smiled at Peter, then at Maureen. "Mademoiselle, there is no need to walk."

And as Maureen indicated that she was ready, Roland lifted her out of bed without effort and carried her gently through the château.

Father Peter Healy followed mutely behind the giant who carried the rag doll form of his cousin through the château. He had never felt so helpless in his life, so completely out of control in a situation. He had a sense that Maureen was now somewhere he could not reach. The discovery of the chest had come through some kind of divine intervention; he saw it in her and he knew the others did as well. There was an air of prescience in the huge house. Something monumental was happening, and none of them would come through it unchanged.

Then there was Maureen's medical condition. The doctor had been appalled at the wound in the back of her head; he had called it a miracle that she was alive. Peter contemplated just how literal that might turn out to be. Perhaps Roland was right. In fact, Peter had argued that his cousin should be hospitalized. It was Roland—not Sinclair—who fought this suggestion. The big man was adamant that Maureen should not be taken too far away from the chest. Maureen's contact with the relic may have already worked some kind of divine healing, as her survival was phenomenal.

As they approached the door of Sinclair's study, Peter realized that the grasp he had on the rosary beads in his pocket was causing the chain to cut into his hand.

The chest rested on the floor, next to a sumptuous sofa. Roland placed Maureen gently on the velvet cushions as she thanked him softly. Tammy sat on one side of her, Peter on the other, while Sinclair and

Roland remained standing. No one stirred or spoke for a long moment. The silence was broken by a small sob that escaped from Maureen.

No one else moved as Maureen leaned forward carefully. She placed both hands on the lid of the large trunk and closed her eyes. Tears slid past her eyelids and down her cheeks. Finally, she opened her eyes and looked at each of the faces around her.

"They're in here," she said in a whisper. "I can feel it."

"Are you ready?" Sinclair asked gently.

Maureen smiled at him, a calm, knowing smile that transformed her face. For a moment, she wasn't Maureen Paschal. She was somebody entirely different, a woman brimming with inner light and peace. Later, when Bérenger Sinclair remembered that moment, he would say that he saw Mary Magdalene herself sitting in Maureen's place.

Maureen turned to Tammy with a smile of radiant compassion. She reached out to her friend and squeezed her hand tightly for a moment, then released it. In that second Tammy knew she had been forgiven. They had all been brought here for some divine purpose, some higher good, and everyone in the room knew it. It was that knowing which transformed each of them, and bonded them for eternity at the same time. Tammy buried her face in her hands and cried softly.

Sinclair and Roland knelt beside the chest and looked to Maureen for confirmation. When she nodded, each man hooked fingers beneath the lid and prepared for a difficult opening. But the hinges did not react with the rust of age they all expected. The lid slid open effortlessly, so much so that it almost caused Roland to lose his balance. Not that anyone noticed. They were all too busy gaping at the two perfectly preserved, large clay jars resting within the chest.

Peter was very tense in his place beside Maureen, but he broke the silence first. "The jars—they're almost identical to those used to house the Dead Sea Scrolls."

Roland knelt beside the chest and ran his hand reverently along the top of one jar. "Perfect," he whispered.

Sinclair nodded. "Indeed. And look, there's no dust or erosion and no sign of wear or age. It's as if these jars have been suspended in time."

Roland commented, "They're sealed with something."

Maureen ran her hand along the top of one jar, jumping as if she had been shocked by an electrical current. "Could it be wax?"

"Wait a minute," Peter interrupted. "We need to discuss this for a moment. If these jars contain what you all hope and believe they do, we have no right to open them."

"No? Then who does?" Sinclair's tone was sharp. "The Church? These jars aren't going anywhere until we can all verify their contents. And the last place I want them to end up is in a Vatican vault where they will be hidden from the world for another two thousand years."

"That's not what I mean," Peter said, more calmly than he felt. "I mean that if there are documents in these jars that have been sealed for two thousand years, sudden exposure to the air could damage them, even destroy them. I'm merely suggesting that we find an acceptable neutral outlet—perhaps through the French government—to open these jars. If we ruin them, you have nothing to show for a lifetime of searching. It would be criminal, literally and spiritually."

Sinclair's face showed his dilemma. The idea of damaging the jars' contents was too horrifying to consider. But the temptation of a lifelong dream that was inches from his fingertips was hard to deny, as was his innate suspicion of outsiders involved in bloodline business. He was rendered momentarily speechless as Roland knelt before Maureen.

"Mademoiselle," he began, "this is your decision. I believe that she has brought you to us and that through you she will tell us her will."

Maureen began to answer Roland, but stopped as a wave of dizziness overcame her. Peter and Tammy reached out simultaneously to steady her. Everything went black for Maureen, but only for a moment. And then it came to her with crystal clarity. When the words came out, they were a command.

"Open the jars, Roland."

The instruction issued from her mouth, but the voice that spoke it was not Maureen's.

Sinclair and Roland carefully lifted the jars from the chest and placed them on the large mahogany table.

Roland deferred to Maureen with exceptional reverence. "Which one first?"

Maureen, supported on either side by Peter and Tammy, laid a finger on one of the jars. She couldn't say why she chose this one first; she just knew it was the right choice. Roland followed her directions, running his finger along the rim of the jar. Sinclair retrieved an antique letter opener from his desk and began to work on the wax seal. Tammy stood by, transfixed, never taking her eyes off Roland.

Peter looked petrified. Among them, he was the only one who knew what it was to work with ancient documents and priceless data from the past. The potential for great damage was immense. Even damaging the jars would be a terrible shame.

As if to punctuate his thought, a sickening crumbling noise filled the tense room. Sinclair's letter opener had shattered the lid of the first jar and taken a chip out of the rim. Peter cringed, and put his face in his hands. But he couldn't hide for long. Maureen's sharp intake of breath beside him forced him to take notice.

"My hands are too big, Mademoiselle," Roland said to Maureen.

Maureen moved forward a step on wobbly legs and reached her hand into the damaged jar.

What she removed—slowly and gingerly—resembled two books written on ancient, linen-looking paper. The black ink of the writing stood in vivid contrast to the flaxen pages. The letters were small, precise, and perfectly legible.

Peter leaned over Maureen, unable to hold back his own growing excitement about what was now on the table before them. He looked into the rapt faces around him, but delivered his judgment directly to

Maureen. His voice cracked as he pronounced, "The writing. It's . . . Greek."

Maureen's breath caught in her throat. She asked him hopefully, "Can you read any of it?"

But she knew the answer before he spoke; all the color had drained from his face. It was clear to everyone in the room at that moment that the world Father Peter Healy knew would never look quite the same.

"I am Mary, called Magdalene," he translated slowly. "And . . ." He stopped, not for dramatic effect but because he really wasn't sure if he could continue. One look at Maureen's face and he knew there was no choice but to go on.

"I am the lawful wife of Jesus, called the messiah, who was a royal son of the house of David."

# Chapter Sixteen

*Château des Pommes Bleues*
*June 28, 2005*

Peter worked through the night on the translations. Maureen refused to leave the room, resting periodically on the velvet sofa. Roland brought extra pillows and a coverlet. Maureen smiled assurance at him as he fussed around her with great concern. Strangely, she felt fine. Her head didn't hurt in the least, and she was feeling amazingly strong.

She stayed on the sofa as she didn't want to hover over Peter. Sinclair was doing enough of that for everyone. But Peter didn't seem to mind; Maureen thought he probably didn't even notice. Peter was immersed, completely absorbed in the sacred nature of his task as scribe.

Tammy came in periodically to check on the progress, but retired late—at the same time as Roland. Maureen had been observing them together all day and came to the conclusion that this was not a coincidence. She thought about the night of the party, when she had heard Tammy in the corridor outside her room, joined by a man with an accent. Tammy and Roland. There was definitely something going on there, but it had the feel of a new pairing. Maureen didn't think they had been involved with each other for too long. When all of this calmed down, she would extract the story from Tammy. She wanted to know the whole truth of all the relationships here in the Château des Pommes Bleues.

Her attention was drawn sharply back to the scrolls as Sinclair exclaimed loudly, "My God! Will you look at that!"

He had been standing over Peter nervously, watching. Peter scribbled furiously on yellow legal pads, writing verbatim translations of the Greek words. It wouldn't all make sense immediately. He would need to finish the transcription, then go back and use his expertise in language to modify the sentences into a form that was logical from a twenty-first-century perspective.

"What is it?" Maureen asked.

Peter looked up and ran his hands over his face. "You need to see it. Come here, if you can. I don't dare move this scroll at the moment."

Maureen rose from the couch slowly, still cognizant of her head wound despite her miraculous recovery. She approached the table, and took a place to the right of Peter, who was sitting with his extensive notes spread out before him. Sinclair pointed to the original scrolls as Peter explained.

"These appear at the end of each major segment, we'll call them chapters. It looks like a wax seal."

Maureen followed Sinclair's finger to the symbol in question. The now-familiar pattern of Maureen's ring, nine circles dancing around a central tenth, had been applied to the bottom of the page.

"Mary Magdalene's personal seal," Sinclair said with reverence.

Maureen held her ring up to the image. They were identical. In fact, they could have been made by the very same ring.

By the time the sun rose on the Château des Pommes Bleues, much of the first book, the first-person account of Mary Magdalene's life, had been translated. Peter worked like a man possessed on this gospel of the Magdalene, huddled over the pages. Sinclair had tea brought in for him, but other than a quick break to take a few sips, Peter wouldn't stop. He looked extremely pale, and Maureen was worried.

"Pete, you have to take a break. You need to sleep for a few hours."

"No." He was emphatic. "I can't. I can't stop now. You don't understand because you haven't seen what I've seen yet. I have to keep going. I have to know what else she will say."

They had all decided to wait until Peter was comfortable with the translations before reading any part of them. All respected Peter's ability and the enormous responsibility they understood to be on his shoulders, but it was still hard for them to wait. At that moment, only Peter knew the content of the scrolls.

"I can't leave them," he continued, eyes shining with a fervor that Maureen had never seen before.

"Just for five minutes. Come outside with me for five minutes and walk in the morning air. It will be good for you. Then you can come back in and we'll get breakfast for you here."

"No, no food. I need to fast until the translations are finished. I can't stop now."

Sinclair thought he understood what Peter was feeling, but also saw how physically drained he appeared. He tried a different tactic. "Father Healy, you've done a commendable job, but your accuracy will suffer if you are overloaded. I'll have Roland come in and guard the scrolls while you take a break."

Sinclair rang a bell to summon Roland. Peter looked up at Maureen's worried face.

"Okay," he conceded. "Five minutes, just to get some air."

Sinclair unlocked the gates to the Trinity Gardens, and Maureen entered them with Peter. A dove flew over the rows of rose bushes as the Mary Magdalene fountain gurgled in the morning sun.

Peter spoke first, his voice soft and filled with awe. "What is happening, Maureen? How did we get here, come to be a part of all of this? It's like a dream, like . . . a miracle. Does this feel real to you?"

Maureen nodded. "Yes. I don't know how to explain it, but I feel such a sense of calm about the whole thing. As though it all happened according to plan. And you're as much a part of this as I am, Pete. It's not an accident that you came with me, or that you teach ancient languages and can translate Greek. This was all . . . orchestrated."

"I definitely feel that I'm playing a part in a master plan. I'm just not sure which part yet, or why me."

Maureen stopped to smell one of the gloriously rich red roses in full bloom. Then she turned back to Peter. "How long has this been in the works? Was it planned before we were born? Further back? Was your grandfather destined to work on the Nag Hammadi library to prepare you for this specifically? Or was it planned two thousand years ago when Mary first hid her gospel?"

Peter was silent for a moment before answering. "You know, before last night I would have had a very different answer than the one I have now."

"Why?"

"Because of her, and what she says in her scrolls. She says exactly what you just did—it's astounding. She says that some things are etched in God's plan, that some people are simply destined to play a particular part. Maureen, it's amazing. I'm reading a firsthand account of Jesus and the apostles by someone who speaks of them all in such human terms. There is nothing like this . . ."—he hesitated to use the word for only a moment—". . . gospel in any Church literature. I feel so unworthy of it."

"But you are worthy," Maureen assured him emphatically. "You were chosen for this. Look at how much divine intervention was required to bring us all together, to this place and time, to tell this story."

"But what story do we tell?" Peter looked tormented, and for the first time Maureen saw that he was wrestling with some very strong inner demons. "What story do I tell? If these gospels are authentic . . ."

Maureen stopped in her tracks and looked at him, incredulous. "How can you doubt it? After everything it took to get us here, to this place?" Maureen touched the back of her head where the huge gash was healing.

"It's now a question of faith for me, Maureen. The scrolls are perfectly preserved, not a flaw on them, not a word missing. The jars didn't even have dirt on them. How is that possible? It's one of two things—either it's a modern forgery or it's an act of divine will."

"What do you truly believe?"

"I've spent twenty straight hours translating the most astounding document. And much of what I'm reading is . . . essentially heretical, yet it also provides a vision of Jesus that is beautiful in an extraordinary and human way. But what I think won't matter. The scrolls will still have to be authenticated through rigorous processes for the world at large to accept them."

He paused, taking time to come to terms with it all in his own head. "If they can be proven to be authentic, this challenges the belief system of a large part of the human race for the last two thousand years. It challenges everything I've ever been taught, everything I ever believed."

Maureen looked at the man, her cousin and best friend, for a long moment. She had always known him to be a rock, a pillar of strength and absolute integrity. He was also a man of intense faith and loyalty to his Church.

She asked simply, "What will you do?"

"I haven't had time to think that far. I need to see what the rest of these scrolls say to see how much they contradict, or hopefully confirm, the gospel accounts as we know them. I haven't reached Mary's description of the crucifixion—or the resurrection."

Maureen understood suddenly why Peter was so reluctant to leave the scrolls before finishing the translations. Mary Magdalene's authenticated account of the events following the crucifixion could be critical to the belief system of one-third of the earth's population. Christianity was based on the understanding that Jesus rose from the dead on the third day. And as Mary Magdalene was the first witness of his resurrection, according to Gospel accounts, her first-person version of those events would be vital.

Maureen learned during her research that theorists who had written about Mary Magdalene as Jesus' wife had also overwhelmingly taken the position that Jesus was not the son of God and did not rise from the dead. Various hypotheses existed regarding Jesus surviving the crucifixion; another common theory was that his physical body had simply been moved by his followers. No one had ever theorized that Jesus had been married *and* had been the son of God. For some reason, those two circumstances had always been viewed as mutually exclusive. Perhaps that's why Mary's existence as the first apostle had been so threatening to the Church throughout history.

No doubt all of these things had been running through Peter's mind in the last, intense hours. He responded to Maureen's question.

"It will depend on what official position the Church takes."

"And what if they deny them? Then what? Do you choose the institution of the Church, or do you choose what you know in your heart to be the truth?"

"I hope those things are not mutually exclusive," Peter said with a wry smile. "Perhaps that is overly optimistic. But if that happens, well, then the time will come."

"The time for what?"

"Eligere magistrum. To choose a master."

They had finished their walk and returned to the château, Maureen convincing Peter to at least take a shower to refresh himself before returning to his task. She went back to her own room to wash her face and gather her thoughts. Exhaustion was creeping in, but she couldn't surrender to it, not yet. Not until she knew what was in the scrolls.

As Maureen dried her face on an elegant red towel, there was a knock on her door.

Tammy bounced into her room. "Good morning. Did I miss anything?"

"Not yet. Peter is going to read to us from the first book as soon as he feels the translation is ready. He says it's stunning, but that's all I know."

"Where is he now?"

"He's in his room taking a little break. Didn't want to leave the scrolls, but we insisted on it. He's having a hard time even though he won't admit it publicly. This is a huge responsibility for him. Maybe even a huge liability."

Tammy perched on the edge of Maureen's bed. "You know what I don't understand? Why does it bother people so much, this idea that Jesus was married and had children? How does that diminish him or his message? Why would Christians be threatened by any of this?"

Tammy continued passionately; this was obviously something she had been thinking about seriously.

"What about that famous passage from Mark's Gospel, the one they read in the marriage ceremonies? 'At the beginning God made them male and female and for this shall a man leave his mother and father and cleave to his wife. And the two shall become one flesh, so they are no more two but one.'"

Maureen watched her with surprise. "I would not have expected you to be one to quote the Gospels quite so accurately."

Tammy winked at her. "Mark, chapter ten, verses six through eight. People use the Gospel against us all the time to try and diminish Mary's importance, so I dedicated myself to finding the verses that support our beliefs. And that's what Jesus preaches right there in the Gospel. Find a wife and stay with her. So why would he preach something that would then be wrong for him personally?"

Maureen listened and considered Tammy's question carefully. "Good question. For me, the idea of Jesus married makes him seem more accessible."

Tammy wasn't finished. "And God is referred to as the father so why shouldn't Christ, as the son of God made in his image, father children? How does that impact his divinity? I just don't see it."

Maureen shook her head; she certainly didn't have the answer to such a huge question.

"I suppose that's ultimately a question for the Church, and for individuals according to their faith."

By early evening, Peter announced that he had completed the initial translation of the first book.

Sinclair rose from the table. "Are you ready to translate for us, Father? If so, I'd like to summon Roland and Tamara. They're very much a part of this."

Peter nodded at Sinclair. "Yes, call them." Then he looked directly at Maureen, his eyes an unreadable combination of shadow and light. "Because it's time."

Tammy and Roland hurried down, joining the others in Sinclair's study. When they were all gathered around Peter, he explained that there were still a number of rough patches within the translation that would take time and several other expert opinions. But overall, he had a solid translation and an understanding of who Mary truly was, and what her role was in the life of Jesus Christ.

"She refers to this as the Book of the Great Time."

Picking up the stack of yellow notepads, Father Healy began to read softly to his audience.

" 'I am Mary, called Magdalene, a princess of the royal tribe of Benjamin and a daughter of the Nazarenes. I am the lawful wife of Jesus, the messiah of The Way, who was a royal son of the house of David and descended from the priestly caste of Aaron.

Much has been written of us and more will be written in time to come. Many who write of us have no knowledge of the truth and were not present during the Great Time. The words I will commit to these pages are the truth before God. This is what occurred during my life, during the Great Time, the Time of Darkness, and all that came after.

I leave these words for the children of the future, so that when the time is come they may find them and know the truth of those who led The Way.' "

The story of Mary Magdalene's life unfolded before them in all of its unexpected, stunning detail.

# Chapter Seventeen

*Galilee*
*26 A.D.*

The dirt was soft and cool between Mary's toes. She looked down at her feet, fully aware that her bare legs were absolutely filthy. She didn't care, not a bit. Besides, it was only one of the many unseemly elements of her appearance today. Her glossy auburn hair hung to her waist unbound and in wild tangles; her shift was loose and without a belt.

Earlier, as she attempted to slip unnoticed from the house, she was discovered by a disapproving Martha.

"And where do you think you're going looking like that?"

Mary laughed lightly, undisturbed that she had been spotted in her escape.

"I'm just going out to the garden. And it's *walled in*. No one will see me."

Martha looked unconvinced. "It is unseemly for a woman of your rank and stature to run loose in the dirt like a barefoot serving girl."

Martha's disapproval was more routine than sincere. She was used to her young sister-in-law's free-spirited ways. Mary was a uniquely exquisite creation of God, and Martha doted on her. Besides, the girl had little enough opportunity to be self-indulgent. Hers was a life shadowed by responsibility, and most of the time she shouldered that fact with grace and courage. On the rare day when Mary had a free moment to wander the gardens, it would be unfair to deny her that small pleasure.

"Your brother will be back before the sun sets," Martha reminded Mary with emphasis.

"I know. Don't worry, he won't see me. And I'll be back in time to help you with the meal."

The younger woman gave her brother's wife a quick kiss on the cheek, and scurried out to enjoy the privacy of her garden. Martha watched her go with a sad little smile. Mary was so petite and fine-boned, it was easy to treat her like a child. But she was not a child, Martha reminded herself. She was now a young woman of marriage-able age, a woman with a strong sense of her profound and serious destiny.

Mary had no thoughts of destiny as she entered the garden. There would be enough of that tomorrow. She lifted her head as the spicy scent of October, mixed with the breeze from the Sea of Galilee, filled her nostrils. Mount Arbel stood to the northwest, strong and reassuring in the afternoon sun. She always thought of it as her own personal mountain, a rocky pile of rich, red soil that rose up beside her birthplace. And she had missed it so much. Recently the family had been spending more time in their other home in Bethany, as the proximity to Jerusalem was important for her brother's work. But Mary loved the wild beauty of Galilee and was delighted when her brother announced they would spend the autumn here.

This was her cherished time, these moments alone surrounded by wildflowers and olive trees. Solitude was becoming increasingly rare, and she savored every second of these stolen opportunities. Here she was able to fully enjoy God's beauty in peace, unbound by the strict rules of wardrobe and tradition that were an integral part of her station in life.

Her brother once caught her out here and asked what she had been doing during the hours she had been "missing."

"Nothing! Absolutely nothing!"

Lazarus had looked sternly at his little sister, but then softened. He had been furious when she did not appear for their afternoon meal, an anger that had grown out of fear. It was more than mere sibling concern. He cared deeply for his beautiful, intelligent little sister, but he was also her guardian. Her health and well-being were his first priority. She must be protected at all costs as that was his sacred duty: to his family, to his people, to his God.

When he came upon her lying in the grass her eyes were closed and she was very still, causing him a moment of raw terror. But Mary had stirred, as if sensing his panic. Shading her sleepy eyes from the sun, she looked up into the glowering face of her brother. He looked positively murderous.

Lazarus' anger abated as she spoke to him. He began to understand for the first time how desperately she needed to take advantage of such rare opportunities for solitude. The only daughter in the lineage of Benjamin, her future had been carved out since infancy. Hers was the privileged destiny of royal blood and prophecy. His little sister was destined for a dynastic marriage, one that had been foretold by the great prophets of Israel—a marriage that many believed was no less than the absolute will of God.

Such tiny shoulders for so great a weight, Lazarus had thought as he listened to her. Mary spoke in a manner that she did not usually allow herself, open and with emotion. It made her brother realize with a pang of guilt that she felt real fear about her predestined role in history. It was strange, but he rarely allowed himself to think of her as entirely human. She was a precious commodity, to be protected and cared for. He had seen to all of these tasks with absolute diligence and accomplished them admirably. But he also loved her—although it was not until he met his wife, Martha, that he allowed himself to fully realize that, or emotion of any kind.

Lazarus had been a very young man when his father died. Too young, perhaps, to take on his family's huge dynastic responsibilities in addition to his obligations as a landowner. But the young man had vowed to his father during those final days that he would not fail the house of Benjamin. He would not fail his people and he would not fail the God of Israel.

With an intensity of determination, Lazarus attacked his myriad responsibilities, chief among them the care of his sister, Mary. His was a life of duty and obligation. Lazarus arranged his sister's education and upbringing to befit her noble birthright, but never did he allow himself to feel anything. Emotion was a luxury, and often a dangerous one.

But then, blessedly, God brought Martha to him.

She was the eldest of three sisters from Bethany who had been born to one of Israel's noble families. It had been essentially an arranged marriage, although Lazarus was given the opportunity to choose from the three girls. He had chosen Martha for practical reasons initially. As the eldest, she was level-headed and responsible, with more experience in the running of a household. The younger girls were too frivolous and were slightly spoiled; he was concerned that they would negatively influence his sister in that manner. All of the girls were lovely, but Martha's beauty was more serene. She had an unusually calming effect on him.

The practical match turned into a great love, and Martha opened Lazarus' heart. When his mother died suddenly, leaving the child Mary without a maternal influence, Martha stepped into that role effortlessly.

Mary was thinking of Martha when she stopped to rest beneath her favorite shade tree. Tomorrow, the high priest Jonathan Annas would come and the wedding preparations would begin. There would not be any more opportunities to slip away unescorted for a very long time, so Mary chose to make the most of this. Indeed, the time would come, as they all knew it would, when she would be forced to leave her beloved home to travel south with her future husband. Her husband!

Easa.

The very thought of the man who was her betrothed filled Mary with a warm glow. Any woman would envy her position as future queen to their dynastic king. But it was more than his position that filled Mary with joy; it was the man himself. The people called him Yeshua, this eldest son and heir to the house of David. But Mary called him by a childhood nickname, Easa, much to the chagrin of her brother and Martha.

"It is not fit to call our future king and the chosen leader of the people by a child's nickname, Mary," Lazarus had scolded her during Easa's last visit.

"It is for her," responded the deep, gentle voice that commanded attention without effort.

Lazarus had stopped short at this. He looked behind him to see the Son of the Lion himself, Yeshua, standing there.

"Mary has known me since she was a small child, and she has always called me Easa. I would not have her change it for anything."

Mary's brother looked positively mortified until Easa rescued the moment with his smile. There was magic in that single expression, a transformational warmth that was impossible to resist. The rest of that evening had been wonderful, filled with the people Mary loved most, gathered around Easa and listening to his wisdom.

Lying beneath the greater of two olive trees, Mary drifted to sleep in the afternoon sun, images of her future husband playing in her head.

When Mary first felt the shadow cross her face, she panicked, thinking she had overslept. It was getting dark! Lazarus would be furious.

But as she shook her head to clear it, she realized that it was still full midday, the sun shining brightly over Mount Arbel. Mary looked up sharply to see what object had caused the shadow to cross her dreaming face. She gasped, immobilized with surprise, before launching herself, with all the exuberance of a young girl in love, at the figure before her.

"Easa!" she shrieked with joy.

He opened his arms and wrapped her in a huge embrace for a moment before stepping back to look down at her exquisite face.

"My little dove," he said, using the nickname he had given her as a child. "Is it possible that you grow more beautiful every day?"

"Easa! I didn't know that you were coming. Nobody told me . . ."

"They didn't know. I will be as much of a surprise to them. But I could not allow the preparations for my marriage to happen without me." He turned the full force of that smile on her again. Mary scanned his features for a moment, the intensely dark eyes set off by sharp cheekbones. He was the most beautiful man she had ever seen, the most beautiful man in the world.

"But my brother says it is not safe for you to be here now."

"Your brother is a great man who worries too much," Easa reassured her. "God will provide and protect."

As Easa spoke to her, Mary looked down and realized with horror how absolutely disheveled she was. Her waist-length hair was tangled and filled with bits of grass and a stray leaf, a suitable frame for her bare, dirt-dusted limbs. At this moment she did not even remotely resemble a future queen. She began to stammer an apology about her appearance, but Easa stopped her with a full, ringing laugh.

"Do not worry, my dove. It is *you* I have come to see, not your clothing, nor your station." He reached out to pull one of the leaves playfully from her hair.

She smiled up at him, adjusting her shift and brushing at the dirt. "My brother will not see it that way," she said with mock concern.

Lazarus was very stern with her in matters of protocol and honor; he would have been beside himself if he had known that his sister was currently standing in their garden, unescorted and improperly dressed—and in the presence of the future Davidic king.

"I will handle Lazarus," Easa reassured her. "But just to be safe, why don't you run inside and pretend you didn't see me. I will leave through the back and return this evening after I have been properly announced. That way, neither your brother nor Martha will be caught unaware."

"I will see you tonight then," Mary replied, suddenly shy. She paused for one brief moment, before turning toward the house.

"Act surprised," Easa shouted after her, laughing as he watched the retreating form of his future wife run through the garden toward her brother's home.

That day and the night that followed would burn in Mary's memory for the rest of her life. It was the last time she would know how it felt to be carefree, young, in love, and happy.

Jonathan Annas did come the next day, but he arrived with a new agenda. The political and spiritual climate in Jerusalem showed escalating instability, and plans had changed to avert increased threat from the Romans. The priests had selected a new leader during a secret council, a council that deemed Yeshua unsuitable to take on the duties of the anointed one. Members of that council appeared with Annas to present their findings.

Mary had been sent with Martha from the room upon their arrival, but she refused to remain hidden while her future was discussed by the most powerful of her people. Easa had smiled his assurances at her, but she saw something in his eyes that frightened her. Uncertainty. She had never seen him appear uncertain before, but it was there and it terrified her. Against Martha's wishes, Mary hid in the corridor outside and listened.

There were raised voices, some shouting, men talking over each other. It was often hard to hear precisely what was being discussed. The harsh voice, loud and raspy, belonged to Jonathan Annas.

"You have brought this about yourself by aligning with the Zealots. The Romans will never allow us to show any kind of alliance with you because of the assassins and revolutionaries among your supporters. We would be inviting slaughter on our own people."

The calm, melodic voice that followed belonged to Easa.

"I accept every man who chooses to follow me and seek the kingdom of God. The Zealots acknowledge my descent from David. I am their rightful leader. And yours."

"You don't understand what we're up against," Annas snapped back. "The new procurator, Pontius Pilate, is a barbarian. He will shed as much blood as he feels is necessary to silence even our most basic demands. He flaunts his pagan banners in our streets, stamps his symbols of blasphemy on our coins, and all to remind us that we are powerless against it. He would not hesitate to eliminate any of us here if he sensed that we were supporting insurgence against Rome from within the Temple."

"The tetrarch will support us," Easa said. "Perhaps he would intervene with the new procurator."

Annas spat. "Herod Antipas supports nothing but his own lust and pleasure. Rome butters his bread. He is only a Jew when it suits his ambitions to be one."

"His wife is a Nazarene," Easa said pointedly.

This comment was met with silence. Easa had embraced the liberal teachings of the Nazarene people, of whom his mother was a leader. The Nazarenes did not keep the law in the strict way of the Temple Jews. Among their differing traditions, they included women in their rituals and even acknowledged women as prophets. They also allowed Gentiles to listen to their teachings and participate in their services.

While Annas emphasized the Zealot faction as the council's primary reason for withdrawing their support from Easa, everyone in the room knew that was a smokescreen for the truth. Easa's teachings were too revolutionary, too influenced by the Nazarenes. The Temple priests simply could not control him.

By raising the issue of Herod's wife as a Nazarene, Easa had thrown down a challenge before the Temple priests. He would step into his prophesied role of Davidic king and messiah without them, and do so as a Nazarene. Such a choice was extremely risky. While it could dimish the power of the Temple priesthood, it could also work against Easa if the people withdrew their popular support from him in favor of their traditional leaders.

But Annas wasn't finished with his attack. His voice rang out through the tension of the room.

"He who has the bride is the bridegroom."

Silence dampened the room again, and Mary froze in her position outside the door. Her tongue was dry and thick in her mouth. This was a reference to the Song of Songs, the poem written by King Solomon to celebrate the supreme dynastic union of the noble houses of Israel. Here, it was a pointed and overt reference to the betrothal of Mary to Easa. In order for a king to reign over the people, tradition proclaimed that he have a bride of equally royal lineage. Mary, as the Benjamite descendant of King Saul, was the highest-ranking princess in Israel by blood. As such she had been betrothed to Yeshua, the Son of the Lion of Judah, from infancy. The tribes of Judah and Benjamin had been conjoined since antiquity, and the dynastic marriage of these two lines had been secured since Saul's daughter Michal had married David.

But to be a dynastic king within the law, one had to have a dynastic queen. Annas was issuing a direct threat to the betrothal.

It was Mary's brother who spoke next. Lazarus was a man in total control of his emotions at all times, and only those very close to him would have heard the strain in his voice as he addressed the high priest.

"Jonathan Annas, my sister is betrothed to Yeshua by law. The prophets have shown him to be the messiah of our people. I do not see how we can stray from this course as God chose it for us."

"You dare to tell me what God has chosen?" Annas snapped.

Outside the door, Mary cringed. Lazarus was a righteous man, and he would be mortified at offending the high priest. "We believe that God has chosen another man. A righteous defender of the law, a man who will uphold all that is sacred to our people without creating political offense to the Romans."

There it was, the truth laid out for all to hear it. *A righteous defender of the law.* This was Annas' way of showing Easa that they would not tolerate his Nazarene reforms despite his flawless bloodline.

"And who is that?" Easa asked quietly.

"John."

"The Baptizer?" Lazarus was incredulous.

"He is kin of the Lion," another harsh voice chimed in, one Mary did not recognize. It was possibly that younger priest, Caiaphas, the son-in-law of Annas.

"He is not a David." Easa's voice remained calm.

"No." This was Annas. "But his mother is from the Aaron line of priests and his father from the Zadokites. The people think he is the heir to the prophet Elias. It will be enough to sway the people to follow him, if he is married to the proper bride."

They had come full circle. Annas was here to secure Mary's betrothal to the candidate of their choice for messiah. She was the commodity they all required to legitimize any kingship.

The next voice was angry, shouting. Mary had never met James, a younger brother of Easa, but she guessed that this was who she heard yelling now. This man sounded like Easa, but without the calm control that was always present in his elder brother.

"You cannot just pick and choose your messiahs like items in a bazaar. We all know that Yeshua is the chosen one to lead our people out of bondage. How dare you adopt a substitute because you fear for your own prized positions."

Shouting erupted as men yelled over each other to be heard. Mary tried to discern the voices and the words, but she was shaking now. Everything was about to change; she could feel it in the marrow of her fine bones.

The raspy command of Annas' voice pierced through the others.

"Lazarus, as the guardian of this girl, only you can make the decision to break the betrothal and bestow the daughter of Benjamin upon the candidate we have chosen. It is all in your hands now. But may I remind you that your father was a Pharisee and a loyal servant of the Temple. I knew him well. He would expect you to do what is best for the people."

Mary could feel the heaviness in Lazarus from across the room. It was true, their father was dedicated to the Temple and a servant of the law until his death. Her mother had been a Nazarene, but that would not matter to men such as this. Lazarus had sworn to their father on his deathbed that he would uphold the law and preserve the position of the Benjamites at all costs. He was facing a horrible choice.

"You wish to marry my sister to the Baptizer?" Lazarus asked carefully.

"He is a righteous man and a prophet. And once John is anointed as messiah, your sister will have the same status as his wife that she would have had with this man," Annas answered.

"John is a hermit, an ascetic," Easa interrupted. "He has no desire or need for a wife. He chooses to live in seclusion as he feels this brings him closer to hearing the voice of God. Would you destroy his solitude and end his good work by forcing him into a marriage with all the responsibilities of that under the law?"

"No," Annas replied, "we would force John into nothing. He will marry the girl to confirm his status as messiah with the people. After that, she will live in the house of his kin and John can return to his preaching. She will perform dynastic duties as necessary under the law, and so will he."

Mary listened, praying that the roiling sickness in the pit of her stomach would not overcome her and reveal her hiding place. She knew that "dynastic duties under the law" meant breeding, having children—with John the ascetic. It wasn't bad enough that these men were attempting to strip her of the greatest happiness she had ever dreamed of, which was her marriage to Easa. But with all of that they were attempting to remove Easa from his place as their future king.

And then there was the idea of the Baptizer himself. Mary had never seen this man who preached on the banks of the Jordan, but he was legendary among the people. He was Easa's elder cousin, but the two of them were very different in temperament. Easa revered John, spoke of him often as a great servant of God and a true and righteous man. But Easa also saw John's limits. He had explained this to Mary once when she asked about the fiery preacher who baptized with water. John rejected women, Gentiles, the lame, or any he considered unclean, while Easa believed that the word of God belonged to all people who wished to hear it. It was not an elite message, Easa explained. It was a message of good news for everyone. These differences had been the cause of argument between Easa and John.

John had spent a great deal of time on the barren shores of the Dead Sea after his parents died. He became entrenched with the Qumran Essenes there, a severe sect of ascetics from whom many of his strict observances were derived. The Qumran sect lived in harsh conditions and disdained those they called "seekers after smooth things." They spoke of a Teacher of Righteousness who would bring repentance and ultimate adherence to the law.

Easa had spent time among the Essenes as well, and had explained their ways to Mary. He respected their devotion to God and the law, and praised their good and charitable works. Easa would count many Essenes among his close companions throughout his life, and would retreat to the absolute solitude of Qumran for periods of meditation. But where John embraced the harsh observances of the Essenes, Easa ultimately rejected many of their beliefs as harsh and judgmental.

Easa gave Mary further details of John, about the strange diet he had adopted in Qumran, of locusts mixed with honey, and his odd clothing made from animal skins and coarse camel's hair that itched and tore the skin. He explained how his cousin the Baptizer chose to live in the wilderness, under the sky, where he felt closer to God. It was not a proper existence for a noblewoman or a child. And it was certainly not what Mary Magdalene had been prepared for throughout her young life.

It was all up to Lazarus now, Mary thought sadly. The men were arguing again in the next room, as the tears rolled down Mary's face. She could no longer discern one voice from another. Which was Lazarus and what was he saying? Her brother loved and respected Easa, as a man and as a descendant of David, although he had never taken to the reforms of the Nazarene Way. Lazarus was highly traditional; their father had been a Pharisee as well as a strong financial supporter of the Temple in Jerusalem.

Jonathan Annas was forcing him to make an excruciating choice: support Easa, the rightful dynastic king and heir to all the prophecies, and Lazarus would be severed from the Temple. That was implicit in the high priest's words. Lazarus would have no real option then but to align with the Nazarenes, embracing a reformist credo that he did not believe in.

The more moderate among the people, Lazarus included, had been content as long as Easa had been accepted by both the Nazarenes and the Temple priests. But this was the eve of a terrible schism, a full separation of the two parties that would create hostility among the great dynastic families of Israel and give birth to a bitter rivalry. It required a choice that would prove agonizing for many within the common populace.

But at that moment, Mary cared about only one choice that had to be made.

A decision by Lazarus to uphold the rule of the Temple priests would do far more than shatter Mary's girlhood dreams and force her into an abhorrent marriage. It was a choice that would change the course of history indelibly for thousands of years to come.

Easa made an agreement with Lazarus that night: he wanted to be the one who broke this news to Mary. Lazarus agreed, likely with great relief, and Mary was brought into a private chamber to meet with the man she had always believed would be her husband.

When Easa saw her trembling body and tear-stained face, he knew she had overheard much of the encounter. And when Mary saw the sorrow in Easa's eyes, she knew her destiny had been sealed. She threw herself into his arms and cried until there were no tears left.

"But why?" she asked him. "Why did you agree to this? Why did you let them take the kingdom that is yours?"

Easa stroked her hair to calm her, and smiled down in his comforting way. "Perhaps my kingdom is not of this earth, little dove."

Mary shook her head; she didn't understand. Easa saw this and continued his explanation.

"Mary, my work is to teach The Way, to show the people that the kingdom of God is at hand, that we have the power to free ourselves here and now from all oppression. I do not require an earthly crown or kingdom to do this. I need only reach as many people as I can to share the word of God's Way with them.

"I had always thought that I would inherit the throne of David and that you would sit beside me, but if that is not to occur in the flesh, we must surrender to it as God's will."

Mary considered his words, trying very hard to be brave and accept them. She had been raised as a princess; this was why she was given the name Mary, a title reserved for daughters of noble families within the Nazarene tradition. She had also been trained by the Nazarene women, led by Easa's mother. The Great Mary had taken over the younger Mary's training at an early age, to prepare her for life with the Son of David, but also to school her in the spiritual lessons of their specific reformist creed. Once she was married to Easa, Mary would don the red veil of the Nazarene priestesses, the same red veil worn by the Great Mary.

But now, that was not to be.

Mary could not endure the loss of it and began to cry again. As she did, a terrible thought struck hard and a jerking sob cut through her.

"Easa?" she whispered, terrified to ask the question.

"Yes?"

"Will—who will you marry now?"

Easa looked at her with such astounding tenderness that Mary thought her heart would burst. He took her hands and spoke to her softly, yet firmly.

"Do you remember what my mother said when you last entered our home?"

Mary nodded, smiling through her tears. "I will never forget it. She said, 'God has made you the perfect mate for my son. You two shall become one flesh. There will be no more two, but one. And what God has joined together, no man can tear apart.' "

Easa nodded. "My mother is the wisest of women and a great prophet. She saw that you were made for me by God. If God has decided within his plan that I shall not have you, then I shall have no other."

Relief flooded through her. Of all the things she could not bear, another woman at Easa's side was the most unthinkable. Another reality struck her then with stunning force.

"But . . . if I am to be John's wife . . . he will never allow me to become a Nazarene priestess."

Easa's face grew very serious as he answered. "No, Mary. John will insist that you keep the law in strictest observance. He despises the reforms of our people, and he may be very hard on you and enforce severe penance. But remember what I have told you, and what my mother has also taught. The kingdom of God is in your heart, and no oppressor—not the Romans, nor even John—can take that from you."

He lifted Mary's chin and looked directly into her huge hazel eyes as he spoke. "Listen closely, my dove. We must walk this path with grace, and we must do what is right for the children of Israel. This means that I cannot at this time oppose Jonathan Annas and the Temple. I will uphold their decision so that the teaching of The Way may continue in peace and grow across the land, and I have agreed to do two things as a show of my support. I will attend your wedding to John with my mother, and I will allow John to baptize me in public to show that I recognize his spiritual authority."

Mary nodded solemnly. She would walk the path that was now laid before her; this was her responsibility as a daughter of Israel. Easa's words of love and strength would get her through it.

He kissed the top of her head lightly, then turned to take his leave.

"You are so strong for such a little one," he said gently. "I have always seen that strength in you. You will be a great queen one day, a leader of our people."

He stopped at the door to look at her one last time and leave her with a final thought. He touched his hand to his heart.

"I will be with you always."

John the Baptizer was not as easily manipulated as Jonathan Annas and his council had anticipated.

When they came to him with their proposal, John railed against their lack of righteousness and called them vipers. He reminded them that there was already a messiah in his cousin, a prophet chosen by God, and that he, John, was not worthy to fill such shoes. The priests countered that the people were calling John a greater prophet, the heir to Elias.

But John answered, "I am none of those things."

"Then tell us what you are so we may tell the people of Israel who would follow you as a prophet and a king," they asked.

John answered in his enigmatic way, "I am the voice in the wilderness."

He sent the Pharisees away, but the canny young priest Caiaphas had caught John's strange pronouncement, "I am the voice in the wilderness," as a reference to the prophet Isaiah. Was John actually calling himself a prophet through a maze of scripture? Was he testing the priests in some way?

The priestly envoys returned the next day, and this time they petitioned John for baptism. He insisted on their repentance of all sin before he would consider it. This rankled the priests, but they knew they must play by John's rules or risk losing him as the key to their strategy. Receiving baptism by John would strengthen their position with the multitudes who were announcing John as a prophet, which was precisely the point.

When the priests affirmed their repentance, John immersed them in the Jordan, but reminded them, "I will indeed baptize you with water, but he that comes after will be mightier than I in the eyes of God."

The priests stayed with John that day and spoke to him of their plan once the crowds had diminished at the riverbank. John wanted none of it. Among the objectionable issues, he was entirely opposed to taking a wife and certainly not a woman who had been betrothed to his cousin. But the council was prepared for John's objections and had considered them carefully due to his vehemence the previous day.

They spoke of Lazarus, the righteous and fine noble from the house of Benjamin, and how that good man feared for his pious sister to be married within the Nazarene influence.

The Baptizer flinched at this revelation. This notion was John's weakness. Although he deferred to the prophecies that Yeshua was the chosen one, he had growing concerns about the path his cousin was walking with the Nazarenes and their blatant disregard for the law. John dismissed them and called the discussion to a close.

The priests left without any change in John's resolve.

Later that day, Easa arrived on the eastern banks of the Jordan to fulfill the promise he had made to Annas. A large entourage of followers attended Easa, and this meeting of two such celebrated men attracted the people in throngs along the river. John put out his hand to stop Easa from coming forward.

"You come to me for baptism?" he asked. "Perhaps I have more need to be baptized by you, as you are the chosen of God."

Easa smiled in return. "Cousin, this is how it must be now. It becomes us to fulfill the path of righteousness."

John nodded, showing no surprise or other emotion at Easa's blatant statement of acceptance. This was the first time the two of them had come together since the manipulations of Jonathan Annas and their first opportunity to size up the other. The Baptizer steered Easa away from the ears of the crowd and spoke in carefully considered words, measuring his cousin's perspective.

"He who has the bride is the bridegroom."

Easa showed no reaction to John's words. He simply nodded his agreement to this arrangement.

John continued, "But the friend of the bridegroom who stands and hears him rejoices greatly at the bridegroom's voice. I can take joy in this, your selfless gift of righteousness, if it is true that you give it freely."

Easa nodded his assent once again. "I will be fulfilled to be the friend of the bridegroom. I must decrease for you to increase, and so be it."

It was a word play, a dance of sorts, between the two great prophets as each took notice of the other's political stance. Satisfied that his cousin had agreed peacefully to submit his position as well as his bride, John turned to the assembled throng on the banks of the Jordan. He made a pronouncement to the people before calling Easa forward.

"After me will come this man, who is preferred before me—because he was chosen before me."

Easa was submerged into the river as John's words rang out. These were carefully chosen, indicating that if John were to step into the shoes of the messiah, then Easa would be the heir to his throne if anything were to happen. "He was chosen before me" was a clear indication that John still acknowledged the prophecies from Easa's birth. This phrasing would protect John with the moderates who supported John and were afraid of the Nazarene reforms, yet still honored Easa as the child of the prophecies. His first words, "After me will come this man," were an indication that John was considering taking on the role of anointed one. John, the wilderness preacher with his wild clothing and extreme evangelical style, was perhaps an easy man to underestimate. But his actions and words from the banks of the River Jordan that day marked him as a far savvier politician than many imagined.

As Easa emerged from the water, the crowd cheered these two great men, kindred prophets who had been touched by the Lord. But then there was silence in the valley as a single white dove appeared from the heavens and flew gracefully over the head of Easa, the Lion of David. It was a moment that would be remembered by the people of the Jordan Valley and beyond for as long as the earth endured.

Caiaphas returned to the River Jordan the next day with his contingent of Pharisees. He had planned his strategy regarding John very carefully. The baptism of Easa the day before had not served the purpose that he and Annas had planned. They believed that by submitting to baptism Easa would publicly acknowledge John's authority.

Instead, the event had served to remind the people that the trouble-some Nazarene was the chosen one of prophecy. Now, more than ever, the Pharisees had to reduce the impact of this idea of Easa as Messiah. The only way to do that was to transfer the title of messiah to someone else as quickly as possible, and the sole acceptable candidate was John.

But John was troubled by the sign of the dove. Didn't this bird appearing from heaven following the baptism prove that Easa was God's chosen? John vacillated, returning finally to support of his cousin's position. Caiaphas, who was a great student of his father-in-law, Annas, was prepared for this possibility and moved in to strike.

"Your Nazarene cousin was with the lepers this day," he informed John.

John was stunned. There was nothing more unclean than those wretches who had been abandoned by God. And for his cousin to attend these creatures after his baptism was unthinkable.

"You're certain that this is true?" he asked.

Caiaphas nodded gravely. "Yes, I'm sorry to report that he was in that most unclean place this morning. I am told that he preached the word of the kingdom of God to them. He even allowed them to touch him."

John was astonished that Easa had fallen so far, so fast. He knew well that the Nazarenes had influenced his cousin profoundly. Wasn't his mother a Mary, and a leader of that group? But she was a woman and therefore of little importance except that she influenced her son in a great way. Yet if Easa was immersed in the world of the unclean not even a full day after his baptism, perhaps God had turned his back on him.

And there was the girl to think of, this daughter of Benjamin. John was deeply disturbed that she was called Mary—a Nazarene name, an indication that the girl had been trained in their unseemly ways.

But the prophecy surrounding the girl herself had to be considered in all seriousness for the sake of the people. She was believed to be the Daughter of Zion as described in the book of the prophet Micah. The passage referred to the *Migdal-Eder*, the Tower of the

Flock, a shepherdess who would lead the people: "And thou, O tower of the flock, the stronghold of the daughter of Zion, unto thee shall it come . . . The kingdom shall come to the daughter of Jerusalem."

If Mary was indeed this prophesied female, John had an obligation to see that she stayed on a straight path of righteousness. Caiaphas assured him that the girl was young enough and certainly pious enough to be trained as John saw fit in the most traditional ways of the law. In fact, her brother begged them to do this before it was too late. The betrothal of this Benjamin princess to Easa had been dissolved based on his Nazarene leanings. This was perfectly acceptable within the law. Hadn't the high priest, Jonathan Annas, written the documents of dissolution himself?

Most important, Easa and his Nazarene followers did not object to this decision, and promised to uphold John in his anointed position. Easa even agreed to attend the wedding feast as a show of his support. There was nothing in this proposal that was at all objectionable. If John would marry the Benjamin princess and become the anointed one, his baptism numbers would increase tenfold. He would reach so many more sinners and show them the path to repentance. He would become the Teacher of Righteousness from the prophecies of their ancestors.

Faced with the opportunity to convert more sinners and teach God's path of penance to the children of Israel, John agreed to marry the Benjamin girl and take his place in the history of his people.

The wedding of Mary, the daughter of the house of Benjamin, and John the Baptizer, from the priestly lineage of Aaron and Zadok, took place on the hill of Cana in Galilee. It was well attended by nobles, Nazarenes, and Pharisees. As promised, Easa attended with his mother, his brothers, and a group of their disciples.

John's pious mother, Elisabeth, had been a cousin of Easa's mother, Mary. But both Elisabeth and her husband, Zacharias, had been dead for a number of years by the time of their son's wedding.

There was no immediate relative to make the proper arrangements for the celebration, and John himself was neither knowledgeable nor concerned about the protocol. When the Great Mary observed that the guests were not properly provided for, she stepped in to take charge of the preparations as an elder female of John's kin. She went to where her own son sat with several of his followers and said, "They have not enough wine for the wedding feast."

Easa listened to his mother carefully. "What has this to do with me?" he asked her. "This is not my wedding. It would not be proper for me to intervene."

The elder Mary disagreed and said so to her son. First, she felt an obligation to ensure that the wedding feast was appropriate in memory of Elisabeth. But beyond that, Mary was a wise woman who knew the people and the prophecies. This would be an opportune time to remind the assembled nobles and priests of her son's unique position in their community. Easa agreed with some reluctance.

Summoning the servants, Mary gave them instructions. "Whatever he asks of you, do it without question."

The servants waited for Easa's direction. After a moment he requested that they bring six large pots to him, each filled to the brim with water. The servants did this, placing the clay water pots before him. He closed his eyes and said a prayer, running his hands over each of the containers as he did so. When he had finished, he instructed the servants to draw out the liquid. The first serving woman did so, and dropped her serving cup. The clay pots were no longer filled with water. A rich and sweet red wine filled each one.

Easa instructed a servant to take a cup of wine to Caiaphas, who officiated at the ceremony. Caiaphas lifted his glass to John, the bridegroom, and praised him for the quality of the wine.

"Most serve fine wine early in the day and save the poor quality for the end, when few will notice," Caiaphas joked. "But you have saved the best wine for last."

John looked to Caiaphas with some confusion. Neither he nor the priest had any knowledge of what had transpired. The only inkling that anything was out of the ordinary was the low mumbling of a few servants in the background and a few of the Nazarene disciples. But it would not be long before everyone in Galilee knew exactly what had taken place at the wedding in Cana.

Following the wedding of John and Mary, no one was speaking of the bride and bridegroom. Indeed, the dynastic merge had been completely overshadowed by something more extraordinary. The subject of discussion among the common people was the miraculous transformation of water into wine by the younger prophet. In this, the northern region of Galilee, the name of Easa was on everyone's lips. He was their only messiah, regardless of the manipulations that stemmed from the Temple.

John's power and popularity grew to the south, from the banks of the Jordan near Jericho, through Jerusalem, and down into the desert areas of the Dead Sea. Fueled by the Temple priests, the numbers of John's followers swelled until the banks of the river were overflowing with men petitioning for baptism. John's insistence that these men keep the law in strictest accordance increased the number of sacrifices—and therefore the coffers in the Temple. Everyone was pleased with the outcome of their arrangement.

Everyone save Mary Magdalene, who was now wed to the Baptizer.

It was perhaps a blessing that this was a union desired by neither the bride nor the bridegroom. John wanted only to remain in the wilderness and do God's work. He would abide by the law, which required men to be fruitful and multiply, and visit his wife at the appropriate times for reasons of procreation. But other than those periods specifically dictated by law and tradition, he had no interest in keeping the company of any woman.

Settling on a place for Mary to live had been the first order of business for the newly wed John. He made no secret that she was not welcome in the vicinity of his ministry. Indeed, the Qumran Essenes did not allow women to live with them at all, but exiled them to separate buildings because they were naturally unclean. And John's mother was dead, which was problematic. Had Elisabeth been alive, Mary would have lived in the home of her in-laws.

The issue was discussed by John and Lazarus prior to the wedding, and Mary had prompted her brother on her wishes. Lazarus urged that his sister be allowed to continue to live with him and Martha on their family estates in Magdala and Bethany. This would provide Mary with constant companionship as well as the chaperoning of a pious man and woman. And Bethany was an easy enough distance from Jericho, for those rare occasions when John was required to visit his wife.

It was an appropriate solution and an easy one for John, who had little interest in Mary's general activities other than the assurance that she conduct herself as a pious and repentant woman at all times. If this girl was to be the mother of his son, she must be beyond reproach. Mary assured John that in his absence she would obey her brother as she always had. She tried not to let her joy show when the agreement was made for her to stay with Lazarus and Martha.

But Mary's pleasure was short-lived as John laid down the rest of his laws. He would not suffer Mary to be in the presence of Nazarene teachings. She would not be allowed to visit the home of the Great Mary, her most revered teacher and friend. And she would certainly never appear in public where Easa was speaking. John was rankled by the fact that some of his own disciples had left the banks of the Jordan to follow his cousin. The Baptizer berated them for becoming Nazarenes and called them by the accursed title "seekers after smooth things." A rivalry was developing gradually between the very different ministries of the Nazarene Easa and the ascetic Baptizer. John would not be shamed by his own wife; she must never be allowed in the presence of the Nazarenes. John extracted this as a solemn vow from Lazarus.

Young, naïve, and never exposed to anything but love and acceptance, Mary attempted to argue this with John, but met the first of her husband's blows as she tried to object. John's hand left an imprint on Mary's cheek for the remainder of the day as a firm reinforcement that she would not argue with him about matters of obedience. The

Baptizer abandoned his bride to her home in Magdala the same day without so much as a farewell.

Mary dreaded John's visits and was grateful that they happened seldom and were separated by long periods of time. John came to Bethany only when he was in the vicinity for his own purposes, usually when traveling from his riverside shrine to Jerusalem. He inquired after Mary's health formally, and when it was appropriate under the law he performed the duties of a husband. During these visits John would spend time instructing Mary on the law and providing penitent tasks all the while advising her that the kingdom of God was at hand.

As a princess of the house of Benjamin, Mary knew it was unseemly to compare her husband to another, but she could not help it. Her days and nights were filled with thoughts of Easa and all he had taught her. It amazed her that both Easa and John preached much the same thing—that the kingdom of God was approaching—because the meaning was so different for the two prophets. From John, it was an ominous message, a dire warning of terror for the unrighteous. From Easa, it was a beautiful opportunity for all people who opened their hearts to God.

On the day Mary learned that Easa was coming to Bethany with his mother and a group of Nazarene followers, she felt the joy return to her heart for the first time in many, many days.

"They will not stay here. And you cannot go to see them, Mary. Your husband forbids it." Lazarus set his face like a stone against his sister's pleading.

"How can you do this to me?" Mary wailed at him. "These are my oldest friends—and some of them are your oldest friends as well. The fishermen Peter and Andrew, who played with us on the steps of Capernaeum and the shores of Galilee. How can you refuse them hospitality?"

The strain of the decision showed on the face of Mary's brother. To turn away his childhood friends, as well as Easa and the Great Mary, who were both revered children of David, was an excruciating decision. But Lazarus had orders from the high priest not to admit the Nazarene faction as they passed through on their way from Jerusalem. Further, his sister's husband had given explicit instructions that she was not to be in the presence of Nazarene teachings. Lazarus had taken a vow to keep Mary pious within the boundaries laid out by her husband.

"I do this for your benefit, sister."

"Just as you married me to the Baptizer for my own benefit?" Mary did not wait for his answer or to see the shock on his face. She stormed through the house and into the garden, where she allowed herself to cry.

"He really does want what is best for you."

Mary hadn't heard Martha follow her; she had been too immersed in her misery to pay attention. And as much as she loved Martha, she did not want to hear further lectures on obedience. Mary began to speak, but Martha cut her off.

"I am not here to chastise you. I'm here to help you."

Mary looked at Martha carefully. She had never known her brother's wife to go against his wishes or oppose him in any way. Yet there was a quiet strength that ran through Martha, and Mary saw that look of strength on her sister-in-law's face at that moment.

"Mary, you are like my own sister, in some ways like my own child. I cannot bear to see the pain you have suffered in this passing year. And I am proud of you, as is your brother. I know he doesn't tell you that, but he tells me all the time. You did your duty as a noble daughter of Israel, and all of it with your head held high."

Mary wiped the tears away as Martha continued. "Lazarus is leaving for Jerusalem on business. He will not be back until late tomorrow night. The Nazarenes will be here in Bethany, meeting at the house of Simon."

Mary's eyes grew huge as she listened. Was this really obedient, pious Martha, laying out a plan for subterfuge? "Simon? You mean in that house?"

Mary pointed to the house in question, which was easily visible from their own estate. Martha nodded.

"If you are very careful and entirely discreet, I will look in the other direction if you choose to visit your oldest friends."

Mary threw her arms around Martha and squealed, "I love you!"

"Shh!" Martha broke away from Mary's grip, looking around to be sure they had not been observed. "If Lazarus comes to see you before he leaves for Jerusalem, you must be furious with him. He can suspect nothing or we are both in terrible trouble."

Mary nodded solemnly at Martha, trying hard not to smile. Martha scurried back into the house to see Lazarus off, leaving Mary dancing beneath the olive trees.

Mary approached the house of Simon from a side entrance, covering her recognizable copper hair with one of her heavier veils as she walked. She gave the word of admittance and was allowed inside immediately, where she was delighted to see a number of familiar faces. She looked quickly around the room but did not yet see the most important and beloved faces, as Easa had not arrived with his mother. She had little time to think about this as she was startled from behind by a young woman's voice shouting her name.

Mary turned to see the exquisite smile of Salome, the daughter of Herodias and stepdaughter to the tetrarch of Galilee, Herod. Mary squealed in recognition, as they had trained together at the feet of the Great Mary. They embraced happily and with warmth.

"What are you doing this far from home?" Mary asked her.

"My mother has given me permission to follow Easa and continue my training so that I might take the seven veils." The seven veils were worn only by women who had been initiated as high priestesses.

"Herod Antipas gives my mother whatever she desires, and besides, he is sympathetic to the Nazarenes. It is only the Baptizer he detests."

Salome covered her mouth immediately as the words slipped out. She appeared mortified. "I'm sorry. I forget."

Mary smiled at her sadly. "No, Salome, do not apologize. Sometimes I forget myself."

Salome looked immensely sympathetic. "Is it horrible for you?"

Mary shook her head. She loved Salome like a sister, and indeed they referred to each other by that title, which was traditional for Nazarene priestesses. But Mary was still a princess and schooled to behave as one. She would not speak ill of her husband no matter what the company. "No, it's not horrible. I rarely see John."

Salome rushed through her words as if she felt the need to make further amends for her gaffe. "I hope I didn't offend you, sister. It's just that the Baptizer says terrible things about my mother. He calls her a whore and an adulteress."

Mary nodded. She had heard all of these things. Salome's mother, Herodias, was the granddaughter of Herod the Great and had inherited some of the infamous king's headstrong traits. She put aside her first husband to marry Herod Antipas, who ruled Galilee, and the tetrarch had taken similar action by divorcing his Arabian wife to marry Herodias. John had been outraged that a Jewish monarch would show such blatant disregard for the law and had openly denounced the marriage of Herod Antipas to Herodias as adultery. Thus far, Herod had expressed annoyance but showed little interest in taking real action against John for his condemnation. As tetrarch of Galilee he had enough to do with juggling the whims of a Caesar and the demands of this difficult outpost; he didn't need the added headache of an abrasive ascetic prophet.

The fact that Herodias was a Nazarene certainly didn't help her case with John, nor did it improve John's opinion of Nazarene culture. It further proved why women should never be allowed positions of authority or even social freedoms; clearly, it turned them into wantons. John often used Herod and Herodias as examples of Nazarene corruption.

But while the Baptizer made enemies of the tetrarch, Easa was much admired by Herod's wife. Herodias had sent her only daughter to begin training in The Way when she came of age. Salome and Mary had become very close during their time together in Galilee, further bonded in their spiritual love for the Great Mary and her son.

"Our sister Veronica is here," Salome said, anxious to change the subject. Simon's niece, Veronica, was a lovely and deeply spiritual young woman who had trained with them at the home of Easa's mother. Mary loved Veronica and looked around for the face of her cherished friend.

"There she is!" Salome grabbed Mary's hand and pulled her across the room to a now-beaming Veronica. The three women, sisters in the Nazarene creed, embraced warmly. But they had little further opportunity for discussion as Easa entered the room.

He was followed by his mother and two younger brothers, James and Jude, as well as the fishermen brothers from Galilee and a dour-looking man who Mary believed to be called Philip. Easa greeted everyone in the room but stopped in front of Mary. He embraced her warmly, but with the propriety and respect due to a noblewoman who was another man's wife. He gave her a long look to indicate his surprise that she had disobeyed her brother, but said nothing.

Mary smiled up at him and put her hand over her heart. "The Kingdom of God is in my heart, and no oppressor can take it from me."

Easa returned the smile, an expression of utmost warmth, then moved to the front of the room and began to teach.

It was a beautiful night, filled with the love of friends and the word of The Way. Mary had almost forgotten how important the Word had become to her and what an inspirational teacher Easa was. But to sit at his feet and listen to his preaching was to experience the Kingdom of God here on earth. She could not imagine how anyone could condemn such beautiful words, or why someone would willfully deny those teachings of love, compassion, and charity.

As Easa rose to take his leave, he walked toward Mary and touched her gently on the belly.

"You are with child, little dove."

Mary gasped. John had stayed for a night to fulfill his duties within the last season, but she had no idea that she had conceived. "You are sure?"

Easa nodded. "A male child grows in your womb. Keep well, little one. For I would see you deliver in safety."

A shadow crossed his face for the briefest moment. "Tell your brother that you must spend your confinement in Galilee. Ask that he allow you to leave in the morning at first light."

Mary was puzzled by this. Bethany was close to Jerusalem, and the finest midwives and medicine were at hand if there were any complications. It made sense for her to stay here, and Lazarus wouldn't be back for another full day. But Easa had seen something in that moment of shadow, something that bade him urge her to leave Bethany for the shores of Galilee immediately.

What Mary could not know was that in a clear moment of prophecy, Easa had seen the need to get her as far away from John as possible.

"Whore!" John screamed as he slapped Mary again and again. "I knew it was too late for you and your wanton Nazarene ways. How dare you disobey your husband and your brother!"

Martha and Lazarus were at the far side of the Bethany house, but they could hear the violence unfolding. Martha cried softly from her place on the bed as she listened to the blows fall on Mary's tiny frame. This was her fault. She had encouraged Mary to disobey the explicit orders of her husband and her brother. Martha felt that she was the one who deserved the beating.

Lazarus sat immobile, frozen with fear and helplessness. He was furious with Martha and Mary, but far more concerned with the beating his sister was receiving at the hands of her husband. He was utterly powerless to do anything about it. To intervene would add further insult to John, something he did not dare do. Besides, it was common for a husband to beat a disobedient wife. In the more traditional households, it was even expected. John's actions were in keeping with his interpretation of the law.

They still didn't know how John had come to discover Mary's presence at the Nazarene gathering. Was there an informer among them the previous night? Or was John's gift of prophecy so clear that he saw Mary in his own visions?

Whatever the catalyst, John had come to Bethany the following afternoon in a fit of uncontrolled rage and was determined to punish everyone involved in the deception. He knew his young wife had been sitting devotedly at the feet of his cousin the night before. Worse, she sat with the wanton spawn of the whore Herodias. For Mary to flaunt her Nazarene sympathies and her affiliation with Salome was a source of shame and embarrassment to John. It had the potential to damage his reputation.

Damn the woman! Didn't she understand that any smirch on his name could impact his work and diminish the message of God? This was proof that women had no sense, no ability to think things through to their consequences. Females were sinful creatures by nature, daughters of Eve and Jezebel. John was beginning to conclude that perhaps they were all beyond redemption.

John shouted these things and more as he continued his assault. Mary huddled in the corner with her arms over her head in a futile effort to protect her face. It was too late; a purplish circle was spreading around one eye, and her lower lip was swollen and bleeding where the back of his hand had caused a tooth to tear it open. She managed to cry out, "Stop, you'll hurt the baby."

John stayed his hand from the next blow. "What did you say?"

Mary breathed deeply in an effort to calm herself. "I am with child."

John regarded her coldly. "You are a Nazarene whore who spent the night in the home of another man without a chaperone. I cannot even be sure that the child is mine."

Mary spoke slowly as she attempted to stand. "I am not what you call me. I came to you as a virgin bride, and I have never been with any man save you, my husband under the law." She emphasized these last five words. "You are angry that I disobeyed you, and I deserve your anger."

She stood her ground now. A full head shorter than he, she drew herself up and looked into his face. "But your child does not deserve to be questioned. He will be a prince of our people one day."

John made a guttural noise in his throat and turned his back to leave. "I will deliver the strict terms of your confinement to Lazarus." He opened the door and stalked out into the corridor. Without ever looking back, he issued a final verbal blow.

"If that child is female, I will gladly forsake you both."

It was late the next afternoon when Mary decided to venture into the garden for some air. She had been in bed most of the day, nursing her bruises. The garden was private, enclosed by walls, so there was no chance of anyone seeing the marks of disgrace that covered her face. Or so she thought.

Mary heard a rustling in the bushes that caused her heart to stop. What was it? Who was it? "Hello?" she called out haltingly.

"Mary?" a female voice whispered, followed by more rustling. Suddenly a figure emerged from behind a row of hedges near the garden wall.

"Salome! What are you doing here?" Mary ran to embrace her friend, a Herodian princess who was sneaking around like a common thief.

Salome couldn't answer immediately. She was struck motionless, staring at Mary's battered face.

Mary turned her head. "Is it so bad?" she asked in a whisper.

Salome spat on the ground. "My mother is right. The Baptizer is an animal. How dare he treat you like this! You are a noblewoman."

Mary started to defend John but realized she didn't have the energy. She was suddenly exhausted, worn-out by the events of recent days and by the growing toll that pregnancy was taking on her petite frame. She sat on a stone bench and was joined by her friend.

"I brought this for you." Salome handed Mary a silken pouch. "There's a healing unguent in the jar. It will soothe your bruises."

"How did you know?" Mary asked. It had suddenly occurred to her that Salome knew something that only Martha and Lazarus had witnessed.

Salome shrugged. "*He* saw it." There could only be one "he." "He didn't tell me what happened. He just said, 'Take your finest healing cream to your sister Mary. She will be in need of it immediately.' And then he said to be sure no one else saw me come here because of John."

Mary tried to smile at the revelation of Easa's vision, but the cut lip made her wince instead. Salome's lovely face darkened with anger as she watched her friend in pain. "Why did he do it?" Salome demanded.

"I disobeyed him."

"How?"

"By attending the Nazarene meeting."

The dawn of understanding crept up on Salome. "Ah, so we are the enemy now as far as the Baptizer is concerned. I wonder when he will publicly denounce Easa? That is sure to happen next."

Mary gasped. "They are kin, and John announced Easa publicly at his baptism. He wouldn't do such a thing."

"No? I'm not so sure, sister." Salome was thinking. "My mother says that John is as cunning as a serpent. Think about it. He married you to legitimize his kingship, and now you're pregnant with his heir. He denounces my mother as an adulteress and uses the fact that she's a Nazarene against her, and as a weapon over the rest of us. What's the next step? To publicly withdraw his support of Easa based on what John believes is our Nazarene disregard for the law. He won't be satisfied until he destroys The Way."

"I don't think John would do that, Salome."

"Don't you?" The girl laughed, a hard sound from someone so

young. "You haven't spent as much time around the Herods as I have. What men will do to advance their position is astonishing."

Mary sighed and shook her head. "I know this is hard for you to believe, but John is a good man and a true prophet. I would not have married him if I did not believe that to be so, nor would my brother have agreed to it. John is different from Easa, and he is harsh and rough, but he believes in the kingdom of God. He lives only to help men find God through repentance and the law."

"Yes, he believes in helping *men*. As for women, John would sooner drown us all in his precious river than offer us salvation." Salome made a face to show her disdain. "And he has become a puppet of the Pharisees, if for no other reason than because he has no social or political skills of his own. He goes where they direct him. And I guarantee that he will be directed to question Easa's legitimacy even further if he is not stopped."

Mary looked at her friend. Something about the way Salome was speaking made her nervous, yet it was a fear mixed with respect. Her childhood friend had developed a savvy understanding of politics from her time in the Herods' palaces.

"What do you propose?"

As Mary looked up, a beam of sunlight illuminated her face, showing off the florid purple and black marring of bruises. The Herodian princess shuddered at the sight of Mary's beautiful, fine-boned face with such marks. When Salome spoke, it was with a soft determination. "I will make John the Baptizer pay for his deeds—against you, against Easa, and against my mother. One way or another."

A shudder wracked Mary's body at those words. Despite the heat of a midday sun, she suddenly felt very, very cold.

The swiftness of John's arrest was staggering. Mary was to find out much later that Salome had hastened to the tetrarch's winter palace near the Dead Sea, where a celebration was under way for the birthday of Herod Antipas. Herod had requested that Salome dance for him and his guests—the girl's grace and beauty were legendary, and travelers had come a great distance to pay tribute to Herod. The tetrarch felt it would be a gesture of goodwill to show off his exquisite stepdaughter.

Salome entered the room where the celebration was in full Roman swing. She was dressed in glittering silks and golden chains that had been bestowed by her doting stepfather. As she arrived in the room, she caused a stir among the guests, who craned their necks for a better look at the stunning princess.

"You are the most priceless jewel in my kingdom, Salome," her stepfather announced. "Come, dance for us. It will be a great thrill for these guests to see your grace."

Salome approached Herod's throne, from which he ruled over the banquet. She was a picture of pretty petulance. "I don't know if I can dance, Stepfather. My heart is so heavy with what I have endured while I traveled that I do not believe I have the spirit to dance."

Herodias, perched on a cushion beside her husband, straightened. "What happened that has had such an effect on you, child?"

Salome told them a tearful story, about the horrible man who was called the Baptizer and how his words haunted her and seemed to follow wherever she went.

"Who is this man, this Baptizer?" A visiting Roman nobleman asked the question.

Herod made a dismissive gesture. "Nobody. One of several fashionable messiahs this year. He is a troublemaker, but not an important one."

At this Salome burst into tears and threw herself at her mother's feet. She cried about the terrible names that this man the Baptizer called Herodias. She was frightened because this prophet called for Herod to be displaced and predicted the palace would fall with all of them in it. He incited hatred of the Herods among the people, so much so that Salome could no longer travel safely with the Nazarenes unless she was well disguised.

"He sounds more like an insurgent than a prophet," the Roman noble observed. "It's best to deal with his kind quickly."

Herod was in no mood for politics but could not allow himself to appear weak before a Roman envoy. He called for his guards and issued the order.

"Arrest this man, this Baptizer, and bring him here. I would see if he has the courage to say such things to me in person."

The assembled guests applauded this decision and followed the Roman nobleman's lead by raising glasses to their host. Salome wiped the tears from her eyes and smiled sweetly at Herod Antipas.

"Which dance would you like to see tonight, Stepfather?"

John the Baptizer was a troubling prisoner. Herod Antipas had not anticipated the strength of John's following, which had grown to extraordinary proportions. Petitioners flooded the palace each day, demanding the release of their prophet. They appealed to Herod as a Jew, begging his sympathy as one of their own. Because the winter palace was in the vicinity of Qumran, the Essene community sent envoys daily to ask for the freedom of this righteous prisoner. This was not a simple, regional prophet to be chastised and silenced with ease. John the Baptizer was a phenomenon.

Herod took it upon himself to interview John, and sent for the ascetic preacher to be brought before him. He questioned John personally, expecting self-righteous answers and the wild ravings that often came from these wilderness preachers and self-styled messiahs. This was a type of sport for Herod, and he was particularly looking forward to baiting the man who had so troubled his wife and stepdaughter. After he had had the chance to toy with the prisoner for a time, he would decide what final sentence to pass.

The interview did not go as the tetrarch planned. While this man John was oddly dressed and had an uncivilized appearance, there was nothing of the raving wild man in his words. Herod found him disturbingly intelligent, perhaps even wise. John spoke severely of sinners and of the need for repentance, and did not hesitate to look in Herod's eyes when he warned that someone with the tetrarch's sins would be denied the kingdom of God. But there was still time for re-demption, if Herod would put aside his adulteress wife and repent for his many transgressions.

By the end of the interview Herod was deeply troubled by John's incarceration. He wished to release John, but could not do so without appearing weak and ineffective before Rome. Hadn't a Roman envoy been present during the orders for John's arrest? To release the man now would make Herod appear inconsistent and perhaps even in-competent to deal with Jewish insurgents. No, he didn't dare release the Baptizer, at least not yet. Instead, he lessened the strictness of his incarceration and allowed John to have visitors from among his fol-lowers and the local Essenes.

When she heard of this policy, Mary of Magdala sent a messenger to the palace, asking if her husband would like to see her or have word of the child she carried. John ignored the message completely. The only words that Mary heard from John during his incarceration were ones of condemnation. She heard through his closest followers that John continued to question the paternity of her child and referred to her in the most derogatory terms. He blamed his young wife for his arrest, and the more fanatic of his followers had even sent threats to her family. Finally, Mary convinced her brother and Martha to take her back to Galilee, as far away from the Baptizer and his followers as possible. She did not understand how one night of innocent disobe-dience had translated into a tarnished reputation as a harlot, but that was the reality she now faced. Mary preferred to face it in the sanctu-ary of her home at the foot of Mount Arbel, closer to the Nazarenes and their sympathizers.

John continued his ministry from prison, where his legend and his influence grew in the southern region. But the ministry of his cousin, the charismatic Nazarene, blossomed with increased vigor in the area north of Jordan and into Galilee. John's followers brought word to him in prison of Easa's great works and of the miraculous healings that were attributed to him. But they also told of the Nazarene's con-tinued leniency toward Gentiles and the unclean. He had even stopped an adulterous woman from being justly stoned! Clearly,

John's cousin had lost all grasp of the law. It was time for John to take a stand.

At John's instruction, the followers of the Baptizer set out to attend a large gathering of Nazarenes. When Easa stood before the gathered multitude to begin his preaching, two of the ascetic ambassadors came forward. The first spoke, addressing Easa and then the rest of the crowd.

"We come from the cell of John the Baptizer. He begs that we deliver this message unto you all. He says to you, Yeshua the Nazarene, that he questions you. That where he once believed you were the messiah sent by God, he cannot believe that your acceptance of the unclean is within the law. Therefore he asks of you, are you the one who was awaited? Or should these good people wait for another?"

The crowd grew restless at these words. John's baptism of Easa had been the defining moment for some of the newer Nazarene disciples. The magical day on the banks of the Jordan, when John had announced his cousin as the chosen one and when God had showed his favor in the form of a dove, had transformed many into followers of The Way. Now John the Baptizer was in essence withdrawing his support by publicly questioning his cousin.

Yeshua the Nazarene was unmoved by the question and unaffected by the insult. He silenced the crowd and said to them, "There is no greater prophet on this earth than John the Baptizer."

To the men who had challenged him, he added, "Please give all kind regards to my cousin. Go, and tell him what things you see and hear with us today."

And there would be much to tell. The Nazarene leader went out among the crowd then and ministered to the ill. On that day he was said to have given eyesight to many who had been blind. He cured the infirmities of the elderly; he drove evil spirits and ill humors from the afflicted. And through it all he preached the word of The Way and taught the people about the light of God. He told a story, a parable about a woman who was forgiven for her sins because she had a heart filled with faith and love. This was his final message of the day.

"Sins are forgiven of those who are filled with love. But if the most righteous man has little love in his heart, he will know little forgiveness."

It was a day that would define the ministry of Yeshua the Nazarene as the healing Way of love and forgiveness, a path of salvation available to all people who chose to walk in that light.

Herod Antipas had a problem. The Roman envoy who had witnessed the arrest warrant for John the Baptizer months earlier had returned. When the Roman asked the tetrarch's officials why there were so many Jews surrounding the palace, he was told that the imprisoned prophet continued to attract followers. The envoy was astounded that Herod had not seen fit to take a position on the insurgent Baptizer.

At dinner later in the evening, the nobleman from Rome spoke with Herod sternly about the issue.

"You cannot be seen to be spineless where these rabble-rousers are concerned. You are here because Caesar trusts you to represent Rome and because he feels that you have an advantage with the people as a fellow Jew. But it would be a terrible mistake to appear too soft on them. This man insults Rome daily from the very prison where he is held, and you allow it."

The tetrarch defended his position. "This desert land is overrun by Essene sects and others who call this man a prophet. To execute him would incite rioting."

"You, a Roman citizen and a king, allow yourself to be held hostage by these desert dwellers?" The question was filled with rebuke.

Herod knew when he was cornered. This envoy was returning to Rome the following day, and he could not risk the man reporting any perceived weakness to Caesar. He had plenty of enemies who would like to see the fall of the Herods once and for all; that could not happen. Antipas was not born into the blood of such kings for nothing. Hadn't his grandfather executed his own sons when he perceived a threat to his throne? Herods knew how to fight for what was rightfully theirs.

Herod Antipas clapped twice to call his servants, and ordered the centurions brought forward.

"Carry out sentence on the prisoner, John the Baptizer, immediately. He is to be executed swiftly with a sword."

The Roman envoy nodded his vigorous approval as Herod Antipas moved to take his place in history for the first time—but not for the last.

Before his execution, John asked for just one thing—that a message be sent to his wife in Galilee. He was allowed to receive one follower to act as a courier. To him, John gave his final words of instruction and repentance before the centurion's sword fell swiftly. The head was severed from the body with the first blow, and John the Baptizer, prophet of the Jordan, was sent to the kingdom of God.

Herod had John's head mounted on a pike and displayed high at the front gate of the palace to show the Roman envoy how swiftly and severely he would deal with treason. It stayed there until it had been picked clean by scavenging birds, but disappeared mysteriously one night. The rest of John's body was given to the Essene followers for burial.

It was to a heavily pregnant Mary of Magdala that word was brought of John's execution. The messenger delivered John's last words to her in person.

"Repent, woman. Do penance each day for the sins that have brought us to this place. Do it in memory of me and for the sake of the child you carry. If there is any hope for the child to be accepted into the kingdom of God, you must repent and have the child baptized at birth."

Whether or not John died believing that Mary carried his child, she would never know. That he bothered to send a message as his last request gave her some indication that he may have believed that the child was his. Mary took his words to her heart and prayed every day for the rest of her long life for John's forgiveness. He had been unkind to her, but she did not hold ill will toward him. Easa and the Great Mary taught that forgiveness was divine, and she embraced that principle with all sincerity.

John had been an enigma for her from the very beginning. He was a rough man who had never asked for what was pressed upon him, never intended to take a wife. She did her best to behave in a way that John would determine was obedient, but nothing about her ever pleased him. Sadly, Mary was wed to the only man in Israel who wouldn't have given anything to have her. She was beautiful, virtuous, and wealthy in her own right, and she carried the royal blood of their people. None of those qualities was of interest to John the Baptizer.

The marriage had been a kind of sentence for each of them. The blessing for both was that they were separated most of the time, coming together only when the Pharisees pressured John to create an heir. In the end, the marriage was more abhorrent to John than it was to Mary. Now they were released from it, but Mary would have given anything to change the manner in which she was given her freedom.

Just as Mary had been blamed for John's imprisonment, so was she accused in the execution by his most loyal followers. The only woman more reviled in the land at that moment was Salome. The Herodian princess was accused of terrible acts, including incest with her stepfather. Lurid tales spread of Salome's loose sexuality and how she had used it to demand the head of John the Baptizer on a silver platter. None of these things was true. Salome had used a childish ploy to secure John's imprisonment, but she confessed tearfully to Mary later that she had never anticipated his execution. She merely wanted to stop John for a time, to diminish his growing power among the people so he could not harm Easa or Mary. Salome was ultimately too young and inexperienced in the ways of politics and religion to foresee that John's arrest would lead to his greater popularity among the common people. Worse, she did not anticipate Herod's unfortunate dilemma or its singular solution.

An anonymous messenger from John's camp brought a final and unexpected relic of repentance to his young widow some weeks later. Without a word, the ascetic handed her a woven reed basket and left the house quickly. There was no message attached, and the courier would not meet her eyes as he delivered the package. Curious, Mary lifted the lid to reveal the contents.

Resting on a silk cushion within the container was the sun-bleached skull of John the Baptizer.

Mary went into labor prematurely. It was a blessing in disguise as her tiny frame would not have been able to deliver this baby at full term. Even coming before his time as he did, the child was a strapping infant. He arrived in the world bellowing with great indignity. At a single day old he was the physical image of John. And anyone who heard the insistence in the infant's wail would have recognized him as the legitimate child of the Baptizer.

Mary of Magdala sent word to the Great Mary and to Easa that her child had been delivered safely, along with her thanks for their welcome prayers.

She named the child John-Joseph, after his father.

After John's execution, tremendous pressure was put upon Easa to take a position among the followers. He went into the desert place and met with the Essenes and John's disciples, preaching the kingdom of God in his own way. Some among the Essenes accepted Easa as their new messiah and followed him because he was of the line of David. Yet many others were opposed to his Nazarene reforms because John had spoken harshly of these things at the end of his life. For the majority of the desert dwellers, John was the one and only

Teacher of Righteousness, and anyone who tried to take his position was an imposter.

The deep division between those who would follow John and those who would be faithful to Easa was fashioned in these early days. The Nazarene spirit emerged as one of love and forgiveness, and was accessible to anyone who chose to embrace it. The Johannite philosophy was a very different one, based on harsh judgments and strict rules of law. Where women were welcomed and honored by Easa and the Nazarenes, they were reviled by the followers of John. John had always held women in low esteem, and his depiction of Mary and Salome as the whores of Babylon incarnate cemented the idea of women as lowly.

Inaccurate and unfair portraits emerged of Mary as a repentant sinner and Salome as a decadent harlot. The followers of John the Baptizer fanned these flames of injustice, igniting a conflagration that would burn through several thousand years.

Easa the Nazarene, prince of the house of David, intended to change the public perception of the maligned and newly widowed princess. He, more than any other, knew that this good and virtuous woman had suffered terrible injustice. She was no less a daughter of Benjamin now than before. Her blood was still royal, her heart was still pure, and he still loved her.

Lazarus was taken aback when the Son of the Lion appeared at his door, completely alone and without his followers.

"I have come to see Mary and the child," he said simply.

Stammering, Lazarus called to Martha and invited Easa in. Martha entered the room and made no attempt to disguise either her surprise or her joy. She had long been a Nazarene sympathizer, despite her more conservative family background. She had always loved and revered Easa.

"I'll bring Mary and the baby," Martha said, and scurried out of the room.

When they were left alone, Lazarus attempted to speak again. "Yeshua, I have many things to apologize for . . ."

Easa held up his hand. "Peace, Lazarus. I have never known you to do anything that you did not believe in your heart was right and just. You are true to yourself and true to your Lord. As such, you have no need to apologize to me or to anyone."

Lazarus was tremendously relieved. He had long held the sadness of breaking the betrothal between Easa and his sister, as well as the guilt of denying the Nazarenes lodging on the night in Bethany that had turned out to be such a calamity for Mary. But he had no time to say so, as little John-Joseph announced his arrival in the room with a hearty cry.

Easa turned to smile at Mary and her infant child. He reached out his arms for the baby, who was red-faced from his vocalizations. "He is as beautiful as his mother and as opinionated as his father," Easa laughed, taking the child. At the first touch of Easa's hand, John-Joseph ceased his crying. The infant grew quiet, looking at this new figure with great interest. Little John cooed happily when Easa bounced him gently in his arms.

"He likes you," Mary said, suddenly shy in the presence of this man who had grown into a legend among the people.

Easa looked at Mary seriously. "I hope so." He looked at Lazarus. "Lazarus, dear brother, I would speak privately to Mary about a very serious matter. She is a widow and it is appropriate to speak with her directly."

"Of course," Lazarus muttered and hurried swiftly out of the room.

Easa, still holding little John, motioned for Mary to sit. They sat together for a quiet, happy moment, as the baby continued to coo at Easa and grab at his long hair, worn in the Nazarene style.

"Mary, I have something to ask you."

She nodded quietly, not sure what was coming but in absolute bliss to be near him again. Easa's presence was a balm to her ravaged spirit.

"You have endured much, and done so because of your faith in me and The Way. I would right that wrong for you and for this child.

Mary, I would like you to become my wife and give me permission to raise John's son as my own."

Mary was immobilized. Had she heard him correctly? Surely, this was impossible.

"Easa, I don't know what to say." She paused momentarily, grasping at the thoughts that raced through her surprised mind. "I spent my entire life dreaming of being married to you. And when that was not to be . . . I never thought of that dream again. But I cannot allow you to do such a thing. I would damage you and your mission. There are too many who blame me for John's death, men who hate me and call me sinner."

"That makes no difference to me. Anyone who follows me knows the truth, and we will teach the truth to those who do not yet know it. And the followers of the law cannot oppose it. In fact, it is seemly that I would take you to wife. You are John's widow and I am his kin. I am the nearest related male to John and as such should raise this child. And I would raise him as a prince of his people, as my chosen heir and the son of a prophet. This is a proper union, for the law and for the people of Israel. I am still the son of David and you are still the daughter of Benjamin."

Mary was overwhelmed. She had never expected that anything like this could happen. At best, she had hoped for Easa to baptize this child as John had requested. But to adopt little John as his own and take her as his wife? It was more than she could bear. Mary put her head in her hands and began to weep.

"What makes you cry, little dove? We are no less perfect for each other in the eyes of God now than when He first chose us to be joined together."

Mary wiped the tears from her eyes and looked into the face of the Nazarene, her Easa, whom God had given back to her.

"I never believed I would know what it was to be happy again," she whispered.

Unlike the elaborate affair at Cana, Easa and Mary were wed in a small private ceremony attended by the Great Mary and surrounded by the most loyal of Nazarenes. The event occurred on the shores of Galilee, in the village of Tabga.

Word of the union spread quickly, and the following day throngs of people began to arrive in Tabga. Some were followers, some merely curious at this idea of the bride and bridegroom of Solomon's prophecy coming together. Others were not pleased at the idea of their beloved Galilean prophet joining with this woman of tarnished reputation. But Easa was glad for the presence of all of them. He told Mary over and over again that each day brought a new opportunity to show The Way to someone who had never seen it before, a chance to bring eyesight to the blind.

The news of their wedding attracted thousands over the course of two days.

The Great Mary came to Easa at the end of the second day. She reminded him of the first wedding miracle in Cana, when there was not enough wine for the wedding guests. Now the shores of Galilee were overflowing with travelers who had not eaten in several days, and they had very little food left. His mother bade him to consider his own wedding feast on this day.

Easa called his closest followers to him. He asked for an accounting of the total number of guests, to which Philip replied, "There are near to five thousand and we have only two hundred pennyworths."

Andrew, the brother of Peter, advised, "There is a lad here whom I am acquainted with, a fisherman's son. He has five barley loaves and two small fish, but that is all. It is nothing compared to the number we face here."

Easa told them, "Have them sit down in the grass. Bring the loaves and fishes to me."

This was done by Andrew, who placed the loaves and fishes in a basket at the feet of his master. Easa said a prayer of thanksgiving for abundance over the food, then handed the basket back to Andrew, saying, "Begin with this basket and pass it among the guests. Gather up all the fragments so that nothing is lost. Then place those fragments into new baskets and pass those around as well."

Andrew followed these directions, aided by Peter and the others. They marveled as baskets that had held but a few crumbs overflowed with loaves of bread. Soon, there were twelve large baskets heaped with food. These were passed to the multitudes until each person in attendance had eaten his fill.

All who feasted on the shores at Tabga that day were convinced beyond any doubt that Easa the Nazarene was truly the messiah of prophecy. His reputation as a great worker of miracles as well as a healer continued to spread, as did his following among the common people. And many more were inclined to accept Mary at this time. Surely if so great a prophet had chosen this woman, she must be worthy.

Mary's position and stature presented a problem: her name. In a time when women were defined by their male relationships, hers were tricky and politically difficult. It would not be appropriate to refer to her as the widow of John, nor would it be entirely acceptable to call her simply the wife of Easa. She became known at that time by her own name, as a woman of leadership. She would forever after reign as the Daughter of Zion, the Tower of Her Flock—the Migdal-Eder. Hers was the stand-alone name of a queen. The people called her simply:

Mary Magdalene.

It was this period of ministry following the miraculous feeding of the multitude at Tabga that Mary Magdalene referred to as the Great Time. Shortly after the wedding, the Nazarenes, with Mary now in their number, set out for Syria. Easa healed an astonishing number of people during their journey. He spent time teaching in the synagogues and bringing the word of The Way to new ears. But after a number of months the entourage returned to Galilee. Mary Magdalene was pregnant, and Easa wanted their child born where Mary would be most comfortable—in her home.

A perfect, tiny daughter was delivered to Mary and Easa upon their return to Galilee. They gave her the double name of a princess, Sarah-Tamar. The name Sarah invoked a noble Hebrew woman of scripture, the wife of Abraham. Tamar was a Galilean name; it made reference to the abundant date palm trees that grew in the region, and had been used by royal houses for generations as a pet name for their daughters.

The noble family was expanding, their ministry was growing, and the children of Israel were given a sense of hope for the future. It was, indeed, a Great Time.

# CHAPTER EIGHTEEN

*Château des Pommes Bleues*
*June 29, 2005*

No one spoke immediately after Peter finished reading his translation of the first book. They all sat in silence for a long moment, each absorbing in his or her way the immensity of the information. All of them had cried at varying intervals—the men in a more reserved manner, the women weeping openly at elements of Mary's story.

Finally, Sinclair broke the silence. "Where do we begin?"

Maureen shook her head. "I wouldn't even know where to start." She looked up at Peter to see how he was coping. He looked surprisingly calm, even smiling at her as their eyes met. "Are you okay?" she asked.

He nodded. "Never better. It's very strange, but I don't feel shocked or worried or concerned, I just feel . . . content. I can't explain it, but that's how I feel."

"You look exhausted," Tammy observed. "But you did an amazing job."

Sinclair and Roland chimed in their agreement, each thanking Peter for his tireless approach to the translation.

"Why don't you get some rest and you can start back in on the other books tomorrow," Maureen suggested gently. "Seriously, Pete, you need to sleep."

Peter shook his head, adamant. "No way. There are two more books left—there's the Book of Disciples, and she calls the next one the Book of the Time of Darkness. I think we have to assume that is an eyewitness account of the crucifixion, and I'm not going anywhere until I find out."

When they realized that Peter wouldn't budge, Sinclair had a tray of tea brought in for him. The priest still refused any food, believing that he needed to fast during the translations. They left him alone then, and Sinclair, Maureen, and Tammy adjourned to the dining room for a light meal. Roland was invited to join them but refused politely, stating that he had too many things to do. He caught Tammy's eye across the room, then left.

Dinner was light as none of them had much interest in food. They were still finding it hard to put their reaction to the first book into words. Tammy finally spoke about the John elements.

"After spending the day with Derek, this all makes so much more sense. I now see why the Guild followers of John hate Mary and Salome so much, but it's all so unjust."

Maureen was confused. She had not yet been privy to Tammy's findings. "What do you mean? Are those the people who attacked me?"

Tammy explained all she had learned from Derek on that dreadful visit to Carcassonne. Maureen listened in stunned silence.

"But did you already know that Mary had a son by John the Baptist?" She asked this question to both of them. "Because this is a complete shock to me. I mean, really stunning."

Sinclair nodded. "It will be a shock to most people. It is a tradition that we know of here, but few people outside of our proudly heretical sect are aware of it. There was a concerted effort to remove those facts from history—on both sides. Ostensibly, the followers of Jesus did not want any information about John to overshadow the story of Jesus, so it was carefully and cleverly told by the authors of the Gospels."

Tammy interrupted. "The followers of John don't talk about it because they despise Mary Magdalene. I have started reading through their Guild documents, the so-called *True Book of the Holy Grail*. They call it that because they believe that the only holy blood comes through John and his child. So that makes their bloodline the true Holy Grail, the true vessel of sacred blood. And if they had their way, they would have eliminated all mention of Mary Magdalene not only in scripture but in history. They have a law within the Guild that she is never to be mentioned without the title of whore attached to her name."

"That makes no sense," Maureen said. "She was the mother of John's child, and they acknowledge him as legitimate. Why would they still hate Mary Magdalene so?"

"Because as far as they're concerned she and Salome plotted John's death so that she could marry Jesus—Easa—and so that he could take over the position of anointed one. And so that he could usurp the position of father to John's child and train him in the Nazarene ways. It is actually a part of their ritual to deny Christ by spitting on the cross and calling him the Usurper."

Maureen looked at both of them. "I'm hesitant to bring this up, but it's hard for me to believe that Jean-Claude is a part of that."

"You mean Jean-Baptiste." Tammy dripped disdain on the name.

"When we were in Montsegur . . . he knew so much about the Cathars. Not only that, he was so reverent about them, so respectful. Was that all a show?"

Sinclair sighed and ran his hands over his face. "Yes, and it was only a very small part of a very large show, from what I understand. Roland has discovered that Jean-Claude had been groomed since childhood to infiltrate our organization. His family is wealthy and with the resources of the Guild he was able to create this identity. Granted, he added the Paschal element later, which should have made me suspicious, but I had no reason not to believe him. And the fact remains that he is an accomplished scholar and historian, an expert on our history. But in his case it turns out not to be for reverential purposes, but more along the lines of 'Know thine enemy.'"

"How long has this been going on? This rivalry?"

"Two thousand years," Sinclair responded. "But it's one-sided. Our people hold no ill will toward John and have always welcomed the Baptist bloodline as our brothers and sisters. After all, we're all children of Mary Magdalene, right? That's how we see it here, and always have."

"It's their side of the family who are the troublemakers," Tammy joked.

Sinclair interrupted. "But not all followers of the Baptist are extremists, which is important to remember. These Guild fanatics are a minority. A rabid, frightening group and a surprisingly powerful one, but still a minority. Come outside with me, I'd like to show you something."

The three of them got up from the table, and Tammy excused herself. She asked Maureen to join her later in the media room. "Now that we've come this far, I want to show you a few more things I've uncovered in my research."

Maureen agreed to meet Tammy in an hour, and followed Sinclair outside. The twilight sky was still bright with the remnants of summer sunshine as they strolled toward the entrance gate of the Trinity Gardens.

"Remember the third garden? The one you didn't get to see the other day? Come, let me show it to you now."

Sinclair took Maureen's arm and led her around the Mary Magdalene fountain and through the first archway on the left. A marble path led them into an elaborate garden resembling the grounds of an Italian villa.

"It looks very . . . Romanesque," Maureen noted.

"Yes. We know very little about this young man, John-Joseph. As far as I know there is nothing in writing about him—or at least there wasn't until today. We have only a smattering of local traditions and legends that have been handed down."

"And what do you know?"

"Just that this child was not the son of Jesus—that he was John's. We had his name right, John-Joseph, although some legends refer to him as John-Yeshua and even John-Mark. Legend has it that he went to Rome at some stage, and left his mother and siblings behind here in France. Whether or not that was his own doing or part of a master plan is purely speculation. And what his fate is, we don't know either. There are two schools of thought."

Sinclair led her to a marble statue of a young man in the Renaissance style. He stood before a large cross, but in one hand he held a skull.

"He was raised by Jesus, so it is possible that he remained part of the burgeoning Christian community in Rome. Yet if he did, it is likely that he met an untimely end as many of the early church leaders were wiped out by Nero. The Roman historian Tacitus said that Nero 'punished with every kind of cruelty the notoriously depraved group known as Christians,' and we know that to be true through the accounts of Peter's death."

"So you think he was martyred?"

"Very possibly, perhaps even crucified with Peter. It's hard to imagine that someone of his pedigree would have been anything but a leader. And the leaders were all executed. But then there is the other perspective."

Sinclair pointed to the skull in the marbleized John-Joseph's hand. "Here is another possibility. One legend says that the more fanatic followers of John sought out his heir in Rome and convinced him that the Christians had usurped his rightful place. That John was the one true messiah and John-Joseph as his only son was the heir to the throne of the anointed one. Some say that John-Joseph turned on his mother and his family to embrace the teachings of his father's followers. We don't know where he ended up, but we do know that there is an intense sect of John worshipers in Iran and Iraq, called the Mandaeans. Peaceful people, but very strict in their laws and in their belief that John was the only true messiah. It is possible that they may be direct descendants, that John-Joseph or his heirs ended up farther east following a schism with the early Christians. And of course you are now aware of the Guild of the Righteous, who claim to be the true bloodline descendants here in the West."

Maureen looked intently at the skull while listening to Sinclair's explanation. A thought hit her, and she exclaimed, "It's John! The skull—it's in all of Mary Magdalene's iconography, the paintings. She's always shown with a skull, and no one has ever been able to give me a good explanation for it. Always a vague reference to penance. The skull represents repentance. But why? Now I see why. Mary was painted with the skull because she was doing penance for John—literally with John's skull."

Sinclair nodded. "Yes. And the book, she's always shown with a book."

"But that could just be scripture," Maureen observed.

"It could be, but it's not. Mary is shown with a book because it is her own book, her message that she has left these for us to find. And I hope it will give us insight into the mystery of her oldest son and his fate, because we just don't know. I'm hoping that the Magdalene will put that mystery to rest for us herself."

They walked through the garden in silence for a moment, basking in the twilight sky with its first dusting of stars. Maureen finally spoke. "You said that there were others, followers of John who were not fanatics."

"Of course. There are millions of them. We call them Christians."

Maureen gave him a look as he continued. "I'm serious. Look at your own country. How many churches call themselves Baptist churches? These are Christians who have integrated the idea of John as a prophet in his own right. Some call him the Forerunner and see him as the one who announced the coming of Jesus. In Europe, there were some bloodline families who blended together, mixing the blood of the Baptist with the blood of the Nazarene. The most famous of these was the Medici dynasty. They were integrated, celebrants of both John and Jesus. And our boy Sandro Botticelli was one of these as well."

Maureen was surprised by this. "Botticelli was descended from both bloodlines?"

Sinclair nodded. "When we go back inside, take another look at Sandro's *Primavera*. On the far left you will see the figure of Hermes, the alchemist, holding his caduceus symbol in the air. His hands make the 'Remember John' gesture that Tammy told you about. Sandro is telling us, in this allegory of Mary Magdalene and the power of rebirth, that we must also acknowledge John. That alchemy is a form of integration, and integration leaves no room for bigotry and intolerance."

Maureen watched him closely, a true admiration blossoming for this man who had started off as such an enigma to her. He was a mystic and a poet in his own right, a seeker of spiritual truths. More than that, he was a good man—warm, caring, and clearly very loyal. She had underestimated him, which became more evident with his final words on the matter.

"It is my opinion that an attitude of forgiveness and tolerance is the cornerstone of true faith. In the last forty-eight hours, I have come to believe that more profoundly than ever."

Maureen smiled and put her arm in his, and they walked back through the garden. Together.

*Vatican City, Rome*
*June 29, 2005*

CARDINAL DECARO was finishing a telephone call in his office when the door burst open. It amazed the high-ranking church official that this Bishop O'Connor had not yet realized how tenuous his footing was here in Rome, but the man appeared to be utterly clueless. DeCaro was still unsure if it was pure ambition or complete lack of perception that afflicted O'Connor. Perhaps it was both.

The Cardinal listened with feigned patience and mock surprise as the man babbled on about the discovery in France. But then O'Connor said something that made DeCaro's spine stiffen. This was inside information. No one at this level should know about the scrolls yet—and certainly not of their content.

"Who is your informant?" the Cardinal asked, assuming a casual tone.

O'Connor squirmed. He wasn't yet ready to reveal his source. "He's very reliable. Very."

"I'm afraid I cannot take this terribly seriously if you are unwilling or unable to give me further details, Magnus. You must understand how much misinformation comes through here. We cannot investigate all of it."

Bishop Magnus O'Connor shifted uncomfortably. He dared not reveal his source, not yet—it was his only remaining power play. If he turned over his source, they would no doubt go directly to him, leaving O'Connor with no power or involvement in this most important historical situation. Besides, there were others he would have to answer to besides DeCaro and the Vatican Council.

"I will check with the informant and see if I can reveal him to you," O'Connor offered.

Cardinal DeCaro shrugged, much to O'Connor's annoyance. This nonchalant reception of his earth-shattering news was not what he wanted or expected. "Very well. Thank you for the information," said the elder official dismissively. "You are free to go about your duties."

"But, your grace, don't you want to know exactly what they found?"

Cardinal DeCaro peered over his reading glasses at the Irish cleric. "Unsubstantiated sources do not interest me. Good night, sir. May God bless and keep you."

The Cardinal turned his back and picked up a sheaf of papers, sorting through them as if the Bishop had just told him something as basic as that the sun rose in the morning and set in the evening. Where was the shock? The concern? The gratitude?

Sputtering with indignation, Bishop O'Connor mumbled a reply and waddled out the door. He was finished here in Rome for the moment. He would go to France. Then he would show them.

*Château des Pommes Bleues*
*June 29, 2005*

As PROMISED, Maureen met Tammy in the media room following her stroll in the garden with Sinclair. She first popped her head into the study to check on Peter, who was immersed in the translation of the second book. Her cousin looked up and gave her an unintelligible grunt, his eyes glassy with the work. She knew this was not a good time to interrupt and went out to find Tammy.

Outside the study, there was an exhilaration running through the château, a buzzing sense of history and excitement. Maureen wondered how much the servants knew, but also assumed that they were all highly trusted and loyal. Roland and Sinclair were meeting to discuss security measures until the remainder of Mary's gospel was translated and a decision was made about the proper course of action. No one had discussed this openly yet, and Maureen found herself very curious about what Sinclair intended to do—and when he intended to do it.

"Come in, come in." Tammy beckoned as she saw Maureen at the door.

Maureen plunked down on the couch next to Tammy, allowing her head to roll back with a groan.

"Uh-oh, what's wrong?"

Maureen smiled at her. "Oh nothing and everything. I was just wondering, will my life ever look the same again?"

Tammy answered with her throaty laugh. "No. So you'd better get used to that now." She grabbed Maureen's hand. This time, she spoke more sympathetically. "Listen, I know most of this is new for you and you've had to process a lot in a short period of time. I just want you to know that you're my hero, okay? And so is Peter, for that matter."

"Thanks," Maureen sighed. "But do you really think the world is ready for all this tweaking of their sacred belief systems? Because I don't."

"I disagree," Tammy said with her usual conviction. "I think the timing has never been better. It's the twenty-first century. We don't burn people at the stake for heresy anymore."

"No, we just bash their skulls in." Maureen rubbed the back of her head for emphasis.

"Point taken. Sorry."

"I'm just being dramatic. I'm fine, really." Maureen gestured to the wide-screen television. "What are you working on now?"

"We were sidetracked the other night and I didn't have a chance to show you the rest of this. I think now, more than ever, you'll find it very interesting."

Tammy had the remote in her hand. Pointing it at the television monitor, she continued, "We were looking at bloodline pictures, remember?" She released the pause button as portraits filled the screen. "King Ferdinand of Spain. Your girl Lucrezia Borgia. Mary, Queen of Scots. Bonnie Prince Charlie. Empress Maria Theresa of Austria and her more famous daughter, Marie Antoinette. Sir Isaac Newton." She paused on an image of several American presidents. "And here is where we get into the Americans, starting with Thomas Jefferson. Then we move gradually into modern times."

A modern photograph of a large America family reunion filled the screen.

"What's this?"

"The Stewart family reunion in Cherry Hill, New Jersey. I took this last year. And this one, too. Seemingly regular people in regular locations, but they're all bloodline."

Maureen was struck with a thought. "Have you ever been to McLean, in Virginia?"

Tammy looked puzzled. "No. Why?"

Maureen recounted her unlikely experiences in McLean, and the lovely bookstore owner she had met. "Her name was Rachel Martel, and . . ."

Tammy cut her off. "Martel? Did you say Martel?"

Maureen nodded, to which Tammy burst out laughing. "Yeah, well, no wonder she has visions," Tammy said. "Martel is one of the oldest bloodline names there is. Charles Martel, the line of Charlemagne. If you dig around that part of Virginia, I bet you'll find a huge concentration of bloodline families. Probably came over for asylum during the Reign of Terror—that's how most of the noble French families ended up in the States. Pennsylvania is crammed with them, too."

Maureen laughed. "So that's why there are so many sightings there. I'll have to call Rachel when I get back to the States and let her know."

They returned their attention to the screen, where another reunion photograph appeared as Tammy explained.

"This is the St. Clair family reunion in Baton Rouge last summer. Louisiana has the highest concentration of bloodline families because of the French legacy there. You know that firsthand now. See this guy here?"

Tammy clicked the remote to pause on an image of a young, long-haired street musician, playing a saxophone in the French Quarter. She released the pause to allow some of his hauntingly beautiful sax music to fill the room before halting it again.

"His name is James St. Clair. Homeless. Survives as a street hustler in New Orleans but plays a saxophone that would make you cry. I sat down on the street corner and talked to him for three hours. A brilliant, beautiful man."

"Do all of these people know they're bloodline?"

"Of course not. That's the beauty of it, and it's also the final point of my film. In two thousand years of history and evolution, there are probably close to a million people on earth carrying the blood of Jesus Christ in their veins. Maybe more. There's nothing elitist or secretive about it. It could be the guy who bags your groceries or your teller at the bank. Or the homeless guy who breaks your heart every time he picks up a saxophone."

*Château des Pommes Bleues*
*July 2, 2005*

PETER WORKED TIRELESSLY, but his perfectionism overtook him and it was another two days before he was ready to share the translations of the latest scrolls, the Book of the Time of Darkness.

Maureen had fallen asleep on the couch the afternoon of the second day, content to be in the vicinity of Mary's gospel as it was transcribed.

The sound of her cousin's sobs awakened her.

She looked up to see Peter, his head in his hands, surrendering to the exhaustion and emotion that swept through him. But Maureen couldn't determine immediately what the emotion was. Was it sorrow or joy? Elation or devastation? Maureen looked up at Sinclair, who was sitting opposite Peter at the table. He shook his head at her helplessly. He, too, was at a loss to understand what had triggered Peter's intense reaction.

Maureen approached Peter and put her hand gently on his shoulder. "Pete? What is it?"

Peter rubbed the tears from his face and looked up at his cousin. "I'd rather let her tell you," he whispered, pointing to the translation before him. "Will you get the others, please?

Tammy and Roland hurried to Sinclair's study. They were easy to find because they were now openly together. Nor were they ever far away as neither wanted to be too distant from the scrolls for fear of missing anything. They both noticed the fevered look on Peter's face as they entered the study.

Roland called a housemaid to bring in tea for everyone. Once she was dismissed and the door was closed behind her, Peter picked up where he had left off.

"She calls this the Book of the Time of Darkness," Peter said. "It deals with the last week of Christ's life."

Sinclair started to ask a question, but Peter stopped him. "She tells it far better than I."

And he began to read.

. . . *It is important to know who Judas Iscariot was in order to comprehend his relationship with me, with Easa, and with the teachings of The Way. Like Simon, he was a Zealot and passionate in his desire to drive the Romans from our shores. He had killed for this belief and had been more than willing to do so again. Until Simon brought him to Easa.*

*Judas embraced The Way, but his conversion was neither quick nor easy. Judas came from a line of Pharisees and had a strict perspective on the law. He had followed John as a young man, and was suspicious of all he had heard of me. In time, we became friends, brother and sister in The Way—because of Easa, who was the great unifier. And yet there were times when Judas and his old ways would surface, and this would cause tension among the followers. He was a natural leader and would insinuate his position of authority. Easa admired this, but some of the other followers did not. But I understood Judas. Like mine, it was his destiny to be misunderstood.*

*Judas believed that we should be taking every opportunity to expand our following and that we should do this through donations to the poor. Easa designated Judas as treasurer, and it became his responsibility to raise money for distribution among the needy. He was a man of honesty and conscience when it came to this task, but he was also a man without compromise.*

*The greatest argument occurred on the night I anointed Easa in Bethany, in the home of Simon. I took a sealed alabaster jar that had been sent to us from Alexandria. It was filled with a blend of costly and aromatic spikenard with myrrh. I broke the seal and anointed Easa's head and feet with the balm, proclaiming him our messiah in keeping with the traditions of our people and the Song of Songs as given to us from Solomon. It was a spiritual moment for all of us, one filled with hope and symbolism.*

*But Judas did not approve. He was angry and chastised me before everyone, saying, "That balm was valuable. Sealed, it would have* brought a great price, money we could have allocated to our collections for the poor."

I did not have to defend my actions, as Easa did so for me. He reproved Judas, saying, "You will have the poor always, but you will not always have me. And let me say this further—wherever the deeds of my life are preached throughout the world, so will this woman's name be preached with my own. Let this be done as a memorial to her and the good works she has wrought for us."

It was a moment that showed Judas did not fully comprehend the sacred rituals of The Way and one that upset some of the elect—some who never trusted Judas fully after that.

As I have said, I hold no ill toward him for that or any other act. Judas could not overcome who he was in his heart, and he was always true to that.

I mourn him still.

THE ARQUES GOSPEL OF MARY MAGDALENE,
THE BOOK OF THE TIME OF DARKNESS

# CHAPTER NINETEEN

*I*t had been an eventful day for the Nazarenes. When Easa entered Jerusalem, he had been received with the popular support that they had anticipated. Indeed, his reception had exceeded expectations. When the followers were called to learn the Prayer of the Way—Easa was now calling it the Lord's Prayer—the grotto location on the Mount of Olives proved too small. The followers who attended Easa's preaching spilled out over the hill, waiting for their turn to get close to their anointed one, their messiah, so that he could teach them how to pray as well.

Easa stayed until every man, woman, and child was satisfied that they knew and understood this prayer and took it into their hearts.

On the way down the Mount and moving toward the city, the Nazarenes were stopped by a pair of Roman centurions. The Romans were guards at the eastern entrance to the city, the gate closest to Pilate's residence in the Fortress Antonia. They challenged the group in butchered Aramaic, questioning their destination. Easa came forward and surprised them by speaking in perfect Greek. He pointed to one of the centurions, noticing that the man's hand was heavily bandaged.

"What happened to you?" he asked simply.

The centurion wasn't expecting to be asked this, but answered plainly. "I fell into the rocks during a night watch."

"Too much wine," cracked his watch partner, an unsavory-looking character with a jagged scar slashing across the left side of his face.

The injured centurion glared him into silence and added, "Don't listen to a word Longinus says. I lost my balance."

Easa stated simply, "It is painful for you."

The centurion nodded. "I believe it is broken, but I have not had the chance to be attended by a physician. We are stretched thin with the Passover crowds."

"May I see it?" Easa asked.

The man held out the bandaged hand, which hung at an unnatural angle from the wrist. Easa placed one hand underneath it and another above it, gently. Closing his eyes, he said a silent prayer as his hands closed in gently but firmly over the centurion's hand. The injured Roman's eyes grew large as the assembled Nazarenes watched the healing that was taking place. Even the scar-faced centurion appeared momentarily rapt.

Easa opened his eyes and looked into those of the Roman. "You should feel better now." And as he released the hand it was clear to everyone in view that it was now straight and strong. The Roman stuttered, unable to speak. Instead, he unwrapped the bandages and flexed his fingers. His sky blue eyes grew cloudy with unshed tears as he looked up at Easa. He dare not speak for fear of losing his place among his fellow soldiers. Easa knew this, and saved him from embarrassment.

"The kingdom of God is yours for the taking. Tell others of the good news," Easa said, and continued on a path around the city walls, followed by Mary, the children, and the elect.

Mary was exhausted, but she would not complain. The weight of the child she carried slowed her down a little, but she had such joy in it that she refused to complain. They were settled in the house of Easa's uncle, Joseph, a wealthy and influential man with lands immediately outside the city. She was thankful that both little John and Tamar were asleep. The day had worn them out as well.

Mary had time to reflect on Easa's healing abilities as she sat in the cool shade of Joseph's garden, alone. Easa was with his uncle and some of the male followers, planning their visit to the Temple the following day. Mary chose to leave them to it, seeing the children to their beds and taking a few moments for rest and prayer. The other Marys and the female followers were gathered together tonight in a prayer ceremony, but this Mary chose not to attend. Solitude was an increasingly rare commodity for her and she cherished it.

But as Mary Magdalene recalled the events surrounding the healing of the Roman soldier earlier in the day, she found herself feeling uneasy and disconcerted. She couldn't identify the feeling, and she wasn't sure why it made her nervous. The centurion himself was decent for a Roman soldier, almost pleasant. And she had felt his distress, as Easa had, when he was near tears from the miracle of the healing. The other soldier was a different story altogether. He was hard and coarse, what they had all come to expect of the mercenaries who had spilled so much Jewish blood. This scar-faced man, called Longinus, had been startled by the healing, but he would not be affected by it in any positive way. He was too battle-hardened for that.

But the blue-eyed man had been not only healed, but changed. Mary saw it in his eyes as it happened. As she thought back on it she felt an electric charge run through her, the strange feeling on the edge of prophecy that always warned her she was glimpsing the future. Mary closed her eyes and tried to catch the image, but came up empty. She was too tired, or perhaps she was simply not meant to see this.

What could it be? she wondered. Easa's reputation as a great healer had grown across Israel these last three years. He was renowned and honored for it among the people. And lately it appeared effortless for him. The healing power of God poured through Easa with an ease that was joyous to behold.

Hadn't Easa healed her own brother when the doctors of Bethany had declared him dead? The previous year, Mary and Easa had hurried from Galilee after receiving word from Martha that Lazarus was gravely ill. But the journey had taken longer than anticipated, and by the time they arrived, Lazarus was cloaked with the stench of death. It was too late, they had all feared. While Easa's powers of healing were indeed astonishing, he had never raised anyone from the dead. It was too much to ask of any man, messiah or no.

But Easa entered Martha's house with Mary and told both women to hold tight to their faith and pray with him. Then he entered the chamber of Lazarus alone and began to pray over the dead man.

Easa came out from the chamber and looked into the pale faces of Mary and Martha. He smiled reassurance at them before turning toward the room. "Lazarus, dear brother, arise from your bed and greet your wife and sister who have prayed with such love for you to return to us."

Martha and Mary watched with astonishment as Lazarus emerged slowly through the door. He was pale and weak, but very much alive.

There was a celebration throughout Bethany that night as word spread of the miraculous raising of Lazarus from the dead. The ranks of Nazarene followers swelled as Easa's good works became legendary throughout the land. He continued his path of healing, pausing at the Jordan River near Jericho to baptize new followers in the way that John had taught. The crowds that assembled for baptism were huge, causing the Nazarenes to stay longer than anticipated on the banks of the Jordan.

The fact that Easa had taken up John's mantle was popular with many of the moderates who were praying he was truly their messiah. Herod Antipas, the tetrarch of Galilee, himself had proclaimed that in Easa he saw the spirit of the Baptizer living again. But not everyone was pleased by these developments. Herod's endorsement of Easa was not well received by John's more devoted followers as well as the most extreme of the Essene ascetics. They quietly cursed Easa for usurping John's position. But their most deadly ire wasn't directed at the Nazarene man; it was for the Nazarene woman.

The next day at the river, Mary Magdalene fell to the ground, clutching her stomach. She quickly became violently ill as her followers gathered around her. Easa ran to her side immediately upon hearing that his wife had fallen.

The Great Mary was present with them at this time, and she too attended to Mary Magdalene. She watched her daughter-in-law carefully, gauging her symptoms and nursing her gently. She turned to her son. "I have seen this before," she said gravely. "This is not a natural illness."

Easa nodded his understanding. "Poison."

The Great Mary confirmed her son's assessment and added, "Not just any poison. See how her legs are paralyzed? She cannot move her lower body at all, and her insides are set to come out with her retching. This is an Eastern poison, called the poison of the seven devils. It is named for the seven deadly ingredients that it contains. It kills, and it does so slowly and painfully. There is no antidote for it. You shall have to work with God to save your wife, my son."

The Great Mary cleared the area to create peace and privacy for Easa to work the healing on his wife. Easa held her hands and prayed there, prayed until he felt the poison evaporating from her body and the flush of health returning to her. While Easa performed the work of God, his disciples set out to determine who had poisoned Mary Magdalene.

The culprit was never discovered. They assumed that a fanatic follower of John had arrived at the Jordan disguised as a convert and had slipped the deadly poison to a trusting Mary. From that day forward Mary Magdalene was very careful not to drink or eat in public unless she knew exactly where the food had come from. She spent the rest of her eventful life under attack from those who despised or envied her.

Easa's healing of Mary Magdalene from the poison of the seven devils spread as one of the great legends of the Nazarene's ministry.

Like so many elements of Mary Magdalene's history, this event, too, would be misconstrued and used against her.

Mary's memories were interrupted by a cry in the courtyard. It was Judas, and he was desperately looking for Easa. Mary rushed out to him. "What is it?"

"My niece, the daughter of Jairus." Judas was panting and out of breath. He ran all the way from within the eastern walls to get to Easa. "It may be too late, but I need him. Where is he?"

Mary led him to where the men were meeting in Joseph's house. Easa saw the agitation on Judas' face and rose immediately to greet him. Judas explained breathlessly that his niece had been struck with a fever that was afflicting the children of Jerusalem and its boundaries. Many were dying. By the time Judas heard the news and got to Jairus, the doctors were already saying it was too late. Because of his position in the Temple and his closeness to Pontius Pilate, Jairus had access to the finest doctors. Judas knew that if these physicians had given up then the girl would likely be dead by now. Still, he had to try.

Judas had more softness in his heart than he allowed others to see. And as a man who had rejected the path of family life for the way of a revolutionary, he had grown to adore his nieces and nephews. Twelve-year-old Smedia, the child who was ill, was his favorite.

Easa saw Judas' fear and anguish over losing this child and looked over at Mary Magdalene. "Are you able to travel tonight?"

She nodded. Of course she would go. There would be a grieving mother in this house, and Mary would be there to support the woman in any way possible.

"We will go now," Easa said simply. He never hesitated, as Mary knew he would not. It did not matter what the hour, it did not matter how tired Easa may have been. He would never refuse a person in true need of him.

Judas followed them out, giving Mary a long look of gratitude as they left. It warmed her to see it. *Perhaps Judas will come around to The*

*Way more completely in his heart this night,* she thought, the hope very great in her spirit.

Jairus' position in the community was a unique one. He was a Pharisee and a leader in the Temple, but he was also the special envoy to the procurator. As such he met weekly with Pontius Pilate to discuss the affairs of Rome as they related to a smooth and peaceful relationship with the Temple and the Jerusalem Jews.

Jairus had developed a bond with Pilate, and the two of them would argue politics for hours at a time. Rachel, the wife of Jairus, accompanied him to the Fortress Antonia and spent these hours with Pilate's wife, Claudia Procula. The friendship between Rachel and Claudia grew despite their innate differences. Claudia was a Roman woman of immense stature in her own right. Not only was she the wife of the procurator of Palestine, she was the granddaughter of one Caesar and the favored foster daughter of another. In contrast, Rachel was a Jewish woman from one of Israel's noble families. But these women of differing backgrounds came together in their commonality as wives of powerful men and, most of all, as mothers.

Rachel's daugher Smedia came often to the Fortress Antonia with her mother. Smedia loved to play in the elegant rooms, and as the girl got older Claudia allowed her access to her lotions and cosmetics. At twelve, she was on the way to developing into a beautiful young woman.

Claudia held a special warmth for Smedia as the girl had been a kind playmate to her own child, Pilo. The seven-year-old son of Pontius Pilate and Claudia Procula, Pilo was a mystery to most of Jerusalem. There were few who were even aware that Pilate had a son. The deformity of Pilo's twisted left leg limited his activity and he was confined to the fortress. Pilate did not announce his son to the world as he knew this boy would never grow into a soldier; he would never follow in his father's footsteps as a procurator of Rome.

A child born into such obvious displeasure of the gods was a bad omen.

But Claudia saw a side of Pilate that others did not. She knew how he wept for the boy in those darkest hours when he thought no one could see or hear. Pilate had spent half of their fortune on expensive doctors from Greece, limb straighteners from India, and healers of every description. Each of these sessions ended with Pilo in tears of pain and frustration. Claudia held the boy as he sobbed himself to sleep; his father stormed out of the fortress for long hours and stayed away from both of them each time this happened.

Young Smedia had infinite patience with the boy, and she would sit with him for hours, telling him stories and singing him songs. Claudia smiled to herself as she watched them out of the corner of her eye while working on embroidery with Rachel. What would Pilate say if he heard his child singing in Hebrew? But Pilate was rarely here in her quarters, and she knew they would not have to worry about such a thing.

It was on one of these visits that Claudia Procula first heard of Easa, the Nazarene. Rachel was positively enamored of this man and his deeds. She regaled Claudia with the stories of Easa's healings and his miracles. Rachel's husband, Jairus, would not allow her to rhapsodize of the Nazarene—he was considered something of an adversary of Jonathan Annas and Caiaphas. Those men considered Easa to be a renegade who was disrespectful of Temple authority. Jairus could not be seen to have anything to do with this man.

And yet Jairus' cousin, Judas, was now one of Easa's elect followers. This was sometimes awkward for Jairus, but so far he was balancing it very well. And Rachel was delighted as she now had more firsthand accounts of Nazarene miracles.

"You should take Pilo to see this Easa," Rachel said one day.

Claudia's eyes grew cloudy with regret. "How can I? My husband would never allow us to be seen in the company of a traveling Nazarene preacher. It would be unseemly."

Rachel did not mention it again out of sensitivity to her friend.

But Claudia never stopped thinking about it. Then Smedia was struck with the terrible wasting fever, and it was only a few days later that Pilo fell ill with it as well.

The mourning throngs were already crowded around the city home of Jairus. Families attached to the Temple and the many citizens of Jerusalem who had been touched by Jairus and Rachel came out to show support. Smedia, their beloved daughter, was dead.

Judas pushed through the crowd, moving urgently toward the home of his cousin. Easa and Mary followed close behind him, Easa grasping her hand tightly so as not to lose his diminutive wife in the crowd. Andrew and Peter followed behind them as extra protection. It was obvious to the arriving Nazarenes that the child had succumbed to her fever, but they were not deterred. They pressed on and into the house of Jairus.

At the Fortress Antonia, Pontius Pilate and Claudia Procula had been given a death sentence for their only child. The doctors had given up. There was no more they could do for the child; besides, wasn't he weak to begin with? Pontius Pilate left the room without a word and closeted himself for the rest of the night with his stoic philosophers. He had to come to terms with this loss in his own Roman way.

Claudia was left alone with the withering Pilo. She held him in his bed and cried softly that her sweet, brave boy was dying. This was how the Greek slave found her mistress as he entered the room.

"My poor boy is leaving us," Claudia said softly. "What will we do? What will I do without him?"

The slave rushed to the side of his mistress. "My Lady, I come bearing news from the home of Rachel and Jairus. These are tidings of great sadness, but perhaps they are draped in greater hope. The lovely Smedia has died."

"No!" Claudia cried. Certainly this was all too much to bear. What justice was there when such a beautiful girl as Rachel's daughter had departed the world, perhaps on the same night as her beloved son?

"But wait, Lady, for there is more. Rachel bid me tell you that the Nazarene healer, Easa, will come to their home tonight. Even if it is too late for Smedia, it may not be too late for Pilo."

Claudia had little time to consider the consequences. Pilo was clearly on his last breaths. "Bundle him up. Let's get him to the chariot. Quickly, please go quickly."

The Greek, who was also a tutor for the boy and loved him greatly, wrapped Pilo gently and carried him to the chariot, with Claudia running behind them. She did not stop to leave word with Pilate, but didn't think he would notice she was gone. Besides, she was perfectly capable of making such an important decision on her own. Wasn't she herself the granddaughter of a Caesar?

Pilo held on, still breathing as the Greek and his mother held him. Claudia was heavily veiled, not wanting to appear obviously imperial upon arriving at the home of a Jewish family in mourning. The Greek slave drove the chariot as far as he could take it in the crowd, then abandoned it to help his mistress and the child make their way through the mass of people. It was difficult. Beyond the mourners, word had spread that the miracle-working messiah from Galilee was on his way, and the streets were filling with the curious as well as the faithful. But the little party from the Fortress Antonia was determined, and pushed until they reached the vestibule door.

"We would see Rachel, the wife of Jairus," the Greek slave announced. "Please tell Rachel that it is her dear friend, Claudia."

The door opened, but they were not readily admitted. Judas stood guard at the inside door. He told the exterior guard that no observers would be allowed in the room until Easa had left. Judas wanted no witnesses, and this was for Easa's protection. Jairus was a Pharisee, and there were others from the Temple surrounding the house waiting to see what would transpire—others who were not friendly to the Nazarene mission. If Easa was unable to raise Smedia, they would condemn him as a fake. If he was successful in his efforts, they could claim witchcraft or trickery of some sort, a charge that would damage not only Easa but Jairus—and an eyewitness account of such a charge by a Pharisee with an agenda could carry a death penalty. The safest course of action was to keep witnesses out of the room, other than the immediate family.

Claudia Procula heard only Judas' curt "No visitors yet" instruction. But as the door opened, she had a glimpse of the activity in the room. She saw Smedia on her deathbed, white and lifeless in the thick incense. Rachel sat at her side, holding the still hand of her child, head bowed in surrender to excruciating grief. A woman in the red veil of a Nazarene priestess stood beside Rachel, a tower of strength and compassion in the tragic setting. Jairus, a man Claudia had known as proud and strong, was collapsed in a heap on the floor at the feet of Easa the Nazarene. He was begging the Nazarene to heal his daughter.

Later, when everything from that night had settled, Claudia spoke of her first vision of Easa. "I have never felt like that before," she said. "Seeing him filled me with a sense of calm, as though I was in the presence of love and light itself. Even in that brief moment, I knew what he was—that he was more than human, that we were all blessed for eternity to be in his presence even for those few seconds."

The door did not close as Claudia had anticipated. Judas was attending to the grief-stricken Jairus, and the external guard was too fascinated by the proceedings to be effective. Claudia watched with utter fascination as Easa moved to the side of the bed. He looked at the woman in red, who Claudia would learn later was his wife, Mary Magdalene, then put his hands on Rachel's shoulders. He whispered something into her ear that no one else could hear, but for the first time Rachel lifted her head. Then Easa bent over the child and kissed her forehead. He took Smedia's hand in both of his and closed his eyes to pray. After a long and silent minute when no one in the room took a breath, Easa turned to Smedia and said, "Arise, child."

Claudia did not recall everything that happened next. It was like a strange dream that is never remembered quite the same way twice. The child, Smedia, stirred very slowly at first, but then sat up and cried for her mother. Rachel and Jairus screamed as they ran to embrace their daughter. At some stage Claudia fell to her knees, just as the crowd surged forward. There was chaos from the mob around the house. There were cheers as followers of the Nazarene and friends of the family celebrated the miracle of Smedia's resurrection. But there were jeers and hisses as well, from Pharisees and opponents of the Nazarene who yelled out his blasphemy and called him a black magician.

Claudia was in a panic. She and the Greek had been pushed out of the doorway and were being carried away by the surging crowd. Pilo was desperately ill, and she knew he might die here on the steps of Jairus' house. It had been risky, even cruel, to bring Pilo out here when he could have drawn his last breaths in the comfort of his own bed. And now it looked futile. The Nazarene was being ushered out by his followers, and Claudia could not reach him.

But as all hope was draining from Claudia, she saw Mary Magdalene stop in the crowd. Something happened between the two of them then, the mystical communication between mothers in difficult times. Their eyes locked for a long moment, and then Mary's gaze moved to the child in the Greek's arms. Silently, Mary placed her hand on Easa's shoulder. He stopped, turning to see what Mary was asking of him. Easa's eyes met Claudia's for a brief moment and he smiled at her then, an expression of pure hope and light. Claudia was never able to say how long this lasted as she was distracted by the voice of her son shouting for her.

"Mama! Mama!" Pilo squirmed in the arms of the Greek. "Put me down!"

Claudia could see the color returning to Pilo's face. He appeared healthy and strong again. In less than an instant, the dying son of Pilate and Claudia had been completely restored. And there was more. As the child's feet touched the ground, it was apparent to both Claudia and the Greek that Pilo's leg was no longer twisted. He walked to her, straight and strong. "Look, Mama! I can walk!"

Claudia hugged her beautiful boy as she watched the retreating form of the Nazarene healer and his tiny wife blend into the raucous Jerusalem crowd.

"Thank you," she whispered to them. And strangely, though they were now too far to be seen, she knew they had heard her.

The healing of Pilo was a double-edged sword for Pontius Pilate. He was delighted to have his son restored and healed completely. The boy was whole in a way that neither he nor Claudia had ever imagined was possible. He was now a proper heir to a Roman legacy, a child who could become a man and a soldier. But the method of his healing was disturbing. Worse, both Claudia and Pilo were now obsessed with this Nazarene, who was something of a thorn in the sides of both the Roman authorities and the Temple priests.

Pilate had met with Caiaphas and Annas, at their request, earlier in the day to discuss the mob scene at the eastern gates. The Nazarene had arrived on an ass in the manner predicted by one of their Jewish prophets, upsetting the priests with what they felt was a declaration of messianic proportions. While the religious squabbles of the Jews were not Pilate's immediate problem, this Nazarene was rumored to be calling himself a king of the Jews, which was treason against Caesar. Pilate was feeling pressure to take some action against this Easa if he made one more controversial move in Jerusalem as Passover approached.

To complicate matters, Herod, the tetrarch of Galilee, had come out against Easa privately in a message to Pilate. "I have information that this man would make himself king over all the Jews. He has become dangerous to me, to you, and to Rome."

Those were Pilate's logistical problems. His philosophical issues were another matter entirely.

What force did this Nazarene control or channel that allowed him to do such things as raise a child from the dead? Had it not been for Pilo, Pilate would have thought Easa's miracles were pure trickery and conceded to the Pharisees' accusations of blasphemy. But Pilate knew better than anyone that Pilo's illness and deformity were very real. Or at least they had been. Now they were simply gone.

There was something here that had to be explained. Roman reason demanded an answer, an understanding of what had occurred. Pontius Pilate was very frustrated when he could not find one.

But his wife needed no such convincing. She had witnessed two great miracles, had basked in the presence and glory of the Nazarene and his God; Claudia Procula was an instant convert. She was both displeased and disappointed when her husband refused to allow her to attend any of Easa's preachings in Jerusalem. She wished to take Pilo, to allow her son to meet this amazing Nazarene who was more than a man. Pilate forbade it, vehemently.

The Roman procurator was a complex man, filled with doubt, fear, and ambition. The tragedy of Pontius Pilate would come when all of these things outweighed whatever he had once possessed in love, strength, or gratitude.

It was very late by the time the Nazarenes arrived at Joseph's house. Easa, as ever, was wide awake and preparing for one more gathering with his closest followers before retiring. They were weighing their options in Jerusalem the following day. Mary stayed to hear the discussion to get an indication of what the next day would hold. The incident at Jairus' house made it clear that the people of Jerusalem were divided on the issue of Easa the messiah. There were more supporters than detractors, but they all suspected that the detractors were powerful men attached to the Temple.

Judas spoke to the assembled men. He appeared drawn and exhausted, yet the exhilaration of what he had witnessed at Smedia's deathbed was keeping him going.

"Jairus took me aside as we were leaving," he told them. "He is far more inclined to support us now that he has seen that Easa is truly the messiah. He warned that the councils of Pharisees and Sadducees were disturbed by the throngs of Nazarene supporters who entered the city. We are stronger in number than they ever imagined. They are afraid of us and likely to take action if they feel we pose a threat to them or to the peace of the Temple during Passover."

Peter spat on the floor in disgust. "We all know why. Passover is the most profitable time of the year at the Temple. The greatest number of sacrifices are made and the most money is exchanged."

"It's harvest time for the merchants and moneylenders," added his brother Andrew.

"And the chief profiteers among them are Jonathan Annas and his son-in-law," Judas agreed. "It won't surprise any of you that those two are at the head of the campaign to discredit us. We have to tread very carefully here or they will push Pilate to issue an arrest warrant for Easa."

Easa held up his hand as the men began to talk over each other in their agitation. "Peace, my brothers," he said. "We will go to the Temple tomorrow and show our brothers Annas and Caiaphas that it is not our intention to challenge them. We can exist peacefully together and do not need to exclude each other. We will go as celebrants in a holy week, along with our Nazarene brothers. They cannot deny us admittance, and perhaps we will find a truce with them."

Judas was uncertain. "I don't think you will get any compromise out of Annas. He despises us and everything we teach. The last thing Annas and Caiaphas want is for the people to believe that they don't need the Temple to reach God."

Mary rose from her place on the floor and smiled warmly at Easa across the room. He caught her eye and returned the expression as his wife turned quietly to leave by the rear door. She was too tired for strategy now. Besides, if Easa was determined to make a showing at the Temple the following day, she had a strong feeling that they would all need some rest.

Mary was sharing a room with the children, as she always did when they traveled. She believed this gave them a sense of security, a necessary element for children who had an often nomadic existence. They were both angelic in their sleep: John-Joseph, with his sweeping, dark eyelashes resting on his olive cheeks, and Sarah-Tamar, nestled in a cloud of shiny, auburn hair.

Their mother resisted the urge to kiss them. Tamar particularly was a light sleeper, and she did not want to wake either of them. The children would need their rest if they wanted to accompany her into Jerusalem tomorrow—they found the city so exciting and colorful. As long as it remained safe for them in Jerusalem, she would allow it. But if circumstances became tumultuous for Easa, she would need to get the children away from the city. If the worst were to happen, even Joseph's lands would not be safe. She would have to get them to Bethany and into the safety of Martha and Lazarus' home.

Mary finally settled in her own bed and closed her eyes to the eventful day. But sleep would not come easily, although she desired it and needed it badly. There were too many thoughts and images in her head. In her mind's eye she saw the woman in the heavy veil, the one who had been carrying the child outside of Jairus' house. Mary knew two things instantly upon seeing that woman's face. First, she was neither a Jew nor a commoner. There was something in the way she held herself and in the quality of the veil that belied any attempt to blend in with the common folk. And Mary knew full well when a woman was trying to disguise herself; hadn't she done it herself many times when the situation warranted?

The second thing Mary had noticed was the woman's utter despair. She had felt the desperation flowing from her; it was almost as if the grief itself had called out for Easa's help. When Mary looked into the woman's face, she had seen the same sense of loss that every mother feels when she is helpless to save her child. It is a pain that knows no race, creed, or class, a grief that can be shared only by suffering parents. During the last three years of their ministry Mary had seen that face numerous times. But many times she had also watched as that face changed from despair to joy.

Easa had saved many of Israel's children. And now, it appeared, he may have saved one of Rome's.

Easa and his followers went to the Temple as planned the following day. Mary took the children into Jerusalem with her, stopping to witness the activity and debate occurring outside the hallowed walls. Easa was in the center of a large and growing crowd, preaching the kingdom of God. Men in the crowd challenged him and asked questions, all of which he answered with his usual calm. Easa's answers were thorough and incorporated the teachings of scripture. It was not long before it became obvious to all that his knowledge of the law could not be challenged.

Later, through information supplied by Jairus, they would discover that Annas and Caiaphas had planted their own men in the crowd. The were instructed to ask deliberately challenging questions. If any of Easa's answers could be interpreted as blasphemous, particularly in such close proximity to the Temple and with so many witnesses, the high priests would have further evidence to use against him.

One man came forward to ask a question on the issue of marriage. Judas saw the man and recognized him; he whispered into Easa's ear that this was a Pharisee who had put aside his older wife to marry a younger one.

"Tell me, Rabbi," the man asked, "is it lawful for a man to put his wife away for any cause? I have heard you say it is not, and yet the law of Moses says otherwise. Moses wrote of a bill of divorcement."

Easa spoke out so that his voice rose loud and clear over the crowd. His reply was harsh because he knew of the man's personal transgressions. "Moses wrote this precept because of the hardness of your heart."

The crowd consisted primarily of men from Jerusalem to whom this Pharisee was known. There was a rumble through these men at the implied insult. But Easa wasn't finished. He was tired of these corrupt Pharisees who lived like decadent kings off the donations from poor and pious Jews. He viewed this current batch of priests, men who were charged to uphold the law with utmost integrity, as hypocrites. They preached a holy life but certainly did not live one. During the recent years of his ministry Easa had come to realize that the people of Jerusalem had been cowed by these men; they feared the Pharisees' power as much as they did that of Rome. In many ways these men of the Temple were as dangerous to the common Jews as the Romans because they had the authority to affect their everyday existence in as many ways.

"Have you not read the scriptures?" Easa's question was another assault on the man he knew to be a priest. Then he turned to address the crowd at large. "He who made them at the beginning made them male and female, and said, 'For this cause shall a man leave father and mother and cleave unto his wife, and the two shall become one flesh, wherefore they are no more two but one. What God has put together let no man tear asunder.' And I say unto you whoever puts away a wife, other than for adultery, commits adultery himself."

"If this is the case, perhaps it is not good to marry," joked a man in the crowd.

Easa did not laugh. The sacrament of marriage and the importance of family life were cornerstones of the Nazarene way. He spoke out against this idea. "Some men are born eunuchs and others have been made eunuchs. For those men alone is marriage unacceptable. Let all men who are able to receive the sacrament of marriage receive it, for it is the will of the Lord our father. And let him cling unto his wife until death do them part."

Stung, the Pharisee fought back. "And what of you, Nazarene? The law of Moses says that any man who would be an anointed one must marry a virgin, and never a harlot or even a widow." It was an overt attack on Mary Magdalene, who stood back from the crowd with her children. She had elected to dress plainly to blend into the crowd and was not wearing the red veil of her station. She was glad of it at that moment as she waited for Easa's reply.

His response was another question to the Pharisee. "Am I a David?"

The man nodded. "That is not in question."

"And was David a great king and an anointed one of our people?"

The Pharisee replied in the affirmative, aware that he was being led into a trap but unsure how to extricate himself from it.

"Would you not ask that I emulate David if I am to be his heir? Who here would not think it a fine and honorable thing to walk in the steps of David?" Easa's question rang out through the crowd, who acknowledged with nods and gestures that it would indeed be a fine thing to model oneself after the Great Lion of Judah.

"For that is exactly what I have done. As David wed the widow Abigail, who was a fine and well-bred daughter of Israel, so have I wed a widow with noble blood."

The Pharisee knew he had been snared by his own trap and sunk back into the crowd. But the men of the Temple power structure were not easily deterred. As questions were fired at Easa, his answers became like sharp, pointed arrows fired back at the Pharisees. Another man, this one dressed openly in priestly garb, came at Easa with open aggression. "I have heard that you and your disciples transgress the tradition of the elders. Why do they not wash their hands when they eat bread?"

The crowd had been stirring during these last exchanges. There was dissent in the air, and Easa knew he would have to take a stand. These men of Jerusalem were not the same as those of Galilee and the outer regions. Here in the city the men required action. They might follow a king who could lead them out of bondage, but he would have to prove his strength and his worthiness first.

Easa's rich voice rang out, not in defense of the Nazarenes so much as in condemnation of the priests. "Why do you transgress the commandments of God by your tradition, you hypocrites?" The open insult rang off the stone walls of the Temple. "My cousin John called you vipers, and he was right to do so." The reference to the Baptizer was a canny inclusion to gain the support of the more conservative men in the crowd. "John was known as Isaiah incarnate, and it was Isaiah who said, 'These people honor me with their lips, but their hearts are far from me.' Now I see that you Pharisees make yourselves clean on the outside, but internally you are full of greed and wickedness.

Did not the Lord who made what is without also make what is within?"

Easa raised his voice to make a final point. "And this is the difference between my Nazarenes and these priests," he said. "We care for the cleanliness of our souls, that we may keep God's kingdom on earth as it is in heaven."

"This is blasphemy against the Temple!" one man shouted from the crowd. Then a great roar erupted—with some in agreement, others in opposition.

The noise and commotion in the crowd were escalating. Watching from an elevated space above the Temple walls, Mary thought at first that this was solely a reaction to Easa's bold words. Indeed, much of the consternation among the men of Jerusalem did stem from that. But several of the Nazarene disciples were pushing through the throng to get to Easa, leading a huddled group of men and women who had heard of the miraculous healings. They were a wretched lot, tragedies who were considered less than human in their blindness or their lameness.

The moneylenders and the merchants raised objections as these damaged ones moved through the Temple complex. This was their most profitable week, and this crowd was now encroaching on the business of the Temple. When a blind man fell into a merchant's table, scattering his wares, tempers flared. The merchant came after the blind man with a stick, shouting insults at the poor wretch and at the Nazarenes. Easa came to the aid of the blind man, setting him on his feet gently and whispering something into his ear. Motioning to his disciples to move the injured masses to the side, Easa turned over the other tables of the cruel merchant who had attacked the blind man. He yelled to be heard over the growing din. "It is written that God's Temple should be a house of prayer. You have made it a den of thieves."

Other merchants shouted at Easa in defiance as he moved through the Temple complex. The chaos bordered on rioting until Easa held up his hands and asked his disciples to follow him to the front of the Temple complex. Here, the unfortunates with their infirmities, diseases, and lameness were brought forth. Beginning with the blind man, Easa healed each and every one of them.

The crowds around the Temple grew to great numbers. Despite Easa's daring words, or perhaps because of them, the men and women of Jerusalem were very interested in this Nazarene, this man who healed in seconds the illnesses of many decades. Mary could no longer see him from her vantage point. Besides, Tamar and John were restless with the energy of small children in an exciting environment. Mary moved away from the spectacle to take the children into the marketplace.

As they walked through the cobbled roads, Mary saw the black robes of two Pharisees ahead of her. She was certain she had overheard Easa's name on their lips. Pulling her plain veil to cover most of her face, she kept pace with them, pushing the children forward. The men were speaking openly, but they were doing so in Greek—likely because they knew the common people around them would not understand the more worldly language. But Mary, an educated noblewoman, spoke Greek fluently.

She understood completely when one of the men turned to his companion and said, "As long as this Nazarene is alive, we will have no peace. The sooner we are rid of him, the better for us all."

Mary found Bartolome in the marketplace; he had been sent to purchase provisions for the other disciples. Mary told him to go back to Easa and tell him and the followers that they should not stay with Joseph that night. They would need to get out of Jerusalem for the sake of Easa's safety. Mary believed that the home she once shared with Lazarus and Martha in Bethany was the best choice. It was a safe distance from Jerusalem, yet it would not take too long to get back into the city—or out of it quickly.

Easa met Mary and the children in Bethany later that evening. Some of the disciples stayed with them at the home of Lazarus, while others went to the neighboring home of Simon, their trusted friend. It had been at Simon's house that Mary had disobeyed Lazarus and John with such disastrous consequences years ago. The disciples gathered on this night to discuss the events of the day and plan for what awaited them.

Mary was worried. She sensed that the opinion in Jerusalem was split—half in favor of the brilliant Nazarene who was a miracle worker and a defender of the poor, and half opposed to an upstart who would challenge the Temple and their traditions in such an unapologetic way. She repeated the conversation of the priests as she had overheard it in the marketplace. As she spoke, Judas arrived from the home of Jairus with more news.

"She is right. Jerusalem is growing very dangerous for you," he said to Easa. "Jairus says that Caiaphas and Annas are calling for your execution as a blasphemer."

Peter was disgusted. "Rubbish," he spat. "Easa has never spoken a blasphemy and could not if he so desired. They are the blasphemers, those vipers."

Easa did not look concerned. "It matters not, Peter. The priests have no authority to put a man to death," he told them, calling on his extensive knowledge of the law. "Only Rome can do that, and the Romans do not recognize the blasphemy laws of the Jews."

The men talked into the night about the best course of action for the following day. Mary wanted to keep Easa out of Jerusalem for a day to allow some calm to return to the city. But he would not hear of it. Even larger crowds were expected the following day as word spread through Jerusalem of Easa's bold teachings and extraordinary healings. He would not disappoint those who would travel to Jerusalem to see him. Nor would he bow to the pressure of the priests. Now, more than ever, he needed to be a leader.

The following day, Mary elected to stay in Bethany with the children and Martha. The weight of her pregnancy was taking its toll, and the long walk back to Bethany in such haste had exhausted her. She kept the children busy in the household, all the while trying to keep her own mind off the possible dangers that Easa might face within the city walls.

Mary sat in the front garden, watching Tamar play in the grass, when she saw a woman approaching the house, veiled heavily in black. Her face and hair were covered, and it was impossible to determine if the visitor was known or not. Perhaps it was a friend of Martha's or a new neighbor that Mary was unaware of?

The woman drew closer and Mary could hear the stifled laugh. "What's the matter, sister? You don't recognize me after all this time?"

The veil came down to reveal the woman as Salome, the Herodian princess. Her face had lost the roundness of childhood; she was entering the full bloom of maturity. Mary ran to embrace her, and they held each other for a long moment. Following John's death it had become too dangerous for Salome to be seen in the company of the Nazarenes. Her presence was dangerous for Easa. If her supporters hoped to win over John's followers, they could not be seen to be consorting with the woman who was reviled for causing his arrest, if not his death.

The enforced separation had been hard on the two women. Salome was crushed that she would not be allowed to complete her training as a priestess and would be separated from the people she had grown to love more than her own family. For Mary, it was another bitter aftereffect of the unfair judgment that had been made on both of them following John's execution.

Salome squealed when she saw little Tamar in the grass. "Look at her! She is the double of you!"

Mary nodded, smiling. "On the outside. But inside, she is already developing into the image of her father." Mary recounted some of the stories of little Tamar and how she had shown herself to be special from the time she began to walk. She had healed a lamb that had fallen into a trench in Magdala with the touch of her infant hand. She was just over three years old now, but her speech was phenomenal—she spoke easily in both Greek and Aramaic.

"She is indeed a fortunate child to have two such parents," Salome said, her face darkening. "And we need to keep both of those parents safe, which is why I'm here. Mary, I have word from the palace. Easa is in serious danger."

"Let's go inside, where we know there are no other ears, and where little ears such as these"—she gestured to Tamar—"can be otherwise occupied."

Mary leaned over to lift Tamar, but her growing belly made it difficult to bend. Salome held her arms out. "Come to your sister Salome," she said. Tamar paused, looking up at the unknown woman, then at her mother for reassurance. A perfect little smile spread across Tamar's face as she jumped into the arms of the Herodian princess.

As they entered the house, Mary signaled for Martha to take Tamar.

Martha took the little girl from Salome. "Come, little princess, we will go find your brother."

John was out walking the lands with Lazarus. Martha indicated that she would take her niece outside to allow privacy for the conversation between Salome and Mary. When they were out the door, Salome turned and grabbed Mary's hand.

"Listen to me; this is very urgent. My stepfather was in Jerusalem today at the home of Pontius Pilate, and I with him. He is leaving for Rome to see the emperor in two days' time and needed a full report from the procurator. I used the excuse of wanting to see Claudia Procula, Pilate's wife, to obtain his leave to come with him. Claudia is the granddaughter of Caesar Augustus, and I knew my stepfather would not say 'no' to that. But of course, that is not why I wanted to come. I knew that you and Easa and the others were here. Where is the Great Mary?"

"She is here," Mary answered. "She is staying with Joseph's family tonight with some of the other women, but I will take you to her tomorrow if you'd like."

Salome nodded and continued her story. "I used the excuse of seeing Claudia to see what news there was in Jerusalem of the Nazarenes. Little did I know how much Claudia had to tell me! Mary, isn't it amazing?"

Mary was unsure of what Salome was referencing. "What?"

Salome's exotic, dark eyes grew larger. "You don't know? Oh, Mary, this is too much. On the night that Easa raised Jairus' daughter, do you remember a woman in the crowd as you were leaving? She was with a Greek man who carried a sick child, a little boy."

The entire scenario flooded back to Mary now. She had seen that woman's face for the last two nights before she went to sleep. "Yes," she answered. "I told Easa, and he turned to her to heal the child. That's all I know with any certainty, other than the woman did not appear to be common or a Jew."

Salome laughed openly at this. "Mary, that woman was Claudia Procula. Easa healed the only child of Pontius Pilate!"

Mary was astonished. Now it all made sense—the feeling of pre-science, of knowing at that moment that something was happening beyond the healing itself.

"Who knows this, Salome?"

"No one but Claudia, Pilate, and their Greek slave. Pilate has forbidden his wife to speak of it and has told anyone who asked about the boy's miraculous recovery that it was the will of the Roman gods." Salome made a face to show her distaste. "Poor Claudia was bursting to tell someone, and she knew I had once been a Nazarene."

"You still are a Nazarene," Mary said kindly as she stood to allow the growing babe in her belly to adjust his position. She needed to contemplate this important information. It was exhilarating, but she didn't dare invest too much in it yet. Surely, such an occurrence had to be part of God's master plan for Easa. Had he given Claudia an ill child so that Easa could heal him and prove his divinity to Pilate? And if Easa's fate ended up in the hands of Pontius Pilate, surely he could not pass sentence on the very man who had healed his own child?

"But there's more, sister." Salome darkened again. "When I was there, the horrid Jonathan Annas and his son-in-law came to see Pilate and my stepfather. They are making a case against Easa." She gave Mary a sly smile. "I heard them announced and then begged Claudia to tell me the best place to hide so I could listen."

Mary smiled at Salome, who was as impetuous as ever.

"Pilate wanted none of it, and tried to brush it off as unimportant so he could finish his meeting with Herod. Pilate cares only about a good report going to Rome concerning his abilities as a governor. He wants a post in Egypt."

Mary was listening patiently, heart pounding, as Salome continued. "But my stepfather—arrogant Herod that he is—sided with these idiot priests. They played to him, told him that Easa was calling himself king of the Jews and meant to supplant the Herods from their throne."

Mary shook her head at this. It was nonsense, of course. Easa had no desire to sit on any earthly throne. He was the king in the hearts of the people, the one who would deliver the kingdom of God to them. He needed no palace or throne for that. But an insecure Herod was feeling threatened because of the manipulations of Annas and Caiaphas.

"I heard Pilate come in to Claudia shortly after that—he could not see where I was hiding—and he said to her, 'My dear, I'm afraid the fates are against your Easa the Nazarene. The priests are crying for his head, and they will see him arrested before their Passover.' To which I heard Claudia say, 'But of course you will see that he is spared.' Pilate said nothing, and I heard Claudia ask again, 'Won't you?' and then I heard nothing until Pilate left the room. When I was sure he was gone, I came out to find Claudia in a terrible state. She said her husband would not look at her as he left. Oh, Mary, she is very worried about what will happen to Easa. And I am as well. You must get him out of Jerusalem."

"Where does your stepfather think you are now?"

She shrugged. "I told him I would spend the day shopping for silks. He is too preoccupied with his excursion to Rome to know or care where I spend the night. He has amusements of his own in Jerusalem."

Mary was trying to devise a strategy. She must wait until Easa returned home tonight, and then she would tell him everything, of course. She knew it would take little enough encouragement to get Salome to stay and provide details.

Salome did stay, and was overjoyed when the Great Mary came to them later in the afternoon. Easa's esteemed mother brought with her the other elder Marys—her sister, Mary Jacoby, and their cousin, Mary Salome, who was the mother of two of Easa's most loyal followers. It was an honor for Salome to be in the company of these wise women, the strong if often silent leaders of the Nazarene tradition. But her joy was fleeting, as was Mary Magdalene's.

"I have seen a great darkness on the horizon, my daughters," the Great Mary told them. "I have come to meet with my son. We must all be prepared for the test of strength and faith that this Passover will bring to us."

The news from Jerusalem was certainly troubling. Larger crowds had greeted Easa and the Nazarenes upon their entrance to the city that morning, causing unease among the Roman guards. The Nazarenes had set up outside the Temple where Easa preached and fielded the questions and challenges that were hurled at him. Just as they had the previous day, representatives of the high priest and the Temple had planted their own within the crowd. The unrest increased as the chastised merchants and moneylenders from the day before came forward to protest the Nazarene presence. Finally, in an effort to keep the peace and prevent potential bloodshed, Easa took his leave and left with his most loyal Nazarene followers.

Later that night in Bethany, the combination of Salome's observations, intelligence from Jairus, and the prophecy of the Great Mary created an atmosphere of consternation and worry. Only Easa seemed unaffected by the increasingly dire circumstances as he set out the plan for the following day.

Simon and Judas, who had spent the day meeting with their brother Zealots, had a plan of their own. "There are enough of us to do battle with anyone who comes for you," Simon said. "The crowds at the Temple tomorrow will be overwhelming. If you emphasize to the people that the kingdom of God as we know it will free Jews from the oppression of Rome, the crowd will follow you."

"To what end?" Easa asked calmly. "The result of such an action would be the bloodshed of many innocent Jews. That is not The Way. No, Simon, I will not incite a riot that will spill the blood of our people on the eve of a holy day. How can I show that the kingdom of God is in each and every man and woman if I ask them to bleed and die for it? You are missing the meaning of The Way, my brothers."

"But there is no Way without you," Peter snapped. The strain of these past days was showing on Peter more than on any of the other disciples. He had sacrificed everything for his belief in Easa and The Way. It was too much for him to contemplate any unfortunate outcome.

"You are wrong, my brother," Easa said. There was no reproach in his tone as he turned to Peter and continued warmly. "Peter, I have said this to you from the time we were children. You are the rock on which our ministry will flourish. Your legacy will live as long as my own."

Peter did not look comforted, nor did the other disciples. Easa saw this and held up his hands.

"My brothers and sisters, hear me. Remember what I have given you, and that is an understanding that the kingdom of God lives within you, and no oppressor can ever take that away. If you hold that one truth in your hearts, you will never know a day of pain or fear."

Then he held out his hands to the disciples and led them in the Lord's Prayer.

Easa left his followers that night to confer privately with the Great Mary. When they were finished, he bade his mother good night and sought out his wife.

"You must not be afraid of what will happen, little dove," he said gently.

Mary searched his face. Easa often concealed his visions from the followers, but rarely from her. She was the one person he shared almost everything with. But tonight she sensed his restraint.

"What do you see, Easa?" she asked quietly.

"I see that my father in heaven has laid out a great plan and we must follow it."

"To the fulfillment of the prophecies?"

"If that is his will."

Mary was silent for a moment. The prophecies were specific—they stated that the messiah must be put to death by his own people.

"And what of Pontius Pilate?" Mary asked with some hope. "Surely you were sent to heal his child so that he would see for himself who and what you are. Do you not think that is part of God's plan?"

"Mary, listen closely to what I am about to tell you, for it is a great understanding of the Nazarene Way. God creates his plan, and he puts each man and woman into their place. But he does not force them into action. Like any good father, the Lord guides his children, but then gives them the opportunity to make their own choices."

Mary listened intently, applying Easa's philosophy to the current situation. "You believe that Pontius Pilate was put in this place by God?"

Easa nodded. "Yes. Pilate, his good wife, their child."

"And whether or not Pilate chooses to help us . . . that is not God's determination?"

Easa shook his head. "The Lord does not dictate to us, Mary. He guides us. It is up to each person to choose his or her master, and that comes down to a choice between God's plan and earthly desires. You cannot serve God and also serve these earthbound needs. The kingdom of Heaven comes to those who choose God. I cannot say which master Pontius Pilate will choose to serve when his time comes."

Mary listened carefully. Although she was well versed in Nazarene ideas, Easa's example of Pontius Pilate made this tenet clear and powerful. In a flash of prescience, she felt the need to savor her husband's words, to remember them exactly as he spoke them. The time would come when she would teach others precisely as he had taught her.

"The high priest and his supporters are determined to have me arrested—we know now that we cannot escape that," Easa continued. "But we will ask that they send me to Pilate, and I will plead my case before him. It will then be upon his faith and his conscience to make a decision. We must be prepared for whatever that choice may be. No matter what it is, we must show by our actions what we know to be the truth—that when we allow the kingdom of God to live inside us, nothing on earth can change that, neither an empire, nor an oppressor, nor pain. Not even death."

They talked well into the night as Easa discussed his plans for the following day. Mary asked the heaviest question in her heart just once.

"Can we not just leave Jerusalem tonight? Go back to our preaching in the hills of Galilee until Annas and Caiaphas find some other quarry to chase?"

"You of all people know better, my Mary," he chided gently. "The people are watching us closely now. I must show them by example."

She nodded her understanding, and he continued, telling her about his discussion with the Great Mary. They had decided that an appearance at the Temple in Jerusalem the following day would be too dangerous. Too many innocents stood to be injured if there was rioting. Easa's primary concern was the protection of his disciples. The high priest wanted him, not the others. They had heard as much from Jairus. There was no need to endanger the others unnecessarily. Instead, the closest of the followers would meet privately in the afternoon at a property of Joseph's for a Passover meal. There Easa would issue instructions to each as to what their role in the ministry would be if he faced a long period of incarceration as John had—or if something worse were to transpire. They would spend the night in Joseph's lands at Gethsemane, under the sacred stars of Jerusalem.

And there Easa would allow himself to be arrested.

"You are going to surrender to the authorities of the Temple?" Mary was incredulous.

"No, no. I cannot do that. The people would lose all faith in our Way if that were the case. But I must see that my arrest happens away from the city and in such a manner that there is no blood spilt and no rioting. I will have one of our own 'betray me' and go to the authorities to give away my position. The guards will come to Gethsemane, where there will be no crowds and therefore no rioting."

Mary's mind was racing. All of this was happening so fast. She was struck by a terrible thought. "Oh, Easa. But who? Who of our own would have the stomach to do such a thing? Surely you can't think that Peter or Andrew would be able. Certainly not Philip or Bartolome. Your brother James would shed his own blood first, and Simon would shed that of others."

The answer came to her then, and they said it in unison. "Judas."

Easa's expression was grave. "And that is where I must go now, my dove. I must speak to Judas and tell him that he has been chosen for this task because of his strength."

He kissed his wife's cheek as he rose to take his leave. She watched him go with a growing sense of dread for what the next day would bring.

They assembled the following afternoon, as planned, for their meal together: Easa, his twelve chosen, and all of the Marys. The children stayed in Bethany with Martha and Lazarus.

Easa began the evening with the ritual of anointment. This was his own version, a role reversal wherein he bathed the feet of each person in the room. He explained that this was to acknowledge each person as a child of God who had a special mission to preach the word of the kingdom.

"I have given you this example, that you will do to others what has been done here to you. That you will acknowledge others as your equals under God. And a new commandment I will give you this night—that you will love each other the way that I love you. For when you go out into the world I would have people recognize that you are Nazarenes by the way you love each other."

When he had bathed the feet of each follower in the room, Easa led them to the table for the Passover supper. Breaking a piece of the unleavened bread, he blessed it first, then said, "Take this and eat, for this bread shall be as my body." And taking a cup of wine, he said thanks over it before passing it around the table. "This is my blood of the new testament, which is shed for many."

Mary watched quietly along with the others. Only she and the other Marys knew the full details of the events that were to come. When Judas was given the signal by Easa, he would leave the supper and go to Jairus. Jairus would take him to Annas and Caiaphas, presenting Judas as the betrayer. Judas would ask for thirty pieces of silver; this would make his betrayal appear authentic. In exchange for the money, he would lead the priests to Easa's private retreat, where, away from the unpredictable crowds of the city, it would be easy to arrest him.

The tension was plain on Judas' face for those with eyes to see it. The other disciples were not told of this plan as Easa did not want to take any chances. He did not want it argued, and he certainly didn't want the men to resist. Later, Mary would weep for Judas and the unfairness of it all. She would defend him to the other disciples, who saw him only as the betrayer. But by then, it would be too late by far for Judas Iscariot. God had created a place for him, and he had chosen to take it.

Easa turned to Judas now. He handed him a piece of bread soaked in wine, giving him the predetermined signal.

"What you must do, do quickly."

As Mary watched Judas retreat from the room, her heart sank. There would be no going back now. She looked up in time to catch the eye of the Great Mary, who was also watching Judas walk out the door with Easa's fate in his hands. The two women held each other in their gaze in that moment, each praying silently that God would protect their beloved Easa.

The guards came in greater numbers and with a force that Mary had not anticipated. It was well into night when Judas appeared over the rise with the soldiers of the high priest. There was chaos as the commotion of the extensive and heavily armed arresting party appeared on the scene, waking the male apostles. The women were holding vigil at a distance by a fire. All but Mary Magdalene, who waited with Easa.

Peter jumped from his position on the floor, grabbing a sword from one of the shocked younger soldiers. "Lord, we shall fight for you!" he cried, and went after a man he recognized, Malchus, the servant of the high priest. He cut the man's ear badly with the sword, and blood flowed freely from the wound.

Easa rose and walked calmly toward the group. "Enough, brothers," he said to Peter and the others. To the high priest's cohort he said, "Put away your weapons. No man here will harm you. You have my word."

He went to Malchus, who had fallen to his knees, and held his robe against his ear to stanch the blood. Easa placed his palm over the ear and said, "You have suffered enough for this." When he removed his hand, the ear was healed and the flow of blood stopped.

Easa helped Malchus to his feet and addressed him. "Caiaphas sends out this group of armed men against me as he would to a thief or a murderer. Why? When I came every day to the Temple he made no attempts to arrest me nor to indicate that I was a danger. This is indeed an hour of darkness for our people."

One of the soldiers, a man wearing the badges of a leader, stepped forward and demanded in a guttural attempt at Aramaic, "Are you Easa the Nazarene?"

"I am," he answered plainly in Greek.

Several of the followers yelled accusations and questions at Judas. Easa had advised him not to speak if this happened, and Judas remained obedient. Instead, he kissed Easa gently on the cheek, hoping that by this sign some of the disciples might understand what he had been charged to do.

The soldier wearing the badges of his rank read out the charges for arrest, and Easa was led away to his fate at the hands of the high priests.

Mary Magdalene kept vigil with the other Marys late into the night. They could not get too close to the men—it was too risky. Emotions were running very high, and the women could not let on how much they knew about the night's events.

The Marys led each other in prayer and offered each other quiet comfort. It was deep in the night when they saw a torch coming across the Kidron Valley toward their retreat. It was a small party, two men and what appeared to be a small woman. Mary got up from her place as she recognized the Herodian princess. She ran to Salome, embracing her. It was only then that she realized the man carrying the torch was a Roman centurion in plain clothes—the blue-eyed man whose painful broken arm Easa had healed.

"Sister, there is little time." Salome was breathing heavily. They had obviously rushed to get here. "I have come from the Fortress Antonia. Claudia Procula sent me to you with her kindest regards and her deepest sympathies for the unjust arrest of your husband."

Mary nodded, encouraging Salome to continue and swallowing the swelling fear in her gut. If the wife of the Roman procurator was sending out royal messengers in the middle of the night, something was terribly wrong.

"Easa will go to trial before Pilate in the morning," Salome continued. "But Pilate is under terrible pressure to put him to death. Oh, Mary, he doesn't want to. Claudia says that Pilate knows Easa healed their child, or at least he is willing in his Roman way to try to accept that. But my abominable stepfather is calling for Easa's death as quickly as possible. Herod goes to Rome on the sabbath. He told Pilate he wants this 'Nazarene problem' sorted out before he leaves. Mary, you need to understand how serious this is. They may execute Easa. Tomorrow."

This was all happening too fast. None of them had expected it, not like this. They expected an incarceration and a period when Easa would have the time to argue his case before Rome and before Herod. There had always been a possibility that the worst could happen, but not this fast.

Salome continued breathlessly. "Claudia Procula has sent us to fetch you. These two men are her trusted servants." Mary looked up and saw the light reflect off the face of the silent man behind the torch. She recognized him now. He was the Greek who had held the ailing boy outside of Jairus' house.

"They will take you to where Easa is being held. Claudia has seen to the situation with the guards until dawn. This may be your last chance to see him. But we have to go, and quickly."

Mary asked them for one moment, and went to the Great Mary. She knew the older woman would never be able to make the required haste to get to Easa in time, but it was respectful to offer her place to Easa's mother.

The Great Mary kissed her daughter-in-law on the cheek. "Give that to my son. Tell him I will be there tomorrow, come what may. Go with God, my daughter."

Mary and Salome hurried to keep up with the silent men, who were moving quickly to the eastern edge of the city. Mary had taken an extra moment to change the red veil that identified her as a Nazarene priestess for a plain black one, as Salome wore. The Herodian princess informed Mary as they walked. "I have sent a messenger to Martha. Easa wants to see the children; he told Claudia's servant as much." She indicated the Greek slave. "Easa knew that you would not have time to go out to Bethany and bring them back if you were coming to see him."

Mary's thoughts were racing. She didn't want Tamar and John to witness anything traumatic on the morrow, yet if the worst were to occur, Easa would need to see his children one final time. Little John was as much his own as Tamar; Easa loved them both unconditionally. The protection and safety of all of them would be an issue when the sun rose. Mary prayed silently for a moment but had little time to consider these issues now. They had arrived outside the area of Easas' detainment. So far, the darkness had sheltered them and they had attracted no attention, but they would be forced to walk down a long flight of external stairs that were well lit by torches.

The centurion whispered instructions to them, and they waited for the Greek to survey the area quickly. The slave ran to the bottom of the stairs and gave the signal to come forward. Salome remained at the top of the stairs to act as watch, while the Greek filled the same role below. Mary and the centurion hurried down the stairs and into the prison corridors. He held the torch ahead of him to light the way in the subterranean space. Mary followed quickly behind, trying to block the sounds of men in pain and despair that echoed from the stone walls around her. She knew none of these sounds came from Easa—no matter what pain was afflicted upon him, he would never cry out; it was not in his nature. But she felt deep compassion for the other poor souls who awaited their fates in a Roman prison.

The centurion pulled a key out from under his tunic and slipped it into the door, releasing the lock and allowing Mary entrance to her husband's cell. Mary discovered many years later how Claudia and Salome had accomplished this feat of securing the keys and removing the guards—it had involved massive bribery and no small personal cost to the Herodian princess. Mary would be grateful for the rest of her life to the Roman woman Claudia Procula and to her friend, the misunderstood Salome—not just for the events of this night, but also for those on the terrible day that would follow.

Mary had to resist the urge to cry out in despair when she saw Easa. He had been beaten—badly. There were bruises on his beautiful face, and she saw him fight back the wince as he rose to embrace her. She whispered her question as she looked over his battered face.

"Who did this to you? The men of Caiaphas and Annas?"

"Shh. Listen to me, my Mary, as there is little time and much to say. There is no place for blame, as blame brings only vengeance. When we forgive we are closest to God. That is what we are here to teach the children of Israel and the rest of the earth. Take this with you and teach it to everyone who will listen, in memory of me."

It was Mary's turn to wince. She couldn't bear to hear Easa speaking of himself this way, as if his death were assured. Sensing her despair, he spoke to her gently.

"Last night in Gethsemane, I went to pray to the Lord our father. I asked him to take this cup away from me, if that was His will. But He did not. He did not because *this* is His will. There is no other way, don't you see? The people are not able to understand the kingdom of God without a supreme example. I will be that. I will show them that I can die for them and do so without pain or fear. Our Lord showed me the cup and I drank from it and did so joyously. It is done."

Mary could not stop the flow of tears, but she was trying hard not to sob. Any noise could give them away. Easa attempted to comfort her.

"You must be strong now, my dove, because you will take the true Nazarene Way with you, and you will teach it to the world. The others will do their best as well, and I gave each of them instructions after the supper. But only you know everything that is in my heart and my head, so you must become the next leader of our people, and our children after you."

Mary was trying to think clearly. She needed to be focused on Easa's last requests, not on her own grief. She would have time to mourn later. Now she had to be worthy of his trust as a leader of the Nazarenes.

"Easa, not all of the men love me, as you know. Some of them will not follow me. Although you have taught them to treat women as equals, I fear that once you are gone . . . that understanding will wane. How would you have me tell them that you have chosen me to lead the Nazarenes?"

"I have been thinking of this tonight," he answered. "First, you alone have the Book of Love."

Mary nodded. Easa had spent a large part of his ministry writing the Nazarene beliefs and his own understandings in a volume they referred to as the Book of Love. The other disciples knew about it, but Easa had never shared it with anyone but Mary. It was kept safely under lock and key at her home in Galilee.

"I have always said that the Book of Love would never see the light while I lived on earth, for as long as I was here, it was incomplete," Easa continued. "Every minute of every day that I have lived, God has brought me a new understanding. Every person I have ever encountered has taught me more about the nature of God. I have written these things in the Book of Love. When I am gone, you must take it and make it the cornerstone of all teachings that will follow."

Mary nodded her understanding. The Book of Love was indeed a beautiful and powerful memorial to all that Easa had taught in his life. His disciples would be honored and awed to learn from it.

"There is something else, Mary. I will give the men a sign, something that tells them clearly that you are my chosen successor. Fear not, little dove, for I will let the world know that you are my most beloved disciple."

Easa placed his hands on Mary's swollen abdomen. There was so much to say yet. "This child you carry, this son of ours, he has the blood of prophets and kings, as our daughter does. Their descendants shall take their place in the world, preaching the kingdom of God and the words contained within the Book of Love so that all people will know peace and justice the world over." The babe kicked in answer to the prophecy that his father spoke. "This child has a special destiny in the western islands where the word of The Way will spread. I have given my uncle, Joseph, instructions on this child's upbringing. You must trust Joseph and allow this child to go where God takes him."

Mary accepted this. Joseph was a great man, wise and strong and worldly. He traveled extensively in his trade as a tin merchant. As a young man, Easa had accompanied Joseph to the misty green isles

west of Gaul. He once told Mary that while there he had a premonition of the Nazarene Way growing among the fierce, blue-eyed people
who inhabited the islands.

"And you must name him Yeshua-David, in memory of me and
the founder of our royal line. The greatest king to rule on earth will
come from his blood."

Mary agreed to Easa's request, asking next, "What would you instruct me regarding our Sarah-Tamar?"

Easa smiled at the mention of his precious daughter. "She must
stay with you until she is a woman grown, and then she will make her
own choice. She has your strength, our Tamar. But Israel will not be
safe for you and the children, I have seen this. Joseph will take you to
Egypt, along with as many of the others who choose to leave. Alexandria is a great center of learning and is safe for our people. You may
choose to stay there or go farther away, to the west countries. I will
leave that to you, Mary. You must decide what is best in order for the
teachings of the Nazarenes to go on into the world. Follow your heart
and trust in God to guide you."

"And what of Little John?" Mary asked. Easa had always treated the
child as his own son, but his blood and destiny would always be different; they both knew that.

Easa's eyes clouded with knowing. "Even at this age, John is
strong-willed and unsettled. You are his mother and you will guide
him, but John will need the influence of men to shape his restlessness.
He is much loved by Peter and Andrew. When John is older, he may do
well to foster with Peter or his brother."

Easa didn't need to elaborate; Mary knew what he meant by this.
Peter and Andrew had once been followers of the Baptizer, and they
had all known each other since they were children in Galilee, attending the temple at Capernaeum. Peter and Andrew revered Little John
as the son of a great prophet in his own right as well as Easa's foster
child.

"I have words of thanks and comfort for one more person," Easa
said. "To the Roman woman Claudia Procula, I would have you say
that I left this world in her debt. She sacrificed much to get you here to

me, and I thank her. Tell her she must not judge her husband too harshly. Pontius Pilate must choose his master, and I have seen that he will choose poorly. But in the end, his choice will fulfill God's plan for us all."

Easa gave further directions to his wife, some of a spiritual nature and some practical, before his final words of comfort to her. "Be strong, no matter what comes tomorrow. Do not fear for me, as I feel no fear for myself. I am content to take the cup of our Father and join Him in heaven, Mary. Be a leader of the people and be not afraid. Remember who you are at all times. You are a queen, you are a Nazarene, and you are my wife."

A shattered Mary stumbled through the streets of Jerusalem behind Salome as the sky began to grow lighter with the first essence of dawn light. The princess had a house that would be safe for them, and it was there that she had instructed the messenger to take Martha and the children. Once Mary was safely ensconced in the house, waiting for her sister-in-law to come with John and Tamar, Salome set off to find another messenger to send to the Great Mary and the others at Gethsemane.

Elsewhere in Jerusalem, another noble woman, the lady Claudia Procula, was feeling the enormous burden that awaited her family that day. She slept fitfully when exhaustion finally claimed her late in the night. Once the Greek had come to tell her that their mission to the Nazarene's wife had been successful, she allowed herself to close her eyes.

Claudia awakened in a cold sweat. The haunting dream had her in its throes. She could feel it swirling around her in the room. She closed her eyes, but the images remained, as did the sound of a chant that filled her head. A chorus of voices, hundreds strong, perhaps

thousands, repeated the phrase "crucified under Pontius Pilate, crucified under Pontius Pilate." There was more to the chant, repeated obediently by the voices in her dream, but she heard nothing else, just
those four words.

As disturbing as the nightmare sounds were, the sights were
worse. It had started out as a beautiful dream, with children dancing
on a grassy hill in the springtime sun. Easa stood in the middle of a
circle, surrounded by children who were all dressed in white. Pilo was
among the children who laughed and danced, as was Smedia. The hill
was filling now with people of all ages dressed in white, smiling and
singing.

Claudia recognized one of the arriving men in the dream as Praetorus, the centurion who had been healed of a broken hand. The man
had confided in her about his own healing after hearing the whispered rumors of Pilo's miracle. But as she came to the realization that
every one of the smiling souls in the dream, adults and children, had
been healed by Easa, the landscape changed. The dancing stopped
and the sky grew dark as the sound of the chant grew louder and
louder: "crucified under Pontius Pilate, crucified under Pontius Pilate."

Claudia watched in the dreamscape as her beloved Pilo fell to the
ground. The last image before she awoke was that of Easa bending
over to lift him. He carried Pilo away without looking back as the others fell to the ground around them. She saw her husband then,
screaming in futile agony at the retreating form of Easa the Nazarene
as he departed with Pilo's lifeless body. Lightning ripped the sky as the
sound of the chant followed them down the hill.

"Crucified under Pontius Pilate."

"Crucify him!" This was a new sound. Not the eerie chant from the
nightmare, but the real sound of hate coming from beyond the walls
outside the Fortress Antonia. "Crucify him!"

Claudia rose to dress as the Greek slave rushed into the room.

"My lady, you must come before it is too late. The master sits in the
judgment seat and the priests are baying for blood."

"Who do I hear outside?"

"A great mob. It is early for so many to be here. The men of the Temple must have worked through the night to ensure a large crowd. The sentence will be passed before the rest of Jerusalem has the chance to rally for your Nazarene's sake."

Claudia dressed quickly and without her usual care. She had no interest in her appearance today; she simply had to be decent enough to appear before the men attending the tribunal. As she glanced quickly in the mirror, a thought struck her hard.

"Where is Pilo? He is not awake yet, is he?"

"No, my lady. He is still in his bed."

"Good. Stay with him and see that he remains there. If he awakens, keep him as far away from the walls as you can. I do not want him to see or hear anything that is happening in the city."

"Of course, my lady," the Greek slave answered, as Claudia ran from the room on the most important mission of her life.

Claudia Procula did her best to hide her despair and disgust as she entered the patio that had become a makeshift judgment chamber. Pilate had made this concession to the high priests, who would not enter the formal Roman chambers and risk being defiled on Passover. This area was enclosed and private, not exposed to the mob scene that was growing outside the walls. Pontius Pilate had had his chair brought in and sat high on the judgment seat of Rome. Behind him stood two of his trusted guards, the blue-eyed Praetorus and the harsh man Claudia disliked called Longinus. Pilate was flanked on the dais by Caiaphas and Annas on one side, an envoy of Herod on another. The Temple envoy, Jairus, was conspicuous by his absence.

On the floor in front of them, bound and bleeding, was Easa the Nazarene.

Claudia stared at Easa from behind the curtain. He looked up as if he sensed her before he saw her. Their eyes locked for a long moment that seemed to stretch into eternity, and Claudia knew the same feeling of pure love and light that she had felt on the night that Pilo was healed. She had no desire to break the gaze or turn away from the warmth of this man before them. Could these others not feel it? How was it possible for them to stand in this enclosed space and not be affected by the brightness of the sun that shone from such a holy being?

She cleared her throat to alert her husband to her presence. Pilate looked up from his chair and acknowledged Claudia. "Gentlemen, if you will excuse me," the procurator said as he rose from the judgment seat to join his wife. Claudia took him out of earshot and felt panic shoot through her as she looked at her husband's ashen face. Sweat trickled across his forehead and down his temples, yet it was a mild morning.

"I do not see an easy outcome here, Claudia," he said quietly.

"Pontius, you cannot allow them to kill this man. You know what he is."

Pilate shook his head. "No, I do not know what he is, and that is what makes it difficult for me to pass judgment."

"But you know he is a just man who has wrought good works throughout the land. You know he has committed no crime that requires severe punishment."

"They are calling him an insurgent. If he is seen as a threat to Rome, I cannot allow him to live."

"But you know that is not the truth!"

Pilate looked away from her for a long moment. He took a deep breath before facing his wife. "Claudia, I am in torment. This man defies all Roman reason and logic. Every philosophy I have ever studied is challenged by this situation that we face. My heart and my gut tell me he is innocent and I should not condemn an innocent man."

"Then do not! Why is that so difficult? You have the power to save him, Pontius. Save the man who gave us back our son."

Pilate ran his hands over his face to push the sweat away. "It is difficult because Herod calls for his execution, and he is calling for it early in the day."

"Herod is a jackal."

"True, but he is a jackal who departs for Rome this evening and has the power to destroy me with Caesar if I displease him. This man can bring us down, Claudia. Is it worth it? Is the life of one more Jewish insurgent worth throwing away our future?"

"He is not an insurgent!" Claudia cried.

They were interrupted by the envoy of Herod, who called Pilate back to the tribunal space. As he turned to leave his wife, Claudia grabbed him by the arm.

"Pontius, I had a terrible dream last night. Please, I fear for you and for Pilo if you do not save this man. The wrath of God will fall upon us all."

"Perhaps. But which God? Am I to believe that the God of the Jews holds sway over Rome?" he questioned. As the other men called for him to return to the seat of judgment, Pilate looked intently at his wife. "This is a dilemma, Claudia. The most challenging I have ever faced. Do not think that I feel this burden any less than you do."

He returned to the dais to question the prisoner as Claudia watched from behind the curtain.

"The chief priests of your nation have delivered you to me, asking for your death," Pilate said to his Nazarene prisoner. "What have you done? Are you the king of the Jews?"

Easa answered with his usual calm. A stranger watching would never guess that his life was forfeit based on the answer. "Do you ask this question yourself, because of what you know of me? Or did others tell you this of me?"

"Answer the question. Are you a king? If you say you are not, I shall give you back to the priests to charge under your own laws."

Jonathan Annas jumped in at this. "We have no laws to put a man to death, procurator. This is why we have come to you. If he were not a malefactor and dangerous, we would never have bothered your excellency with this matter."

"The prisoner will answer the question," Pilate said, ignoring Annas.

Easa did so, looking only at Pilate. As Claudia watched the exchange she had a strong sense that the two of them did not see or hear the others in the room. What was playing out was between the two of them alone, a dance of destiny and faith that would change the world. Claudia felt it in the shiver that ran through her body.

"I came into the world that I may show people The Way of God and bear witness to the truth."

The Roman philosopher in Pilate jumped at this. "Truth," he mused. "Tell me Nazarene, what is truth?"

The two of them stared at each other for a long time, locked in their intertwined fates. Pilate broke the gaze and turned to the priests.

"I'll tell you what is true. The truth is that I find no fault in this man at all."

Pilate was interrupted by the announcement of an arrival. The proceedings stopped as Jairus entered the room and greeted the other priests. He apologized to Pilate for his late entrance, citing urgent Passover business.

"Good Jairus." Pilate was relieved to see the envoy who had become his friend. They had a shared secret, and each man knew it of the other. "I have informed your brothers here that I see no fault in this man and I cannot pass judgment on him."

Jairus nodded sagely. "I see."

Caiaphas shot a look at Jairus and said, "You know how dangerous this man is."

Jairus looked at his brother priest and back at Pilate, trying with all his might not to look at the prisoner. "But it is Passover, my brothers. A time for justice and peace among our people." To Pilate he said, "You know of our custom at this time of year?"

Pilate caught a glimpse of what Jairus was trying to do and seized the opportunity. "Yes, of course. Each year at this time I allow your people to choose one prisoner to receive clemency and release. Shall we take this prisoner out to the people and ask for their point of view?"

"Excellent!" Jairus said. He knew that Caiaphas and Annas were cornered and could not refuse this generous offer from Rome. He also knew that the crowd was stacked with supporters of the high priests—and more than a few mercenaries who had been well paid to create a mob scene against the Nazarene if such a thing proved necessary. Jairus could only hope that the Nazarenes and their supporters had arrived by now and brought their own followers in great numbers.

Pilate signaled to the centurions to bring the prisoner out onto the rampart walls. Caiaphas and Annas excused themselves, indicating that they could not be seen in the presence of the Romans this morning, but would return once the decision had been made to release a prisoner. Pilate suspected the high priests were rushing to secure their position with their followers in the mob, but could do nothing about it. Jairus caught his eye as he, too, excused himself. The two men exchanged a meaningful look just before each turned to perform their duties.

Pilate made the Passover announcement before the swelling crowd. "You have a custom," his voice rang out in the Jerusalem morning, "that I shall release unto you one of the prisoners in honor of your Passover." Easa was dragged up roughly alongside Pilate. The procurator glared at Longinus for his unnecessary brutality. "Enough," he hissed under his breath before returning to the crowd. "Shall I release this man, the king of the Jews?"

There was frenetic activity in the crowd as raised voices battled over each other to be heard. A distinct voice yelled, "We have no king but Caesar!" Another called, "Release Barabbas the Zealot." This suggestion was met with cries of approval in the crowd.

Valiant voices cried out, "Release the Nazarene," but to no avail. The followers of the Temple had been well coached, and the chant to release Barabbas swelled to a great roar. "Barabbas! Barabbas! Barabbas!"

Pilate had no option but to release the prisoner called for by the crowd. Barabbas the Zealot was set free to celebrate Passover, and Easa the Nazarene was sentenced to be scourged.

Claudia Procula intercepted her husband as he descended the ramparts. "You will scourge him?"

"Peace, woman!" Pilate snapped, pulling her roughly to the side. "I will beat him publicly and have Longinus and Praetorus make a show of it. It is our last chance to save his life. Perhaps that will satisfy their blood lust and they will cease to scream for his crucifixion." He sighed hard, releasing his grasp on his wife. "It's all I have left, Claudia."

"And if it's not enough?"

"Don't ask the question if you don't want the answer."

Claudia nodded. She had suspected as much. "Pontius, I would ask one further thing of you. This man's family—his wife and his children—are at the rear of the fortress. I would have you delay the scourging just long enough for him to see them. It may be his last chance to speak with his loved ones. Please."

Pilate nodded curtly. "I'll hold them off, but not for long. I'll have Praetorus take the prisoner. He is trustworthy where your Nazarene is concerned. I will send Longinus to prepare for the public display."

Pontius Pilate was true to his word and allowed Easa to be taken to quarters at the rear of the fortress for a brief meeting with Mary and the children. Easa embraced Little John and Tamar, telling them both to be very brave and to take care of their mother. He kissed both of them and said, "Remember, my little ones, no matter what happens, I will be with you always."

When their time was nearly gone he embraced Mary Magdalene one final time. "Listen to me, my dove. This is very important. When I have left my body of flesh, you must not cling to me. You must let me go with the understanding that I am always with you in spirit. Close your eyes, and I am there."

She attempted to smile through her tears, trying so hard to be brave. Her heart was shattered, and she was numb with pain and terror, but she would not show him that. Her strength was the final gift she could give him.

Praetorus arrived in the room then to take Easa away. The centurion's blue eyes were ringed in red. Easa saw this and comforted the man. "Do what you must."

"You will regret that you healed this hand," the centurion said, choking on the words.

Easa shook his head. "No. I would rather know that the man on the other end was a friend. Know now that I forgive you. But please, may I have one more moment?"

Praetorus nodded and left to wait outside.

Easa turned to the children and put his hand to his heart. "Remember, I am right here. Always." They both nodded solemnly, John's dark eyes huge and grave, little Tamar's filled with tears if not with understanding of the dire situation.

He turned then to Mary and whispered. "Promise me you will not let them see anything else that happens today. And I would not want you to witness what happens next. But at the end . . ."

She did not let him finish. She grabbed him and held him tightly to her for one last moment, searing into her brain and body exactly what he felt like in the flesh. She would hold this last memory to her for as long as she lived. "I will be there for you," she whispered. "No matter what."

"Thank you, my Mary," he said as he pulled away from her gently. He spoke his final words to her with a smile, as if he would be back for dinner at the end of the afternoon.

"You will not miss me because I will not be gone. It will be better than it is now, because we will never be apart after this."

Mary and the children were led from the rear of the Fortress Antonia by Claudia Procula's Greek slave. Mary asked to meet Claudia and thank her in person, but the slave shook his head and spoke to her in his native tongue.

"My mistress is much distressed by the events of this day. She tells me she cannot face you. She tried everything she knew to save him."

"Tell her I know that. And Easa knows as well. And tell her that I hope one day we will meet and I will be able to look into her face and give her my thanks, and his."

The Greek nodded humbly, and left to attend his mistress.

Mary and the children emerged into the chaos that was Jerusalem on this holy Friday. She needed to get the children away from this area, needed to get as far away as possible before the sounds of the scourging reached their ears. The safe house that Salome had provided was nearby. Mary decided to go there to find Martha and instruct her to get the children back to Bethany.

The Great Mary and the two elder Marys were at the house, but Martha was not. She was out searching for the Magdalene and the children, not realizing that they were coming back to the house. Mary Magdalene had the difficult task of relaying the morning's events to Easa's mother. The Great Mary nodded, tears filling her aging eyes that held so much wisdom and compassion. "He saw this long ago. We both saw it," she said finally.

The women made the decision to face the mob in Jerusalem. They would find Martha and see that John and Tamar were taken to safety—and then they would find Easa. If he were to be sentenced and crucified today, they would not leave him. Mary had promised. He had asked only for her and for his mother in these final hours.

As they prepared to leave the house, the Great Mary came to her daughter-in-law holding the rich red veil of their rank. She handed it to Mary Magdalene. "Wear this, my daughter. You are a Nazarene and a queen, now more than ever."

Nodding slowly, Mary Magdalene took the full-length red veil and draped it over her body, fully aware as she did that her life on earth would never be the same again.

"Crucify him! Crucify him!" The crowd swelled with the chant. Pilate watched with a mixture of helplessness and disgust. The vicious bloodletting of the Nazarene had not satisfied them. Indeed, it had functioned only to urge the mob into more of a frenzy as they called for the prisoner's life. A man had come forward carrying a crown twisted from the razor-sharp branches of a whitethorn tree. He threw it at Easa, who was still slumped against the whipping post, back laid open to the glaring morning sun. "Here's your crown, if you are a king," the man yelled as the crowd laughed derisively.

Praetorus unshackled Easa and was in the process of moving him from the whipping post when Longinus picked up the crown of thorns and shoved it cruelly onto Easa's head. The flesh of his scalp and forehead ripped, causing blood mixed with sweat to pour into his eyes as the hostile crowd whooped approval. "That is enough, Longinus!" Praetorus growled at his watch partner.

Longinus laughed, a harsh and bitter sound. "You're getting soft." He spat at Praetorus' feet. "You showed no sport at all in the flogging of this king of the Jews."

When Praetorus replied, it was in a voice so deadly that it caused a chill to run up the spine of the hardened Longinus. "Touch him unnecessarily again," Praetorus said, "and I will match that scar on your other cheek."

Pilate stepped between them then, sensing real danger within his own men. He couldn't have that, not today. What these two chose to do to each other later, out of sight of the mob, was one thing, but he had to take control now before things became worse. The procurator held up his hands to address the crowd.

"Behold the man," Pilate said. "The man, I say. But I think not a king. I see no fault in this man and he has been scourged under Roman law. There is no more for us to do here."

"Crucify him! Crucify him!" came the chant, again and again as if it had been rehearsed and staged. Pilate was furious at the manipulation of the crowd and at the position he found himself in because of it.

He put his hand on Easa as he bent to speak to him. "Listen to me, Nazarene," he said quietly. "This is your last chance to save yourself. I ask you, are you a king of the Jews? Because if you say that you are not, I have no grounds to crucify you under Roman law. I have the power to release you." The last sentence was said with utmost urgency.

Easa looked at Pilate for a long moment.

*Say it, damn you! Say it!*

It was as if Easa read the thoughts of Pontius Pilate. He replied in a whisper, "I cannot make this easier for you. Our destinies were chosen for us, but you must now choose your own master."

The tension in the crowd was escalating as more screaming rang in Pontius Pilate's brain. There were cries in favor of the Nazarene, many of them. But they were drowned out by the bloodthirsty shouts of the mercenaries who had been paid heartily to accomplish this task today. Pilate's nerves were drawn as tight as a bow as he balanced his duties, his ambition, his philosophy, and his family on the shoulders of this frail Nazarene. A shout to his left startled him, and he looked up to see the envoy of Herod, the tetrarch of Galilee.

"What is it?" Pilate snapped at him.

The man handed Pilate a scroll with Herod's seal. The procurator snapped the wax and read the scroll.

"Have done with this Nazarene matter immediately for I would set out early to Rome knowing that I may give Caesar a fine report of how you deal with threats against His Imperial Majesty."

It was the final blow for Pontius Pilate. He read the scroll again and realized that it was covered in blood—the blood of the Nazarene, which coated Pilate's hands. He called for a servant, and a silver basin filled with water was brought to him. Pilate submerged his hands in the water, scrubbing the stains from them, trying not to witness the water turning red with the blood of the prisoner before him.

"I wash my hands of this man's blood!" he yelled at the crowd. "Crucify your king, if that is what you are determined to do." He turned without another glance at Easa and stormed into the Fortress Antonia.

But it wasn't over for Pontius Pilate. Caiaphas came to see him moments later with several men of the Temple in tow.

"Haven't I done enough for you in one day?" Pilate shot at the priest.

"Almost, your excellency." Caiaphas smiled smugly.

"What more do you want from me?"

"It is the tradition for a sign to hang on the cross, a title to show the world what crime the man has committed. We would have you write that he was a blasphemer."

Pilate called for the materials to create the title for the cross. "I will write what I have sentenced him for, not what you ask of me. That is the tradition."

And he wrote the abbreviation INRI, and under it the meaning— Easa the Nazarene, King of the Jews.

Pilate looked to his servant. "See to it that this is nailed above the prisoner on his cross. And have the scribe write the same in Hebrew and Aramaic."

Caiaphas was taken aback. "It should not say that! If you must, write, 'He claimed he was king of the Jews', so the people will know that we do not honor him as such."

Pilate was finished with this man and his manipulations, today and forever. He dripped venom in his reply. "What I have written, I have written."

And he turned his back on Caiaphas and the others, retreating to the quiet of his quarters, where he locked himself in for the remainder of the day.

The crowd swelled and moved as a living thing, taking Mary and the children along with it. She clung to John and Tamar, one on each hand, as she struggled to move through the crowd in search of Martha. Mary was able to tell from the talk in the crowd that Easa had been sentenced and was on his way to the hill of Golgotha to be executed. Gauging the movement in the crowd, she had an idea of where Easa was in the procession that marched through the street. Desperation was growing in her. She had to find Martha, had to see her children to safety so she could spend this final time with Easa.

And then she heard it. Easa's voice in her head as clearly as if he stood beside her. "Ask and it shall be given to you. It is so simple. We must ask the Lord our Father for what we want, and he will provide it for the children he loves."

Mary Magdalene squeezed the hands of her children and shut her eyes. "Please dearest Lord, please help me find Martha so I may deliver my children to safety and be with my beloved Easa in his time of suffering."

"Mary! Mary, I am here!" Martha's voice cut through the crowd to reach her sister-in-law within seconds of the prayer. Mary opened her eyes to see Martha pushing toward her in the crowd. They threw their arms around each other in an emotional embrace. "You are wearing your red veil. It is how I found you," Martha said.

Mary fought the tears. There was no time, but Martha's presence was such a comfort to her. "Come, my little princess," Martha said to her niece, scooping up Tamar. "And you too, my young man," she said as she grabbed John's hand.

Mary hugged each of her children tightly to her for a moment, assuring them she would meet them in Bethany as soon as possible. "Go with God, sister," Martha whispered to Mary. "We will keep the children until you can come home to us. Be safe." She kissed her younger sister-in-law, now a woman and a queen in her own right, and moved to fight the crowd once more, children in tow.

It had been a struggle for Mary Magdalene to make her way through the crowd. She was able to stay parallel with the surging mob, but could not get close to Easa. She saw the red veils of the Great Mary and the other Marys within the crowd and followed them on the winding path to Golgotha, trying to reach them, but she was pushed farther and farther back as the multitude surged to follow their quarry.

As the centurions reached the top of the hill known as the Place of the Skull, she saw that they were at least a hundred meters ahead of her. There was the huddled figure of Easa and the red veils of his mother and the other Marys. The crowd was still dense on the path, blocking Mary's way. She no longer cared; there was no time to think of anything but getting to Easa. She skirted the mob, left the path, and began to climb the rocky hillside. It was jagged with sharp stones and encrusted with nettles, but none of this mattered to Mary Magdalene. Her body felt nothing as she moved with absolute determination to reach Easa.

Mary was so intent on her destination that she didn't notice at first that the sky was growing darker. She slipped on a rock, tearing the lower portion of her veil and a large section of her leg on a thorn bush. As she fell, she heard the sound, the sickening, heart-wrenching din that would haunt her every night for the rest of her life—metal on metal, hammer striking nail. There was a shriek of agony as Mary slipped again, but it wasn't until later that she realized the scream had emanated from her own lips.

She was so close now, she couldn't let anything stop her. As Mary picked herself up she realized numbly that the rocks were slippery with water. The sky had turned black, and rain trickled like divine tears on the scorched, doomed earth, where the Son of God had just been nailed to a wooden cross.

Mary Magdalene reached the foot of the cross moments later, joining her mother-in-law and the other Marys in their vigil there. There were two other men suffering on the Hill of Golgotha today on crosses that flanked Easa's. Mary did not look at them; she could see nothing but Easa. She was determined not to look at his wounds. Instead, she focused on his face, which appeared serene and calm, eyes closed. The women stood there together, holding each other up, praying to God to release Easa from suffering. Mary looked around and realized that she knew no one else in the crowd that stood behind them—and she had seen none of the male disciples during the course of the day.

The Romans kept the crowd at large away from the execution site. Looking across at the centurions, she saw Praetorus at their head. She said a silent prayer of thanks to him—no doubt he was responsible for allowing the family this privacy at the foot of the cross.

They froze as they heard Easa attempt to speak from his place.

It was difficult as the hanging weight of his body over the diaphragm made it nearly impossible to breathe and speak at once. "Mother . . . ," he whispered, "behold thy son."

The women moved closer to the cross to hear his words. Blood flowed from his battered body, mixing with droplets of rain that fell on the faces of the women. "My beloved," he said to Magdalene, "behold thy mother."

Easa closed his eyes and said softly yet clearly, "It is finished." Bowing his head, he grew very still.

There was silence, a perfect stillness as no one moved. The heavens grew completely black then, not the color of a rain-filled sky, but black as pitch—totally devoid of light.

The crowd on the hill began to panic; screams of confusion filled the air. But the blackness lasted only a moment, lightening to a dull gray as two soldiers approached Praetorus.

"We have orders to hasten the death of these prisoners so that their bodies may be removed before the Jew's sabbath."

Praetorus looked up at Easa's body. "There is no need to break this man's legs. He is already dead."

"Are you certain?" asked one of the soldiers. "It normally takes men many hours to suffocate from crucifixion; sometimes it takes days."

"This man is dead," Praetorus growled. "You will not touch him."

The two soldiers were astute enough to understand the threat in the tone of their leader. They took their clubs and went about the unpleasant task of breaking the legs of the other two crucified men, thus hastening the process of suffocation.

Praetorus was preoccupied with giving orders and didn't see Longinus approach on the other side of the cross. By the time he had turned his blue-eyed gaze back to where Easa hung, it was too late. Longinus, spear in hand, shoved it into the side of the Nazarene prisoner. Mary Magdalene screamed her objection.

Longinus' laugh in reply was hard and sadistic. "Just checking. But you're right. He's dead." He turned to Praetorus, who had gone white with rage. "What are you going to do about it?"

Praetorus started to speak but then stopped himself. When he finally did, it was with great calm. "Nothing. I need do nothing. You have created your own curse by what you have done."

"Take this man down!" Praetorus ordered.

A runner from Pilate's fortress had come with a message to remove the Nazarene's body and deliver it to his people for burial before the sun set. This was highly unusual as crucifixion victims were normally left to rot on their crosses as a warning to the people. But the case of Easa the Nazarene was different.

Easa's wealthy uncle, Joseph the tin merchant, had arrived with Jairus at the Fortress Antonia and met with Claudia Procula. It was she who had obtained permission for them to remove the body immediately for burial. When Joseph reached the cross, he comforted the Great Mary as her son was removed from the instrument of his execution. Easa's mother held out her arms as the soldiers picked up the body.

"I would hold my child one last time," she said.

Praetorus took Easa's body and laid it gently across the lap of the Great Mary. She held him to her then, allowing herself to weep openly for the loss of her beautiful son. Mary Magdalene came to kneel beside her, and the Great Mary held them both then, an arm around her daughter-in-law, the other cradling the head of her Easa.

They remained together in that position of mourning for a very long time.

Joseph had purchased a sepulcher for his family in a burial garden not far from Golgotha. It was here that the body of Easa was taken by the Nazarenes. Myrrh and aloes were brought to the tomb by Nicodemus, a young Nazarene employed by Joseph. The Marys began the preparation of the body for burial by positioning the burial cloth, but when it came time to anoint Easa with the myrrh, the Great Mary presented the jar to Mary Magdalene. "This honor is for you alone," she said.

The Magdalene performed the duties of a widow in the burial ritual. She kissed Easa on the forehead and said good-bye to him as her tears mixed with the myrrh oils. As she did so, she was sure she heard his voice, faint but certain, in the sepulcher with her. "I am with you always."

Together, the Nazarene women said their good-byes and left the inner tomb. An enormous stone slab had been selected to seal it for the protection of Easa's remains. It took many men, aided by a pulley made of rope and planks, to secure the slab against the tomb. Once this final task was complete, the downcast group retreated to the safety of Joseph's house. Mary Magdalene collapsed upon her arrival there, and slept well into the following day.

On Saturday afternoon, a number of the male apostles assembled at Joseph's to meet with Magdalene and the elder Marys. They shared their stories of the previous day's events while they mourned together and consoled each other. It was a time of despair, yet it was a time that bonded them, bringing everyone closer together. It was too early to contemplate the future of their movement, but this spirit of unity was a balm to their wounded psyches.

But Mary Magdalene was concerned. No one had seen or heard from Judas Iscariot since Easa's arrest. Jairus came to Joseph's home asking for word of him, explaining that Judas was in a terrible state following the arrest. He had cried to Jairus late that night, asking, "Why did he choose me for this act? Why was I the one selected to perform this crime against my people?"

While Mary explained to the inner circle of disciples that Easa had instructed Judas to turn him in to the authorities, those outside did not—and could not—know the truth. Therefore the name of Judas was becoming synonymous with the word "betrayer" throughout Jerusalem, and that word was spreading quickly. The reputation Judas had earned was another in a long line of injustices that occurred on this path of destiny and prophecy. Mary prayed that she would one day be able to restore the name of Judas. But she did not yet see how to do so.

Judas would never know if Mary would be able to return honor to his name. The disciples would discover later that it was already too late, that another tragedy had occurred on that black afternoon. Unable to accept that his name would be linked forever to the death of his lord and master, Judas Iscariot took his own life on the Day of Darkness. He was found hanging from a tree outside the walls of Jerusalem.

Mary Magdalene slept fitfully that night. There were too many images in her head, too many sounds and memories. And there was something else. It started as a feeling of uneasiness, a vague understanding that something was wrong. Mary rose from her bed and walked quietly through Joseph's house. The sky was still dark; it was still at least a full hour before dawn. No one was awake, and there was nothing amiss in the house.

Then she knew. Mary felt that instant flash of prophecy that combines knowing with seeing. Easa. She had to get to the tomb. Something was happening where Easa was buried. Mary hesitated for a moment. Should she awaken Joseph or one of the others to accompany her? Peter, perhaps?

*No! This is for you alone.*

She heard the answer in her head, yet it echoed all around her. Wrapped in her faith and a mourning veil, Mary Magdalene crept quietly to the door. Once she was out of the house, she ran quickly to the tomb.

It was still dark when Mary arrived in the garden that held the sepulcher. The sky was purple rather than black; dawn would be coming soon. There was just enough light for Mary to see that the enormous stone—the slab that had required the strength of almost a dozen men to lift—had been moved away from the tomb.

Mary raced to the open entrance, her heart pounding in fear.

She lowered her head to enter the tomb and saw as she did that Easa was gone. Strangely, there was light in the sepulcher, a strange glow that illuminated the chamber. Mary clearly saw the linen burial clothes laying on the slab. An outline of Easa's body was visible on the cloth, but that was the only evidence that he had been here.

How had this happened? Did the priests hate Easa so much that they would steal his body? Surely that wasn't the case. Who would have done such a thing?

Gasping for air, Mary stumbled out of the tomb and into the garden. She collapsed there, weeping for what she believed was another indignity suffered by Easa. As she cried, the rays of the sun began their journey of light across the sky. The first sunbeams of a brighter morning danced across her face as she heard a man's voice behind her.

"Woman, why weepest thou? Who is it you are looking for?"

Mary did not look up immediately. She thought perhaps a gardener had come in the early morning to tend to the grass and flowers around the tombs. Then she wondered if he had witnessed something and might help her. She spoke through her tears as she lifted her head. "Someone has taken away my lord, and I do not know where they have laid him. If you know where he is, I beg of you to tell me."

"Mary," came the simple answer from behind her, spoken in a voice that was unmistakable. She froze, afraid for a moment to turn, unsure of what she would see behind her. "Mary, I am here," he said again.

Mary Magdalene turned as the earliest rays of morning sun illuminated the beautiful figure before her. Easa stood there, clothed in a pristine white robe and perfectly healed from his wounds. He smiled at her, his beautiful smile of warmth and tenderness.

As she moved toward him, he held up his hand. "Do not cling to me, Mary," he said gently. "My time on earth is gone, although I have not yet ascended to my Father. I had to give you this sign first. Go to our brothers and tell them that I will ascend soon to my Father, who is also your Father and theirs, in heaven."

Mary nodded, standing in awe before him and feeling the pure and warming light of his goodness radiating all around her.

"My time here is gone. It is your time now."

# CHAPTER TWENTY

*Château des Pommes Bleues*
*July 2, 2005*

*M*aureen sat outside in the garden with Peter. The fountain of Mary Magdalene gurgled softly behind them. She had to get him out into the air and away from the others. Her cousin's face was white and drawn with the sleeplessness and stress of the week's events. These past days appeared to have aged him by a decade. Maureen even noticed that there were gray streaks at the temples of his dark head that had not been there before.

"You know what the hardest part of all this is?" Peter's voice was barely a whisper.

Maureen shook her head. For her, this was the most exhilarating of all possible circumstances. But she knew that much of what Peter believed, even lived for, was challenged by things he had read in Mary's gospels. And yet, her words confirmed the most sacred premise of Christianity, the resurrection.

"No, what? Tell me," Maureen responded.

Peter looked at her, his eyes red and bloodshot as he tried to make her understand what he was thinking. "What if . . . what if for two thousand years we have been denying Jesus Christ His final wish?

What if that was what the Gospel of John was trying to tell us all along, when Jesus appears first to Mary Magdalene—that she is his chosen successor? How ironic would it be that in His name we have denied her a place, not only as an apostle, but as the leader of the apostles?"

He paused for a moment, trying to sort through the challenges that had been presented to his mind as well as his soul. " 'Do not *cling* to me.' That's what He says to her. Do you know how important that is?"

Maureen shook her head and waited for the explanation.

"The Gospels are not translated that way—they translate the words as 'Do not *touch* me.' Arguably the Greek word in the originals could have been 'cling' rather than 'touch,' but no one ever sees it that way. Do you see the difference?" This whole idea was a revelation to Peter as a scholar and linguist. "Do you see how a translation of even one word can change everything? But in these gospels the word is definitely 'cling,' and she uses it twice as she quotes Jesus."

Maureen was trying to follow Peter's intense reaction to the single word. "There certainly is a difference between 'Do not touch me' and 'Do not cling to me.' "

"Yes." Peter was emphatic. "That translation of 'Do not touch me' has been used against Mary Magdalene, to show Christ pushing her away from Him. What we see here is Him telling her not to cling to Him when He is gone because He wants her to stand on her own." His sigh was heavy with exhaustion. "It's huge, Maureen. Huge."

The ramifications of Mary's story were only beginning to set in for Maureen. "I think the depiction of women as leaders in the movement is one of the more important elements of her story," she said. "Pete, I hate to make matters worse for you right now, but what about this perspective on the Virgin? She calls her the Great Mary and refers to her clearly as a leader of their people. Mary is obviously a title given to a female leader. And then there's the red veil . . ."

Peter shook his head hard as if doing so would clear it. "You know," he answered, "I once heard the argument that the Vatican declared that the Virgin would be depicted only in white and blue as a way of diminishing her power, of hiding her original importance as one of the Nazarene leaders—who, as we have seen, wore red. Honestly, I always thought that was rubbish. It seemed obvious to me that the Virgin was shown in blue and white to show her purity.

"But now," Peter said, rising wearily, "nothing seems obvious to me anymore."

*Cape Cod, Massachusetts*
*July 2, 2005*

ACROSS THE ATLANTIC on Cape Cod, real estate mogul Eli Wainwright sat staring out the window across the lawn of his sprawling estate. He hadn't heard from Derek in almost a week, which deeply concerned him. There was an American contingent in France for the feast day of John the Baptist, and the leader of that group had telephoned Eli when Derek did not join them in Paris.

Eli wracked his brain, trying to think like Derek. His son had always been a bit of a maverick, but the boy knew how important this was. All he had to do was stick to the plan, stay close to this Teacher of Righteousness and learn as much as he could about his movements and motivations. After they had a full intelligence report, the Americans could begin to plan their coup to wrestle the power structure of the Guild away from the European contingent.

At their last meeting here in the States, Derek had been displeased with the lengthy timeline Eli proposed to achieve their goals. Eli was a strategist, but his son did not inherit the qualities of patience and planning that had made the Wainwrights billionaires. Was it possible that Derek had done something rash and stupid?

The answer, of sorts, came to Eli Wainwright that afternoon as his wife's scream tore through the tranquil sea air of the Cape. Eli sprang from his chair and ran into the entry hall, where his wife was collapsed on the floor in a shivering heap.

"Susan, for God's sake. What happened?"

Susan could not answer him. Her sobs were hysterical, her attempt to speak a gibberish as she gestured toward the international Federal Express box on the floor beside her.

Steeling himself for the contents, Eli slid a small wooden casket out of the box. He opened the lid to reveal Derek's class ring from Yale.

The ring was attached to what remained of the severed index finger from Derek Wainwright's right hand.

*Château de Pommes Bleu*
*July 3, 2005*

EVEN UNDER NORMAL CIRCUMSTANCES, Maureen was a light sleeper. With so many issues pertaining to the scrolls rattling around in her head, she found sleep elusive despite her overall weariness. She heard footsteps in the corridor outside her room and sat up in bed. The steps were very light, as if someone were trying hard not to be heard. Maureen listened carefully but didn't move. It was a huge house with many rooms and servants she probably didn't even know about, she rationalized.

She lay down and tried to go back to sleep, but was disturbed again by the sound of a car engine outside the chateau. The clock said it was nearly 3:00 A.M. Who could it be? Maureen got out of bed and moved to the window that faced the front of the house. She rubbed her eyes to be sure she was seeing clearly.

The car driving past the window and out the front gate of the château was her rental car—with someone who looked like her cousin, Peter, at the wheel.

Maureen rushed out her door and down the hallway to Peter's room. A flick of the light switch confirmed the absence of Peter's things. His black bag was gone, as were his glasses, his Bible, and his rosary beads, all items he kept out next to his bed.

Maureen looked frantically for another minute to see if he had left any information for her. A note? Anything? But her search turned up nothing.

Father Peter Healy was gone.

Maureen tried to sort through the events of the last twenty-four hours. Their last conversation had been the one by the fountain when Peter explained the importance of the words "Do not cling to me." He had seemed distressed, but Maureen had attributed that to the emotionalism and sleeplessness of the week. What caused him to bolt in the middle of the night, and where did he go? This was entirely out of character for Peter. He had never deserted her or even let her down, ever. Maureen felt panic creeping in. If she lost Peter, she would have no one. He was her only family, the one person on earth whom she trusted implicitly.

"Reenie?"

Maureen jumped at the voice behind her. Tammy was standing in the doorway, rubbing the sleep from her own eyes. "Sorry. I heard the car and then I heard movement up here. Guess we're all a little jumpy at the moment. Where's the padre?"

"I don't know." Maureen was trying not to sound frantic. "The car was Peter leaving the château. I don't know why or where. Damn! What does it mean?"

"Why don't you call him on his cell phone and see if he answers?"

"Peter doesn't have a cell phone."

Tammy looked at Maureen, puzzled. "Sure he does. I saw him on it."

It was Maureen's turn to look confused. "Peter hates them. He has no time for technology and finds cell phones particularly distasteful. He wouldn't carry one even when I begged him to for emergency purposes."

"Maureen, I have seen him on a cell phone twice. Come to think of it now, both times he was sitting in the car. I hate to say this, but I think there's something rotten in Arques."

Maureen felt like she was going to be sick. She could see from the look on Tammy's face that the two had the same thought at the same time.

"Let's go," Maureen said as she turned to run through the château corridor and down the stairs toward Sinclair's study. Tammy followed behind her by a half step.

They stopped at the door. It was ajar. Ever since the scrolls had been in the study, it had been closed and locked, even if one of them was in the room. Maureen swallowed hard and braced herself as she entered the dark room. Behind her Tammy found the switch that illuminated the study—and revealed a bare study table. The mahogany surface gleamed in the light. It was empty.

"They're gone," Maureen whispered.

She and Tammy searched through the room, but nothing remained of Mary Magdalene's scrolls. The yellow legal pads were all gone as well. Not a scrap of paper was left, not even a pen. The only proof that the scrolls existed were the clay jars that remained in the corner, where they were out of the way of traffic. But the jars were empty. The real treasure was gone.

And it appeared that Father Peter Healy, the most trusted person in Maureen's life, had taken them.

Maureen moved on wobbly legs to sit on the velvet sofa. She couldn't speak, didn't know what to say or what to think. She simply sat on the sofa, staring straight ahead.

"Maureen, I need to find Roland. Will you stay here? We'll be right back."

Maureen nodded, too numb to reply. She was sitting in the same position when Tammy and Roland returned, followed by Bérenger Sinclair.

"Mademoiselle Paschal," Roland said gently as he knelt by the sofa, "I am sorry for the pain this night will cause you."

Maureen looked at the big Occitan, who leaned over her with concern. Later, when she had the luxury to remember this time in detail, she would think of what an extraordinary man he turned out to be. The most valuable treasure of his people had been stolen and his primary concern was for her pain. Roland, more than anyone Maureen would ever meet, taught her a great deal about true spirituality. She would come to understand why these people were called *les bonnes hommes.* The good men.

"Ah. So, I see Father Healy has chosen his master," Sinclair said calmly. "I suspected he would. I am sorry, Maureen."

Maureen was confused. "You expected this to happen?"

Sinclair nodded. "Yes, my dear. I suppose it must all come out now. We knew your cousin was working for someone. We just weren't entirely sure who it was."

Maureen was incredulous. "What are you saying? That Peter betrayed me? That he planned all along to betray me?"

"I cannot claim to know what Father Healy's motives are. But I did know that he had motives. I suspect that before the end of the day tomorrow we will know the truth."

"Will somebody please tell me what is going on?" This was Tammy, who Maureen now realized was also out of the loop. Roland sat calmly beside her as she looked at him accusingly. "There's a lot you've been keeping from me, I see," she snapped at the big man.

Roland shrugged his huge shoulders. "It was for your own protection, Tamara. We all have secrets, as you know. They were necessary. But now, I think, it is time for us to reveal ourselves to each other more plainly. I believe it is only fair for Mademoiselle Paschal to know everything. She has proven herself more than worthy."

Maureen wanted to scream in her stress and confusion. The frustration must have shown on her face as Roland reached over and took her hand. "Come, Mademoiselle. I have things to show you." Then he turned to Sinclair and Tammy and did something she had never seen before—he gave them orders. "Bérenger, have the servants bring coffee and then join us in the Grand Master's room. Tamara, come with us."

They walked through the winding corridors and into a wing of the château where Maureen had never been.

"I must ask that you be a little bit patient, Mademoiselle Paschal," Roland said over his shoulder. "I must explain a few things first before I can answer your most important questions."

"Okay," Maureen said, feeling a little inadequate as she followed Roland and Tammy, not really knowing what else to say. She thought of the day back in southern California when she had met with Tammy at the marina. She had been so naïve then; it seemed like two lifetimes ago. Tammy had compared her to Alice in Wonderland. How apropos that comparison seemed now, as Maureen felt as though she had walked through the looking glass. Everything she thought she understood about her life had been turned completely around.

Roland unlocked the enormous double doors ahead of them with a key he wore around his neck. A piercing beep sounded as they stepped into the room and Roland punched in a code to shut off the alarm. The activated light switch revealed a huge and ornate hall, a beautiful meeting room fit for the kings and queens of France. In its elegance it resembled the throne rooms of Versailles and Fountainbleu. Two matching carved and gilded armchairs stood on a dais in the center, each sculpted elaborately with blue apples.

"This is the heart of the our organization," Roland explained. "The Society of Blue Apples. Everyone who is a member is of the royal bloodline, traceable through the Sarah-Tamar line specifically. We are the descendants of the Cathars, and we do our best to keep their traditions alive and in the purest form possible."

He led them to where a portrait of Mary Magdalene hung behind the thronelike chairs. It was similar to the painting of the Magdalene by Georges de la Tour that Maureen had seen in Los Angeles, with one important difference. "Do you remember the night that Bérenger told you that one of de la Tour's most important paintings was missing and not on view to the public? That's because it is here," he said. "De la Tour was a member of our society, and he left this painting to us. It is called *Penitent Magdalene with the Crucifix.*"

Maureen looked at the portrait with awe and admiration. Like all of the French artist's work, it was a masterpiece of light and shadow. But in this painting, Mary Magdalene was posed differently than in any other Maureen had seen. This version depicted Mary resting her left hand on the skull, which she now understood to be the skull of

John the Baptist, and in her right hand she held a crucifix and gazed at the face of Christ.

"The painting was too dangerous to leave in public. The reference is clear for those with eyes to see—this is Mary doing penance for John, her first husband, and looking with love upon Jesus, her second husband."

He guided both women to a huge painting on another wall. This depicted two elder saints sitting in a rocky landscape having what appeared to be a spirited discussion or debate.

"Tamara can tell you the history of this painting," Roland said, smiling at Tammy as she stood beside him. Maureen looked to her for the explanation.

"This is by the Flemish artist David Teniers the Younger," Tammy said. It's called *Saint Anthony the Hermit and Saint Paul in the Desert*. That's not the same Saint Paul who wrote in the New Testament, but another regional saint who was also a hermit. Bérenger Saunière, the infamous priest at Rennes-le-Château, acquired this painting for the Society. Yes, he was one of us."

Maureen looked closely at the painting and began to see elements that were now becoming very familiar. She pointed to them. "I see a crucifix and a skull."

"Right," Tammy replied. "This is Anthony here. He's wearing that symbol that looks like a letter 'T' on his sleeve, but it's actually the Greek version of the cross, called the Tau. Saint Francis of Assisi popularized it among our people. Anthony is looking up from his book, which is a representation of the Book of Love, and gazing at the crucifix. And look at Paul over here, he is making the 'Remember John' gesture with his hand and debating his friend about who the first messiah was, John or Jesus. There are books and scrolls scattered around their feet to indicate that there is much material to consider in this discussion. It's a very important painting—in fact, these two are arguably the most significant paintings in our tradition. That village represents Rennes-le-Château up on the hill, and over in the landscape—look who's here?"

Maureen smiled. "It's a shepherdess and her sheep."

"Of course. Anthony and Paul are debating, but the shepherdess looms behind them to remind that The Expected One will one day find the hidden gospels of Mary Magdalene and end all the controversy by delivering the truth."

Bérenger Sinclair entered the room quietly as Roland said, "I wanted to show you these things, Mademoiselle Paschal, so that you would know that my people do not bear any ill will to the followers of John, and they never have. We are all brothers and sisters, children of Mary Magdalene, and we wish we could all live in peace."

Sinclair joined in the discussion. "Unfortunately, some of John's followers are fanatics and have always been so. They are a minority but a dangerous one. It is the same anywhere in the world where any group of fanatics overshadows the peaceful people who believe the same thing. But the threat of these men remains very real, as Roland can tell you."

Roland's expressive face darkened at this. "It is true. I have always tried to live the beliefs of my people. To love, to forgive, to have compassion for all living things. My father had the same belief, and they killed him."

Maureen felt the Occitan's deep sadness at the loss of his father, but also at the intense challenge to his belief system that came from the murder. "But why?" Maureen asked. "Why would they kill your father?"

"My family goes back a long way in this area, Mademoiselle Paschal," Roland said. "Here, you have only heard me called by the name Roland. But my family name is Gélis."

"Gélis?" Maureen knew the name was familiar. She looked at Sinclair. "My father's letter was written to a Monsieur Gélis," she said, remembering.

Roland nodded. "Yes, it was written to my grandfather when he was Grand Master of the Society."

It was starting to come together. Maureen looked at Roland and then back at Sinclair. The Scotsman answered her unasked question. "Yes, my dear, Roland Gélis here is our Grand Master, although he is too humble to tell you this himself. He is the official leader of our people, as were his father and his grandfather before him. He does not serve me, nor do I serve him—we serve together as brothers, as that is the law of The Way.

"The Sinclair and Gélis families have been pledged to serve the Magdalene for as long as any of us can trace the lineage."

Tammy jumped in. "Maureen, remember when we were up in the Tour Magdala at Rennes-le-Château and I told you about the old priest who had been murdered back in the late eighteen hundreds? His name was Antoine Gélis—and he was Roland's great-great uncle."

Maureen looked to Roland for an answer. "Why all of this violence against your family?"

"Because we knew too much. My great-great uncle was the keeper of a document, called 'the Book of The Expected One,' in which the revelations of every shepherdess for over a thousand years had been recorded by the Society. It was our most valuable tool for attempting to find the treasure of our Magdalene. The Guild of the Righteous killed him for it. They killed my father for similar reasons. I did not know it then, but Jean-Claude was their informant. They sent my father's head and his right finger to me in a basket."

Maureen shuddered at the gruesome revelation. "Will it end now, this bloodshed? The scrolls have been found. What do you think they will do?"

"It is hard to say," Roland replied. "They have a new leader who is very extreme. He is the man who killed my father."

Sinclair added, "I spoke to local authorities earlier today, the ones who are, shall we say, sympathetic to our beliefs. Maureen, we haven't told you all of this yet, but do you remember meeting Derek Wainwright, the American?"

"The one dressed like Thomas Jefferson," Tammy explained. "My old friend." She shook her head sadly at the memory of Derek's years of deception—and at his fate.

Maureen nodded and waited for Sinclair to continue.

"Derek has disappeared under somewhat grisly circumstances. His hotel room was . . ." He looked at Maureen's increasing pallor and decided to spare her the details. "Let's just say that foul play was clearly indicated."

Sinclair continued. "The authorities feel that with the unpleasantness surrounding the American's disappearance—and almost certainly his murder—the Guild of the Righteous will have to lay low for a while. Jean-Claude is in hiding somewhere in Paris, and their leader is an Englishman who we suspect has returned to the U.K., at least temporarily. I do not suspect that they will bother us in the immediate future. At least, I hope not."

Maureen looked up at Tammy suddenly. "Your turn," she said. "You haven't told me everything, either. It took me long enough to figure that out, but now I'd like to know the rest. And I'd also like to know what's going on with you two," she said, pointing at Tammy and Roland, who were standing within an inch of each other.

Tammy laughed in her throaty way. "Well, you know how we love to hide things in plain sight down here," she said. "What's my name?"

Maureen frowned. What was she missing? "Tammy." And then it hit her. "Tamara. Tamar-a. My God, I am an imbecile."

"No, you're not," Tammy said, still laughing. "But I was named for the Magdalene's daughter. And I have a sister named Sarah."

"But you told me you were born in Hollywood! Or was that a lie, too?"

"No, not a lie. And 'lie' is such a harsh word. Let's call them necessary untruths. And yes, I was born and raised in California. My maternal grandparents were Occitan and deeply involved in the Society. But my mother, who was born here in the Languedoc, went to Los Angeles to work in costume design after breaking into film through her friendship with the French artist and director Jean Cocteau—another Society member. She met my American father and stayed there. Her mother came to live with us when I was a child. Needless to say, I have been very influenced by my grandmother."

Roland turned to point at the two chairs, side by side. "In our tradition, men and women are complete equals, just as Jesus taught through his example with Mary Magdalene. The Society is run by a

Grand Master, but also by a Great Mary. I have chosen Tamara to be my Mary and sit beside me here. Now I must try to get her to move to France so I can ask her to become an even greater part of my life."

Roland put his arm around Tammy, who snuggled in close to him. "I'm thinking about it," she said coyly.

They were interrupted by two servants who brought silver trays of coffee into the room. There was a meeting table at the far side, and Roland signaled for them to follow. The four of them sat as Tammy poured strong, dark coffee for each of them. Roland looked at Sinclair across the table and nodded his head for him to begin.

"Maureen, we're going to tell you what we know about Father Healy and the Magdalene's gospels, but we felt you needed all of the background to understand the situation here."

Maureen sipped her coffee, grateful for the warmth and strength of it. She listened closely as Sinclair explained.

"The fact is, we allowed your cousin to take the scrolls."

Maureen nearly dropped her coffee cup. "Allowed it?"

"Yes. Roland left the study unlocked intentionally. We had suspicions that Father Healy might try to take the scrolls to whomever he is working for."

"Wait a minute. Working for? What are you saying? That my Peter is some kind of spy for the Church?"

"Not exactly," Sinclair answered. Maureen noticed that Tammy was listening intently as well—she didn't have all of this information, either.

"We don't know for sure whom he is a spy for, which is why we allowed him to take the scrolls—and why we're not terribly concerned about them. Yet. There is a tracking device on your hired car. We know exactly where he is and where he is going."

"Which is where?" Tammy asked. "Rome?"

"We think Paris." The answer came from Roland.

"Maureen." Sinclair put his hand lightly on her arm, "I'm sorry to tell you this, but your cousin has been reporting your actions to

Church officials since the day you arrived in France, and probably for much longer."

Maureen reeled visibly; she felt as though she had been slugged in the face. "It's impossible. Peter wouldn't do that to me."

"Over this past week, as we have watched him work and had the chance to get to know him, it became increasingly hard for us to reconcile this idea of a spy with your charming and scholarly cousin. Initially, we believed that he was just trying to protect you from us. But I think he was too firmly entrenched with the people who employ him to break free, even after reading the truth in the scrolls."

"You didn't answer my question. Is it the Vatican that you believe he's working for? The Jesuits? Who?"

Sinclair sat back in his chair. "I still don't know, but I can tell you this. We have people in Rome who are looking into it. You may be surprised by just how high our own influence reaches. I am certain we will have all of our answers by tomorrow night, the following day at the latest. Now, we just have to be patient."

Maureen took another sip of her coffee, staring straight ahead of her at the portrait of the penitent Mary Magdalene. It would be almost twenty-four hours before she had all of her answers.

*Paris*
*July 3, 2005*

FATHER PETER HEALY was beyond exhaustion by the time he arrived in Paris. The drive from the Languedoc had been a tough one. Even without the late-morning traffic in the city, the trip required a full eight hours. He had also stopped to prepare his package for Maureen, which had taken longer than anticipated. But the emotional energy required to make this choice had been enormous, and he felt as though the life had been sucked out of him.

Peter transported his precious cargo carefully in his black leather carry-on bag. He crossed the river on his way to Notre-Dame, where he was met at a side entrance by Father Marcel. The Frenchman ushered Peter in and crossed with him through the rear of the cathedral, where they entered a chamber door camouflaged by an ornate choir screen.

Peter entered the room, expecting to see his handler, Bishop Magnus O'Connor. Instead he was met by another official of the Church, an imposing Italian wearing the red robes of a cardinal. "Your Grace," he gasped, "forgive me. I did not expect this."

"Yes, I understand that you were expecting Bishop Magnus. He will not be coming. I believe he has done quite enough already." The Italian official kept his face expressionless as he held out his hands for the bag. "You have the scrolls in there, I assume?"

Peter nodded.

"Good. Now, my son," the Cardinal said as he took the bag from Peter. "Let us talk about the events of these past weeks. Or perhaps we should talk of the events of these past years? I will let you decide where to begin."

*Château des Pommes Bleues*
*July 3, 2005*

THERE HAD BEEN FRENETIC ACTIVITY at the château all day. Sinclair and Roland were buzzing around, chattering in French and Occitan with each other, with the servants, and with various people by telephone. On two occasions Maureen thought she heard Roland speaking Italian, but she wasn't certain and didn't want to ask.

She joined Tammy for a while in the media room, looking through some footage for her documentary on the bloodline. They talked about how Mary Magdalene's scrolls would change Tammy's perspective as a filmmaker. Maureen gained added respect for her friend as she saw how capable and creative she was, and how Tammy was able to throw herself into her work when she was stressed, as they all were at the moment.

Maureen, on the other hand, felt absolutely useless. She couldn't concentrate on anything, had absolutely no focus. She felt she should be scribbling notes furiously, trying to capture from memory as much as she could about the Magdalene material. But she was simply unable to do it. She was too disheartened by the personal betrayal of Peter. Whatever his motives, he had left without saying a word, and he had taken something that was not his to take. Maureen thought it would be a very long time before she recovered from this.

Dinner that night was a quiet affair with just three of them—Maureen, Tammy, and Sinclair. Roland was out but would be returning shortly, according to Sinclair and Tammy. He was picking up a guest from the private airport in Carcassonne, Tammy explained. Once this mystery guest arrived, they would have more information. Maureen nodded her understanding. She had long since learned that pushing an issue here didn't get her anywhere. They would reveal their secrets in their own time; it was part of the culture here in Arques. But she did notice that Sinclair appeared more tense than usual.

Shortly after they adjourned for coffee in the study, a servant came in and spoke to Sinclair in French.

"Good. Our guest has arrived," he translated for Tammy and Maureen.

Roland came through the door with an equally imposing man. He was dressed in dark clothing, casual but elegant and of the finest Italian fabrics. This man had the air of an aristocrat and was clearly comfortable with his power and influence. He commanded the energy in the room from the moment he entered.

Roland stepped forward. "Mademoiselle Paschal, Mademoiselle Wisdom, it is my pleasure to introduce you to our esteemed friend, Cardinal DeCaro."

DeCaro held out his hand to Maureen first and then to Tammy. He smiled warmly at both women. "It is a pleasure." He gestured to Maureen and asked Roland, "This is our Expected One?"

Roland nodded.

"I'm sorry, did you say 'Cardinal'?" Maureen asked.

"Do not let the simple clothes fool you," Sinclair said from behind her. "Cardinal DeCaro is an official of immense influence in the Vatican. And perhaps his complete name will be helpful to you. This is Tomas Francesco Borgia DeCaro."

"Borgia?" Tammy exclaimed.

The Cardinal nodded, a simple answer to Tammy's unspoken question. Roland winked at her from across the room.

"His Excellency would like to spend some time with Mademoiselle Paschal alone, so we will leave the two of them for now," Roland said. "Please ring if you require anything."

Roland held the door for Sinclair and Tammy as Cardinal DeCaro gestured to Maureen to sit at the mahogany table. He took a seat opposite her. "Signorina Paschale, I want to tell you first that I have met with your cousin."

Maureen was taken aback by this. She didn't know what she had expected, but this wasn't it. "Where is Peter?"

"On his way to Rome. I was with him in Paris earlier today. He is well, and the documents that you discovered are safe."

"Safe where? And with who? What . . ."

"Patience, I will tell you everything. But there is something I would like to show you first."

The Cardinal reached into an attaché case he had carried into the room and removed a series of red folders. They were labeled EDOUARD PAUL PASCHAL.

Maureen gasped as she saw the labels. "That's my father's name."

"Yes. And in these folders you will see photographs of your father. But I need to prepare you. What you are about to see is disturbing, yet very important for you to understand."

Maureen opened the top folder, dropping it onto the table the first time as her hands started to shake. Cardinal DeCaro narrated as she looked slowly through the graphic photos of her father's wounds.

"He was a stigmatic. Do you know what that is? He manifested the wounds of Christ on his body. There are his wrists, his feet, and the fifth point here, below his ribs, the wound where Longinus the centurion pierced Our Lord with a spear."

Maureen stared at the photos, dumbfounded. Twenty-five years of speculation about her father's alleged "illness" had corroded her opinion of him. Now it was falling into place—her mother's fear and hostility, her anger toward the Church. And this explained the letter from her father to the Gélis family that was in the archives here at the château. He was writing to the Gélises because of his stigmata—and because he wanted to protect his child from the same tortured fate. Maureen looked at the Cardinal through her tears.

"I—I was always told that he took his own life due to mental illness. My mother said he was insane when he died. I had no idea, no one ever told me anything like this . . ."

The churchman nodded solemnly. "Your father was misunderstood by a great many people, I'm afraid," he said. "Even those who should have been able to help him, his own Church. This is where your cousin comes in."

Maureen looked up, listening with her full attention. She could feel the chills running down her back and all the way to her toes as the Cardinal continued.

"Your cousin is a good man, Signorina. I think you will not judge him for what has happened when I tell you this. But, you see, we must begin back when you were a child. When your father developed the stigmata, the local priest he went to for help was part of a rogue organization within the Church. We are like all people—we are human. And while most of us within the Church are dedicated to the path of goodness, there are some who would protect certain beliefs at any cost.

"Your father's case should have been brought directly to Rome, but it was not. We would have helped him, worked with him to find the source or understand the holy significance of his wounds. But the men who intercepted him made their own determination that he was dangerous. As I said, they were rogues within the Church, operating on their own agenda, but they had influence that stretched into the upper ranks, which is something I have only recently discovered."

The Cardinal continued to explain the vast network that emanates from the Vatican, the tens of thousands of men who work throughout the world to preserve the faith. With such enormous numbers spread over the face of the earth, it was impossible to track the personal motives of individuals or even groups of men. An extremist shadow organization had developed following Vatican II, a cadre of priests who vehemently opposed the reforms of the Church. A young Irish priest called Magnus O'Connor was recruited to join this organization, as were a number of young Irish men. O'Connor was working in the parish outside New Orleans when Edouard Paschal contacted the Church for help.

O'Connor had been spooked by Paschal's stigmata, but even more disturbed by his visions of Jesus with a woman by his side, and Jesus as a father with children. The Irish cleric had evaluated the case within his own secret organization rather than through official Church channels. After Edouard Paschal took his own life out of despair and confusion over his stigmata, this shadow organization within the Church continued to watch his wife and daughter. Little Maureen Paschal had visions like those of her father from the time she was a toddler. O'Connor convinced her mother, Bernadette, to distance the child from the Paschal family. It was then that Maureen's mother moved them back to Ireland and reverted to her maiden name of Healy. She attempted to change her daughter's name, but at almost eight years old Maureen was already extremely strong-willed. The child refused, insisting that Paschal was her name and she would not change that for any reason.

It proved immensely convenient for Magnus O'Connor, now elevated to the rank of bishop, that the Paschal girl had a close relative with a vocation. When Peter Healy entered the seminary, O'Connor worked the Irish angle to get to Peter in the same way they had worked on Bernadette. Peter was informed of Edouard Paschal's history and asked to keep a close eye on his cousin and make regular reports on her progress.

Maureen stopped the Cardinal to ask for clarification. "You're telling me that my cousin has been watching me and reporting my actions to these men since I was a child?"

"Yes, Signorina, that is the truth. However, Father Healy did not do so out of anything but love. These men manipulated him, led him to understand that this was all in the interest of protecting you. He did not know that they had refused to help your father or, worse, that they were perhaps to blame for his sad demise."

The Cardinal looked at her with compassion. "I believe that your cousin's motives where you are concerned are pure and commendable, in the same way that I believe he chose to turn over the scrolls to the Church for the right reasons."

"But how can that be? He knows what's in them. How can he want to suppress that?"

"It would be an easy thing to misjudge him based on the limited information that you possess. But I do not believe that Father Healy wanted to suppress anything. We have reason to suspect that Bishop O'Connor and his organization put pressure on him by threatening your safety. Please understand that this is entirely outside of official Church business and is not sanctioned by Rome. But your cousin took the scrolls to O'Connor to trade for your safety."

Maureen was allowing it all to sink in, not sure how she should feel. There was a sense of relief that Peter, the only true and trusted ally in her life, had not betrayed her in any real sense. But there was so much new information to digest.

"And how did you discover all of this?" Maureen wanted to know.

"O'Connor's ambition got the best of him. He was hoping to utilize the discovery of Mary's gospel for his own advancement within the accepted hierarchy of the Church. In turn, he would have more power and access to higher-level information for his shadow organization and their intolerant agenda." Cardinal DeCaro's smile was just the slightest bit smug. "But don't worry. We are working to reassign O'Connor and his associates now that we have identified them all. Our intelligence network is second to none."

This did not surprise Maureen, who had always thought of the Catholic Church as an omnipotent organization with arms that stretched all the way around the world. She knew they were the richest organization on the planet and had the best resources that money could buy.

"What will happen to Mary's scrolls?" she asked him, preparing herself for an unpleasant answer.

"If I am to be honest with you, it is hard to say. I am sure that you can understand that this discovery is the most important of our time, if not the most important in Church history. It is a matter that will need to be discussed at the highest levels once they are authenticated."

"Peter told you what was in them?"

The Cardinal indicated affirmatively. "Yes, I read some of his notes. Signorina Paschale, this may surprise you, but we do not sit on silver thrones in the Vatican and plan conspiracies all day."

Maureen laughed with him for a moment, then asked very seriously, "Will the Church try to stop me if I write about my experiences here—and more important, if I write about what is in the scrolls?"

"You are free to do whatever you choose and go where your heart and conscience guide you. If God is working through you to reveal Mary's words, it would not be anyone's place to stop you from that sacred duty. The Church does not set out to suppress information, as many believe. That may have been true in the Middle Ages, but it is not today. The Church is interested in the survival and propagation of the faith—and it is my personal belief that the discovery of Mary Magdalene's gospel may give us a new opportunity to bring more and younger people into our fold. But"—he held up his hand as he said this—"I am only one man. I cannot speak for the others, nor for the Holy Father himself. Time will tell."

"And until then, what happens?"

"Until then, the Arques Gospel of Mary Magdalene shall be preserved in the Vatican library, under the observation of one Father Peter Healy."

"Peter is going to stay in Rome?"

"Yes, Signorina Paschale. He will oversee the team of official translators. It is a great honor, but one that we feel he deserves. And do not think we have forgotten your contribution," he said, handing her a calling card from his attaché case. "Here is my personal line in Vatican City. When you are ready, we would like to invite you to be our guest. I would like to hear from your lips the entire journey that brought you here to this place. Oh, and you can reach your cousin at this number until his own is established. He will be working for me directly."

Maureen looked at the name on the calling card. "Tomas Francesco Borgia DeCaro," she said aloud. "If you'll forgive me for asking . . ."

The Cardinal laughed now, a true smile spreading across his face. "Yes, Signorina, I am a son of the bloodline, just as you are a daughter. You'll be surprised at how many of us there are—and just where you will find us when you know where to look."

"The moon is full and the night is perfect. Would you do me the honor of joining me for a walk in the gardens before retiring?" Bérenger Sinclair asked Maureen after the Cardinal had taken his leave.

Maureen agreed. She was entirely at ease with him now, comfortable in the unique manner that comes to people who have endured extreme circumstances together. And there were few things more beautiful than a summer night in the southwest of France. With the floodlights illuminating the majestic château and the lunar light reflecting on the marble paths, the Trinity Gardens were transformed into a place of pure magic.

Maureen told him everything she had discussed with the Cardinal, and Sinclair listened with sincere interest and attention. When she was finished, he asked her, "And what will you do now? Do you think you will begin a book about this experience? How do you intend to reveal the words of Mary's gospel to the world?"

Maureen walked around the perimeter of the Magdalene fountain, running her finger along the cool, smooth marble as she thought about her answer.

"I haven't decided what form it will take yet." She looked up at the statue. "I'm hoping she'll give me some guidance. Whatever it becomes, I only hope I can do her justice."

Sinclair smiled at her. "You will. Of course you will. She chose you for a reason."

Maureen returned the expression of warmth. "She chose you, too."

"I think all of us were selected to play roles in our own way. You, me, certainly Roland and Tammy. And, of course, Father Healy."

"So you don't all despise Peter for what he did?"

Sinclair answered quickly. "No. No, not at all. Even if Peter did the wrong thing he did it for the right reasons. Besides, what kind of hypocrite would I be if I felt hatred for a man of God after discovering this treasure? Our Magdalene's message is one of compassion and forgiveness. If everyone on earth could embrace those two qualities, we would have a much nicer planet to live on, don't you agree?"

Maureen looked up at him with admiration, and the dawning of an emotion that was new to her. For the first time in her eventful life, she felt safe. "I'm not sure how to thank you, Lord Sinclair."

The Scottish burr came out with greater force, rolling the "r" in her name as he spoke it. "Thank me for what, Maureen?"

"For this." She gestured to the lush surroundings. "For introducing me to a world that most people have never even dreamed of. For showing me my place in all of it. For making me feel that I'm not alone."

"You will never be alone again." Sinclair took Maureen's hand and led her deeper into the rose-scented lushness of the gardens. "But you must stop calling me Lord Sinclair."

Maureen smiled then, and called him "Berry" for the first time, right before he kissed her.

The following morning, a package for Maureen arrived at the château. It had been sent from Paris the day before. There was no return address, but she didn't require one to know who the sender was. She would know Peter's writing anywhere.

Maureen ripped open the box, anxious to see what Peter had sent. Although she had no anger toward him for anything he had done, he wouldn't know that yet. They would have to get through an awkward period of apologies and undertake some serious discussions about

their shared history, but Maureen had no doubt they would come
through this as close as ever.

Maureen let out a small scream of surprise and delight when she
saw the contents of the box. Inside were photocopies of each page of
Peter's notes from all three books of Mary Magdalene's gospels. All of
his notes were here, from the first transcriptions to the final translations. On the top page, written on a page torn from one of his yellow
legal pads, Peter had written:

*My dear Maureen:*

> *Until I can explain everything to you in person, I will entrust
> these to you. In the end, you are their rightful keeper, far more
> so than the people I am finding myself forced to give the
> originals to.*
>
> *Please extend my apologies as well as my thanks to the
> others. I hope to do this in person as soon as possible.*
>
> *I will contact you very soon.*

*Peter*

*. . . It was many years later when I had the chance to thank Claudia Procula in person for the risks she had taken for Easa. The tragedy of Pontius Pilate and his decision to choose Rome as his master was that it did not save his career or serve his ambitions in the end. Herod did indeed go to Rome the day following Easa's passion, but he did not speak well of Pilate to the emperor. A true Herod until the end, he had another agenda, a cousin he wished to see in the position of procurator. He spoke poison in the ears of Tiberius, and Pilate was recalled to Rome to stand trial for his misdeeds while he was the governor of Judea.*

*Pontius Pilate's own words were used against him at his trial. He had sent a letter to Tiberius telling him about Easa's miracles and the events of the Day of Darkness. The Romans used his words against him, to not only eliminate his title and position, but to exile him and confiscate his lands. If Pilate had pardoned Easa and stood up against Herod and the priesthood, his fate would have been no different.*

*Claudia Procula remained loyal to her husband through the most terrible times. She told me that their little boy, Pilo, died within a few weeks of Easa's execution. There was no explanation for it; he simply wasted away before their eyes. Claudia told me that at first it had taken all of her strength not to blame her husband for the death of their child, but she knew that Easa would not want that. She had only to close her eyes and see Easa's face on the night he healed her son—that was how Claudia Procula found the Kingdom of God. This Roman woman of royal blood had an extraordinary understanding of the Nazarene Way. She lived it effortlessly.*

*Claudia and Pilate moved to Gaul, where she had lived as a child. She said that Pilate spent the rest of his life attempting to understand Easa—who he was, what he wanted, what he taught. Over many years she told him often that Easa's Way was not something that he could apply his Roman logic to. One had to become like a little child to understand the truth. Children are pure, open, and honest. They are able to accept goodness and faith without question. While Pilate did not think* it was in him to embrace *The Way* in the manner that Claudia had, she felt that he was, in his own way, a convert.

Claudia related an extraordinary story to me about the day before she and the procurator left Judea forever. Pontius Pilate had gone to the Temple in search of Jonathan Annas and Caiaphas, demanding that they see him. He asked them both to look him in the eyes on the most sacred ground of their people and tell him: did we or did we not execute the Son of God?

I do not know what is more extraordinary—that Pilate sought out the priests to ask the question, or that both of the priests confessed that they had made a terrible mistake.

Following Easa's resurrection to our Father in Heaven, a number of men came forward to say that our followers had moved his physical body. These men had been paid to do so by the Temple, who now feared a terrible backlash if people were to learn the truth. Annas and Caiaphas confessed to this. Pilate told his wife that he believed these men were truly repentant, that they would suffer every day for the rest of their lives on earth as they lived with the knowledge of their terrible deeds.

If only they had come to me and told me this. I would have given them the teachings of *The Way*, and assured them of Easa's forgiveness. For on the day that the Kingdom of God is awakened in your heart, you need never suffer again.

THE ARQUES GOSPEL OF MARY MAGDALENE,
THE BOOK OF DISCIPLES

# Chapter Twenty-One

*M*aureen drove the rented car through the pastel dusk hours of the southern summer. As she pulled into the parking lot alongside the suburban cemetery, the fading light illuminated the little church within the cemetery gates.

This time, she did not skirt the gates. The daughter of Edouard Paschal entered through them, head held high. No one with loved ones buried here would ever have to visit their final resting places in a misfit and overgrown graveyard. The gates had been moved to incorporate the previously pathetic plots, thanks to the influence and a grant from a particular Italian cardinal.

The white marble of her father's new grave marker seemed to glow from within as Maureen approached. An elaborate wreath of roses and lilies rested against the marble, just below the large gilded fleur-de-lis and the inscription that read:

EDOUARD PAUL PASCHAL
BELOVED FATHER OF MAUREEN

She knelt before the grave and had a long overdue conversation with her father.

The sense of peace that Maureen experienced internally was entirely new to her, and very welcome. She had butterflies about what tomorrow would bring, but overall she felt more excited than afraid. Tomorrow in New Orleans she would meet members of the Paschal clan—aunts and cousins she had never known—for a lunchtime reunion. Following that event, she would fly to Shannon Airport in Ireland and drive to a little western Galway town and stay at the Healy family farm. Peter was meeting her there. It would be their first meeting since her cousin left the Château des Pommes Bleues. They had spoken on the phone a number of times, but they had not seen each other. Peter had requested that they meet in Ireland, far away from crowds and curious eyes. There, they could talk at length and he would have the time and opportunity to fill her in on the official status of the Arques Gospel.

Maureen was thinking of all these things as she strolled through the French Quarter, which was coming to life on a beautiful Friday evening. As she walked, the distant sound of saxophone music floated on the southern breeze. Rounding a corner, drawn by the music, Maureen caught her first glimpse of the musician. He wore his dark hair long, which emphasized his gaunt and soulful appearance. As she drew closer to him, he looked up at her, and their eyes locked for a moment.

James St. Clair, the street musician from New Orleans, winked at Maureen. She smiled at him as she walked by, the saxophone strains of "Amazing Grace" floating behind her through the air of the French Quarter.

# CHAPTER TWENTY-TWO

*County Galway, Ireland*
*October 2005*

*T*here is a stillness that exists within the heart of the Irish countryside, a hush that sweeps across the land as the sun sets. It is as if the night demands silence, devouring any enemy to tranquillity, without bias.

For Maureen, this peace was a necessary respite from the chaos of the previous months. Here she was safe in her seclusion—a solitude that included her own heart and mind. She had not allowed herself to process recent events from a personal perspective; that would come later. Or perhaps it would not come at all. It was too overwhelming, too far-reaching . . . and too absurd. She had fulfilled her role as The Expected One, for whatever bizarre quirk of fate or destiny or even divine providence she had been chosen.

Her job was finished. The Expected One was a spectral creature, tied to time and space in the wilds of the Languedoc—and left happily behind in France. But Maureen Paschal was a flesh-and-blood woman, and an exhausted one at that. Breathing in the sweet still air of her childhood home, Maureen retired to her bedroom for a long-awaited rest.

Her sleep would not be dreamless.

She had witnessed a similar scene before—a figure in shadow huddled over an ancient table, a stylus scratching as words flowed from an author's pen. As Maureen watched over the writer's shoulder, an azure glow seemed to emanate from the pages. Fixated on the illumination shining from the writing, Maureen didn't see the writer move at first. As the figure turned and stepped forward into the lamplight, Maureen caught her breath.

She had been given glimpses of this face in previous dreams, fleeting moments of recognition that were over in an instant. He now fixed the full force of his attention on Maureen. Frozen in the dream state, she stared at the man ahead of her. The most beautiful man she had ever seen.

Easa.

He smiled at her then, an expression of such divinity and warmth that Maureen was suffused with it, as if the sun itself radiated from that simple expression. She remained motionless, unable to do anything but stare at his beauty and grace.

"You are my daughter, in whom I am well pleased."

His voice was a melody, a song of unity and love that resonated in the air around her. She floated on that music for an eternal moment, before crashing down to the sound of his next words.

"But your work is not yet finished."

With another smile, Easa the Nazarene, the Son of Man, turned back to the table where his writing rested. Light from the pages grew brighter, letters shimmering with indigo light, blue and violet patterns on the heavy, linenlike paper.

Maureen tried to speak, but the words would not come. She could not function in any human manner. She could only watch the divine being before her as he gestured to the pages. Easa returned his focus to Maureen and held her gaze for an eternal moment.

Gliding effortlessly across the space that separated them, Easa came to stand directly in front of Maureen. He said nothing more. Instead, he leaned forward and placed a single, paternal kiss on the top of her head.

Maureen awoke, drenched in sweat. Her scalp burned as though branded, and she felt dizzy and disoriented.

Glancing at the bedside clock, she shook her head to clear it. The first light of morning crept threw the heavy draperies, but it was still too early to call France. She would allow Berry a few more hours of sleep.

Then, she would call him—and demand to hear every detail regarding the last known resting place of the Book of Love, the one true gospel of Jesus Christ.

# AFTERWORD

## What is Truth?
PONTIUS PILATE, JOHN 18:38

My journey along the Magdalene Line in search of the answer to Pontius Pilate's question began with Marie Antoinette, Lucrezia Borgia, and a first-century Celtic warrior queen. Known to history as Boudicca, the latter's impassioned battle cry "Y gwir erbyn y byd" translates from Welsh to mean "The truth against the world." I have carried these words as my personal mantra on a quest that has spanned my adult life and led me down a tortuous path through 2,000 years of history.

I have long been driven to unearth the great untold stories, layers of human experience that are buried silently and often deliberately beneath academic accounts. As my protagonist, Maureen, reminds us, "History is not what happened. History is what was written down." More often than not, what we know and accept as history was created by an author with a committed political agenda. This understanding turned me into a folklorist at an early age. I derive immense satisfaction from exploring cultures firsthand, seeking out the local historian or storyteller to uncover the real human chronicles that are unavailable in libraries or textbooks. My Irish heritage gives me an

enormous appreciation for the power of oral records and living traditions.

My Irish blood also drove me to become a writer and activist, and
as such I was immersed in the tumultuous politics in Northern Ireland throughout the 1980s. It was during this period that I developed
an increasingly skeptical perspective on recorded, and therefore accepted, history. As an eyewitness to historic events, I realized that the
reported version rarely resembled what I had watched occur before
me. In many cases, the recounting of these occurrences in newspapers
and television broadcasts, and later in "history" books, was nearly un-
recognizable to me. All of these documented versions were written
through layers of political, social, and personal bias. The truth was
lost forever—except, perhaps, to those who had observed the events
firsthand. Overall, these witnesses were working-class people who
wanted only to get on with their lives; they would not write letter after
unprinted letter to the national newspapers or seek out a publisher to
record their version for posterity. They would bury their dead, pray
for peace, and do their best to keep going. But they would also preserve their experience as witnesses to history in a personal way,
through the retelling to family and community.

My experiences in Ireland reinforced my belief in the importance
of oral and cultural traditions, and why they are often our richest
source for understanding the human experience. These localized
events on the Belfast streets became my microcosm. If they were
deemed important enough to be reconstituted and altered by major
newspapers and broadcast accounts, what did this mean when that
concept was applied to the macrocosm of world history? Wouldn't
the tendency to manipulate the truth become greater and more absolute as we looked farther back to the past, to a time when only the
very wealthy, highly educated, and politically victorious were able to
record events?

I began to feel an overwhelming obligation to question history. As
a woman, I wanted to take this idea one step further. Since the dawn of
written records, the vast majority of materials that scholars consider
academically acceptable have been created by men of a certain social

and political strata. We believe, usually without question, in the veracity of documents simply because they can be "authenticated" to a specific time period. Rarely do we take into account that they were written during darker days when women held a status lower than livestock and were believed to have no souls! How many magnificent stories have been lost to us because the women who starred in them weren't deemed important enough, even human enough, to merit mention? How many women have been removed completely from history? And wouldn't this apply most certainly to the women of the first century?

Then there are those women who were so powerful and instrumental in world governments that they could not be ignored. Many who did find their place in the history books were remembered as notorious villains—adulteresses, schemers, deceivers, even murderers. Were those characterizations fair, or were they political propaganda used to discredit women who dared to assert their intelligence and power? Armed with these questions and my escalating sense of mistrust for what has been academically accepted as historical evidence, I set out to research and write a book about infamous women who had been maligned and misunderstood through time. I started researching the aforementioned notorious ladies—Marie Antoinette, Lucrezia Borgia, and Boudicca.

Mary Magdalene was initially just one of multiple subjects in my research. I set out to gain a greater awareness of this New Testament enigma in terms of her importance as a follower of Christ. I knew that the idea of the Magdalene as a prostitute was prevalent in Christian society and that the Vatican had made some effort to correct that injustice. This was my starting point. It was my intention to incorporate Mary Magdalene's story as one of many within the context of an entire body of literature that spanned twenty centuries.

But Mary Magdalene had a different plan for me.

I began to experience a series of haunting, recurring dreams that centered on the events and characters of the Passion. Unexplainable occurrences, like those that Maureen experiences, led me to investigate research leads surrounding the legends of Mary Magdalene from locations as disparate as McLean, Virginia, and the Sahara Desert. I traveled from the mountain of Masada to the medieval streets of Assisi, from the Gothic cathedrals of France to the rolling hills of southern England and across the rocky Scottish islands.

I fought hard to balance the increasingly surreal elements of my life, walking a Dali-esque line between suburban Little League mom and Indiana Jones. I would come to understand that most of my life had been lived in preparation for this specific journey of discovery. Seemingly random personal and professional experiences began to fall into an elaborate pattern, leading me to uncover a series of family secrets that would have been unimaginable to me previously. I even dealt with the shock that much of what I was raised to believe about certain members of my family turned out to be completely untrue. Nearly two decades after their passing, I discovered that my conservative and highly traditional paternal grandparents—my sweet southern belle grandmother and her devoted Southern Baptist husband—had been deeply involved in Freemasonry and secret society activity. I learned that my grandmother was related in blood to some of the oldest families of France, a fact that would change the course of not only my research, but my life. The ultimate shock came with the revelation that my own birth date was the subject of a prophecy related to Mary Magdalene and her descendants—the Orval Prophecy as spoken by Bérenger Sinclair. These personal "coincidences" became the skeleton key to unlock doors that had been barred to researchers who preceded me.

My interest in Mary's folklore turned to obsession as I experienced fascinating ancient cultural traditions that have been preserved with love and a fervent passion throughout western Europe. I was invited into the inner sanctum of secret societies and met with guardians of information so sacred that it astonishes me to this day that they, and the information they protect, exist—and have done so for 2,000 years.

I most certainly did not set out to explore issues that called into question the belief system of a billion people. It was never my intention to write a book that tackled a subject as weighty as the nature of Jesus Christ or his relationship with those closest in his life. Yet, like my protagonist, I discovered that sometimes our path is chosen for us. Once I discovered the Greatest Story Ever Told from Mary Magdalene's perspective, I knew there would be no turning back. It possessed me then as it does to this day. I am certain that it always will.

Two millennia of controversy have made Mary Magdalene the most elusive character of the New Testament. In my quest to find the real woman behind the legend, I realized that I had no desire to rehash all of the traditional sources as interpreted by the usual suspects. I wrapped myself in the warm cloak of the folklorist and went in search of a deeper mystery. I discovered that the extensive folklore and mythology surrounding Mary Magdalene in western Europe is as rich as it is ancient. *The Expected One* and the subsequent books in this series explore theories about the identity and impact of this controversial Mary as inspired by subcultures in the south of France and elsewhere in Europe.

The folklore and traditions of Europe also provided new insight into some of Mary's mysteries, those that have never been explained in any way that I could find palatable through traditional scholarship. An excerpt in Mark's gospel (16:9) has been used against Mary for centuries: *"Now when Jesus was risen early the first day of the week, he appeared first to Mary Magdalene, out of whom he had cast seven devils."* This single line has led to extreme claims about Mary's mental state, including books dedicated to the idea that she was either possessed by demons or mentally ill. It was not until I became familiar with the Arques perspective as presented here—that Jesus healed Mary after she had been poisoned by a lethal concoction known as the poison of seven devils—that Mark's line made real sense for me.

In a time when women were defined by their relationships, Mary Magdalene is not identified as anyone's wife in the New Testament, much less the spouse of Jesus. This fact alone has led scholars to assert definitively that the idea of Mary and Jesus as married is an impossibility. But this creates another conundrum as she is also the only woman in the four Gospels to be identified entirely as her own person. She is a stand-alone character, indicating that her name would have been easily recognized by the people of her time and immediately after. I believe that Mary's complicated relationships—her status as a noblewoman who becomes both widow and bride—were problematic. It would have been awkward and even politically incorrect to attempt to identify Mary in terms of her relationships with men. As a result, she became known by her name and title: Mary Magdalene.

Further, Magdalene's iconography has always puzzled me. Despite the enigmatic nature of her legend, she evolved into one of the most popular subjects for the great artists of the Middle Ages and of the Renaissance and Baroque periods. Hundreds of portraits exist of Mary Magdalene, from Italian masters like Caravaggio and Botticelli to those of modern Europeans like Salvador Dali and Jean Cocteau. One common thread runs through the vastly different portrayals of Magdalene; she is depicted over and over again with the same props: a skull, said to represent penance, a book, believed to symbolize the Gospels, and the alabaster jar she used to anoint Jesus. Always, she wears red—a tradition that reaches back into history and is generally believed to relate to the idea of her as a harlot.

But I believe now that the iconography is linked to this secret version of her story as it has been preserved throughout the European underground. The skull is, for me, clearly a representation of John, for whom she will always do penance. The book is either a reference to her own gospel or to Easa's work, the Book of Love. And the red robes and veils are representative of her queenly stature in the Nazarene tradition. I believe wholeheartedly that many of the great artists and authors of Europe were immersed in the "heresy" of Mary Magdalene—and the rich heritage that she left on the Continent.

Along this road the untold stories of other New Testament heroes and anti-heroes unveiled themselves in stunning detail. The reader finds a very different—and I hope a very human—interpretation of the role of the infamous Salome in these pages. John the Baptist is a different man when seen through the eyes of Mary Magdalene, and of those who have revered her for 2,000 years. It is my fervent hope that the reader will not feel that I was harsh in this portrayal of John. Both Mary and Easa reiterate that John the Baptist was a great prophet. I also believe that he was a man of his time and his place, a man committed to his law in an uncompromising way, a man who was unbending in his opposition to reforms. While I am certainly not the first writer to suggest a rivalry between the followers of John and Jesus—and I won't be the last—I am aware that this idea of John as Mary's first husband is shocking to many. It literally took years for me to process that revelation before I was prepared to write about it. John's legacy, through his son with Mary Magdalene, will continue to reveal itself in my future books.

I fell in love with the apostles Philip and Bartholomew during this process. As seen through Mary's eyes, they were extraordinary heroes. Peter came to life for me in a way that was far beyond "the man who denied Jesus," just as I developed a new perspective on Judas and his tragic, eternal role in the passion.

I was perhaps most excited by the information that came to light regarding Pontius Pilate and his heroic, heartbreaking wife, a Roman princess known as Claudia Procula. Catalogued documents in the Vatican archives and a fascinating French royal tradition exist to support the extraordinary story of Jesus' involvement with the Pilate family, an account that authenticates his miracles and explains Pilate's more enigmatic actions in John's gospel. I believe that the Pilate material is critical to a new understanding of the events surrounding the passion, and I was fascinated to discover that Claudia is a saint within Orthodox traditions, as is Pontius Pilate within the Abyssinian/Ethiopian churches.

I worked to corroborate the new Magdalene material from many different angles, using the first-century correspondence of Claudia Procula as published by the Issana Press, multiple versions of New Testament apocrypha, early writings by Church fathers, a number of invaluable Gnostic sources, and even the Dead Sea Scrolls. I understand that this version of events may be surprising to the point of stunning, and it is my sincere hope that readers will be inspired individually to explore their own understanding of these mysteries. A treasure trove of information exists, most written from the second to the fourth centuries, that is not included in the traditional Church canon. There are thousands of pages of material to discover—alternate gospels, additional Acts of the Apostles, and other writings that reveal details and insights into the life and times of Jesus that will be completely new to readers who have never before looked beyond the four evangelists. I believe that exploring all of this material with an open mind and heart can build a bridge of light and understanding between the many divisions of Christianity, and beyond.

Through my years of research, I have discussed, questioned, argued, and even conceded many points with clerics and believers from a number of faiths. I am blessed to have friends and associates from many spiritual arenas, including Catholic priests, Lutheran ministers, Gnostic practitioners, and pagan priestesses. In Israel, I encountered Jewish scholars and mystics, as well as Orthodox guardians of Christianity's sacred sites. My father is a Baptist, my husband a devout Catholic. All of these individuals became a part of the mosaic of my belief system, and ultimately a part of this story. Despite the myriad differences in their philosophies, each of these people blessed me with the same gift—the ability to exchange ideas and engage in dialogue freely and without anger.

There are elements of this story that I cannot corroborate through any of the "acceptable" academic sources. They exist as oral traditions and have been preserved for centuries in highly protected environments by those who have feared repercussions. In crafting this book I have taken the approach of building a case for my theory via 2,000 years' worth of circumstantial evidence. While I cannot produce a smoking gun, I have many interesting witnesses and a staggering array of corroborating exhibits, many created by no less than the great Renaissance and Baroque masters. I present my case within the context of such evidence and allow the jury of readers to establish their own verdict.

I must be circumspect about the primary source of the new information presented here for reasons of security, but I will say this: The content of the gospel of Mary Magdalene as I interpret it here is taken from previously undisclosed source material. It has never been released to the public before. I have taken poetic license in the interpretation to make it more accessible to a twenty-first-century audience, but I believe that the story it tells is genuine, and entirely her own.

In my need to protect the sacred nature of this information and those who hold it, I had no choice but to write this, and the subsequent books in this series, as fiction. However, many of my protagonist's adventures and virtually all of her supernatural encounters are based in my own life experiences. In numerous cases, Maureen receives information in precisely the same way that I did during my research—as does Tammy. While my modern-day characters are all fictional, I have done my best to provide the reader with an authentic experience. There are certainly places where I have taken literary liberties, which will no doubt be recognized by readers who have followed these mysteries on their own. The Arques tomb as painted by Poussin no longer exists—it was destroyed with dynamite by the local landowner who had grown tired of the trespassing that it encouraged! There are other allowances for which I must beg the reader's indulgence. Certainly, Peter's translation of the Arques Gospel happens in record time. In reality, the translation of such a document would take months, even years.

This book was almost two decades in the making, and along the often treacherous path I have received invaluable assistance from many intrepid souls. I am so grateful for the knowledge that has been shared with and entrusted to me by the most phenomenal individuals, some of whom took enormous risks to help me. There were many, many times when I wondered about my worthiness to tell this story. I don't think I've slept through the night in more than ten years as I have agonized over the details in this book and its potential repercussions.

While we were preparing this book for press, the controversial Gospel of Judas was released to the public for the first time. I began to immediately receive mail from readers who recognized that there are elements of this exciting new discovery that corroborate and support my own assertion that Judas didn't "betray" Jesus—that Judas was, in fact, carrying out the difficult and painful orders of his friend and teacher. The injustice done to Judas and his reputation is perhaps even greater than that which has been endured by Mary Magdalene for twenty centuries. It is my belief that it is well past time to restore those who were close to Jesus to their rightful places in history. As Father Peter Healy asks, "What if we have been denying Jesus his final wish for two thousand years?" In my effort to address that possibility, I submit my own portrait of Judas as loyal friend, even as hero; of Mary Magdalene as spouse, mother, soul mate, and life partner; of Peter as one who denied his friend and teacher only because he was ordered to do so. I also believe that past and future archaeological discoveries will continue to come to light and prove these portraits to be accurate and just.

I can only hope that the final product is worthy of those guardians of Mary Magdalene's truth who are depending on me to tell her story. Most of all, I hope it conveys Mary's message of love, tolerance, forgiveness, and personal accountability in a way that the reader might find inspirational. It is a message of unity and nonjudgment for all people of all belief systems. Throughout this process, I have remained devoted to Christ's teachings of peace and to the belief that we can create heaven on earth. My faith in Him—and her—has kept me going through some very dark nights of the soul.

I realize that I will come under fire from scholars and academics, and many of them will call me irresponsible for presenting a version that cannot be corroborated through their acceptable sources. But I will not apologize for the fact that I have opposed accepted scholarly practices in the telling of this story. My approach is based in my personal and perhaps radical belief that it is, in fact, irresponsible to accept what was written down. I will wear the scarlet label of the "antiacademic" with no small degree of pride and arm myself with Boudicca's battle cry. Readers will make the determination regarding the version of Mary's story that resonates within their spirit.

Yet to all the writers and seekers who have theorized, postulated, argued, speculated, and forged intrepidly through 2,000 years of clues and red herrings on the path of understanding the nature of Mary Magdalene and her children, I extend my hand in friendship. The spirited disagreements over the role of our Magdalene—and the many writers and artists who have portrayed her—are perhaps at the very essence of the search for truth. I hope they will see fit to call me their sister when all is said and done.

Two thousand years later, and it's still the truth against the world.

KATHLEEN MCGOWAN
MARCH 22, 2006
CITY OF THE ANGELS

# Acknowledgments

To thank every person individually who has helped me over two decades is a task worthy of a book unto itself, and unfortunately not possible in such finite space. I will do my best to include as many as possible of those who have been instrumental in helping me to complete this book.

To my agent and friend Larry Kirshbaum, who became my personal archangel through this process, I offer my unlimited admiration and gratitude. His passion for Mary's story and his determination to help me bring it to the world was the guiding force that made everything happen.

I am grateful beyond words for the staunch support, professional guidance, and sisterly advice of my editor, Trish Todd. My appreciation for her, and for the extraordinary team of professionals at Simon & Schuster/Touchstone Fireside, is limitless.

It has taken an enormous amount of sacrifice for my family to support me through years of research. During this process my husband, Peter McGowan, put the "faith" in "faithful." He supported me fiscally and emotionally, holding down the fort and keeping the family together while I traveled. He never doubted my experiences or lost faith in my discoveries, no matter how wild they appeared at first— which is far more than I can say for myself. My beautiful boys, Patrick, Conor, and Shane, have put up with a mother who was at times absentee and missed too many Little League games. And yet my husband and children have witnessed so many miracles with me along this path of discovery that we all felt we had no choice but to follow it to a conclusion, despite the often considerable risks. I hope this book proves worthy of their sacrifices.

This was indeed a family affair, and a piece of everything I do and everything I am belongs to my parents, Donna and Joe. Their love and support has been the cornerstone of my life, and they have suffered through some very difficult times as a result of their daughter's gypsy spirit. I thank them for everything, but am particularly blessed by the unconditional love they show for their grandchildren.

I share this and my future work with my brothers, Kelly and Kevin, and their families. I hope the revelations in this book will one day inspire my extraordinary nieces and nephews, Sean, Kristen, Logan, and Rhiannon, as they fulfill their unique destinies. On the day that I concluded this final version of the manuscript, we welcomed my newest niece, Brigit Erin, into the world. She was born on March 22, 2006. I will watch with loving interest as her tiny feet grow to fill the shoes of the Expected Ones who have come before her.

My entire family owes our happiness to the staff of the UCLA Neonatal Intensive Care Unit for saving baby Shane. In fact, they really saved all of us. I suggest that anyone who doubts miracles spend a few days in that particular NICU. There, one can see that angels truly exist on earth. They wear lab coats and are disguised as doctors, nurses, and respiratory therapists. Shane's miracle was the catalyst that forced me to finish this book.

I traveled countless miles of this journey with Stacey K, who has been my sister, research partner, and cherished friend. She deserves special mention for accepting the most bizarre tasks without flinching—like following disembodied voices calling "Sandro" through the Louvre, and chasing strange little men through the Basilica of the Holy Sepulcher. I could not have completed this without her faith and loyalty.

I have endless appreciation and indebtedness to "Auntie Dawn"

# Acknowledgments

for superhuman generosity and for acting as an amazing anchor of friendship and loyalty.

Literally eternal gratitude goes to Olivia Peyton, my spiritual sister and research master. I bow to her genius as a woman and a cybersybil, and pay homage to her brilliant novel, *Bijoux,* which holds the key to so many mysteries.

Special thanks to Marta Collier for her contribution to and belief in the music of Finn MacCool as well as her stalwart support of the McGowan clan through thick and thin.

Sincerest appreciation goes to my great friend and all around courageous Grail knight, Ted Grau. I don't think he really understands just how important his contribution has been. But I do.

Thanks to Stephen Gaghan for his insightful—albeit agonizing—comments on the earliest drafts of this story. His unabashed honesty forced me to make critical improvements.

*Go raibh mile math agat* to Michael Quirke, the woodcarving mystic of County Sligo, who also happens to be the greatest storyteller on earth. From the day I walked into his shop "accidentally" while lost in the summer of 1983, I have lived on the other side of the mirror. More than any single person or event, Michael made me understand that history is not what was committed to paper, but what was written in the hearts and souls of human beings—and etched into the land where they lived their greatest joys and deepest sorrows. A thousand thanks for giving me eyes to see and ears to hear.

Additional thanks go to:

Patrick Ruffino, who taught me the meaning of friendship and for keeping me from straying down Zsx Avenue;

Linda G, who juggles the archetypes of Martha and Vivienne with such grace;

Verdena, for embodying the spirit of Magdalena and teaching me more than a few things about faith, miracles, and staggering courage;

R. C. Welch, for acting as translator in the Moreau museum and for a great conversation about life and writing in the pews of Saint-Sulpice;

Branimir Zorjan, for bringing his friendship, light, and healing to our home;

Jim McDonough, the most lovable media mogul on the planet and a great friend to us;

Carolyn and David, who are only just beginning to see their role in all of this;

Joyce and Dave, my newest old friends;

Joel Gotler, for fighting the good fight and working to get Mary's story to a wider audience;

Larry Weinberg, my lawyer and friend, for believing in me as well as the book;

Don Schneider, for making me laugh;

Dev Chatillon, for her thorough professionalism;

Glenn Sobel, for his limitless patience and support in the past;

Cory and Annie, who bought the very first copy.

I also owe a debt to the illustrious ram queen, Linda Goodman, the late astrologer and author who first whispered this secret into my ear long before I was ready to comprehend it. She altered the course of my life with that piece of information, and by leaving me her Emerald Tablets translations (which will show their importance in later books). My destiny remains strangely intertwined with Linda's, a fact that has brought both surprising pain but also great joy. I wish she had stayed with us long enough to see the proof I uncovered of her own bloodline connections.

I am also grateful that the path through Linda's life brought me to another great author and astrologer, Carolyn Reynolds. Carolyn was my rock through some very dark days with her battle cry of "No one can steal your destiny." I thank her with all my heart.

Special thanks to the enlightened ladies of the Emerald Tablets Forum for their support and love over the years.

Sometimes it takes half a lifetime to understand why certain events shape your destiny. Jackson Browne changed my impressionable young life on my seventeenth birthday backstage at the Pantages Theater, and I truly believe if he hadn't, this book wouldn't exist. As a teenage activist, I was the recipient of his impassioned speech about

Acknowledgments

the power of one person to make a difference in the world—and of his praise for my youthful need to question an unjust status quo. He grabbed me by the shoulders as he emphasized, "Never stop doing what you do. Never." I thank him for that catalyst (although my parents probably wouldn't), and for a lifetime of inspired music, but particularly for "The Rebel Jesus." I believe that Easa would approve.

Heartfelt thanks to Ted Neeley and fondest memories of the late Carl Anderson; both have moved me and countless others with their divinely inspired portrayals of Easa and Judas. (Is it a coincidence that Andrew Lloyd Webber was born on March 22?) Anyone fortunate enough to spend time in Ted's glowing presence knows just how much he embodies the beauty of the Nazarene spirit.

The talented members of the Screenwriter's Refuge have provided group therapy and tremendous support to me for the last few years. So to Cindy, Robert, James, Mel, Kathy, Fitchy, Teddy, Chris, and Wenonah—well, you guys have my admiration and sincerest thanks. It's great to be in the trenches with such trusted friends.

My heart lives in Ireland, and my gratitude is in County Cavan specifically, where my in-laws, John and Mary, have always treated me as their own. My love and thanks to all of my extended Irish family: Brian, Bridie and Pat, Susan, Philomena, Pam and Paul, Geraldine and Eugene and Peter and Laura, and Noeleen and David and Daniel.

Thanks to the whole gang in Drogheda for showing me the essence of the city that survived Cromwell. These are very special people and wonderful friends. And that landmark is called Magdalen Tower for a reason, isn't it?

Over the course of this research, Los Angeles was my home, Ireland my refuge, and France my inspiration. I am grateful to the staff of the Hotel Place du Louvre, who always make me feel welcome in Paris, and for introducing me to the story of the Caveau du Mousquetaires. There are so many people in France who have given little pieces of their hearts and souls to me, and there isn't a day that goes by when I don't sigh over the beauty of the Languedoc, the Camargue, Midi, and Provence—and the extraordinary people who inhabit those magical regions.

# Acknowledgments

The essence of the Magdalene is one of compassion and forgiveness, and in that spirit I would offer this book as an olive branch to those whom I may have offended along the way—specifically to my uncle, Ronald Paschal, as his passion for our unique French heritage was something I was unable to grasp at the time he tried to show it to me.

I would also offer this to Michele-Malana. Our friendship did not survive the tumultuous path that we were set upon, but her generosity and inspiration will never be forgotten. If she ever reads this—and her love of our Magdalene indicates that she may—I hope she will find me.

I must acknowledge the wonderful people at Issana Press for publishing the translations of Claudia Procula's letters. I recommend their "Relics of Repentance" booklet highly—it is very small, but certainly mighty. I thank them for confirming for me that Pilo was, indeed, the name of Pilate's son—and for challenging my brain with the knowledge that there may have been other Pilate children . . . !

I think it is necessary for writers to honor those pioneers who opened the door for all of us to step through. As such, I must acknowledge the often controversial authors Michael Baigent, Henry Lincoln, and Richard Leigh, who brought *Holy Blood, Holy Grail* to the world in the 1980s. This book was the earthquake that awakened the public to the idea that something important was going on in the southwestern corner of France. I have obviously come to different conclusions and found an alternate focus for my own research. Still, I nod to the courage, tenacity, and pioneering spirit of these three honorable gentlemen and what they were able to achieve—and for introducing the esoteric world to an enigmatic and sly muse in Bérenger Saunière.

Finally, to all of the brilliant artists who longed for this information to be discovered in their own lives, I extend my gratitude for giving us the maps and clues that were required to find it. Particularly to Alessandro Filipepi, who was truly a "cherished child of the gods" and continues to enchant me across time and space.

I'll meet you all soon in Chartres Cathedral at the entrance to the labyrinth as we begin our search for the Book of Love. You already have a map. But you may want to bring your most well-worn copy of the collected works of Alexandre Dumas and wrap yourself in a uni-corn tapestry . . .

Lux et veritas,
KDM

### Et in Arcadia Ego

On the road to Sion, I met a woman
A shepherdess so fair
She spoke these words in a secret whisper
Et in Arcadia ego

I traveled east through the red mountains
By the cross and this horse of God
Saint Anthony the hermit said,
"Begone, begone"
I hold the secrets of God

In the harvest time I rested
seeking the fruit of the vine
in the midday sun I saw them
blue apples, blue apples
Et in Arcadia ego

In the shadow of Mary
I found the secrets of God

From the album *Music of The Expected One*, by Finn MacCool,
words and music by Peter McGowan and Kathleen McGowan.
Visit www.theexpectedone.com to hear the audio.